NEON
MIRAGE

Books by Max Allan Collins

THE MEMOIRS OF NATHAN HELLER
True Detective
True Crime
The Million-Dollar Wound
Neon Mirage

NOLAN AND JON NOVELS
Bait Money
Blood Money
Fly Paper
Hush Money
Hard Cash
Scratch Fever
Spree

QUARRY NOVELS
The Broker (retitled: *Quarry*)
The Broker's Wife (retitled: *Quarry's List*)
The Dealer (retitled: *Quarry's Deal*)
The Slasher (retitled: *Quarry's Cut*)
Primary Target

IN THE MALLORY MANNER
No Cure for Death
The Baby Blue Rip-Off
Kill Your Darlings
A Shroud for Aquarius
Nice Weekend for a Murder

OTHER NOVELS
Midnight Haul
The Dark City

CRITICAL/BIOGRAPHICAL STUDY
One Lonely Knight: Mickey Spillane's Mike Hammer (with James Traylor)

COMIC STRIP COLLECTIONS
Dick Tracy Meets Angeltop (with Rick Fletcher)
Dick Tracy Meets the Punks (with Rick Fletcher)
Dick Tracy's Wartime Memories (with Dick Locher)
The Files of Ms. Tree (with Terry Beatty; three volumes)

EDITOR
Tomorrow I Die (Mickey Spillane collection)
Mike Hammer: The Comic Strip (two volumes)

NEON MIRAGE

MAX ALLAN COLLINS

A Thomas Dunne Book

St. Martin's Press
New York

Although the historical events in this novel are portrayed more or less accurately (as much as the passage of time, and contradictory source material will allow), fact, speculation and fiction are freely mixed, here: historical personages exist side by side with composite characters, and wholly fictional ones—all of whom act and speak at the author's whim.

Library of Congress Cataloging-in-Publication Data

Collins, Max Allan.
   Neon mirage / by Max Allan Collins.
      p.   cm.
   ISBN 0-312-01484-8 : $18.95
   I. Title.
PS3553.04753N4   1988
813'.54—dc19   87-29939
                                                                          CIP

First Edition

10 9 8 7 6 5 4 3 2 1

For Mike Gold—
a friend as good as

"Life is a game of chance."
—Arthur "Mickey" McBride

ONE
A KILLING IN CHICAGO
JUNE 24 – AUGUST 31, 1946

CHICAGO LOOP—STATE STREET

I was riding shotgun, and that wasn't just an expression: there was a goddamned sawed-off twelve-gauge in my lap, and I didn't like it. At all.

When you're the boss of a business, the owner of a company, the fucking *president* of A-1 Detective Agency, you're not supposed to draw duty like this. I had six operatives for that; I was thirty-eight years old and had been at this racket long enough, and was successful enough, to pick and choose which jobs I wanted to go out on. If I wanted to spend all day behind my desk, I could do that (and these days I frequently did). I was good on the phone, and that's eighty percent of being a good private detective. If I ever had any thirst for adventure, Guadalcanal had taken it out of me. I rarely carried a gun, in this glorious post-war world.

But nonetheless, here I was: riding literal shotgun in the bodyguard car following James Ragen and his fancy Lincoln Continental down State Street, filling in last minute for an op of mine who took sick, wondering if today would be the day the Outfit decided to blow my tough little Irishman of a client to kingdom come.

Dealing with the mob was something that couldn't be avoided in Chicago, if you were in my line, but the last couple years I'd done my best to do less and less of it. I used to know Frank Nitti fairly well—better than I wanted to, really—and had more than once found an unlikely ally in the diminutive, dapper, one-time barber who had been Al Capone's successor.

Since Nitti's death, however, I'd with a couple of exceptions kept arm's length from Outfit guys. Nitti was, compared to those who came before him and those who came after, a relatively benevolent figure. He killed less often, and often schemed, like a master chess player, to have those he did want dead killed by somebody else—the cops or the FBI, for example. He tried to stay out of the headlines—it brought too much "heat," it was bad for business.

And to him the Outfit *was* a business; and he was a businessman, and you could trust him. As much as you can trust any Chicago businessman, anyway.

Former pimp Jake Guzik, he of the greasy thumb, was in charge of the Outfit these days, while Paul "The Waiter" Ricca and Louie "Little New York" Campagna sat in stir trying to buy their way out of the sentences they got for their part in the Hollywood extortion racket, the exposure of which had led to Nitti's demise—a suicide if you believe what you read in the papers. Fat Guzik, mob treasurer for several decades now, who would do anything for money, was somebody I'd *never* feel close to, though he did owe me a debt of sorts. I hoped that debt would be enough to let me survive acting as protector to Jim Ragen.

I'd tried to keep my distance from the job, assigning various ops to the bodyguard duty—even though Ragen had, from the beginning, wanted me aboard personally.

"Jim," I'd told him, as we sat in my nicely furnished office in an admittedly less than nice building at Van Buren and Plymouth, speaking over the rumble of the El rushing by, "it's against my better judgment getting involved in this at all. If we weren't friends . . ."

"It's because we're friends I come to you," Ragen had said. He wasn't a big man; my six feet and one-hundred-eighty pounds was enough to make him look small, despite the bull neck and broad shoulders. You might even mistake him for mild, this balding, bespectacled, ruddy-complected Irishman whose tiny eyes were as blue and benign as a summer sky. Only the dimpled jutting chin hinted at the toughness and determination that had made him one of the most feared and effective circulation sluggers during the great newspaper wars early in the century.

Today this Back-o'-the-Yards, South Side boy was arguably the most powerful, important man in gambling in America. Yet he never gambled, not in the wagering sense; nor did he drink or smoke.

His Continental Press Service was the country's dominant racing wire service, transmitting all pertinent racing information to bookmakers nationwide. That included track conditions, changes in jockeys, scratches and, as post time approached, up-to-the-minute racing odds. And, of course, results of the races themselves, transmitted immediately as the horses crossed the finish line. A bookmaker without this service, operating under the delay of officially transmitted results, would be easily prey to past-posting—that is, bets placed after post time by a sharpie who has been phoned the results by an on-track accomplice, thus allowing said sharpie to bet on a horse that has already won a race.

Ragen's Continental service relayed its information from telegraph and telephone wires hooked into 29 race tracks and from those tracks into 223 cities in 39 states (tracks that didn't cooperate were spied upon by high-powered telescope from trees and buildings). For legal reasons, Continental buffered itself, allowing several dozen "distributors" to supply the wire info to the nation's thousands of bookie joints.

Ragen, like Frank Nitti, was a business executive in the world of crime. I'd done jobs for him before, and I liked him.

But I'd never seen this tough, irascible little Irishman in a state like this. He seemed shaken as he came into my office, unannounced, no appointment, which was also not like him; he was nothing if not businesslike. Even his gray suit was rumpled, his red and blue striped tie askew.

Of course that day had been no ordinary one in the life of James M. Ragen. That day, in April, James M. Ragen was convinced he'd narrowly missed being bumped off.

That morning two men in a car had trailed Ragen's Lincoln Continental, from his home, and when he sensed he was being shadowed, he increased his speed to sixty miles an hour, and still they came, still they clung to him. They chased him through the city streets until finally Ragen pulled up in front of, and scurried into, a precinct house—the would-be assassins whooshing by.

It was in the aftermath of that that he came to me, Nathan Heller, president of A-1 Detective Agency, looking for bodyguards. Trustworthy ones.

"Who can I trust in this town but a friend?" Ragen said, his oblong face a dour mask. "The cops offered to provide me 'protection'—of a sort I'd be safer *without*, goes without saying. You can buy a Chicago cop and get change for a five—everybody knows that. And most of the private dicks in this town, even them that's employed by the big agencies, is ex-cops."

"So am I, Jim," I said.

"Yeah, but you ain't for sale, my lad. Not when a friend is what they're buying."

I sighed. I think he thought of me as Irish, despite the Jewish last name my father left me. It's what my Irish Catholic mother bequeathed me that fools people—her blue eyes, regular features and

reddish brown hair. Of course, where the latter's concerned, mine is
graying some, at the temples, the only temples I attend, by the way,
which'll give you an idea of about how Jewish I am. Papa was apos-
tate, he didn't believe in God, Hebrew or whatever else you got,
though he tried to see some good in his fellow man; I guess I inher-
ited that from him, too, minus the part about my fellow man. As for
my mother, she didn't live long enough for her hair to go gray at all,
which may explain why I'm not very Catholic, either. Just the same, I
was Irish enough for Ragen.

"Well," I said, shrugging, "I can fix you up with some bodyguards.
But if the Outfit wants you, I'm afraid they're going to get you. You
know that. You know what you're up against."

"If they kill me," he said, chin jutting, eyes slitting, "there's a
Ragen to take my place."

"Your son Jim, Jr."

He nodded curtly.

I didn't think the boy had near the stones his old man had, but I
said only, "And if Jim should go the way of all flesh, as well?"

"I have two more sons."

Oh brother.

"Is it worth it, Jim?"

"Nobody has ever stood up to these dago sons of bitches. If I stand
up to 'em, they'll back down."

"You really think so?"

"Let 'em run their competing wire service. They'll never deliver
the quality product I can, so they'll never put me under. I caught 'em
tapping my phones, pirating my news, and got a court order against
'em!"

Jesus, I thought. *Does this guy* really *think the courts is where he
can win against the Outfit?*

But he was ranting on: "There'll be some poor bastards operating
handbooks out there, feelin' they gotta pay for both services, letting
themselves be shook down . . . but if *they* want to knuckle under to
the Capone crowd, that's up to *them.*"

Coming from most people, talk of standing up to the Outfit would
go past suicidal into idiotic. But Ragen had coexisted with the Outfit
for years; despite all the talk of "dagos," he'd been cordial with Guzik
and thick with Dan Serritella, the longtime state senator and longer-
time Capone mob crony. Serritella even had business ties with
Ragen, who had taken control of the horse-race wire service business

in 1939, shortly before Moe Annenberg, his mentor, got sent up for tax evasion. Since then, the Outfit had been content to pay the price for Ragen's service; but of late they'd been trying to buy in. Ragen had been resisting all offers, despite Guzik's assurances that the little Irishman would be kept on as a partner.

"Those greasy sons of bitches would need my know-how at first," Ragen told me, "but then some fine morning you'd find me gutted in an alley, with my dick stuffed in my mouth."

"And then what would you have to say for yourself?" I asked.

"And this guy Siegel is a fruitcake," Ragen said, distastefully, ignoring my remark, shifting in the client's chair across from my desk. "They call him 'Bugsy' and it fits."

It seems Guzik, in response to Ragen's rebuffs, had set up a rival wire, Trans-American, in cooperation with the East Coast version of the Outfit, the Combination; the West Coast branch of Trans-American was under this fellow Ben Siegel.

I nodded. "I've heard of the guy. Out of the old 'Bugs and Meyer' gang in New York. What's he doing in California, anyway?"

Ragen snorted. "Hanging around with movie stars. Screwing starlets. Pushing his wire service down people's throats. He's a thug in a two-hundred dollar suit."

"Have you had any run-ins with him?"

"His people roughed up my son-in-law out there—pretty bad," he said, referring to Russell Brophy, who ran the L.A. Continental office. "The lad went to the hospital over it."

"No offense, Jim," I said, with gentle sarcasm, "but there was a day when you used the strongarm approach yourself—back when you were circulation chief for the *Herald and Examiner*? It proved successful, as I recall."

Ragen waved that off; then he smirked humorlessly, saying, "Well, the crazy bastard *has* cut into me, some—in California and other points west. He owns a horse store downtown in Las Vegas, and he's got that little desert flyspeck in his pocket . . ." Some humor drifted into the smirk. ". . . though some of the Vegas boys *are* paying for *my* wire, too."

I tapped my finger on my desk. Said, "I think you should consider selling out. You're, what? Sixty-five? You can retire and take the Outfit's dough and get your sons into something legitimate."

Ragen's face turned redder than usual and he clutched the arms of the wooden chair, like a guy in the hot squat when they turned on the juice. "My business *is* legitimate, Heller! But it *wouldn't* be if those dago bastards bought their way in! You think Hoover would put up with that? The mob running the interstate race wire business? Why, we'd have the FBI all over us like flies on horse manure—"

"But you'd be out of it. I didn't say go in business with them. I said sell out to 'em—take their money, and run. You've had your fun."

The red faded but his mouth became a tight line, which parted, in a barely perceptible manner, as he said, "You think I'm getting old, Nate?"

"You're not getting any younger. Hell, neither am I. But you *are* rich. Christ, if I had a tenth your dough, I wouldn't work another hour!"

The tight line curved upward into the slightest smile. "Bullshit, Heller. You love your work."

"I love to eat, Jim. Without working, I don't get to."

"You love your work, you love bein' in business. What would you do with your time, lad, if you didn't have your work, your business? Where would you go? What would you do?"

"I'd think of something," I said, lamely.

"You'll die in harness, just like me. Christ! I'm not gonna let a bunch of wop pricks muscle me out of my business! Now, are you in, or are you out?"

Quite frankly, I would've been out, friendship or not. And what Ragen was calling a friendship was more a friendly acquaintance. But he had a niece named Peggy, about whom I'll tell you later. At which time you'll better understand why I said:

"Yeah. I'll play bodyguard for you. Or anyway, I'll put two of my ops on it. I don't want to be around when the bullets start to fly. *I'm* not anxious to die at all, let alone 'in harness.'"

But here I was, two months later, a hot late June afternoon at rush hour, just before six o'clock, cruising down State Street in a black Ford behind Ragen's dark blue Lincoln Continental.

We'd started on foot, at Ragen's office at 431 South Dearborn; it was hot and muggy and our clothes were sticking to us. Few of the men on the street were wearing their suitcoats; we stood out, some, accordingly. Of course Ragen—wearing a crisp-looking light brown suit and a green and yellow striped tie and a dark brown snap-brim— looked cool, unbothered by the heat. Except for that one day in my office, I'd never seen the little hardass otherwise.

When we reached the parking lot, two blocks later, Jim had

climbed into his car alone (once a week his staff bodyguard, a racing
sheet truck driver, got the day off, and this was the day) and we—me
and Walt Pelitier, an ex-pickpocket detail dick, like most of my ops—
got into the bodyguard car, Walt behind the wheel, me riding with
shotgun in my hands, my nine millimeter automatic snug under my
shoulder, an old friend I'd rather not get reacquainted with.

For fifteen minutes or so, we'd had an uneventful journey. We'd
just passed through the remnants of the once-proud Levee district,
reduced from its former red-light and saloon glory to a handful of
rundown bars and weedy vacant lots. We were heading south on
State, making our way to Beverly, a nice neighborhood on the far
South West Side, one of those sedate upper-middle-class areas that
whispered money. Ragen and his family lived there, in a spacious
two-story with a sprawling lawn, at 10756 Seeley. So, for two months
now, in the apartment over the garage, had Walt Pelitier.

We were not, at the moment, in a nice neighborhood. We were, in
fact, in the midst of a colored corridor that might charitably be described as a slum; we were at the west end of the South Side
Bronzeville, and the black faces that watched Ragen's fancy car slide
by were not sympathetic. Several blocks to the right, across the
tracks, yet worlds away, was a nice neighborhood. A white neighborhood.

A certain irony, here, was not lost on me: Ragen's late brother
Frank had, in the first couple decades of the century, ruled "Ragen's
Colts," a vicious street gang which began, as so many gangs in those
days did, as a baseball team. Frank, the star pitcher, offered his
team's slugging services to the local Democratic Party, for whom they
won votes in much the same muscular manner as brother Jim won
readers for the *Trib* and, later, the *Herald and Examiner*.

To my knowledge, Jim had never been a part of the notorious
Colts, but it still chilled me, momentarily, to be gliding through the
very black area where the Colts had, back in 1919, started the city's
biggest race riot. It should be kept in mind that one member of the
Colts publicly derided the Ku Klux Klan as "nigger lovers." On this
very street, not so many years ago, blacks had been shot on sight,
residences had been burned and dynamited, shops looted. That
"nice" white neighborhood, a few blocks over, had been the scene of
reprisals, as colored world war veterans dug out their service weapons and returned fire, attacked streetcars, turned over autos, de-
stroyed property. In four days, twenty whites died, fourteen colored

died, and a thousand-some others of both races were injured. My father, an old union man who had no truck with bigots, had told me the story many times. It was his favorite example of "man's inhumanity to man." In my time I've seen plenty more.

This stretch of Bronzeville was so shabby that the riot might have taken place here last week, instead of a few decades ago. Some storefronts were boarded up, as if the depression were still here. For many of these people, it still was, of course. Always would be, probably. An occasional prosperous business—a barber shop, a laundry, a drugstore—seemed the exception, not the rule; the streets were thick with hot, sweating coloreds, men mostly. The curbs were all but empty of parked cars. This was a poor neighborhood. The cars on this street were moving.

Actually, ours was slowing to a stop; maybe it makes me a bigot, too, but in a neighborhood this colored, this poor, I feel uncomfortable whenever a traffic light insists I stop. For a moment I was glad I had a shotgun in my lap.

Up ahead, a gray Buick sedan had stopped at the light; a shabby-looking green Ford delivery truck, with a tan tarp covering its skeletal frame, some orange crates visible in the back end, rolled past Walt and me and came to a slow stop in the righthand lane. I sat up.

"That truck," I said, pointing.

We were poised just behind Ragen's car. I had to speak up, because a train was rumbling by on the nearby El; it was to our left, just back of these ramshackle buildings along State Street.

"Huh?" Walt said. He was a puffy-looking, heavy-set man of fiftysome, with hooded eyes. Despite all that, despite the "huh" as well, he was a hardnosed, alert dick.

"No license plates," I shouted, over the El.

Walt sat forward. "They're slowing next to Ragen—"

They were indeed; rather than pulling up to the intersection of State and Pershing, next to the gray sedan, they had stopped next to the Lincoln.

And the tan tarp on that same side was parting, down the middle, like theater curtains.

The barrels of two shotguns slid into view. Shiny black metal caught some dying sun and winked at us.

"Christ!" I said, and hopped out, shotgun in my hands, feet slapping cement, firing at the truck.

Or trying to.

The sawed-off jammed. I didn't even know the fucking things *could* jam! But the trigger simply wouldn't squeeze back. I knew the thing was loaded; it wasn't mine, it was Bill Tendlar's, the op I was replacing, but I had checked it and it was loaded when I left the office . . .

And now the afternoon was interrupted by shotgun fire, but not mine, not mine, as the two barrels extending like long black snouts from the side of the delivery truck delivered on Ragen's car, ripping the metal of the front right door, just under the absent rider's open window, but you could barely hear the blasts, what with the roar of the El. The train made a great silencer.

Up ahead the traffic light had changed, but the gray sedan before Ragen was keeping its position. Whether the driver had panicked (in which case you'd think the asshole would hit his gas pedal and high-tail it away) or was in on the hit, I couldn't say.

In fact all I could think to say was, "Shit! You bastards," as I moved quickly toward the truck, yanking the nine millimeter from under my arm and firing on them, three times, right into that fucking tarp.

From which one of the barrels turned upon me and fired and I dove for the cement, between the two cars, as the windshield of the bodyguard car just behind me caught the brunt, spiderwebbing. As if sliding toward home, I landed in the next of the four lanes, sprawled in front of oncoming traffic. Despite the El's rumble, I heard the screech of tires and wondered if I'd wind up so much spaghetti sauce on the Bronzeville pavement; but I seemed to be alive and rolled into the next lane, the sidewalk my goal, as another shotgun blast ate into the side of Ragen's once-proud Lincoln, repeatedly puckering the top of the car, entering the rider's window. I heard a scream, which had to be Jim, and then I screamed something, "Fuck," I think, and got to my feet and started firing the nine millimeter again. Walt had climbed out of the bodyguard car, which shielded him some as he was shooting, ripping off shot after shot from his revolver, right at the truck. Traffic had finally had sense enough to stop and I stood there, feet apart, gun gripped in both hands, planted in the middle of the empty left lane like the world was my target range. I ripped three off and then a shotgun barrel was aiming my way, in the hands of an indistinct figure in a white sportshirt, but that shotgun was distinct enough, the guy standing up in the truck now, visible over the shot-up Lincoln, and I dove and rolled onto the sidewalk.

The blast that followed blew across the top of the Lincoln and shattered the window of the corner drugstore. The colored pedestrians were running for cover, screaming their lungs out as if needing to be heard over the El, feet doing their stuff and it didn't have anything to do with being colored. The blast went over my head into that window and I stayed down but shot the nine millimeter up and at the side of that truck, knowing that my bullets were probably too high, having to shoot across two empty lanes of State Street and over the Lincoln, but hoping against hope to get a piece of something, somebody . . .

Then the nine millimeter was empty and the truck was gone. So was the gray sedan.

Even the El had passed by. The street was silent, but for the occasional outbursts from the colored pedestrians, coming up for air, "Mercy!" "Judas Priest!" "Mama!"

That sedan, which turned right on Pershing, did have plates: Indiana plates, though neither Walt nor I had caught the numbers. Maybe one of the colored witnesses had. The truck was heading on south, gears grinding as it picked up speed.

Walt, who also was out of ammo, helped me up off the sidewalk, and then we were at the Lincoln, looking in, where James M. Ragen, gambling czar, was slumped behind the wheel, teetering between winning and losing, the front of him blood-spattered, his right shoulder and arm a scorched, red, sodden mess.

"Jim," I said, leaning in the window.

He looked up at me and the little blue eyes damn near twinkled.

"Well, my lad," he grinned, "you were right . . . I guess if they want you, they're going to get you."

And he either passed out or died.

At that moment I couldn't tell which.

The year before, in May of '45, I had taken on another job for Jim Ragen; it, too, had the taint of the Outfit. But it did bring Peggy Hogan back into my life.

I didn't even know she was Ragen's niece when he pitched me the job. We had just finished lunch at Binyon's, a no-nonsense, businessman-oriented restaurant on Plymouth, just around the corner from the seedy building my growing private investigative firm was trying to escape from. He'd had the finan haddie, I the corned beef and cabbage plate. We were sharing one of the wooden booths, drinking coffee.

"I made a mistake," Ragen said, tiny blue eyes staring into the steaming black cup; he was the kind of man who could admit a mistake, but couldn't look you in the eye doing it. "I trusted Serritella."

"That does sound like a mistake," I said. "He'd sell out God if the devil was buying."

"I know, I know," Ragen said, waving it off. Wearily, he said: "Couple years back, I went partners with the senator, on a tip sheet."

"The Blue Sheet?"

"Yeah. I thought he was operating for himself, but he was playing his usual tricks, fronting for Guzik and company. I don't mind doing business with those wops, but I don't want to be *in* business with 'em."

"A fine distinction, don't you think?"

"Not at all, my lad. Not at all. As customers, I got 'em where I want 'em—putting their money in my pocket. As partners, I wouldn't trust 'em far as I could throw 'em."

"You think they've been using Serritella to worm their way into your business? Into Continental Press?"

"Hell yes. They've had their hand in my pocket ever since I went with Serritella; bilking me right along. Of course, I can't lay my hands on the books to prove it. And that's why I'm suing the bums. Serritella and Guzik both."

JAMES RAGEN

"Suing them? Outfit guys?"

"It's the only way I can get an accounting."

I shook my head. "Sounds dicey to me."

"Where would they be without Continental? They're making noises about starting up their own wire—let 'em try it!"

I sat forward in the booth. "I don't know where you think *I* fit into this, Jim, but I don't do mob-related work. I gave that up the day Frank Nitti blew his brains out."

He smiled his tight smile. "You played intermediary in the Guzik kidnapping, I hear."

"Yeah, but it wasn't my idea."

"I hear Greasy Thumb thinks you're aces."

"Let's keep it that way. And let's keep him a distant admirer."

He frowned. "They're trying to spook my lawyer, Nate. He's been getting threatening calls; nasty notes."

"Telling him to drop the case."

"Yes."

"Sounds like swell advice to me."

"His secretary's been getting the calls. It's a small office—there's no receptionist; just one girl, and him. And they've threatened *her,* too."

"That's a little nasty, I'll grant you."

He leaned forward; spoke softly. "The secretary is my niece. I feel a responsibility, here: I *got* her this job. Her father died last year, and the family business went with him. I'm trying to help the lass out." He sighed. "She's a good girl, though she has a bit of a wild streak that gets away from her sometimes."

"And you mean to straighten her out," I said.

"Yes. But my concern right now is her safety. Her family's had enough tragedy . . . they lost the only son in the war."

I sucked some air in. "Yeah, well."

"Bataan," Ragen added.

I winced. "What do you want me to do?"

"Spend some time with her."

"If you're looking for a bodyguard, I'll put one of my men on it . . ."

"I want *you,* Nate. What's your rate these days?"

"Twenty-five a day, unless you insist on the boss himself, in which case it's thirty-five. And even if you do, I still have to run the office; I can't be on her all the time. I'd talk to the girl, spend the first day with her, then put an op on it. I don't work just one job at a time, you know—we have sixty-some clients, at the moment."

"Make it hundred a day, with a week's retainer."

That raised my eyebrows and lowered my standards. "What do you expect to accomplish? What do you expect *me* to accomplish?"

He shrugged elaborately. "I think the threats are so much hot air. Those dagos can't afford to fuck with Jim Ragen. They're just makin' noise."

"So do guns."

He smirked humorlessly and waved that off as well. "We go to court next week. That'll be the end of it."

"You didn't answer me, Jim. What do you want from me, exactly?"

"Be at her side. Make her feel safe. *Make* her safe."

"Have you talked to her about this?"

"Yes. She insists she's not afraid, though I can tell she *is* . . . though she resisted the notion of protection, at first. But, who can predict a woman; headstrong lass that she is, she up and turned around and said she'd go along with it."

"Why, do you think?"

"She said she'd heard of you. You've a certain notoriety, after all."

I'd made the papers a few times. Most of the occasions had been bad for my health but good for business.

"What's her name?" I asked.

"Margaret."

"Ragen?"

"Hogan. She's my wife's little sister's girl. Pretty little lass. You should pay me, for the pleasure." He raised a stern finger, the tiny eyes getting tinier. "Which isn't to give you no ideas, lad. Don't ye lay a hand on 'er, now."

They always get more Irish when they're warning you.

"For a hundred bucks a day," I said, "I can leave my dick in a drawer, if you like."

"Fine," he smiled, picking up the check. "And leave the key with me."

It's funny I didn't recognize her name. Hell, I didn't recognize *her*, at first, as she sat at a typing stand near her desk in the little wood-paneled outer office on the tenth floor of the Fisher Building. She was small, and what you saw about her first was all that dark brown hair, the sort of dark brown that looks black till you study it, piles of curls cascading to the squared-off shoulders of her yellow dress, a startling dress with black polka dots, shiny cloth, silk perhaps. It hadn't come cheap, this dress, but it seemed out of place in a law office, even a cubbyhole like this.

She turned to me and smiled, in a business-like way, and then the smile widened.

"Nate," she said, standing, extending a hand. "It's been a long time."

She had pale, pale skin, translucent skin, with the faintest brown trail of freckles over a pert nose. She had a wide full mouth with cherry red lipstick, and big violet eyes. Her eyebrows were rather thick, unplucked, unfashionably beautiful, and she had a couple pounds of eyelashes, apparently real, and the whitest teeth this side of Hollywood. She looked about seventeen, but she was ten years older than that—a few laugh crinkles around the enormous eyes were almost a giveaway—and she had a very slim but nicely shaped frame. The hand she extended, in an almost manly fashion, had short nails with bright red polish, the color of her lipstick.

She was a stunning-looking girl, and in 1938, I'd slept with her once. Well. That was *part* of what we'd done together that night. . . .

"Peggy," I said, amazed. "Peggy Hogan."

Her hand, as I grasped it, was firm and smooth and warm.

Her big grin, dimpling her slightly chubby cheeks, was one of amusement and pleasure.

"You're still a private eye," she said.

"You're still a dish," I noted.

"You told me I shouldn't sleep with strange men."

"I waited till the next morning to give you that advice, though."

Her smile closed over those white teeth and settled in one dimple; she gestured to a chair, which I pulled up, and she sat behind her desk.

"I was a pretty wild kid," she said, echoing her uncle's words.

"I remember."

"I never did sleep around much, Nate. You were one of a select few."

"It was my honor. My pleasure, actually." I felt awkward about this, but was immediately taken with this older version of the fresh young girl I'd once bedded and then lectured and sent on her way.

I'd met her at a party at a fifth-floor suite in the Sheraton. My boxer friend Barney Ross, who'd grown up on the West Side with me, and some other big shots in the sporting world were going to a

wingding tossed by Joe Epstein, who ran the biggest horse-race betting commission house in Chicago. Epstein was an overweight, meek-
looking little guy in his early thirties, with hornrimmed glasses and a
disappearing hairline; but he was a sucker for the night life, and when
he wasn't hitting the local night spots he was throwing his own
bashes.

Epstein had a girl friend who'd been around town since the
World's Fair in '33. She'd danced a pretty fair hootchie-koo for a kid
from the sticks—an Alabama girl with a sultry lilting accent and lots
of chestnut hair and baby-fat curves and a full pouty mouth. Her
name was Virginia Hill and she was looking pretty sophisticated these
days, greeting Joe's guests with a smile and giving them a look at a
couple of yards of creamy white bosom; her clingy black gown didn't
leave much of the rest of her to the imagination, either.

"You're Nate Heller, aren't you?" Virginia had said, taking my
hand. You could've camped out on this girl's tits.

"Yeah. Surprised you remember me."

"Don't be silly," she beamed. "You used to catch pickpockets at the
fair."

"You used to attract crowds," I shrugged. "That attracts pickpockets."

She walked me into the suite, a modern-looking job appointed in
black and white, the furnishing running to armless sofas and easy
chairs, on which were poised pretty girls in their early twenties,
wearing low-cut gowns, drinking stingers and the like, waiting for
male guests. Paul Whiteman music was coming from a phonograph,
louder than a traffic jam.

"Afraid I never gave your girl friend Sally Rand much of any competition," she said, talking over the music.

She was still holding onto my hand. Her hand was hot, a friendly
griddle.

"Sally isn't my girl friend, I said. "Never was. We're just pals."

"That's not what *I* hear," she said, wrapping her accent around the
words, making them seem very dirty indeed.

"Last I saw you, Ginny, you were a waitress at Joe's Place."

Joe's Place was no relation to Joe Epstein: it was a one-arm joint at
Randolph and Clark where the waitresses were pretty and wore
skimpy skirts and V-neck blouses. A lot of men ate there.

"That's where Eppy met me," she said, finally letting go of my
hand, her smile a self-satisfied one.

"I heard," I said, with an appreciative nod for her accomplishment. "You been seeing a lot of him, huh?"

"He's a wonderful guy, Eppy. A real genius."

"Where did he find these girls? They look a little young and fresh to be pros."

Barney and his pals were mixing with the quiff. Drinks and dancing and laughter. Loud men and giggly girls.

"Skilled amateurs," she explained, walking me to a nearby bar, behind which a colored bartender in a red vest mixed drinks dispassionately. "Party girls."

"Secretaries and business-college gals and the like, you mean."

She nodded. "Get you something?"

"Rum," I said.

"Ice?"

"No ice. No nothing. Rum."

"Rum," she said, shrugging, smiling, nodded at the bartender, who poured me a healthy snifter.

"Just girls who want a good time, huh?" I asked.

"Some of 'em might take some money if you forced it on 'em. Why?"

"Some of 'em look a little young to me. You can go to jail for having *too* much fun, you know."

She shrugged. "Most of these girls have been around some. They all do some modeling on the side."

"Oh?"

"Yeah. For the local calendar artists. A friend of mine's tight with the boys who run Brown and Bigelow, the St. Paul advertising firm?"

I nodded. "They put out all those calendars."

"Right. Several of their regular artists are here in Chicago, and I scout up models for 'em."

"These little dishes look like they walked off them calendars, I'll grant you that."

"See one you'd like to meet?"

"I sure do."

And the girl had been one Peggy Hogan, who was a little sloshed when we were introduced, but very cute nonetheless. She told me about her ambitions to be an actress, despite her family's insistence that she go to business school, and I listened. I was a little sloshed myself by the time we wandered into the Morrison Hotel, where I kept a residential apartment, and she was more than a little sloshed when we tumbled into bed together. Despite my condition, that sweet roll in the hay was a memorable one, one I can look back on fondly even now, practically smell her perfume, which was like roses; but the next morning I had been hung over, guilty, and took it out on the girl.

"You should be ashamed of yourself," I told her.

She'd looked at me sad-eyed, sitting up in bed, covers gathered around her, her eye make-up smeared from sleep, putting racoon circles around the impossibly violet eyes.

"I had help," she pouted.

"I'm not proud of myself, either," I said. I was standing next to the bed, looming over her like God in His underwear. "You're a nice kid. You shouldn't oughta sleep with strange men. Where are you from, anyway?"

"I live on the North Side."

"Yeah, yeah, you got one of them flats behind the Gold Coast, right? Right. But where's your *family* live?"

"Englewood."

"That's a nice little neighborhood. White lace Irish. Your father own his own business?"

She nodded.

"And he's sending you to business school, so you must've finished high school."

She nodded. "With honors."

"Figures. You're a smart kid, so you can go to parties every night and still cut the mustard in your classes. You oughta be ashamed."

She swallowed.

"This is no life for you. That guy Epstein, he's a glorified bookie."

Ingenuously she said, "I thought he was an accountant."

"He is. From what I hear, he works for the Capone mob, on the side—helping Jake Guzik with the books. Making sure nobody else goes to jail over income tax."

She smiled a little. "I met Al Capone before."

That didn't make any sense. Capone was sent up in '32. She was about nineteen years old.

"We go to the same church," she explained. "I've seen his wife a lot. St. Bernard's. I dated one of her bodyguards."

"Swell! That sort of life appeals to you, huh? Do you know my name?"

She thought hard. Then she said, "Nat?"

"Close but no cigar. Nate. Don't sleep with strange men. My name's Nathan Heller, and I'm a private detective. I carry a gun sometimes."

She smiled, showed me her wonderful white teeth; first thing in the morning and they looked brushed without brushing. "Really?"

"You think that's swell, I suppose?"

She shrugged. "I don't see why life has to be dull."

"Take my advice," I said, throwing her blue satin gown at her. "Go to school. Find a job. Find a husband. Stay away from Virginia Hill. She'll make a whore out of you."

That made her mad.

She got out of bed and stood there stark naked and shook her finger at me. I'd never seen a girl—or a woman for that matter—just stand before me naked like that without a thought about it. As she shook her finger, her delicately-veined, perfect little breasts bobbled. Her pubic triangle was bushy and near black and a gentle trail of hair tickled its way up to her belly button.

"Don't you call me a whore, you crummy louse. I never took a dime from *any* man."

I was wearing shorts and a T-shirt. Watching her was having an effect on me. She noticed and stopped being mad. She smiled, covered her mouth, catching the laugh.

"You're pretty self-righteous, aren't you, Nathan Heller—for a man whose dirty mind is sticking out."

That embarrassed me, and I went in the other room and got dressed. She came out a few minutes later, wearing the flimsy satin blue gown, sweet little boobs bobbling, and said, "You wouldn't happen to have a car, would you?"

"Yeah," I said, "but it's parked behind my office. That's only a couple blocks from here, though."

"Would you pick me up out front, and take me home? I can't hop a streetcar like this"—she gestured sweepingly toward herself—"and I don't have cab fare."

"I could give you cab fare."

Her jaw tightened. "I don't want any money from you, Nat. Nate."

"Sure I'll give you a ride."

She smiled; no teeth, but plenty of dimples. She had a face like an angel and a hell of a body.

"Sorry I was so rough on you," I said, later, picking her up out front, as she slid in on the rider's side of my '32 Auburn.

"It's okay. It's nice that you care."

"You should stay away from these gamblers and gangsters. And Virginia Hill."

"You were friendly enough with her."

"Yeah, but I'm a lowlife. You find some other social circle to move in. Don't go taking off your clothes posing for no calendar artists, either."

"It pays pretty good money. Times are hard."

"You've done okay. I don't imagine your family fell on hard times much. I bet you get an allowance."

"Is that what you think."

"I think you're a spoiled brat, is what I think."

"Really?"

"Yeah. And check back in with me after you grow up."

"Why?"

"I'd like to spoil you a little myself."

And I'd dropped her at her flat, young Peggy Hogan, and hadn't seen her since, though I'd thought of her from time to time, and her perfume that smelled like roses.

Now here she was, some eight years later, looking older but not much older. She did seem wiser. That was my impression, anyway. Later I'd learn better.

For right now, I sat across from her desk in the lawyer's cramped outer office and said, "You look like you took my advice about school."

"Yes—but I didn't find a husband."

Yet hung in the air. It didn't scare me. If she was on the lookout for a husband, I could think of worse ways a man could invest his life.

"Well," I said, "you did find a right proper job."

She smiled sadly. "It took me a while. I've only been working a little over two years."

"Oh?"

"Only since Dad's first stroke. I tried to be an actress, after I graduated from Sawyer Secretarial. Lived in an apartment in Tower Town; made the Little Theater scene."

That made me flinch. "I, uh, used to have a girl down there who did the same thing."

"Oh? Who?"

I told her; it was an actress whose name she recognized.

"I've seen her pictures!" she said, the violet eyes getting even larger.

"Me too," I admitted. "When did you give up acting?"

"Like I said—when Dad died. I have five sisters, Nate, of which I'm the oldest. I had one brother."

"I know. Your uncle mentioned it. I'm sorry."

She nodded gravely. "Johnny was the valedictorian of his class. He was all set to go to college and the war came along."

"He was drafted."

"Enlisted."

"I suppose your dad intended for him to take over the business."

"Yes he did. Dad always liked a drink of whiskey, but after we lost Johnny, he . . . he got to like it a little too much. The business slipped, and pretty soon Dad was gone. Stroke. Two strokes, actually. The second one killed him."

She was telling this flatly, not the faintest quaver in her voice; but her eyes were close to overflowing.

"So your uncle helped you out," I said. "Got you this job."

"Yes," she said, brightening, using a tissue from a box on her desk to dab her eyes. "I'd never used the skills I'd learned, way back at Sawyer . . . and I've been surprised to find out I still have those skills, surprised more than that to find I enjoy using them."

"That's nice. I'm glad things are working out for you."

"If things were working out, Nate, you wouldn't be here, would you?"

"I guess not. You want to tell me about the notes, and the phone calls?"

"I can show you the notes," she said, getting into a desk drawer. Very business-like, she had them in a manila file folder.

There were three of them; your standard ransom-style, letters-cut-from-papers-and-magazines threats: DROP THE RAGEN CASE OR ELSE; LAY OFF THE BLUE SHEET OR WAKE UP DEAD; FIND A NEW CLIENT OR DIE. Not very original, but the point came across.

"None of these are addressed to you," I said.

"I've been on the end of the phone calls. Most of them have been messages for Mr. Levinson. But they've from time to time threatened me, too."

She didn't seem very bothered.

"If it's not too difficult for you, what have they said?"

"Oh, no death threats, not at me. Just that they'll cut my face up. That kind of thing."

She was pretty blasé about it, and looking at her close, I didn't think it was a pose. This little dame had balls. So to speak.

"What would you think about me tagging along with you," I said, "for the next week or so?"

She smiled wryly; one deep dimple. "I'd like that fine. I don't have a boy friend . . . at the moment. So you wouldn't be getting in the way of anything."

"I'm going to put a man right here in the office with you. I'm personally going to escort you to and from work. We'll go out for lunch and supper together, too."

She arched an eyebrow. "Dutch treat?"

"Your uncle's buying. I'm on an expense account."

"You know, I'm living at home, now. In Englewood. I've been taking the streetcar to work . . ."

"We'll put you up at the Morrison."

"You don't still *live* there?"

"Actually, yes. Different room, though. I moved in when I got back from service, temporarily, and I'm still there. I'm looking for something else, but you know the housing situation."

She nodded. "Do you have a couch?"

"Yes."

"I could move in with you."

"That'd be ideal, really. If you think you could trust me . . ."

"Do you think you could trust *me*, is the point?"

"I could find out."

We began sleeping together that night. She made me promise not to tell her uncle. I accepted those terms; I wasn't crazy. I took his hundred bucks a day, charged him expenses, and slept with his niece. I said I was a lowlife.

On the fourth of our days together, we had just dined at the Berghoff and were walking down West Adams, heading back to the Morrison, when a figure stepped out of the alley. He meant to scare us, and he did, planting himself like an ugly tree before us. He was big and he was pasty-faced and hook-nosed, wearing an ugly blue-and-white checked sportcoat over a white sportshirt and baggy light blue pants. He looked like a bouncer in a circus museum.

"Tell your boss to drop the case," he said, and he jerked a thumb at the alley. "Or the next time I come outa one of these, I'm gonna drag yas back in."

He didn't seem to know me; hell, he didn't seem to notice me. I didn't know him, either, but you didn't have to be Jimmy Durante to smell mob on this guy.

I eased myself in front of Peg, gently pushing her behind me, shooing her back toward and into the Berghoff, and as I did, the guy frowned at me, as if trying to place me.

Both his big hands were at his side, so there was little risk when I pulled the nine millimeter out from under my shoulder and shoved it in his fat gut and said, "Let's you and me go in the alley, right *now*, bozo."

He swallowed and we did. I smacked him once with the automatic, along one side of his head, and he went down and sat amongst the garbage cans and was out, or pretended to be. His ear was bleeding. He had a gun, too, which I took from under his arm and tossed down the alley, skittering on the bricks into the darkness. I took out one of my business cards and, before sticking it in the guy's breast pocket, jotted a note on the back of it: ASK GUZIK TO CALL ME.

The next morning Guzik did.

"You slapped the Greek around," Guzik pointed out in his detached monotone.

"If you'd seen how he was dressed, you'd have helped."

Guzik grunted; it seemed to be a laugh.

I said, "I'd appreciate it if you'd lay off the girl."

I didn't ask him to lay off Ragen. That would be going too far; that wouldn't be my business.

"She's your girl?" Guzik asked.

"She's mine. I'll kill anybody who touches her."

Long pause.

Then: "I'll see to it she's left alone."

"Thanks, Mr. Guzik."

Guzik grunted and hung up.

So did I, trembling.

Peg's lawyer boss didn't make it to court: he had a nervous breakdown first. But Ragen found somebody else to take the case (which was still in litigation at the time of the shooting at State and Pershing) and gave Peg a job in his own office in the meantime. We'd been seeing each other, off and on, since then; but with Peg living at home, being the dutiful daughter, and under her uncle's watchful eye at work and all, we were taking it slow.

And that's why I went along, when Jim Ragen leaned on me to provide him protection in his ill-advised struggle with the Outfit: I was in love with his goddamned niece.

3

Ragen wasn't dead; just unconscious. But the way he was bleeding, he'd be dead soon enough if Walt Pelitier and me didn't move our couple of asses.

First things first: I crossed State to a corner barber shop, where (now that the shooting was over) coloreds were milling, murmuring amongst themselves, pointing over at the shot-up cars. None of them spoke to me, possibly because I still had a gun in my hand. It was a bus stop, and there was a bench; several colored youths were standing on it, to get a better look. No cops had shown yet. This neighborhood wasn't patrolled much—that no doubt was one of the reasons why it had been chosen to host the hit. I walked quickly to the modest newstand along the Pershing side of the barber shop and handed the boy a buck and grabbed a bunch of papers. Then I went out into the street and got in on the pellet-puckered rider's side of the Lincoln, having to yank at the mangled door some to do it, and began wrapping the bloody, unconscious Ragen's wounded right arm in newspapers, like the limb was a big dead fish. The papers soaked up the blood. Black and white and red all over.

I used a few pages to clean the blood off my hands. Then I left Ragen with Walt and danced back through the moderate State Street traffic, most of which was slowing for a look (but not stopping— whites didn't stop in this neighborhood unless, like me, they were shot at or something), and ducked into the drug store, where a thin, white-haired, colored gentleman in a white smock and wire-frame glasses stood behind the prescription counter. He seemed damn near serene, as if his window got shot out every day.

"Has anybody in here called the cops yet?"

The druggist nodded, slowly. "Yes, sir," he said. "I did."

"When they get here," I said, handing him one of my business cards, "give 'em this, and tell 'em I'm driving the victim to the nearest hospital."

"All right," he said, still nodding, not glancing at the card.

BILL DRURY

"That'd be Michael Reese, right?"

He just kept nodding, and I went out, the glass of his window crunching under my shoes.

Michael Reese Hospital was at 29th, a little over ten-block drive, and we'd have to head back north to get there. We took Ragen's Lincoln—the bodyguard car's windshield was shattered, and a tire had been flattened, though I was able to pull it over to the curb and park it—and this time I drove while Walt rode figurative shotgun, Ragen between us, leaned against Walt. I turned left on Pershing and floored it and ignored traffic lights, just slowing a tad as I crossed the intersections while oncoming cars climbed curbs and screeched to stops to allow my passage, and I was going fifty, six blocks later, when I took a hard, careening left on South Park Avenue, a wide boulevard with a parkway down the middle where colored kids paused in their play to look with wide eyes upon the shot-up car full of white people that went streaking by.

The gray-brick complex of Michael Reese Hospital stretched along Ellis Avenue like a fortress in a foreign land; to the rear, separated from the hospital only by Lake Park Avenue, the wide W of the central building and its two major wings faced the downward slope of the Illinois Central tracks, beyond which was the lake. Nothing fancy to look at, the six stories of Michael Reese nonetheless towered over the rundown colored neighborhood at its feet, crumbling three-story buildings that huddled together as if only their close proximity kept them from falling down.

The big privately owned hospital had enough specialists on its staff to attract patients the likes of Ragen, even if he weren't being dragged into the emergency room shot-up, even if it wasn't just the closest, handiest hospital. But that emergency room was populated by street people, almost exclusively colored, victims of the casual violence their neighborhood bred. The South Side Irish seeking their health in this hospital were upstairs in the small private rooms; the emergency room's darker clientele would wind up in a charity ward in Reese's Mandel Clinic or, more likely, be treated as out patients.

As we dragged Ragen in, Walt on one side of him, me on the other, bloody newspaper sheets dropping to the floor like petals from a grotesque flower, a couple orderlies took over and ushered him into the emergency examination room at left, where they eased him onto an examination table and shut a curtain around him. I left Walt to fill in the attending physician, and went back out to the 29th street ambulance ramp, where we'd left the shot-up Lincoln, doors open, motor running, and parked it in one of the nearby Staff Only stalls. I locked the sawed-off in the trunk; this was no neighborhood to be leaving weapons in the back seat of cars. Of course, what neighborhood in Chicago was?

In the phone booth in the corridor outside the emergency room, I called Ragen's home first. His wife Ellen answered.

"He's been shot," I told her, "but he's alive."

There was a long pause.

"Where is he?" she asked; her voice was husky. It tried to be strong, but didn't make it.

"Michael Reese," I said, and she said thank you and hung up.

She didn't ask for any details. There would be time enough for that. I didn't know Ellen very well—we'd only met a few times—but she wasn't naive. That much I knew. Jim winding up on the end of a shooting was inevitable. That much she knew.

Then I called my office. It was late—almost seven, now. I knew Gladys Fortunato, my secretary, would be long gone—she was a dedicated girl, Gladys, until five o'clock rolled around, at which point she couldn't care less about A-1 Detective Agency, and who could blame her?

But Lou Sapperstein might be there. Lou had been out in the field today, investigating loan applicants for a Skokie bank. He was conscientious, and would likely stick around to do his paper work, while the afternoon's interviews were fresh in his mind. If I let it ring long enough . . .

"A-1," Lou's voice said, finally. It was a soothing baritone; Bing Crosby, only Lou couldn't carry a tune.

"It's your boss," I said.

"And you love it," Lou said.

He always said that, or words to that effect, when I reminded him who the boss was. He had been *my* boss on the pickpocket detail, back in the early thirties, when I was the youngest plainclothes dick on the department and he still had hair, or anyway some hair. Lou was pushing sixty, but was still a hard, lean cop. Don't let the tortoise-shell eyeglasses fool you.

"Drop everything," I told. "You're working tonight."

"That's why you put me on salary, isn't it? To get sixty hours a week out of me. So what's up?"

"Jim Ragen's time. Or it pretty soon will be. Lou, they hit us."

"Shit! Where? How?"

I gave it to him.

"Now here's what I want you to do . . ." I started.

"Don't waste your breath," Sapperstein said. "I'll tell *you*: you want me to go to Bill Tendlar's flat over on the near Northwest Side and see just how sick he really is."

Tendlar was the op who'd called in sick; whose shotgun I'd used.

"If he isn't sick," I said, "he's going to be."

"And if he is sick," Sapperstein said, "he's gonna be sicker."

"You got it. This was an inside job, and it wasn't Walt. He was under fire just like I was."

"What about that truck driver pal of Ragen's who had the day off?"

"I want him checked out, too. Maybe you can put Richie on that. But my nose says Tendlar. Of all the guys we got working for us, him I know the least about."

"He was on the pickpocket detail," Lou said, "but after both our times. We had mutual friends, though. He came recommended."

"Judas looked good to Jesus, too. It was Tendlar's shotgun that jammed and almost got me killed. Find him. Sit on him. 'Cause I want him."

"You'll have him, if he's still in town to be had."

And Lou hung up.

Then I dialed the detective bureau at the Central Police Station, at 11th and State in the Loop. And asked for Lt. Drury.

Bill Drury was another former pickpocket detail dick—only he had stayed on. Recently he'd been acting captain over at Town Hall Station, till he and a handful of the other honest detectives got railroaded out of their jobs by the Civil Service Commission, over supposedly tolerating bookie joints on their beats.

"Drury," he said.

"Welcome back," I said.

He laughed. "I been wondering when you'd get around to congratulating me."

"Well, give me a chance. They only reinstated you Friday. And this is your first day back on the job."

"It's not the greatest shift," he admitted, "but it beats unemployment."

"How long you been on?"

"Since five o'clock. Where you calling from? Why don't you come over and I'll buy you a cup of lousy coffee?"

"I'm calling from Michael Reese. Get your reinstated butt over here and I'll give you more than a cup of coffee."

"Oh?"

And I told him, very quickly, about Ragen getting shot up at the corner of State and Pershing.

"Guzik," Drury said, with a smile in his voice.

"Probably. But remember—I don't want to end up in the middle of this, now . . ."

"You're already in the middle of State Street, exchanging fire with a couple of shotguns—and you don't want to be in the middle of this?"

"Well, I don't. Get over here, if you can."

"Who's going to stop me?"

I joined Walt in the emergency room, where Ragen, still unconscious but now stripped down to his waist, his pasty Irish flesh even pastier than usual, his wounds dressed, was being rolled out on his back on what looked like a mobile morgue tray, a young fair-haired intern on one side of him, an older heavy-set dark nurse on the other. They were giving him a bottle of plasma.

We followed them out into the corridor, toward an elevator, where they wheeled him on and the intern looked out at me and said, "Who are you?"

"I'm his bodyguard. Let's hope you're better at your job than I am at mine."

I squeezed onto the elevator and so did Walt.

"You can't come along," the intern said.

"Watch me," I said.

It was one of those self-operated elevators.

"What floor?" I asked the nurse, pleasantly.

"Second," the nurse said, warily.

I pushed the button and we went up.

Walt and I waited outside the surgery, down at one end of a narrow, rather dark corridor, where footsteps echoed on the tile floor and the cool disinfectant-institutional smell constantly reminded us where we were. Ten minutes after Ragen had been wheeled in, two uniformed cops and a detective from the third district joined us.

The detective, a Sgt. Blaine, was a pot-bellied guy in his forties with dark, stupid eyes in a round, stupid face. He pushed his porkpie hat back on his head, to let us know he was appraising us. Big deal. I didn't know him from Adam, but he'd heard of me.

"Heller," he said, his humorless one-sided smile buried in a pocket of puffy cheek. "You're the guy who sided with Frank Nitti over your brother cops."

"If you're going to be mean to me," I said, "I might just bust out crying."

Now he tried to sneer. "Nobody likes a cop who rats out other cops."

"Hey, that was twelve, thirteen years ago. And they weren't cops, they were a couple of West Side hoods Mayor Cermak hired as body-guards. Okay? Can we move onto new business? Like the guy bleeding to death in the next room? Or do you wanna read the minutes of the last meeting?"

He looked at me like he was thinking of spitting, and maybe he was, but the hospital floor looked too clean. So instead he posted the two uniformed cops at the surgery's double doors, and got out his little notebook, licked the tip of his pencil, and started asking questions. I knew we'd have to make a more formal statement later on, but I answered the questions, anyway. There was nothing better to do.

"Where's this shotgun that wouldn't shoot?" he wanted to know. The first vaguely pertinent question in nearly five minutes of piss-poor interrogation.

"In the trunk," I told him, and dug out the keys for him. "You'll be impounding the heap, anyway, right?"

"Yeah, right," he said, like he'd thought of it too. He tucked the little notebook away, and the Lincoln keys. "I guess you boys can find your way home without it."

"We're not going anywhere," I said. "We work for Ragen."

"Oh yeah, I forgot," he smirked. "You're *protectin'* him."

"That's right. And we're sticking, or anyway somebody else from my agency will be sticking, till Ragen or his family sends us away."

"Listen, buddy." He prodded the air with a forefinger. "You just take a hike." He jerked a thumb over one shoulder. "You let the cops do their job." He pointed at himself with the other thumb.

"Do their job," I said. "Like look the other way, if the price is right. A fin, say."

The stupid eyes narrowed, tried to get smart. Without any particular success. He was trying to summon some indignation and come up with something clever or nasty to say, when a finger tapped his shoulder.

"You better call in, sergeant," Bill Drury said. "I can take over on this end."

Drury wasn't big, really, but his broad shoulders and sheer physical presence turned his five-foot-nine, hundred-sixty pound frame into something formidable. His eyes were just as dark as Blaine's, but infinitely more intelligent. His hair was thinning, but combed so as to spread what little there was around. His nose was somewhat prominent and his jaw jutting. And, as usual, he was nattily dressed, wearing (despite the heat) a vest with his dark blue suit, the breast pocket of which bore a white flourish of handkerchief, his wide tie a light blue with a yellow sunburst pattern. He was easily the best-dressed honest cop on the Chicago P.D.

Blaine, about the same size as Bill, nonetheless seemed dwarfed by him. He probably felt dwarfed by him, too. The sergeant swallowed, said, "Yes, lieutenant. I should call this information in. You're right about that."

And he clip-clopped down the tile floor toward the elevator, and went away.

Drury grinned at me, nodded at Walt. Walt had splotches of Ragen's blood on his brown suit. I had some on my brown suit, too, I noticed.

Walt excused himself to go grab a smoke. Drury dispatched one of the uniformed cops to stand by the window near the fire escape down the hall, and the other to guard the elevator. Then it was just me and Drury and the surgery double doors.

"Well, Nate," Drury said. "For a guy who swore off gangsters, you sure pick a hell of a boyo to play bodyguard for. What's a big executive like you doing work like that for, anyway?"

I smiled at this sarcasm, stalled on the answer; I wanted Lou to have a chance to track Tendlar down before I gave all the details to the cops, even to the honest exception of a cop that was Bill Drury.

"Nobody else was available," I explained. That wasn't a lie. It was only marginally the truth, but it wasn't a lie.

Bill folded his arms, leaned back against the cool brick wall. "I've got warrants out on Guzik and Serritella. Also, Murray Humphreys and Joe Batters. And Hymie the Loud Mouth, too."

"Dago Mangano's lucky he's dead," I said, "or you'd have a warrant out on him, too."

"I considered it," Drury said, arching an eyebrow.

"Those guys are just going to love getting hauled in for questioning."

"Not as much as I'm going to love questioning 'em."

Bill hated the Outfit boys. It had started back in the early thirties, when he first came on the job; unlike most cops in Chicago, Drury had pulled no political strings to get on the force—no Outfit-beholden ward committeeman, alderman or judge had played a role in his appointment. He'd made it by scoring record high marks on the police entrance exams; and his reputation as a Golden Gloves boxer hadn't hurt, either. Also, his brother John was a reporter on the *Daily News*—and the department courted good publicity. So Bill had been allowed on.

Naively, Bill had in his early days treated some of the town's top Outfit guys like gangsters; imagine. Whenever he met 'em, even if they were dining with their wives and kids, he would make them assume the position against the nearest wall and pat them down like common criminals (as opposed to uncommon criminals). Those Outfit guys began to wonder what they were paying good money to Bill's superiors for, and soon Bill was forbidden to leave the station house on his tour of duty.

So he'd made a crusade out of it. On his off-duty hours he would stroll Rush Street and Division and various Loop thoroughfares. The time he rousted Guzik himself just outside Marshall Field's on State Street at high noon, before a jeering crowd, was the capper: Guzik had blown a gasket, screaming, cursing, as Drury cooly frisked him, saying: "Two more words out of you, Jake, and I'll put the cuffs on you. Two more sentences and I'll call the Black Maria and get you fitted for a straitjacket."

Shortly after, Guzik headed for the county building and soon a judge had placed Drury under a peace bond, to prevent future molestation of good citizen Greasy Thumb.

Ever since, Bill had had a hard-on where the Outfit was concerned, in general, and where Guzik was concerned, in particular.

"Did you see who did it, Nate?"

"They were just shapes behind shotguns. Wearing white shirts. Sport shirts, I think—I remember seeing their bare arms holding the shotguns. Aren't you glad a trained detective was on the scene to pick up on all these details?"

Drury smiled faintly. "I've sent a colored cop down to question the eye witnesses."

"Good idea. Who?"

"Two-Gun Pete."

"Christ, he won't question 'em, he'll kill 'em."

Drury laughed shortly. "Well, they won't hide any information from him, that's for sure. We're going to nail Guzik's hide on this one, Nate. I can feel it. I can smell it."

"That's disinfectant, Bill."

"If that tough little bastard pulls through in there," Drury said, grinning, nodding back at the double doors, "we'll have Guzik cold."

"Why, you think Jim'll cooperate with you?"

"Sure as hell do. He already gave the State's Attorney's office a detailed statement."

"The hell you say—when the fuck was this?"

Drury shrugged. "Last May. Or late April. Right after that car chased him to the Morgan Park police station."

"He never said a word about it to me! What's in this statement?"

"Quite a bit. It runs almost a hundred pages in transcript. It's mostly about Capone."

"Capone! Capone is ancient history. Capone has the mind of a twelve-year-old kid—and the twelve-year-old kid wants it back."

"Well, frankly, very little of the statement is anything that can be used. He talks a lot about the 'Capone mob.' Not quite naming names. It mostly indicates how pissed off Ragen was that they made an attempt to hit him."

"In other words, it was a message he was sending to the Outfit. That if they tried it again, he'd *really* talk."

Drury nodded. "That's about how I see it. He gave the statement to State's Attorney Crowley, after all."

"Ha. Was he *ever* sending 'em a message. Jesus."

Crowley was a close personal pal of George Brieber, Guzik's attorney.

"He warned 'em not to try it again," Drury said, matter of factly, "but they tried it again, anyway, didn't they? And failed."

"Maybe," I said. "Jim was shot up pretty bad."

"You said it was his arm, mostly."

"His chest was bleeding, too. Don't forget, he's not a kid, either."

The surgery's double doors swung open and a doctor in a blood-spotted smock appeared; he lowered his mask like a bandit surrendering and said, "Which of you gentlemen represents Mr. Ragen's family?"

"I guess I do," I said. "I'm in his employ. I called his wife—she'll be here soon, if she's not downstairs already."

The doctor sighed. He was obviously tired. He said, "We haven't done much yet, except stop the bleeding. He's had several transfusions already, and we're just getting started. He may lose that arm. And his collarbone is shattered. He'll be crippled for life. No doubt of that."

"But he will live, doctor?" Drury asked.

"These are nasty wounds, gentlemen," the doctor said. "But there's no forseeable reason why they should prove fatal."

The doctor excused himself and moved down the corridor, disappearing around a corner.

Drury looked at me, grinning.

"Your concern for Ragen's health has me all choked up," I said.

Drury was laughing softly.

"Now the fun begins," he said.

4

Ragen was in surgery for over two hours. Drury left early on, but said he'd be sending up several more boys in blue to help stand guard—and he'd do his best to hand pick 'em. I sent Walt home and kept watch myself. A little after eight-thirty, Drury's extra cops showed up; he'd actually told the trio to check in with me for deployment. That meant finding places for them to stand. I kept two of them with me at the double doors, and sent the other one outside, to maintain a patrol, particularly the side alleys.

Not long after that I was approached by the hospital's medical director, Dr. Herman Siskin, a well-fed middle-aged doctor with salt-and-pepper hair and matching mustache. He wore a well-tailored dark gray suit and shades-of-blue striped silk tie—no hospital whites for this boy.

"Mr. Heller," he said, offering his hand, which I shook. "I understand you're in charge of Mr. Ragen's security."

"That's right."

"The facts are these. Mr. Ragen's wounds are extensive. He's had five blood transfusions thus far, and penicillin has been administered. Whether or not his right arm can be saved, we don't yet know. His age, the loss of blood, and the resultant shock condition . . . well, let's just say he's not in for a short stay here at Michael Reese."

"I see."

"We have a private room ready for Mr. Ragen," he said, pointing down the hallway, "and we're prepared to accomodate his and your needs."

"Thanks. But let's start by getting him on a higher floor than the second."

"Why's that?"

"You can throw a bomb through a second-floor window."

That opened his eyes. "Perhaps he'd be better off outside the main building." Then, as if to assure us both his concern wasn't for his facility, he added, "Somewhere not as easily accessible to the general public."

"How about a private wing, where we could maintain tighter security?"

He nodded down the hallway to the left. "I'd suggest the Meyer House—which a patient of Mr. Ragen's means might prefer, anyway. It's connected by an enclosed walkway between buildings. You'd have a stairway and an elevator to watch—and the connecting corridor. That's all."

"Okay," I said. "Let's have a look."

Drury's coppers stayed on duty and I let Dr. Siskin walk me down the hall, through an archway into the connecting corridor to the Meyer House, where we took the elevator to the third floor. Siskin led me down a well-lit, vaulted corridor and showed me to a spacious, warmly appointed room—maple furnishings, a lounge chair upholstered in flowery chintz, wall-mounted electric fan, writing desk, chest of drawers, private bath with tub; it was fancy enough to make you sick, or anyway wish you were sick. From the window I saw a wrought-iron-fence-enclosed lawn, beyond which was Lake Park Avenue and the I.C. tracks. It seemed okay, from a security standpoint. The only drawback was a standing fire escape down the hall on the south end wall, maybe thirty feet from Ragen's door.

"No getting away from fire escapes in a hospital," the medical director said, with a little shrug.

"We'll keep a man posted by it," I said. "Does this building have a separate kitchen?"

"Yes. As a matter of fact, the food service in Meyer House is its pride and joy. This wing was built to serve our wealthier patients—Mr. Ragen can, when he's up to it, have lobster if he likes. Why do you ask?"

"They may try to poison him."

He blinked. "I can give you my personal assurance that the head dietician herself will prepare Mr. Ragen's meals."

"Your personal assurance is just swell, Doc, but are you willing to prove it by tasting his food before he does?"

His mustache twitched; he found that a little impertinent, I guess, and I guess it was.

"I don't mean to offend you, Dr. Siskin, and I appreciate your willingness to discuss security measures with me. But I must warn you I'm going to suggest that the Ragen family be extremely cautious. I'll advise that they use their personal family physician, if possible. I'm also going to suggest that they hire private nurses."

"Why?"

"Because you have a big staff here. If we don't do it my way, then anybody in a white uniform will be able to get in that room."

"And not everyone in a white uniform," he said, nodding, "is necessarily a doctor."

I nodded back. "We'll put together a list of names. Nobody whose name isn't on that list is going to get past the guards."

"Mere association with the hospital won't guarantee admittance, in other words."

"If you want to put it that way, yeah. We got to be able to monitor who goes in and out of that room—just as carefully as you people are going to monitor his vital signs."

"Understood."

"Don't feel insulted about my keeping the hospital staff out, Doctor. I'm going to try to keep the cops out, as well."

"Well . . . I can understand that."

I grinned. "Chicago born and bred, Doc?"

Under the mustache, a small smile formed. "Yes. And if I can be of help, where keeping the police at bay is concerned, say the word."

"All you got to do is tell anybody official that Mr. Ragen isn't ready to receive visitors yet. That he's not up to the strain."

"How long would you like me to maintain that posture?"

"Till I say otherwise. Or Ragen himself, of course. He's the boss."

Siskin nodded. Then he said, "I'm impressed, Mr. Heller. You seem to know your job. And I can assure you we know ours, as well."

"I'm sure you do. And don't be so impressed with me. I'm the schmuck who was bodyguarding him when the shit hit the fan, remember."

He had to put some things in motion here, so I walked myself back to the main building, where I found Ellen Ragen and two of her sons waiting outside the double doors of the surgery, the two Drury-picked cops still on watch.

Mrs. Ragen was a small, pudgy woman with a lot of dark curly hair—undoubtedly dyed. I didn't know who she'd been before she married Jim—just some simple Back o' the Yards gal, or a chorus girl or what; but it was clear she'd been a looker once, before age and weight made her face puffy. Now she wore too much bright red lipstick and too much make-up in general, giving her the clown effect of the older woman who was once pretty and keeps trying to get pretty again by applying more and more pancake and rouge. A losing battle. So was the one she was having with her mascara, which was running down those heavily made-up cheeks like narrow black ribbons. Her dress was black, too—premature mourning weeds—with a small gray hat perched amidst the mound of hair and a sort of gray and black speckled vest with a big sparkly brooch.

Her son Jim was a younger (37 or 38, I'd guess) version of his father, minus the glasses and plus hair; he wore a dark suit and kept an arm around his mother. Younger son Daniel, in his early twenties, wore a blue sportshirt and slacks and looked like a college kid, which he was, at DePaul. Facially he resembled his mother, though he was taller. But then so was a fireplug. Daniel—or Danny, as the family called him—looked concerned enough but was fidgeting, hands in pockets.

"Mr. Heller," Mrs. Ragen said, garish red lips trembling, "what am I going to do if I lose my dear husband?"

The formality of that sounded silly, or it would have if she hadn't meant it so deeply.

"You're not going to lose him," I said.

Jim, Jr., released her and she came toward me, wanting to be hugged, so I hugged her. She smelled like face powder. Her cosmetic-counter efforts to forestall getting older were as ill-advised as her husband's attempt to beat the Outfit, and just as futile. They had a lot of money, these people, and they were old enough to retire, and young enough to enjoy it. Why didn't they? As I patted her in a "there, there" manner, she seemed very small, despite her bulk. Like a child.

It embarrassed me, holding this pudgy little woman who I barely knew; but I felt a strange affection for her at that moment. I don't know how guys feel about their mothers, because I never knew mine. But maybe this was something like that.

Only you couldn't tell it from Danny.

"Mom," he said, turning it into a whining two-syllable word, "can I just check in with you and Pop later? The doctor said he was going to pull through okay. Margie's waiting downstairs. We were supposed to meet some friends tonight, at Riccardo's—"

If he were my kid, I'd have decked him. But she just eased out of my grasp, a graceful woman despite her heft, and patted him on the cheek and said, "You were a good boy to come by here, Danny. Don't you worry. Your pop's going to be all right."

Danny grasped one of her hands with both of his and put some warmth into his words: "I know he is, Mom. He's a tough old guy. They aren't going to get him."

She beamed at him and he smiled and waved and headed down the hall. Jim, Jr., seemed faintly disgusted by all this. So was I. Even the two coppers guarding the double doors rolled their eyes at each other.

"He's a good student," she said to me, smiling, proud, face streaked black by mascara. "He'll make a wonderful lawyer someday, Mr. Heller."

"I'm sure he will, Mrs. Ragen."

"I hope his father lives to see it."

"Me, too, Mrs. Ragen. I'm sorry I didn't do a better job today for him. I'm sorry I let this happen."

She smiled at me sympathetically and patted my cheek like she had her son. Neither of us deserved the treatment.

I showed her and Jim, Jr., to Ragen's private room in the Meyer House wing. Settled Mrs. Ragen in the lounge chair and her son at the writing desk, and explained the security measures I'd already taken and intended to take, including that they use their own family physicians to attend Jim.

"I'm sure Dr. Graaf will be glad to help out," Jim, Jr., said.

"And Dr. Snaden is in town," Mrs. Ragen said, looking at her son eagerly, as he nodded back with a small smile. "He's been our doctor in Miami for years." She looked at me and needlessly added, "We have a place down there."

"Is Snaden going to be in town long?"

"He's moving his practice out to California someplace," the son said, nodding. "His practice in Miami has fallen off some, and some of his patients have moved to the West Coast. He was from here originally—still has a place here, in fact—and told me he was going to be on hand for several months, settling various matters."

"Good. Lucky break. If he and your other doctor will cooperate, it'll help us keep close tabs on Mr. Ragen's recovery. I want only a few trusted parties able to get into this room—including medics."

Mrs. Ragen smiled up at me like I was somebody really special; it was a nice smile, even streaked black like that.

"Mr. Heller," she said, "I can understand why my niece is in love with you."

That damn near made me blush; first time this decade.

"Well, I don't know about that," I said.

"Neither do I," a hard-edged yet melodic voice said.

I turned and looked at Peggy Hogan, who was standing in the doorway of the room, her violet eyes red from crying, her jaw tight but trembling. She was wearing a dark blue dress with a white floral pattern; her hands, at her sides, were fists.

She whisked past me and went to her aunt and said a few words of comfort to her, putting a hand on her shoulder; she smiled and nodded at Jim, Jr., and then she turned to me and said, "Let's talk in the hall."

I followed her out there; we walked down to a lounge area between corridors. There were several chairs and couches, but we didn't sit.

"I should be very angry with you," she said, lower lip trembling.

"You're doing a damn good job of faking it, if you aren't."

"You promised me you wouldn't take any dangerous jobs. You promised me that was behind you."

"Something came up . . . I had to fill in . . ."

"People shooting at you in the street! You shooting at them!"

"You used to like life not to be dull."

"I was a kid, then. I was attracted to danger."

"Here I thought it was my boyish charm."

Then she clutched me, held me to her, hugging for dear life.

"Nate, Nate," she said. She was sobbing. Christ, she was sobbing! What was this about?

She moved back to look at me, keeping her arms around me. Freckles on her nose made her look like a kid. "I was so worried when I heard."

"How did you hear, anyway?"

"Lou Sapperstein. He called."

"What did he call you for?"

"He didn't. He called you and got me. I was waiting for you. At the Morrison. We had a date tonight, remember?"

She had a key.

"Oh, hell. I forgot all about it . . ."

"Never mind that. Just let me hold you." She held me. "Hold you."

I squeezed her tight. She smelled good. Not like face powder, or roses, either. Probably the Chanel #5 I bought her.

Then I broke the clinch.

"Peg, what did Lou want?"

"He said he'd found the guy you were looking for."

"Tendlar?"

"I think so. Who's that?"

"A guy that works for me. A guy that used to work for me, anyway. What else did Lou say?"

"He said he was sitting on the guy for you."

I smiled. "Good. Anything else?"

"He said to tell you this guy wasn't feeling good and needed some special medicine." Peggy made a confused face. "He said to tell you you were going to have to feed this guy . . . this doesn't make sense . . . a certain fish."

I laughed. "It makes sense to me. I'm going to have to make a call, and get somebody to take my place, here."

"Aren't you going to look after my uncle?"

"I can't do it twenty-four hours a day, Peg . . . but I'm going to do my best to keep him alive."

"You didn't do so good this afternoon, did you?"

"Are you scolding me?"

"No." She came back into my arms. "I was sick when I heard. Worried for you. Scared to death for Uncle Jim. He's been so good to me, Nate."

"What am I, chopped liver?"

She kissed me; sweet and long.

"You don't taste like chopped liver," she said.

"Neither do you," I said, and kissed her back.

She pulled away, straightened her dress and said, "Those gangsters did this, didn't they?"

"Sure."

"What are we going to do about it?"

"I'm going to try to keep your uncle alive, for the immediate future. And then convince him to sell his business to them."

The violet eyes popped open like windows whose shades got yanked. "Give *in* to them?"

"Of course, give in to them. What else?"

She shook a fist. "Well, fight them, of course! Like Uncle Jim!"

"Yeah—just like Uncle Jim. Who's on his back with his collarbone shattered and his arm mangled, throwing down transfusions like a drunk with a fifth of whiskey and a water glass."

She shook her head, shook her head. "I don't believe you're saying this. Surely you want to get the people who shot Uncle Jim—who tried to kill you! Don't you think they ought to be brought to justice?"

"What justice is that? They own the cops, or most of the cops, anyway."

"I don't know . . . it just doesn't seem right. We should do something."

"You should do nothing but give your relatives some moral support. I'm going to do my job and see if I can't keep your uncle alive."

She sighed. She shrugged. "I suppose you're right."

"But you're disappointed in me."

"No. Not really."

"What happened to not wanting me to take dangerous assignments?"

"This is different. This is personal. This is family."

"This is nuts."

"I just wish you . . . we . . . could *do* something, damnit!"

"I'm not Gary Cooper, honey. Nobody is."

"Gary Cooper is," she said, with a little pout.

"I don't think so," I said. "I think his real name is Frank."

That made her smile, and she came over and gave me another hug. About then, Jim, Jr., came and found us.

"Pop's back in his room," he said. He looked ashen. I think the sight of his wounded father had shaken him pretty bad. "He's awake—wants to see Mr. Heller."

I walked down there. The little room was crowded. Ellen Ragen was standing holding her husband's left hand, gently; a bottle of plasma was feeding that left arm some life, trying to put some color in the white little Irishman. A nurse was tending the plasma, while a doctor was writing something down on a clipboard. The doctor, a somber chap in his mid-forties, glanced at the three of us as we squeezed in, and said, "Everyone, including Mrs. Ragen, needs to clear the room. We're going to be bringing in an oxygen tent momentarily."

"Give me a minute with my friend here, Doc," Jim said, nodding—barely, but nodding—toward me.

"No more than that," the doctor said, sternly, and he went out, taking everybody but the patient, nurse and me with him.

"They'll try to kill me here, lad," he said. His eyes, for the first time since that afternoon he hired me as his bodyguard, showed fear. "I'm a dead man, sure."

"Not yet you aren't," I said, and I quickly filled him in on my security plans. He smiled, narrowing his eyes in little facial ascents to all of it.

"Can you protect my family?" he asked.

"You bet. I'll put every op I have on this."

"God bless you. God bless you."

"What's this about a statement to the State Attorney's office?"

"I thought that would warn the bastards off."

"Don't think it worked, Jim."

"It should've. It should've. They know I made affidavits."

"Affidavits?"

"I fuckin' read 'em to Serritella! Three affidavits in my safe deposit box. Had my lawyer write 'em up."

"What's in those affidavits, Jim?"

He smiled his thin smile. "Everything. I name all the names, lad. Every dirty deed I've been privy to, and I've been privy to more than a few. Those affidavits, they're my insurance policy."

"From the looks of you, you missed a premium."

His eyes tightened. "That's what I don't understand . . . but I want the word put out: if I die, if they kill me in my hospital bed, those affidavits will go to the feds!"

"Okay, Jim. Okay. But, look—don't talk to anybody. Not the papers, and particularly not the cops."

"I said the *feds*, didn't I?"

"Yeah, and I think, when the time comes, that's the way to go. The cop who seems to be heading up this investigation happens to be an honest one—Bill Drury—and he hates Guzik maybe more than you do. He's an ally. But he's one fish surrounded by sharks. If you deal with him, remember what he's up against, in his own organization."

"So I should duck Drury, too, you think."

"For right now. And when you feel up to talking, we'll get you somebody federal."

"You know they won't beat me, Nate. I will not give in."

"Take it easy, Jim—"

"If they kill me, my associates, my family, will carry on. They may kill others—but somebody in my organization will always be left to fight. I have told my boys this over and over. If we stand together, they can't take us."

"Okay, Jim. What do you say we talk about that later?"

"You know what they say, Nate?"

"No. What do they say?"

"The first hundred years are the hardest."

And the sixty-five-year-old wounded son of a bitch winked at me.

JAKE GUZIK

5

An op of mine named O'Toole showed up a bit after nine to spell me. O'Toole, tall, thin, bored, was a few years older than me and I'd worked with him on the pickpocket detail back in '32. I trusted him.

I left Peggy to comfort her aunt and found my way down to the main floor lobby and stepped out into an unusually cool evening for late June. I stretched; to my left was a statue of stocky, mustached Michael Reese himself, whoever the hell he was. Odors mingled in the breeze—from the nearby Keeley Brewery, and the stockyards, and the slum. Nasty odors, but I didn't mind. I'd been on the South Side before.

Visiting hours were getting over and cabbies were picking up their white fares; I considered grabbing a cab myself, though it's generally against my religion—not giving cab drivers my money is about all the religion I have, actually—but I was in a hurry to get to Bill Tendlar's flat on the near Northwest Side, where Lou was probably getting tired of sitting on the guy. And I was on expense account, so what the hell.

But the cabs were full up, and rather than wait and see if another would pull up, I wandered back over toward 29th, and the Mandel Clinic, where I noticed a jitney driver loading up colored passengers in his seven-passenger Chrysler. I walked up and asked the driver, a skinny Negro of maybe twenty-five wearing a brown army uniform stripped of all insignia, if he could take me to Cermak Road.

"If ya got a deece, jack, you got a ride," he said.

That meant even if I was white, if I had a dime I was welcome aboard, so I flipped him one and his hand caught it like a frog would a fly and I climbed in back of the limo. A burly black guy who might've been a beef-lugger from the yards was in the seat next to me; in the seats facing us, a pretty colored gal sat next to a dark heavy-set woman who might have been her mother; the probable mother had a handbag you could hide a head in. The girl, whose hair had been chemically straightened, smiled at me nervously and the mother, whose hair was presumably under her yellow and blue floral scarf, gave me a dirty look that had no nerves in it at all. I stared between them at the back of a male passenger in the front seat.

I didn't work Bronzeville often, but when I did I used jitneys and instructed my ops to, as well. They drove a little fast, but it was safer than standing on the sidewalk. If you stayed on the line, which was whatever boulevard the jitney driver was working, you could travel four blocks or forty for a dime (side trips cost a little more). But you couldn't ride past 22nd—graft only bought these illegal overloaded taxis rights to the South Side streets.

As I got out at Cermak, I risked a wink at the pretty colored gal and she smiled at me, momentarily improving race relations; if the mother caught it, you wouldn't be able to say the same for family relations.

I took the El back to the Loop, adding another twelve cents to my transportation costs, and I got off at Van Buren and Plymouth, right at the doorstep of my office. I would rather have gone straight to the Morrison and my comfortable bed. I was tired. I'd been shot at and scolded; I'd driven a shot-up Lincoln and lugged its shot-up bloody owner into an emergency room; I'd had to teach the director of medicine at Michael Reese what security was about; I'd even taken a jitney ride. But this day, this night, was not yet over.

For one thing, I needed to go up and reload my nine millimeter, and grab a rubber hose while I was at it. We had a little box of such things, saps and brass knucks and the like, on one of the closet floors. Every office has a "miscellaneous items" file, after all.

I headed for the door nestled between the pawn shop and the men's only hotel, opened it, relieved not to find a wino sleeping it off there, thinking for perhaps the thousandth time that moving to better digs was way overdue for the A-1 Detective Agency. True, we'd taken over the better part of the fourth floor; but it was becoming an embarrassment to have clients drop by. The block had never been classy—despite Binyon's and the Standard Club being just around the corner—but my business *had* come up in the world.

Still, certain things about my business never seemed to change.

He was waiting for me at the top of the first flight of stairs; he was sitting on the floor, hook-nosed and pale, black greasy hair combed back, cigarette dangling from his lips, a pile of butts before him at the center of the V made by his long legs. He was tearing a matchbook with his hairy hands, making something out of it. He wore a green and white-checked sportcoat and brown slacks and a pale green shirt and a green and yellow and orange tie that was an offense against nature. His socks were green argyles with some ungodly pattern and his shoes tan loafers. He looked like the golf pro at a country club for felons.

I hadn't seen the guy—who Guzik, on the phone, had once referred to as "the Greek"—since the night he approached Peggy and me on the street. His eyes flickered as he saw me, and he straightened his spine.

"Don't get up on my account," I told him, thinking about the unloaded automatic under my arm.

He got up slowly—like a building reassembling itself in a newsreel played slow-motion and backwards—and glowered at me.

"Mr. Guzik wants to see you."

This wasn't a point worth discussing.

"All right," I said.

"Now," he said, as if I'd refused.

"Fine. Where?"

"The restaurant."

"Oh," I said. "Okay."

We walked the few blocks silently. The lake was in the summer breeze. Nice night or not, he was unhappy; he had a constipated look. I figured Guzik had told him not to rough me up or anything, and that ruined the Greek's evening. It wasn't the first time I'd ruined his evening, after all.

On narrow Federal Street, at the foot of the Union League Club, was St. Hubert's English Grill, where I had once lunched with General Charles Gates Dawes himself, former vice-president of these United States, mover and shaker behind Chicago's Century of Progress, one of the biggest bankers in the city. Dawes had been concerned about Chicago's image—he was outraged by the Capone gang, this "colony of unnaturalized persons" who "had undertaken a reign of lawlessness and terror in open defiance of the law." I wondered if Dawes, who undoubtedly still lunched here from time to time, was aware that another powerful figure in Chicago, one Jake "Greasy Thumb" Guzik, sat nightly in this same Dickensian-style inn dispensing graft to district police captains (or the sergeants who collected the payoffs for them) and to the bagmen (often plain-clothes cops) of numerous Chicago politicians, including various Mayors over the years.

Jake Guzik grew up in the rough Levee district on the near South Side, one of five brothers, and it was said he made his first nickel by running an errand for a prostitute. He was a pimp before he was a teenager and owned several whorehouses before he was twenty. His self-taught accounting skills attracted the attention of notorious Levee aldermen "Bath House" John Coughlin and "Hinky Dink" Kenna, who schooled Guzik in the art of the payoff, the place where politics and the underworld met.

He'd moved up in the Outfit, it was said, by virtue of his account-ing wizardry, and because he had once warned Al Capone—who he barely knew at the time—of an impending visit by a pair of hitmen. Later, when Jake was roughed up by a hardass thief named Joe Howard—who stuck around the bar where it happened bragging about "making the little Jew whine"—Capone repaid the debt, by confronting Howard at the bar, holding a gun to the man's cheek, instructing him, "Whine, you fucking fink." Howard begged a little and Capone shot him in the face. Six times.

Now Capone was crazy as a bedbug, syphillis nibbling his brain while he fished in his swimming pool down in Florida, and Jake was still here. Here in St. Hubert's, sitting alone at a table for four near an unlit fire place, cutting off his next bite of lamb chop. The low, open-beamed ceiling and prints of fox hunts and other sporting events made this a warmly masculine room. At tables nearby, coldly masculine bodyguards sat, lumpy-faced men in loose-fitting suits un-der which guns lurked, men with the blank expressions of somebody who could kill you in the morning and forget about it by noon.

Guzik did not look like a killer; he looked like a prosperous, gone-to-seed accountant, which is what he was. He was chubby but small, flesh hanging loose on him everywhere like the underside of a fat lady's arm. His pouchy eyes huddled behind dark gray tinted wire-rimmed glasses; his flesh was a lighter gray, mottled, aged beyond his perhaps sixty years. His suit was dark blue, nicely tailored but noth-ing fancy, his tie a solid color blue as well, a shade lighter. He was eating the lamb chop slowly but single-mindedly.

They say the night that Capone threw the testimonial banquet for Scalise and Anselmi at Robinson's Restaurant in Cicero, only to sur-prise the boys by pulling a baseball bat out from under the table and clubbing them to death, Guzik just kept calmly eating his dessert while the fatal beating went on. And when Capone, bloody bat in hand, began giving a speech to the stunned assemblage, pointing to the fresh corpses, saying, among other things, "This should teach you to keep your traps shut—and to be loyal," Guzik tugged Capone's sleeve and paused between bites to say, "Okay, Al—that's enough. You made your point."

"Heller," Guzik said, glancing up from his plate, his mouth tightening between the jowls into what passed for a smile on that ravaged face.

"Hello, Mr. Guzik."

A pink-coated waiter, whose English accent struck me as about as real as Mayor Kelly's campaign promises, had ushered me here, to this side room which Guzik and his retinue had to themselves.

"Sit." The fat little man gestured. On his pudgy fingers there were no fancy rings—just his wedding band.

"Thanks," I said, and pulled up a chair across from him.

He nodded to the Greek who'd accompanied me here and the man took a seat at one of the nearby tables with his fellow (if less spectacularly attired) bodyguards.

"How did you and the Greek get along tonight?"

"I didn't slap him around, and he didn't kill me. I consider that a fair exchange."

Guzik grunted his laugh. "Frank got a charge out of you. I can see why."

He meant Nitti.

"How did you know I'd be going to my office?" I asked.

"I didn't. I posted a man there and another at the Morrison."

Fat little bastard thought of everything.

"Mr. Guzik, before we get into anything, there's something you ought to know: Lt. Drury has a warrant out for your arrest right now."

Guzik shrugged gently. "I'll talk to my lawyer. Go in to the station, tomorrow or the next day."

"But you're in a public place . . ."

"Don't be silly, Heller. Are the police going to bother me here? Who is Drury going to get to make the collar?"

He was referring to the fact that St. Hubert's was where Guzik acted as paymaster for the police, prosecutors and political bosses of the eight-county metropolitan area. So that pretty much made it hands off. He felt safe here. That was more than I could say.

"I have a job for you," he said, cutting the lamb.

"I guess you know I'm working for Jim Ragen," I said, carefully. "I don't mean to insult you, Mr. Guzik, but there's such a thing as a conflict of interests."

"I like you, Heller," he said, but I didn't figure he liked me. I didn't figure he liked anything or anybody, except maybe his family, money and food. Of course that's true of a lot of people.

He went on: "Loyalty is important. Al was loyal to me, and now I'm loyal to Al. He's down there in Miami nutty as a squirrel, and a lot of the boys think there's no need to keep him on the payroll. There's not a lot of call for brain-damaged people in our business. But I keep him on the payroll. That's loyalty."

He ate a bite of lamb, leaving a place for me to say something, but I couldn't think of anything to say. I could feel the eyes of the body-guards on me.

"We aren't friends," he said. "I don't expect loyalty from you. If you do a *job* for me, I expect it. But you and me—well, I think you and Frank had an understanding. But to be truthful, to me you're just a guy who did me a favor once. A guy who can be trusted. That's a lot. I don't mean to play that down."

"I already asked you for a favor, Mr. Guzik," I said, meaning when I asked him to lay off Ragen's niece because she was my girl. "I don't figure you owe me anything."

"I don't know about that. When those bookies snatched me, we needed somebody both sides trusted to deliver the dough. And when things got ugly, during the exchange, you came through for me. You did right by me. I don't forget things like that."

He was finished with his lamb chop. Since it was after ten o'clock, I wondered if this had been a late supper for him or just a snack.

He poured himself some Mosel wine; then he poured me some. "Jim Ragen is a friend of mine," he said. "This has all been a mis-understanding."

"Mr. Guzik, I was there. I had shots fired on me. I took Ragen's body to the hospital—he's been crippled for life from this. Excuse me, but that's not a misunderstanding."

Guzik's eyes went hard behind the gray glass. He pointed a stubby finger at me; it was as steady a finger as has ever been pointed my way.

He said, "That wasn't my hit. It was that crazy bastard Siegel."

I felt my face tighten. "Siegel? Bugsy Siegel?"

"Don't ever call him that or he'll have you killed."

Yeah, and you don't like being called "Greasy Thumb," either, do

you, Jake? But you can't peel off all those bills without getting some
ink on your thumb . . .

"Why Siegel?" I asked.

"Siegel wants Ragen gone. He figures when Ragen goes, Continental Press will close up shop. The survivors will be too afraid to
compete with him and his Trans-American."

"I thought that was your operation. I thought Siegel was your boy."

Guzik's mouth twitched. "He's supposed to be working for us, and
for his Eastern friends." He shook his head, frustrated. "He was their
idea."

Meyer Lansky's idea, probably; but I thought it best to leave that
unsaid. I was already hearing more from Guzik than I cared to, my
curiosity aside.

"I like Jim," he said. "We've had our disagreements. But I think
we can come to terms."

"You'd still like to buy him out."

"Or go partners. Heller, you got to understand our point of view.
Back in 1940, after Jim was convicted on that tax rap, he was on
probation—he was ordered by the court to stay out of the racing
information business. We ran Continental for him, while he was on
probation—we sank money in that we lost. Large sums of money,
getting this new business off the ground, after Annenburg had to fold
up. Of course Continental went on to be a big success, but without
our backing, it couldn't have gotten started. We feel we already own
a part of Continental, based on this indebtedness."

"None of this is on the books, though. You couldn't go to court over
it."

"No." Guzik's thin smile connected his jowls again. "I get a charge
out of Jim, taking us to court, on this, on that. He's just taking a page
out of my book—he knows I sue at the drop of a hat." He grunted.
"I'm paying those judges—why shouldn't I put 'em to use?"

I sipped my wine.

Guzik sipped his, got reflective, said: "You know how you buy a
judge, Heller? By weight—like iron in a junkyard. A justice of the
peace or magistrate can be had for a five spot. Municipal court
judge'll cost you ten. Circuit or superior courts, he wants fifteen. And
you can't buy a federal judge for less than a twenty-dollar bill."

"Ragen got a court order against you, though. And he's got you tied
up in litigation right now."

Guzik shrugged. "I'm not the only guy in town with money. Jim's got money, too. Judges don't care who's paying."

"I've already advised him to retire. To sell to you."

"That's wise. I think Jim will come to his senses, too. He needs to understand that we—I—did not do this thing. He needs to understand that he's up against a man who is sick in the head."

"Siegel, you mean."

"They don't call him Bugs because he has fleas. You know me, Heller. You've known me a while, and you knew of me before you knew me. Am I lying when I say that it's well-known I stand for a sound business approach? That I always say, don't kill a guy when you can pay him off?"

"I've heard that," I said. And I had.

"All I want to do is negotiate with Jim. Reason with him." He shook his head again. "These Irishmen. I remember when Dion O'Bannion got himself in hot water. He was running twenty-some handbooks, forty-some speaks, seventy-some houses. I was ready and willing to buy him out. I offered him a six-figure sum for his territory. Said we'd pay him two grand a month, take in all his people in our Outfit. But he wouldn't budge. Not an inch. These Irishmen."

The aforementioned Scalise and Anselmi, they of the baseball bat banquet, had, of course, assassinated O'Bannion in his flower shop back in '24. So despite all this talk of business and negotiation and reason, Guzik was still threatening to kill Ragen, if he didn't sell.

"What do you want from me, Mr. Guzik?"

"I want you to do what you did for me before. Be a neutral intermediary."

"I'm not neutral. I work for Jim. His niece is my girl. I'm just giving it to you straight, Mr. Guzik."

"I appreciate that. But I only mean that you're somebody both parties can trust. All I want you to do is get the message to Jim that we did not do this thing. That it is Siegel's work—that Siegel is a madman and will try it again. I can't stop it. Maybe someday somebody will stop Siegel; but right now his stock is high with his friends out East. I need to maintain good business relations with them."

"So Siegel is Jim's problem."

"He would be my problem—one I could handle—if Jim were to sell us half interest in Continental. I believe Siegel's Eastern friends would tell him to shut Trans-American down."

"Would Siegel go along with that?"

"He'd have no choice. His friends out East aren't going to say much of anything if he wants to go having a Jim Ragen shot up. But if he goes against *us*, he would be in effect going against them."

"I see."

"Here." Guzik dug deep into his right pants pocket. He withdrew the fattest roll of paper money I have ever seen, bound by a thick rubber band. You couldn't begin to get your forefinger and thumb around that wad. He peeled off five bills, like a hand of poker. I looked at them the same way: I had five of a kind. All hundreds.

I swallowed; my tongue felt thick. "Isn't carrying a roll like that a little dangerous, Mr. Guzik? Even for a guy with bodyguards . . ."

"Just the opposite. I always carry ten or twenty grand with me." He said that like ten or twenty bucks.

"With a roll like this, I don't have to worry about getting kidnapped no more. I just give the dough to the guys who want to snatch me and they go away more than satisfied."

"All you want for this five hundred is for me to tell Ragen about Siegel?"

"Yes. And tell him we're prepared to double our last offer to him."

"Double it?"

"Yes. That's two hundred grand for fifty-one percent of the business."

That sounded like a lot of dough to me.

"What," I asked, "if he wants to sell out altogether?"

"We'd make a fair offer. All I ask is to negotiate and reason."

And then, failing that, shoot you dead.

"Okay," I said. I rose, sticking the five hundred in my wallet. "Is that all you wanted, Mr. Guzik?"

"Yes. Report back to me. I'll give you a number." He took a card from his breast pocket and handed it to me. There was no name on it, just a phone number.

"I'll send flowers, as well," he said. "He's in Michael Reese, I understand. I was in there for pneumonia, oh, ten or fifteen years ago, myself. Good hospital. I had 'em put me in that Meyer House wing. Better for security."

"Really," I said, slipping his card in my wallet next to the five C-notes.

I was just turning to go when I heard a commotion in the adjacent room.

One of the waiters, in his mock English accent, was saying, "You

can't go back there, sir," and somebody else was saying, "Oh yes I
can."

And then, big as life, there was Bill Drury standing there in his
natty vested blue suit. He was grinning like a fox; of course, the
sporting prints on the walls around him were all about foxes getting
killed, but that probably didn't occur to him.

"Jake," he said, not acknowledging my presence, "stand up. Everybody else, stay seated."

"Drury," Guzik said, standing slowly, a dirigible lifting off, "why
don't you wise up. Look at the record."

"And what will I see if I do, Jake?"

"You'll see I always reward my friends and punish my enemies."

"Assume the goddamn position, Jake. That wall will be fine."

Guzik's gray face turned pink. He said, "Must I suffer that indignity?"

"Oh, yeah," Drury said.

"You know I never carry a gun. I never carried a gun in my life."

"How do I know tonight isn't the first night? Maybe you didn't
hear—Jim Ragen got shot. You're a suspect. Assume the fucking position, Jake."

Guzik's face tightened—an unlikely sight, considering how flabby
that pan of his was—and he shook his head at the two tables of bodyguards, who sat on the edge of their chairs, ready to wade into this;
but Guzik's gesture meant for them to sit it out. He leaned against
one wall, a fox hunt print just above his pudgy, splayed hands.

Drury patted him down hard. Came across the fat roll of bills and
held it up to look at it, like a piece of evidence he was considering.

"What's this, Jake?"

"More money than you see in a year. Why don't you get smart and
let me give you some of it?"

"Are you bribing me, Jake?"

Guzik turned away from the wall and looked at Drury with an expressionless expression that somehow oozed hatred. He said, "You
came alone, Lt. I don't think anything I say here is going to hold up
in court, now, do you?"

"Well, then, we'll just settle for hauling you in for questioning, for
the moment. Okay? I think we'll have a little lie detector test . . ."

"If I took a lie test, twenty of Chicago's biggest men would jump
out of windows."

Drury threw the roll of dough at Guzik, whose fat hands clapped at it, caught it.

"I'll try to make sure there's a window nearby when we test you, then," Drury said. "Do I have to cuff you, Jake, or will you come along quietly?"

Guzik glared at him, and Drury hauled him out of St. Hubert's. I followed them out, watched Drury deposit Guzik in the back of an unmarked car pulled up against the yellow curb. A uniformed cop was driving.

"Excuse me, Jake," Drury said pleasantly. "I need to talk to your little friend for a minute."

Then he came over and took me by the arm and walked me out of ear shot, up against the front window of St. Hubert's.

"What the hell are you doing here?" Drury said, edgily.

"Guzik sent for me, by way of armed messenger. I decided to go willingly—I'd already been in a shoot-out today."

Drury shook his head. "I didn't know you were in there, Nate—I wouldn't want to put you on the spot. I'd have waited till you come out."

"Thanks, but you're the one putting yourself on the spot. You just had to bust Guzik personally, didn't you?"

Drury grinned. "Hell, it's no secret my pal Jake holds court at St. Hubert's. He just didn't think any cop would have the balls to beard him in his den."

"You're crazier than Ragen," I said, shaking my head.

"We found your green truck, by the way. Over on 43rd Place and Union Avenue. It was built up with quarter-inch steel plates all 'round."

"No wonder I never got a piece of them. Anybody seen ditching it?"

He nodded. "Witness saw two white men in white sportshirts get out of it. That's the extent of the description. It was after dark."

"Great."

"Here's something you're going to like even less: that shotgun of yours? The one you said jammed?"

"What do you mean that I *said* jammed? And it wasn't *my* shot-gun . . ."

"Whoever's it was, it's working now. Sgt. Blaine tested it out this evening, over at the third district station. It fired first time out."

"What? Somebody pulled a switch, Bill! That sawed-off was rigged against me."

"Well, so is this, apparently. It's not going to make you look good. And if the papers get wind of you meeting with Jake tonight . . ."

"The hell with that. Witnesses saw me charge that truck with a gun in my hand, shooting. Nobody can say I was bought off on this one."

"People say a lot of things in Chicago."

"People can go fuck themselves."

He smiled sympathetically. "Where those colored witnesses are concerned, I got Two-Gun Pete on the job. He'll come up with something. Hey—you look beat. Why don't you go home and get some sleep?"

I sighed. "Not a bad idea."

And I walked back toward the office, while Drury joined his "pal" Jake in the unmarked car. I would have loved to take Drury up on his advice, and head for my warm bed in the Morrison. Only I wasn't ready to sleep just yet.

I still had a trip to make, over to the Northwest Side.

Had to see a man about a shotgun.

6

It was nearly midnight by the time I got to the Polish neighborhood near Wicker Park where Bill Tendlar's flat was. I drove my blue '41 Buick straight up Milwaukee, leaving the Loop behind, ending up on this narrow, dirty side street just south of Division, in the shadow of a huge, ornate Catholic church. God had it great in this neighborhood, but the residents in these sagging two- and three-story frame buildings sure as hell didn't.

I parked behind a tipped-over trash barrel and locked up the Buick and stood on the sidewalk, the street as quiet as death, the breeze as soothing as the thought of an afterlife. But the paint-peeling dreariness of the gray three-story building before me was a puzzler. I paid my ops a good wage—there was a housing shortage, yes, but Tendlar should've been able to afford better than this. Not a lot better, maybe, but better.

The building was dark but for a window on the third floor, light peeking out between the sides of and cracks in the green shade. Tendlar's room. Worn wooden steps, half-heartedly bordered by a leaning, rusted iron rail, led me to a heavy, paint-curling, unlocked door. The hall, which seemed more narrow than it was, thanks to walls painted a dirty-chocolate brown, was stuffy, and barely lit by a forty-watt bulb in a corroded copper fixture above an old wooden wall-mounted hatrack that in another part of town might've sold as an antique. I checked the mailboxes on the opposite wall and saw Tendlar's name on 3-A. At the end of the hall, between twin rows of closed doors, stairs rose into darkness. That was okay. I had a rubber hose in my hand, not to mention a loaded automatic under my arm.

I went up to the third floor and another poorly lit, dreary hall, to a gray-painted door next to the metallic 3-A hammered into the nearby woodwork. I rapped once.

Lou Sapperstein let me in. He smiled tightly. He had the sleeves of his white shirt rolled up, his red and blue striped tie loose around his neck. He was sweating, face beaded, loops of sweat on his shirt under his arms. His glasses had slid down some on his considerable nose.

"I was getting worried," Lou said, quietly, stepping out into the hall, closing the door partway behind him.

"Guzik sent for me," I said. "I had to drop by St. Hubert's for a chat."

"Gosh, I wish I could've been there; sounds like a swell way to cap off your day. What did that fat little monster want, anyway?"

I told him; told him about Drury busting Guzik, too. And about the sawed-off that had fired when the cops tested it out.

"What do you figure—they switched guns?" Lou asked.

"That, or unjammed it, then fired it. Either way, it's an obvious attempt to make me look dirty."

"Well, it won't take."

"Maybe. What's been going on?"

Lou shrugged. "I kept it friendly for a while. I found Bill in bed. He's got a bad cold."

"I know. He's been passing it around the office. But this is the first day he's gone home sick."

"Right. We just talked for a while. Then after I gave your girl that message, out on the hall pay phone, I came back in and had Bill sit up at his little kitchen table and have a beer with me. Then I pulled his arms behind him and handcuffed him, and he got pissed off, strangely enough. Really chewed me out, for a while there. For the last hour he's been less indignant and more solicitous."

"Well, let's see what he has to say to his boss."

"His boss," Lou snorted. "Hell, I was working suspects over with a rubber hose when you were in diapers."

"Maybe so, but Tendlar didn't give you a fucked-with sawed-off and send you into battle."

"Good point."

We went in. Tendlar, a medium-size guy in his mid-thirties, was sitting, barefooted, in his gray and white striped pajamas on a wooden chair that Sapperstein had pulled out into the middle of the small room; he looked a little like a convict strapped in the electric chair. His hands cuffed behind him, he was otherwise in no discomfort, except psychological. His baby face was made incongruous by a heavy beard—his five o'clock shadow was midnight black at this point—and his eyes were small and dark blue. Bloodshot dark-blue at the moment.

"Heller," Tendlar said; his medium-pitched voice was hoarse from pleading with Sapperstein for several hours. "You can't believe I'd sell you out."

"Bill," I said, pleasantly. "You used to be a cop. How can you expect me to trust you?"

I glanced around the small, shabby room. You could play a game of poker in here, if you didn't invite more than five players. A cloth-covered brown couch and a cloth-covered brown (but not matching) easy chair and a couple of wobbly end tables were all the furniture in the room. Under my feet was a green Wilton carpet with about as much nap as Sapperstein's skull. Between a closet door and a Murphy bed was an alcove archway, through which a dingy kitchenette could be seen, with the small table from which Sapperstein got the chair Tendlar was trapped in.

"You want a beer, Nate?" Sapperstein asked.

"Sure," I said.

"He's had three of my beers," Tendlar said, almost pouting. "Hasn't let me have a one. It's warm in here."

The room's window was open, but the cracked green shade was drawn. He was right. It was warm in here. I took off my suitcoat. His eyes widened at the sight of the shoulder-holstered nine millimeter. Tendlar knew I didn't carry it often.

"Sapperstein's a hard man," I said with mock sympathy, loosening my tie. "I don't know how you've held up under this torture."

Then, just to be a bastard, I gently slapped the rubber hose with one hand into the palm of the other.

Tendlar gave with a twitch of a one-sided smile.

"I don't buy that," he said. "You're not the type."

"What type, Bill?"

"The type of cop who'd use a rubber hose on a guy."

"You know something, Bill, I've been a cop of one sort or another for a long time. And I've learned one thing in all those years."

Tendlar swallowed. Smiled bravely. "Yeah, and what's that, Heller?"

I smiled. "You never can tell about people."

And I smacked him across the left shoulder with the hose.

He groaned, and it was a little loud.

"Now, Bill," I said, "if you're going to make noise, I'm going to have to find a dirty sock to stick in your mouth. I don't think you'd like that. So you're going to have to keep it down."

And I hit him again, across the other shoulder.

He howled, but softly.

"That's better. We don't want to wake the neighbors—although I got a feeling this isn't the kind of building where the cops get called in, much, even if there is a disturbance."

Tendlar sat there crying, eyes squeezed together, tears rolling down his face. But quietly. He'd gotten the idea.

Lou, who'd come back from the kitchen about midway through all this, handed me a sweating bottle of Pabst. I took a couple of swigs.

"How's Bill holding up?" he asked.

"Not so well," I said. "I don't think anybody ever fed him the goldfish before."

"Fuck you, Heller," Tendlar said.

"You know, I had a couple of tough coppers from East Chicago feed me the goldfish, once. Back in '34, it was. I puked my guts out. I cried my eyes out. And I could barely walk for three days. And the bruises—God, the colors my skin turned. You wouldn't see that many shades at high noon in Bronzeville."

"I didn't sell you out," he said.

I slapped him hard on the right thigh with the hose.

He made a soft crying sound. Then he coughed some. He did have a cold.

"As a guy who used to be on the cops, Bill, you know the whole routine. Good cop, bad cop. We're not going to insult your intelligence. We're not going to subject you to that old wheeze. But we are going to do a variation on good cop/bad cop that we think you'll appreciate."

I took another swig of beer and handed the hose to Lou.

"We're going to both do bad cop," I said, and Lou whapped him across his other thigh.

"I didn't sell you out! I didn't sell you out."

I grabbed him by his pajama front and looked him right in his beady blue eyes, which were dancing with fear, which was just how I wanted them.

"Listen to me, you little cocksucker. You sent me wading into deep shit, this afternoon. You handed me a jammed-up shotgun, knowing I'd take it into a mob hit getting carried out on our client. But what concern was that of yours? You probably figured you'd never see me again, not alive, anyway. Well, I'm alive, and you're dead. You're fuckin' dead."

And I yanked him, by his wadded-up pajama front, to one side, hard, and his chair went crashing on its side to the napless rug. Fortunately, the chair didn't break, and Tendlar didn't, either, at least nothing important. I set him back upright. He was shivering and he was weeping. His nose was running. Those summer colds are the worst.

"You're dead unless you talk," I said through my teeth. "Who bought you. Guzik?"

He was shaking his head side to side, face slick with tears and snot, lips pulled back, teeth showing, and it was not a smile. "I don't even *know* Guzik. I never even met the son of a bitch."

"Give me that fucking thing," I said to Lou, and held out my hand, and Lou filled it with the hose, and Tendlar cried out, "Don't! I can't take any more of it. I don't know anything, Christ! Honest!"

"Honest?" I said. "Swear to God?"

"Don't hit me again. . . ."

I hit him again. In the chest.

He coughed and wheezed and moaned.

I turned to Lou, casually. "Did you know we're only four or five blocks south of the Nitti family deli, Lou? You can spit from Bill's doorstep and, if the wind is with you, hit an Italian."

"Really," Lou said, interested.

I finished my beer, handed the empty to Lou, paced about Tendlar, slapping the rubber hose gently into my palm. "Nice place you got here, Bill. Just you and the rest of the rats."

"It's . . . I know it's a dump, but I got divorced last year. You know that. Alimony. You know."

"I pay you better than this. Alimony or not, why are you living in such a goddamn dump?"

"It's . . . it's hard to find a place . . ."

I went over to one rickety end table where today's Green Sheet, a racing publication, sat under an empty Pabst bottle; various horses were checked off, various notations had been made.

"One of our client's publications," I said, picking up the tip sheet, taking it over and holding it front of him. "He'll be glad to hear you're supporting him."

He sucked some snot up inside him. Tried to pull himself together. Tried to keep his chin from trembling. Couldn't.

"I knew you gambled some, Bill. I didn't know it was this serious." He swallowed. "You know how it is."

"Got in a little deep, did you?"

He nodded.

"Not anymore you aren't. You got out, didn't you?"

He swallowed again. "I don't have anything to tell. Honest to Christ I don't."

"You're thinking they'll kill you if you tell. Well, I'll kill you if you don't."

"You're no killer."

"Ask the Japs."

He looked like he was going to start crying again. "But I really don't have anything to tell you."

"Let's start with the obvious. You did sell me out. Just tell me that much. Never mind who."

"If . . . if I said that I did sell you out . . . I'm not saying I did, Heller . . . but if did say that, you wouldn't make me tell *who*?"

"I wouldn't make you tell who, Bill. Just tell me you sold me out."

He swallowed. He cast his eyes toward the floor. He began to nod.

"You sold me out?"

He kept nodding.

"Say it, Bill."

"I sold you out, Heller." He looked up, with a pleading expression. "It was big dough. You'd've done it in my place, and I wouldn't blame you."

"How much, Bill?"

He coughed. "Damn summer cold," he said.

"How much, Bill?"

"Five gees."

I glanced at Lou. He raised his eyebrows. That *was* a lot of dough.

"It got you out of the hole," I said.

He nodded frantically. "And then some."

"Why didn't you take off? You had to know I'd come around."

"I didn't figure you for this . . . the goddamn rubber hose treatment. You just don't seem the type."

"You'd be surprised how testy I get when people try to kill me."

"No, I wouldn't."

"Did they tell you not to run, Bill?"

He nodded again, not frantically. "Yeah . . . they said if I held up under whatever came . . . cops or you or whatever . . . there'd be another gee in it for me."

"Six thousand to play finger man," I said. And to Lou: "I wonder what the hell the *shooters* got paid?"

"Whatever it was," Lou said, working on a bottle of Pabst, "I bet they have to give it back. They screwed up. Ragen's alive, after all."

"That's true." I smiled at Bill. "Now. Who?"

"What? You said . . ."

"I lied. Who bought you?"

"Don't hit me again."

"Tell me and I won't."

"You won't believe me."

"Try me."

"You'll think I'm lying. You'll hit me again."

"No I won't. Who?"

"I don't know, really. It was all done over the phone."

I hit him again. Across the left bicep.

"You liar," he said, bitterly.

"I can be a real asshole sometimes," I admitted, and hit him again.

"You can hit me all you want," he said, bawling like a baby, "but it's true. It was all done by phone, and money drops. I never saw nobody. They called me, I never called them; I don't have a number or nothing. The voice was male, but it didn't even have no accent. I'm telling the truth."

I looked at Lou. He shrugged.

"Yeah," I said, tossing the rubber hose over on the worn couch. "I think you are."

I told Lou to get a cold wet towel and I wiped Bill's face off. Lou uncuffed him. I took the Murphy bed down and helped him to bed.

"You're going to have a couple of rough days," I said.

He was on his back, pajamas clinging to him damply, eyes closed, arms at his side. He looked like a corpse.

"You're going to hurt like hell," I said, "but don't tip to anybody that we worked you over. We stayed away from your face, so you should be able to pull it off. Don't tip the cops, don't tip the news-hounds, don't tip nobody. Not your phone contact, either."

He nodded. It was barely perceptible, but it was a nod.

"And I wouldn't skip town if I were you," I said. "It just wouldn't look good. In fact, after you had a day in bed, I want you to come back into the office. Business as usual."

He opened his eyes. "Does this mean I'm not fired?"

I looked at Lou and shook my head. Lou was laughing silently.

"Bill," I said. "I'm going to keep you on for the next month or two. Till this blows over. You'll get paid and everything. I'm going to back you when the cops and anybody else, Walt Pelitier for example, asks about your part in this. I'm going to say you're a stand-up guy and clean as a whistle. I don't want any bad reflection on the agency, understand?"

He swallowed and nodded.

"But you're going to stay away from me. Just go to your little cubicle and make your phone credit checks and wait for the day, before very long, when I'm standing before you with a smiling face, telling you to get out of my sight forever or I'll fucking kill you."

He looked at me blankly for a long time.

"Oh," he said, finally. "Then I guess a letter of reference is out of the question?"

7

At one-thirty in the morning, the plush, high-ceilinged lobby of the Morrison Hotel tended to be about dead as its marble floor. A few clusters of out-of-town businessmen were getting in from their evening's entertainment in the big city, talking a little loud, a little drunk; a well-dressed older man in a tux and a good-looking dame in a clingy gown were moving arm-in-arm onto an elevator; the overweight, alcoholic house dick, Matthews, was sitting on a divan almost as overstuffed as he was, next to a palm that was also potted. That was about it.

The night man lurking behind the marble-and-bronze check-in counter—skinny, pockmarked, Gable-mustached Williams, who had been assistant manager for going on ten years now, all the while maintaining the supercilious attitude of one rising fast in his chosen trade—was not glad to see me. He didn't push it, however, because I lived here and took no shit at all off him.

"Messages?" I asked.

He smiled and nodded—which was unusual. I had expected the normal long-suffering sigh of one forced to endure the indignity of the superior doing the bidding of the inferior; instead he rather cheerfully turned to his wall of boxes and came back with a stack of note sheets.

"Reporters," he said, looking down his nose, mustache twitching, as he smiled thinly so we could share his contempt for such lower life forms.

I shuffled through the messages; Davis of the *News* had called every hour. This was typical of the aftermath of an episode like this afternoon's—not that today had been an average day in the life of Nathan S. Heller. If it were, I'd have been dead of old age at twenty-five. Still, I'd been pulled in off the sidelines into the middle of mob activity often enough to know the reporters would swarm in the wake.

"Hold all calls?" Williams asked, almost civilly.

"Yeah, except from Lou Sapperstein. And I guess Lt. Drury; no other cops—if they call, I'm out. Throw these away, would you?"

I pushed the stack of messages his way and he accepted them dutifully if not graciously.

I took an elevator up to the twenty-third floor, which was in the nineteen-story tower atop the Morrison's central twenty-one stories (all of which made it the city's tallest hotel), to "suite" 2317, one rather large room with a kitchenette and a smaller bedroom. Not unlike Tendlar's place, just bigger and nicer.

And, I thought as I worked the key in the door, there was another nice difference: nobody would be handcuffed to a chair waiting for a rubber hose workout from yours truly.

But as the door barely cracked open, I realized somebody had to be waiting in there for me: the light was on, and I hadn't *left* it on.

I had one bad moment, hand drifting toward my nine millimeter under my shoulder.

Then I smiled to myself, thinking *Peggy*, and went on in.

Where, smack in the middle of my floor, face down, kissing the carpet, as if he'd fallen off the nearby couch, was a guy in a lightweight, light brown summer suit. A big guy—not as big as a house, but if he were a garage he'd be the two-car variety. He also had a bloody head, or anyway a bloody back of the head, which otherwise was covered in dark brown, well-greased hair. Around and about his upper torso were the shattered pieces of a porcelain vase and some paper flowers; said vase had once resided on the RCA Victor console radio to the left of the door as you come in.

By this time, I was shutting the door behind me and getting my nine millimeter out, after all. It looked like this ungodly goddamn day wasn't over yet. . . .

I was bending over the guy, hand on his throat, seeing if he was alive or not, when I heard her.

"Nate . . . did I kill him?"

She was standing in the doorway to my bedroom. She was still wearing the dark blue dress with the floral pattern, but neither it nor she looked as crisp as at the hospital earlier. Her eyes were as violet as ever but also wider than ever. She had a .45 Colt automatic in her dainty hand. That hand, which was dwarfed by the gun, was trembling. So was the rest of her, but the hand more so.

"He's alive," I said, rising, going to her, taking the gun from her, tucking my own away, taking her into my arms. "What the hell happened here?"

"I was waiting for you," she said, looking into my eyes apologetically. "I wanted to be with you tonight. I just didn't want to be alone, after what happened to Uncle Jim and you . . ."

"You wouldn't have a key if you weren't always welcome," I said. "Now, what about Kilroy, there? It was you who busted him over the head with my Aunt Minnie's vase?"

"I didn't even know you had an Aunt Minnie!"

"I don't. It's the hotel's vase. I was just trying to keep things light."

Her eyes and nostrils flared. "Light? Light? I've been waiting here with what I thought was a dead body for *hours*, waiting for you, thinking maybe I killed him, wondering what I should do . . . Nate . . . Nate, I'm frightened."

I held her close, glanced back at the guy. "He showed up hours ago?"

She drew away just a little and nodded. "Don't know how long, exactly. I let myself in about eleven and he was already here—after I closed the door behind me, he came out of the bedroom with that gun." She meant the .45 that was now in my hand. "He told me to relax—we were going to wait for my 'boyfriend.' That's you."

"No kidding. So how did you arrange to smack him with the vase?"

"I was just nice to him for about fifteen minutes—smiling, chatting about the weather, just making an inane commentary—he didn't tell me to shut up, either. He was smiling at me. He didn't say much, but when he did, he called me 'cutie.'" She cringed. "And then I asked him if I could turn on the radio. I said I'd be more comfortable with some music playing. He thought that was a good idea."

"And he was sitting on the couch, there, with his back mostly to you, and you clobbered him."

"But good. He fell over like a ton of bricks. Then I got his gun so when he woke up I'd be ready for him—only he never woke up."

I glanced over toward our sleeping guest. "He's hurt pretty bad. I better get some medical help for him, or maybe we will have a corpse on our hands."

"I don't understand . . . all I did was hit him with a vase."

"This isn't the movies, honey. A blow like that to the head'll kill you, as often as not."

"Well, he started it."

I checked his wallet. According to his driver's license, his name was Louis J. Fusco and his address was 7240 South Luella Avenue.

"I know this address," I said, studying the license. "Where do I know it from?"

She raised her heavy dark eyebrows in a facial shrug, as she gazed down innocently at me and my pal Fusco.

"Of course," I said, smiling, standing. "That's Guzik's address!"

Now her eyes narrowed. "Jake Guzik? That Greasy Thumb character that had Uncle Jim shot?" She kicked Fusco; not very hard. "I wish I *had* killed you," she told the slumbering thug. "If that's who you work for."

"Guzik lives in an apartment house at this address," I said. "He owns the place. This guy is probably one of his personal bodyguards, with an apartment in the same building. I should've known right away."

"Why?"

"Guzik sent for me earlier. A man of his—that same clown that accosted us on the street, outside of Berghoff's last year—was waiting in my office building. Guzik mentioned he'd sent a guy here, too. I figured they would've remembered to call him off, once they picked me up. They obviously didn't."

She cocked her head, looking at me like I was the eighth wonder. "You saw Guzik tonight?"

"I'll tell you all about it. Let me make a couple of calls first."

I phoned down to the front desk and Williams answered. "This is Heller. Send Matthews up."

"Why, certainly, Mr. Heller."

"How much did he pay you?"

"Pardon me?"

"How much did this mug who's out cold on my carpet pay you for letting him in with a pass key?"

He gulped. "How can you even suggest . . ."

"I get suspicious when you don't treat me like dirt, Mr. Williams. Of course, it could have been Matthews, or one of the bell boys. I'm just too tired to care, let alone look into it. But if this ever happens again, I'm going to feed you the fucking goldfish."

"The what?"

I cut him off, then called the number on the card Guzik had given me.

"What?" a gruff voice said. Not Guzik's.

"This is Heller. Your boss sent a guy around to pick me up at my place, and forgot to call him off. My girl crowned your boy with a vase and I think he's going to need some stitches."

"Oh. Where are you, the Morrison?"

"That's right. I'm so pleased that you fellas keep up on my whereabouts. I'm sending him down with the house dick. He'll have him in the alley, the loading dock area. You go in off Dearborn."

"I know where it is. I'll send somebody. Twenty minutes, probably."

"Take all night, if you want. He might be dead by morning, but that's your problem."

I hung up. She was looking at me carefully, the violet eyes still narrowed but filled with wonder. She looked like a kid, freckles trailing across her nose.

"How can you talk to people like that," she asked, "like that?"

"I have to talk to all kinds of people in my line."

"No, I mean, get so tough with them. Aren't you afraid of them?"

"Scared shitless. But if you let them push you around, they don't respect you."

"You want the respect of such people?"

"Sure. They leave you alone, more, if they respect you."

She gestured to the unconscious Mr. Fusco on the floor.

"Leave you alone like this, you mean?"

"Tonight's an exception," I said. "Is it Tuesday yet?"

"Technically."

"Good." I sighed. "I've had enough of Monday. You want a beer or something?"

"Please," she said.

I got a couple of bottles of Blatz out of the Frigidaire and poured hers in a glass. We sat at the table in the kitchenette end of the room, by the window, which was open, the breeze wafting through, some traffic sounds too, and drank our beers and waited for Matthews to come up.

Which he did, in several minutes. The red-faced heavy-set dick in the rumpled brown suit had trouble bending over to help me lift the still out-cold Fusco up off the carpet. I got my first look at Fusco's face, at this point, and it was nothing to write home about—he was just another dark, craggy dago stooge from the Guzik camp.

"The least you could do," Matthews said, in his gravelly way, breath like a brewery, "is slip me a fin for my trouble."

"Somebody let this guy in my room," I said, helping Matthews usher the heavy Fusco out into the hall, "and it just might've been you."

"I swear it wasn't, Nate!"

"Well, then why don't you do some detective work tomorrow and get the fin out of whoever it was that did."

He couldn't think of anything to say to that.

So I helped him drunk-walk Fusco to the service elevator, though from the smell of him it was Matthews who should've been drunk-walked by Fusco and me. We sat Fusco in the corner of the cubicle, and I left the slightly dazed house dick and his charge to descend to the alley without any further help from me.

When I got back to my room, Peggy was on her knees trying to clean the blood off the floor with soap and water. She had put the paper flowers on the couch.

"That's good enough," I said, bending, patting her on her padded shoulder, smiling. "I'll get the hotel to take care of that."

She gave me an arch look. "Is it their responsibility to clean up bloody stains off a private detective's carpet?"

"It is when somebody in the hotel let the mug in my room in the first place. I'm going to get some mileage out that, sugar."

I eased her up by the arm. "You want to go out for a bite to eat? Plenty of places still open . . ."

"I couldn't eat after that. How can you still be standing? You look beat."

"I am beat. I plan to sleep till Thursday."

"But Nate—you've got to look after Uncle Jim . . ."

"It was just a figure of speech, honey. I'm going to be on your uncle's door part of the time myself, and the rest of the time my most trusted people will be there."

"You told me once you didn't trust anybody but Nate Heller—and that you sometimes look at yourself suspiciously, in the mirror in the morning."

"True. But there's only one of me and I can't do twenty-four-hour guard duty. Also, I got a business to run. Sometimes you just have to trust people, even if it is against your better judgment."

I put my arm around her and walked her away from the blood-stains.

"Don't send me home, Nate. I want to be with you tonight."

"I'd love you to stay. But let's just sleep. I'm not up to any romance. I barely have enough energy to strip down to my underwear and flop in bed."

She embraced me, put her head against my chest. "I couldn't make love tonight, either, after what happened to Uncle Jim."

"And me. Don't forget. I was there getting shot at too, you know."

"I know. And shooting back. I heard all about it from Uncle Jim tonight. You were very brave."

We moved into the bedroom.

"How was he doing when you left the hospital?"

Her expression was a disheartened one. "He looked deathly pale. He was in an oxygen tent. They're going to operate on his arm tomorrow."

"I hope they can save it—but even if they do, I don't think he's going to be pitching for the Cubs."

She shook her head sadly. "I don't know if he'll be able to hold a spoon. It's really sad. Active man like that."

"Let's go to bed," I said.

"Good idea."

She had a little short powder-blue nightie she kept with some other things of hers in a drawer in my dresser, a lacy thing that decorated rather than concealed her creamy white flesh, small dark nipples. Just the sight of her, radiant in the muted glow of my bedstand lamp, on her side on one side of my bed, half under the sheet, leaning on an elbow, the piles of brown curls framing her sweet face, was enough to get me going. Almost enough. I truly was beat beyond caring about sex. But the events of the day were still churning through my brain; Peg's eyes were bright with thought, too.

I crawled in next to her; wore my skivvies to bed. I don't own anything blue and/or lacy.

"I want you to tell me everything that happened to you tonight," she said.

"Should I start with the blonde or the redhead?"

She pulled my pillow out from under me and hit me with it.

"Okay, okay," I said. "You mainly want to hear about Guzik."

"That's right."

I told her. I wasn't leaving anything out, though I didn't figure to tell her about the rubber hose session; I'd just gotten to the place where Drury barged into St. Hubert's when she barged into my story.

"Do you *believe* what that awful man said? That this character . . . Bughouse Siegel was responsible, not him?"

I shrugged. "It's possible. And it's Bugsy. Actually, it's Ben. I don't think he likes being called Bugsy. None of these gangsters like their nicknames. But then, if your nickname was 'Greasy Thumb' or 'Hymie the Loudmouth,' you might be sensitive, too."

"You know, I get so mad at myself sometimes."

"Why's that?"

"I used to think that men like that were . . . exciting."

"Yeah, you dated one of Capone's bodyguards, didn't you?"

"He was Mrs. Capone's bodyguard. He was very handsome. Dark, like Valentino. Very polite. But he was quiet. You couldn't hold a decent conversation with him. He made me nervous."

"But it excited you that he carried a gun."

"Hey, I was an impressionable kid, then. I looked up to my Uncle Jim, thought what he did was thrilling and dangerous."

"You were right, weren't you?"

"You gotta understand, Nate—I was never very close to my papa. He was one of those hardworking men who provided well for his family but worked eighty hours a week to do it. Well, it wasn't just for us. I think he loved his work, loved poring over numbers and figures."

"It's important for a man to like his work."

"You like your work very much, don't you, Nate?"

"I do as long as it's not today. Getting shot at in the middle of a Bronzeville street by two guys with shotguns isn't my idea of a career. But yeah, I like being a businessman, and the business I'm in, private security, confidential investigations, I like it, yeah. I'm good at it. Of course, it's been a little demanding."

"How so?"

"Well, when you're the boss, and you're building up a business from scratch, you put in a lot of hours, like your dad did. Only at least he managed to marry the girl next door. I haven't had much of a personal life."

"You mean you're thirty-eight years old and still single."

"If I don't settle down soon, people are going to start thinking I'm a fag."

Her face went crinkly with a smile at the thought of that. "I don't think that's too likely. Say, you're not proposing, are you?"

"Not just yet. Not after I saw your work with a flower vase. I bet you'd be murder with a rolling pin."

She flashed those perfect white teeth. She touched the side of my face. "If you ever do get around to asking me . . . well, even if you don't, I'll still love you, you big lug."

Men love it when women call them big lugs. Anyway, I do.

"Why will you still love me?" I asked. Begging for more flattery.

"Because you've really taught me so much."

"Oh?"

"About the kind of man I want to marry. Even if it doesn't turn out to be you. The things I admire about you are the things I saw in my father, and in my Uncle Jim. You care about what you do, and you care about people."

I knew a certain badly bruised party on the Near Northwest side who'd disagree with her on the latter, but I let that go.

"You really love your Uncle Jim, don't you?"

"That's what I started to say . . . I always felt closer to my uncle than to my father. Uncle Jim was always swell—he never treated us kids like kids, more like we were just people."

"I've always had the feeling Jim was the black sheep of your family."

"Well, I don't know about that. But I know Papa wasn't crazy about him. About the business he was in."

"But it seemed kind of glamorous to you."

"I think so. The gambling, the big money, names from the headlines, men with guns, beautiful women with minks and gowns."

"Like your old pal Virginia Hill."

"She's back in town, by the way."

I sat up in bed. "What?"

"She's back in town. Visiting that friend of hers, what was his name? Joe Epstein. They're still thick, after all these years. Imagine that."

"Why, have you *heard* from her?"

"Well, yes. I had lunch with her last Friday. In the Walnut Room at Marshall Field's. She looked me up."

"She looked you up!" I gripped her arm. "Tell me about it."

"Ouch! You're hurting me."

"Sorry," I said. I let go. "Tell me about it."

"It was no big deal. She called me on the phone, at the office. I've

seen her a few times over the years. We've had lunch before. She's
kept in touch with her girls."

"What did she want?"

"To have lunch! Nate, what's the big deal?"

"Did she question you about your uncle, at all? His daily schedule?"

"No," she said, very confused. "Why would she?"

"Did your uncle come up in conversation in any way?"

"Well—yes. She asked about his business."

"What did she ask about his business?"

"How he was doing. How's the tip sheet racket these days, is what
she wanted to know. I said my uncle was doing great and left it at
that."

"That was the extent of it?"

"Yes."

"You're sure?"

"Yes I'm sure! Nate . . ."

"Good girl. Listen, do you remember me telling you, years ago,
that Epstein was Jake Guzik's accountant?"

She rubbed the side of her face; her eyes went dark with worry.
"Oh . . . oh, my. I'd forgotten that . . . I've never seen Epstein, not
in years. I never thought past Virginia herself, when she called. I
never dreamed . . . you don't think she was trying to pump me about
my uncle—for Guzik? Nate, you don't think I inadvertently *aided*
them in setting up Uncle Jim, for that shooting today?"

"If you didn't say anything about his daily routine, no. If you did
. . . yes."

"I didn't." But her eyes were racing, as she thought back, making
sure she hadn't. Then her look became determined and she said: "I
didn't."

"Good. Stay away from the Hill dame. I said it before, and I *hope*
to never have to say it again: she's poison."

She frowned in thought for a while, then said, "I guess this proves
it, then."

"What?"

"That Guzik was the one responsible for what happened to Uncle
Jim."

"Not really. He's not the only one La Hill has connections with.
Haven't you kept up on your old mentor's career?"

"Sure. There's been a lot in the papers about her. Lee Mortimer's column, especially. She's the belle of cafe society—hostess of big cocktail parties in New York and Hollywood. At places like Ciro's on the Sunset Strip."

"Ever been to any of those joints?"

"Nathan, I've never even been to Hollywood."

"It's a great place. The buildings are made of mud and cardboard—you can put your foot through any given wall."

"I can't believe that. You're so cynical. It sounds like a fabulous place to me."

"Why, you still thinking about becoming an actress?"

"No. I let go of that dream a long time ago. But Ginny was in a movie."

"Really? I must've missed that."

"Well, it was her only one. Little role. She's busy with all her social obligations, I guess."

"Where's her money coming from, you suppose?"

"Epstein, other guys like him. She used to have this other sugar daddy, Major Riddle."

I nodded. "He owns the Plantation Club in Moline. Pretty ritzy gambling joint."

It always came back to gambling, didn't it?

"She's done all right," she said, troubled by the thought that her good, old friend might have tried to use her.

"She's had another sugar daddy in recent years," I told her. "Fellow named Joe Adonis."

Her eyes turned into slits. "Isn't he a gangster?"

"He ain't a Greek god. She gets her money from mob guys, baby. Epstein and Riddle, who are tied in through gambling, and the likes of Adonis, who's tied in to every dirty racket you can imagine, from murder-for-hire to peddling heroin."

Her eyes widened. "So then what I said was right: Ginny was after information for Guzik."

"Not necessarily. Adonis is East Coast, and Virginia Hill has been based out in California for years. Hooray for Hollywood, remember? Making movies and tossing parties at Ciro's? She's a goddamn bag man, Peg."

She smiled wryly. "Virginia Hill is no kind of man."

"Oh yes she is. She's a bag man for mobsters—shuttling between New York and Chicago and Hollywood with money and messages. It's no secret."

"So then . . . she could've been looking out for the interests of this Bugsy Siegel person, when she came to me."

"Could be, if she knows him. And she undoubtedly does, since he's the guy running the West Coast end of the mob's wire service. When I say mob, I'm not just talking the local Outfit, either—I mean the East Coast, too. There are men out there who make Guzik look cuddly."

"You've got to find out, Nate."

"Find out what?"

She shook a small fist. "Whether it was Siegel or Guzik who tried to have my uncle killed!"

"Ultimately it doesn't matter."

"How can you say that?"

"Well, it doesn't. Your uncle has to sell out to stay alive. If he doesn't sell, and Siegel doesn't get him, Guzik eventually will."

"You're saying Uncle Jim can't win in this."

"Sure he can. He can win big. He's already a millionaire. He's a winner when he sells to Guzik for big bucks and retires."

"Wouldn't you fight to hold onto your business, if it was being threatened?"

"Not if I was a sixty-five-year-old millionaire."

Her eyes were moving back and forth with frantic thought.

She said, "You know, Virginia's still in town . . ."

"Stay away from her!"

"She's always been my friend. I can't believe she'd try to use me for something . . . criminal."

"Yeah, the mind does boggle trying to picture Virginia Hill using somebody for something criminal."

That stopped her and even made her laugh, a little.

"Why do I love you?" she asked, shaking her head, brown curls shimmering.

"Search me."

"Okay," she said, and she ran her smooth small hands under the blankets, down inside my underwear.

"You're on a fool's mission," I said. "You're not going to find anybody in there—not anybody who isn't sleeping."

"Oh? Who's this?"

"Whoever it is, uh . . . is waking up."

"Turn that lamp off."

"Okay."

"Just let me give you a goodnight kiss."

"Okay."

She crawled up on top of me and kissed me. She put her tongue in my mouth and I told every fiber in my body: everybody up! We weren't tired anymore. I slid my hands under her nightie, under the lacy panties, cupping her small, perfect ass. She reached a hand down and held me, lifted herself, and slid me up in her. She was tighter than a fist but so much smoother. Heaven. Heaven.

"I should use something," I said, moving in her.

"Don't use anything," she moaned. "You'll marry me if I get pregnant."

"I might even marry you if you don't," I said.

Then I didn't say anything; her, either. We just moved together, slowly, her on top, but me driving. I loved her in bed, but I also just plain loved her. She got me into this, goddamn her, shotguns and Jake Guzik and rubber hoses and out-cold bodyguards on the floor with blood and paper flowers.

But I didn't care. I was in heaven. And I wasn't even dead yet.

8

Tuesday afternoon, around three-thirty, against my better judgment, I let Drury pick me up in front of my office in an unmarked car, no police chauffeur, and we headed south on State to Bronzeville. We wound up on the same block where the Ragen shooting had taken place not twenty-four hours before, parking not far from the drug store whose broken window had since been haphazardly patched with cardboard. We had plenty of foul sideways glances and suspicious looks from the men and boys loitering about the street, but, despite the unmarked car, we were so obviously cops that nobody said word one to us, as Drury led me to a hole-in-the-wall saloon a few doors down.

The High Life Inn would have been an apt description for the place if you replaced high with low. The exterior was weathered brick with the peeling ghosts of various pasted-on political campaign posters from the fairly recent past; the words "judge" and "alderman" could still be made out. Above the remains of the posters was a big Coca Cola sign, suggesting a person "Pause . . . drink," to which I mentally added ". . . get mugged." Above it, smaller, was a wooden sign with the joint's name on one line in stubby red capitals against yellow; fairly new sign, a trifle weather-blistered. In front of the place, between an Old Gold poster showing a white society girl in a flowery chapeau selecting just the right cigarette from a pack, a somber colored kid perhaps ten wearing a black derby hat, a short-sleeve plaid shirt and baggy brown pants and black tennis shoes sat on an upended crate next to a card table with a homemade display with tiers of small brown stapled bags, above which in a grease-pencil scrawl it said PEANUTS—5 CENTS. I paused and selected a bag, tossed the kid a dime, waited for my change.

We went on in, past the propped open door, Drury leading the way. The place was dark, as regards both lighting and clientele. In fact, I had the distinct feeling, as numerous eyes at the bar turned our way, that Bill and I might well be the first white people ever to enter. The boxcar of a room had a long counter at left, where eight or ten men stood (there were no stools), some table seating along the right, mostly empty right now, a small band stand with a piano at the back, and a small cleared-away area for dancing. No music at the moment. No sound at all, as these dark men took us white boys in.

The bartender was a big lanky bald man in a black shirt; no apron. Behind the bar, beer cartons lined the wall, with the stack toward the middle only going half way up the wall, so some bottles of whiskey and such would have a place to sit. But the patrons standing at the bar weren't drinking anything but cold sweaty bottles of beer.

In the back of the room, near the bandstand, sitting at a table by himself, was Sylvester Jefferson, the colored cop known variously as "the Terror of the South Side" and "Two-Gun Pete." He was respected and feared in Bronzeville—which in Bronzeville terms was the same thing—and I knew him, a little. He'd been on the job since the mid-'30s and we'd had some friendly run-ins over the years—he'd helped me out, I'd helped him out.

Pete was a handsome, light-complected Negro who had a somber, almost sad expression on his slightly puffy face; he looked a little like Joe Louis, though with an alertness in the eyes that no boxer has. He was damn near dapper, with a mustache about as wide as Hitler's but a third as tall, and his just slightly overweight, five-ten frame was bedecked in a tan suit and white shirt with a wide tie with a tiger-skin pattern. His hat, which had a three-inch brim, was on the table next to a bottle of Schlitz and a poured glass.

He smiled tightly, showing no teeth as we approached, standing, gesturing for us to sit down. Drury said hello, but immediately excused himself to go to the bar and get us some beers. That left me to shake hands with Pete, whose suit coat was open and you could see the two guns on the front of two overlapping belts, framing his police star, clipped to the middle of the lower slung of the belts.

"Those are the biggest revolvers I ever saw, Pete," I said, sitting down.

He grinned and withdrew the guns and set them on the table, like a gunfighter on a riverboat sitting down to play poker at a possibly crooked table. Both guns were nickel-plated and shiny and although light was at a premium in this place, they found some to reflect. One of the guns had a pearl handle and a six-inch barrel, the other a brown handle and a three-inch barrel.

"You're not still packin' that candy-ass nine millimeter?" Pete said to me, huskily, sitting back down.

"'Fraid I am," I said. "Sentimental attachment."

He waggled a thick black finger at me, narrowed the sad eyes. "That's a bad idea. That's the gun your daddy killed hisself with, ain't it?"

"That's right."

"Carrying it, that's your idea of makin' sure you don't use your piece too easy, right?"

"That's it, I guess. I never want to take death too lightly."

"I'll tell you what you don't want to do," he said, patting the pearl handle of the revolver like a baby's butt, "you don't want to have nothing in between you and a shooting situation. You don't want to be thinking about whether or not you should shoot, or this is the gun my daddy killed hisself with. That's bullshit, Heller."

"Well, you may have a point, Pete. But I've been under fire a few times in my time, and I seem to be alive."

He ignored that, saying, "It's like the night I was out driving along 35th—I was off-duty. Just me and my pal Bob Miller, the undertaker. I hear this woman scream and see a kid, maybe nineteen, run out of a store, with a gun in his mitt. I yell for him to halt, but he ducks in the alley and I follow and he starts to shoot back at me. I think, well, hell, least I got an undertaker along—'cause one of us is sure as shit gonna need him. So the kid ducks in back of this laundry, and when I find him, he's locked hisself in the shitter. I yell at him to come out, give hisself up—he says, 'Fuck you, nigger! You want me, you're gonna have to come in and get me.' So I empty this baby into the fuckin' door." He patted the brown-handled gun. "I didn't hear nothing for a while, so I went on in. I got him, all right—more than once. He didn't even make it to Michael Reese. Funny thing, though— when I pulled that poor bastard out of there, dying, holes in his chest, he was puffing on a reefer like a crazy man." He shook his head. "People is strange."

Drury arrived with the beers.

"How's it going, Pete?"

Jefferson stood up, and shook Drury's hand and put the guns back in their holsters. "I was just telling Heller he should toss that old automatic of his in a dumpster. He oughta get one of these .357s like I got."

"I thought those were .38s," Drury said, sitting, pouring some Schlitz in a glass. I was doing the same.

"You can load 'em up with .38s," he said, matter of factly, "but what *I* use can shoot clean through a automobile engine block."

"Lot of call for that, is there, Pete?" I asked, beginning to munch my peanuts. They were pretty good.

He didn't answer me, not directly. He just said, "A .357 Magnum is the world's most powerful revolver. These is the finest guns that money can buy."

"I suppose that's important down here," I said.

"The only way to keep law and order and get respect is to earn a reputation for yourself as bein' as tough or tougher than the roughest s.o.b. on the street." He patted his guns. "People around here know: they don't fuck with Mr. Jefferson."

Like Greasy Thumb and Bugsy and everybody in the world of crime who didn't like his nickname, Two-Gun Pete was the same. He expected to be called Mr. Jefferson and accepted "Pete" only from friends and fellow cops.

He was a good cop, easily the best in his world, and like most Chicago cops took his share of graft—he wasn't interested in hassling the bookies or the numbers runners or numbers bankers or the streetwalkers or their madams; but he was hell on muggers and purse-snatchers and con men and heisters and dope pushers. A bachelor, a ladies' man with a part-time valet and an apartment behind steel bars, Pete Jefferson liked his work.

"So," Drury said, satisfied that Pete had been allowed to flex his muscles and impress his worth upon the two white cops (who already knew damn well what his worth was), "have you found anything out?"

He glanced at his watch. "In a few minutes you'll meet the first of my witnesses."

"How many did you round up?" Drury asked.

"Three so far. Got a line on a fourth."

"These are witnesses who clearly saw the faces of the two men with shotguns?"

"That's a fact," Pete said.

"Did you rough these guys up any?"

"I hardly ever have to rough anybody up no more," Pete said, almost regretfully. "I just come around and they spill their guts."

Better than having a .357 Magnum do it for you.

"Pete," I said, "I have to level with you—I got my doubts. I was there—I was right there in the street shooting it out with those guys, and *I* didn't begin to get a look at either of them."

Pete sipped his beer, licked a foamy mustache off his lip; his real mustache remained. "These boys got a better look than you did. They was on the street. They was not occupied with shooting back."

"I don't mean any disrespect," I said, "but colored witnesses, testifying against white people, in front of a probably mostly white jury and a very white judge, have got to be unimpeachable."

"I know that," Pete said, irritably. "I didn't just fall off a hay wagon, Heller. That's one reason why I'm rounding up four. Taken together, they'll be goddamn hard to impeach."

A few minutes later the first of Pete's witnesses wandered in; he was a thick-set man of about forty, wearing a frayed white shirt and rumpled brown slacks, with gray in his hair and mustache and bloodshot eyes and hands that were shaky, until Pete put the rest of his own beer in them.

"Okay, Tad," he said. "Take it easy."

"Tore one on last night," Tad said. "Tore one on."

"This is Theodosius Jones," Pete said to us. "He used to be a bedbug."

That meant he'd been a Pullman porter.

"Till last year," Tad said.

"Drinking on the job?" I asked, tearing the shell off a peanut.

Pete frowned at me; it wasn't pleasant being frowned at by Pete. I had the feeling he could, if he so chose, tear the shell off me.

But the former bedbug only nodded and gulped at the glass of beer, till it was drained.

I looked at Drury and shook my head, popping the peanut in my mouth.

Drury didn't give up easily, though; he went up and got a fresh beer for Tad and came back with it and said, "I want to hear your story."

"Okay," Tad said, and he reported what he'd seen, very accurately, and described the two white shooters in some detail.

"One was fatter than the other," he said, "but they was both big men. One of 'em had hair that come to a point . . ." He gestured to his forehead.

"A widow's peak?" Drury asked.

Tad nodded. "His hair was black and curly. The other's hair was going. Not bald, but will be. He had spectacles on. I seen their faces plain as day. If you could show me pictures, I could pick 'em out, if they was in there."

"I'll bring you pictures, Tad," Drury said, smiling.

"Tad," I said, "are you up to a court appearance?"

"Pardon?"

"You'd need to be on the witness stand, and you'd need not to have been drinking."

"Got to be sober as a judge," he said, agreeing with me.

"The judge can get away with being drunk," I said. "You can't."

Tad nodded. "Don't matter, really. I been thinkin' of headin' out."

"Heading out?" Drury said, sitting up.

"Detroit. I hear they's jobs up there."

Drury reached in his pocket and peeled a ten off a small money-clipped roll. "Take it, Tad. More to come."

"Thank you kindly," Tad said, smiling.

Pete was looking at me hard. The sullen brown face above the tiger-striped tie seemed to give off heat. He said, "You don't think my witness here has what it takes, do you, Heller?"

"No offense to Mr. Jones, but I wouldn't want to build a case on him."

"No offense taken," Tad said, toasting me with his beer.

Pete nodded toward me and said, "Tad, do you know who this fella is?"

"Sure. He's the guy who was shootin' back at 'em."

Pete smiled and patted Tad's shoulder. "I think you're a damn wonder as a witness, Tad. Why don't you take your beer on up to the bar, and tell the man behind the log to charge your next one to Mr. Jefferson."

Tad nodded, took his ten-spot and beer and went and stood at the bar.

"You're *buying* witnesses, now?" I said to Drury.

"Every cop pays his snitches," Drury said.

"You must want Guzik bad."

"I want him any way I can get him."

"What if it isn't Guzik who bought the hit? What if it's Siegel's contract?"

"Who told you that fairy tale?" Drury snorted, smirking cynically. "Guzik?"

"Whoever it was," I said, "I didn't pay for the information."

The next two witnesses, who came along at roughly fifteen-minute intervals, were admittedly stronger. One of them was a steel worker, a big guy named James Martin who'd gotten his hair cut at the corner barber shop before he wandered over to pick up some cigarettes at the drugstore, just before the shootout. Martin was a crane operator at Carnegie-Illinois Steel's South Works, a union man, a family man, and a church deacon; even colored, this was some witness. Like Tad, he recognized me, immediately. All white people did not look alike to these folks. The other witness was Leroy Smith, a nineteen-year-old clerk from the drug store; he was skinny and a little scared but his description of the two shotgunners matched the others': black curly hair with a widow's peak, balding with glasses; he too recognized me. These latter two witnesses each had a description of the driver of the truck, as well, which tallied.

When all three witnesses had gone, promising to meet with Drury and Pete again when the detectives had suspect pictures for them to sort through, I leaned back in the wooden chair and admitted to the two tough cops that these witnesses weren't all that bad.

"I got one more to round up," Pete said. "We gonna have some depth on our bench."

Drury said, "Pete, I don't know how to thank you. I'd have been lost, trying to work down here without your help."

"My pleasure. I don't like it when those Outfit bums come shooting up my beat. I don't like those Outfit bums, period. Do you fellas have any idea how bad the dope problem is gettin' down here? Not a week goes by we don't haul in a dozen kids, eighteen years old, sixteen years old, some of 'em been on dope two or three years already. I know where the dope comes from. So do you, Lt. They're preyin' on us—ain't it bad enough you got sixteen or twenty families living in a three-flat building, children sleeping four to a bed, in rat-crawlin' firetraps? A man can't find decent quarters for his family, can't stretch a few dollars from his menial damn job to provide food for 'em. Kids playin' in garbage-filled alleys, dirt and filth. And Jake Guzik sends his poison down here so these people can flee into some reefer dream, or stick a needle in themself and go hide in their minds, and pretty soon they're pawning what little they own and after that they're pulling stickups, whatever it takes to get the stuff. Bill, you want my help, going up against these Outfit bums, you got my help. Any time. Any day."

Drury was smiling tightly, drinking that in. Me, I was drinking in the beer. That kind of idealistic talk was fine, in the bar room; in real life, it tended to get you killed.

Up toward the front, at the bar, two colored men were starting to push each other around. A couple of working stiffs in overalls, good size men, both a little drunk at this point.

It was starting to get loud, when Pete got up and said, "Pardon," and took out his long-barreled, pearl-handled, nickel-plated .357 and strode up there.

"Who started this?" he demanded.

Behind the counter, the bartender was leaning against his boxes, smiling. He had a gold tooth.

The two men looked at Pete with wide eyes—they obviously recognized him, and just as obviously hadn't realized he was in the place—and simultaneously pointed each to the other.

He swung the .357 sideways into the gut of the man at his right, and with his left connected with the chin of the other. Both men were soon on the dirty wooden floor, one rubbing his chin, the other doubled over.

"No fighting," Pete told them, and put his gun away and came back to us and said he had to be going.

What a coincidence.

So did we.

NEAR MICHAEL REESE HOSPITAL

9

By the following Saturday a lot had happened and nothing had happened.

I did some time at Meyer House on Ragen's door each day, but mostly turned it over to O'Toole and Peletier, with Sapperstein doing a turn or two, as well. It was a round-the-clock vigil, so some of my boys put in long hours. The police kept three men on at all times, one outside patrolling Lake Park Avenue, another by the fire escape window, and one more sharing the corridor outside Ragen's room with an A-1 man.

We got along with the cops just fine—we were all ex-Chicago P.D. ourselves—but of course didn't trust them far as we could throw 'em. Like I said, we were all ex-Chicago P.D. ourselves.

The fire escape had a landing at each Meyer House floor, trimmed in flowers and plants, making for a regular balcony; Tuesday morning, I'd noticed men in pale green blousy shirts and pants, like pajamas, standing on every level.

"What the hell's that about?" I asked the cop on guard there. "Can't you keep that fire escape clear?"

"Aw, I kinda feel sorry for the poor bastards," the cop said.

They were psyche ward patients, it turned out. The first floor of Michael Reese, where the lobby once was as lavish as that of the finest hotel, had been converted to a psychiatric unit in '39. Some patients were allowed out in the enclosed yard of Meyer House, where they sat in chairs and/or wandered about the small area facing Lake Park Avenue. Hollow-eyed zombies, most of them.

I knew all about it. I'd done some time in a psyche hospital myself, during the war.

"Yeah, you're right—let 'em enjoy themselves," I said. "But if you see anybody on those landings who isn't a psyche patient, clear 'em the hell off immediately. And nobody on *this* landing at all, or I'll hand your ass to Drury. I don't care if it's Freud and his favorite patient."

"Okay, Mr. Heller."

I talked to Drury every day, to see how the investigation was going. The green truck, it turned out, had been stolen last March; the FBI had lent its fingerprint experts to help dust the vehicle, but nothing came of it. Nor did anything come of the gray sedan with Indiana plates, the license number of which no witness seemed to have gotten. Two-Gun Pete did manage to "round up" his fourth witness, a newsboy (possibly the one I bought those papers from, to soak up Ragen's blood); and Drury had gone down to Bronzeville and questioned him, and was satisfied another good witness had been found. Early next week the four would be gathered at the Central Police Station to start going through pictures.

Drury had been less than successful with his frontal attack on the Outfit: Guzik, Serritella and the rest were all kicked loose after questioning. Serritella had been badly embarrassed, however, as Drury—around midnight, Monday night, fresh from his St. Hubert's bust of Guzik—had taken several squads of coppers to surround the home of the First Ward Republican Committeeman (and former State Senator). It got a lot of play in the papers, making Serritella look like the front man for gangsters that he was. Unlike Guzik, though, Serritella submitted to a lie detector test, and passed with flying colors, where complicity in the Ragen shooting was concerned.

At the same time, Mayor Kelly ordered a crackdown on local gambling, handbooks especially; Police Commissioner Prendergast called it "the greatest gambling cleanup" in the city's history. I figured it'd last maybe a week. Possibly even two.

Ragen's family made appearances throughout the week, with all the children, including the three married daughters, putting in regular visits, though Mrs. Ragen herself wasn't seen much from Wednesday on, stopping by during regular visiting hours for an hour or so; she'd collapsed at home on Tuesday after an anonymous phone call came in, a gruff male voice saying, "Tell your old man to get out of the racing business or get fitted for a coffin." Ellen Ragen was (as her husband put it) "a hypertension blood-pressure individual" and her doctor wanted her to stay in bed, and not answer the phone.

Peggy had stopped going in to the office and was keeping her aunt company, playing nurse, although a private nurse was on hand as well; consequently I'd only talked to Peggy a few times since Monday night, mostly over the phone, though tonight, Saturday, we had a date. In the meantime, I had put an op on the Ragen's Seeley Avenue home, too.

Jim, Jr., had taken over the business reins in his father's absence, but to his credit he'd managed to come around every day during visiting hours. He seemed shaken and was not really holding up all that well, but hid it from his pop pretty much—of course, his pop wouldn't have wanted to recognize that, anyway.

I had the enormous pleasure, on Wednesday, of giving the bum's rush to Wilbert F. Crowley, assistant to State's Attorney Tuohy. Confiding in the State's Attorney's Office was like putting up a billboard in Cicero. The staff at Michael Reese, as well as the two Ragen family physicians attending Jim, were going along with me on keeping the cops and such away from him. We'd put word in to the local FBI office that they would be hearing from us—but kept it strictly "don't call us, we'll call you."

It wasn't merely a blind, either. Jim was heavily sedated and in an oxygen tent and mostly just slept, from Tuesday through Friday, at which time, after postponements from day to day waiting for him to get strong enough, the operation on his arm was finally performed in a grueling three-hour session, surgeons probing for pellet after pellet in his shattered arm and shoulder.

On Friday, Mickey McBride showed up. Arthur "Mickey" McBride, that is, the onetime partner of Jim Ragen, in Continental, and who was still in charge of the Cleveland end of the operation.

I'd never met him before, but he'd heard all about me from Jim, he said.

"Jim thinks the world of you," he said, pumping my hand. He was a small man, bigger than Mickey Rooney but just; his face was round, his light brown graying hair thinning some, his face pouchy, his glasses dark-tinted. Physically, he was an Irish, somewhat better preserved version of Guzik. A fairly natty dresser, he wore a gold and brown herringbone suit with a red bow tie and a monogrammed pocket handkerchief.

"He's mentioned you from time to time, too," I said, giving him a polite smile. Jim liked Mickey McBride, but I instinctively didn't. He was too fucking friendly for a stranger. Particularly for a stranger who'd made millions in the rackets.

"You're a pal of Ness', aren't you?"

"That's right," I said.

"He made some waves in Cleveland, I'll give 'im credit for that. Don't think he liked me much." He smiled widely, puffing his cheeks; he looked like an aging leprechaun. "Hated it that I was making legal money off gambling."

"Eliot's idea of a night on the town involves using an ax to go in a front door."

"Ain't it the truth," McBride said, grinning. "Well, he's a nice enough guy. Harmless, now. Private business, these days."

"I don't think you've heard the last of him."

"Maybe not." He made a *tch-tch* sound. "Terrible about Jim. Terrible. Am I gonna get to talk to him today?"

"I don't know. He's being operated on, now."

"He's got balls, the man does. Going up against Guzik and company."

"What's your position on this?"

"Whether he should sell out or not? I don't tell Jim his business. I sold out my interests years ago."

"Doesn't your son still own a piece of Continental?"

"Yes he does."

"But he's not very active in the business."

"He's a college student, Mr. Heller. Pre-law, down at the University of Miami. But he'll need a place to work someday."

"You really want to get your son involved in the race wire business? After what happened to Jim?"

"Mr. Heller, the race wire business has been around for almost sixty years. In all that time, Jim's the first guy to take a hit, and it looks like he's gonna pull through. Now, I know a hundred lawyers that got killed in the last forty years . . . hell, my boy might get hit by a brick from this building and bumped off. Life is a game of chance, my friend."

"Well, you don't seem to be getting in the game, at this point, Mr. McBride."

"Call me Mickey. It's Jim's show, Mr. Heller. I'll back him up, a hundred percent. But I'm not the boss. I'm not even an owner. If Jim wants to go up against Jake Guzik, well he's a better man than I."

"Then why don't you advise him to sell out?"

"I thought you knew Jim, Mr. Heller," McBride said, his smile finally turning nasty like I knew it could. "You think that stubborn mick would listen to me? Just because I taught him everything he knows about this business? Now, if you'll excuse me, I need to find someplace where I can smoke a cigar. Hate the smell of hospitals, don't you?"

He'd spoken to Jim, later that day—night, actually—but I don't know what they spoke about. Me, I hadn't talked to Jim much at all, not since Monday night. And what conversations we'd had were limited to me reassuring him that security here was tight. Between the sedation and the doctor's advice to keep him calm, I figured the time wasn't right to spring Guzik's offer on him.

I took the Saturday morning guard slot. I drove down State, then began cutting over on side streets to avoid the Bud Billikens festivities that would be swarming over the South Side, starting around 29th Street. Bud Billikens was a mythical character concocted by the Chicago *Defender,* the Negro newspaper, to be a sort of colored Santa Claus, and today was the annual parade and festival at which damn near the entire colored population of Chicago would be in attendance.

I arrived at eight, taking over for a bleary-eyed Walt Pelitier, who'd been on since midnight, and met Dr. Snaden for the first time. He was the Ragen's Miami doctor who happened to be in town and who, with Dr. Graaf, their Chicago family doc, was attending Jim. At my suggestion.

He was a thin, very tan man of about forty-five; he wore thick, heavy-rimmed glasses that made his eyes look too big for his face.

"Don't know how we've managed to miss each other," I said, shaking his hand. "I've been here mostly evenings."

"I've been here mostly days," he said with a small smile, though he didn't seem like the type who smiled much.

"You know, I'd swear I know you from somewhere."

"We met a long time ago, Mr. Heller, in Miami."

I snapped my fingers. "You were one of Cermak's doctors."

"That's right," he said. "I was Mayor Cermak's personal physician in Miami. I wish I could have done more for him."

"Well, all the king's horses and all the king's men. How do you think Jim is coming along?"

He shrugged. "Hard to say. He came through the operation yesterday fairly well. He'll have somewhat more use of that arm than was first anticipated. But he has several extensive skin graft operations ahead of him. I don't think he'll see the outside of this hospital for several months."

That was going to be a long haul for the A-1 Detective Agency to provide round-the-clock protection. On the other hand, Jim was a millionaire and there was money in it.

"You think he's up to me talking to him this morning?"

"He's in there, sitting up, drinking juice right now. I think he'd like to see you, Mr. Heller."

"Thanks, Doc. I wish you better luck on Jim's case than you had with the late Mayor."

"I'll see if I can't do a little better this time," he said, a wry smile cracking his parchment tan. "On the other hand, if I recall, you were Mayor Cermak's bodyguard, as well. Do all your clients get shot up like this?"

"Not more than half," I said, with a put-in-my-place grin, and the doc smiled thinly and walked on, and I went in.

Jim was indeed sitting up in bed, sipping orange juice through a long plastic straw. He looked skinnier than I ever saw him, and his right arm was heavily bandaged and in a sling, but his cheeks looked damn near rosy. I guess that's what a dozen transfusions can do for you.

"I feel like a million bucks today, Nate," he said.

"What, green and wrinkled?"

"That joke's older than me," he said, smiling, putting his glass on the bedstand where arrangements of flowers huddled.

"Yeah, but it'll outlive us both." I pulled up a chair. "You given any more thought to selling out?"

"I have."

"And what's your position?"

"Unchanged."

"I had a little talk with Guzik."

His eyes tightened. "When was this?"

"Monday night," I said. "It wasn't my idea—he sent for me."

I gave him the particulars, including Guzik's claim that Siegel did the hit, including Guzik's $200,000 offer. I didn't see any reason to mention I'd been paid five C's to deliver the message.

"Two hundred grand is chicken feed," Jim said, sneering.

"It is?"

"My business is worth $2 million a year."

"It is if you're alive," I said, not showing how impressed I was by that figure, mentally raising his daily rate. "Why not quote Guzik a price? Tell him what you would settle for."

"Whose side are you on?"

"Mostly mine. Then yours. Not Guzik's at all."

Jim laughed. "At least you're honest, lad."

"Don't let it get around. It's bad for business."

"Do you think Greasy Thumb could be tellin' the truth? Do you think this—" he gestured with his left hand toward his bandaged right arm "—could be the work of that crazy Jew bastard instead?"

"Siegel? Sure. It could be."

"Are you looking into it?"

"What do you mean?"

"Are you trying to find out who did this to me?"

"Not really. I'm mostly just trying to keep you alive. I have been cooperating with Drury, who's doing his best to find the shooters."

"You think he'll get the job done?"

"Stranger things have happened." I told him about the trip to Bronzeville and the witnesses that Two-Gun Pete turned up for Drury.

"If the shooters *are* Outfit," Jim said, almost gleefully, "that will prove it was Guzik behind it."

"No it won't. There are plenty of people in this town who do work for Guzik who also take on freelance work, from time to time."

"But if it's out-of-town talent who did it, that would clear Guzik, and point to Siegel."

"Not necessarily. Frank Nitti used to hire out of town talent all the time, for his hits; just to confuse the issue. That's what he did where Tommy Malloy was concerned, and O'Hare, too."

"Damnit, Nate!" He pounded his bed with his good hand. "Give me some good news!"

"Take it easy, Jim. The good news is you're alive. The good news is Guzik wants to buy you out, not kill you."

"He says."

"It's his style. You're not dealing with Ricca or Campagna or Accardo, here. Guzik's favorite weapon is money."

"How can I do business with a man if he tried to have me killed?"

"You don't know that he did."

"I don't know that he didn't. Find out for me."

"What?"

"I want to look into it—work with Drury, but work on your own, as well. You have your contacts, your ways. Find out whether it was Guzik or Siegel who did this; I'll pay a fancy fee."

"I just love fancy fees, but I don't want that job. Jim, I can get away with playing your bodyguard. I have enough clout with Guzik to manage that. But if I go snooping in Outfit business, it could get me killed."

The features of his face squeezed tight as a fist. "You've been saying you think I should sell—well, I'm seriously considering it, now. But I'll only do it, if it's that crazy bastard Siegel who put the hit out on me. How can I sell to Guzik, if he took out the contract?"

"What's the difference who took out the contract? Guzik's willing to buy you out and, apparently, let you walk. Maybe those affidavits of yours, your 'insurance policy,' is working."

Jim rubbed his chin. "That *would* explain it. Siegel could care less about those affidavits coming out. They're no skin off his ass . . ."

"True. And if Siegel's the one gunning for you, well, once you've sold out to Guzik, the heat's off. Siegel would no longer have reason to want you dead. No matter how crazy he is."

"Damnit, Nate! Find out for me! Find out whicha them bastards tried to kill me. Tried to kill *us*!"

I stood. "Jim, I'm just upsetting you. I'm going to have to go. I'll be outside the door, if you need me, till noon. That's when another of my ops comes on for me."

His expression pleaded with me; so did his words: "Nate . . . take the assignment. There isn't a private dick in town, in the country, that knows these Outfit bastards better than you. You're the only man for the job, lad . . ."

"Jim, you're my friend, and more important, my client, and I'm doing my best to keep you alive. It ends there."

And I went out in the hall. Breathed out some air. I felt battered. Even with a clipped wing, that Irish son of a bitch was a handful.

I went down to the lounge area where I'd spoken to Peggy last Monday night and, after bumming a cigarette off a passing doctor, sat and smoked. I don't smoke, as a rule—I picked the habit up overseas, in the Marines, and dropped it when I got back. But now and then I got the craving. Usually when I started getting the combat jitters. I'd been smoking off and on all week.

A few minutes later, just as I was standing up, grinding the cigarette under my heel, ready to go back and help guard Ragen's door, an orderly approached me, a colored kid of maybe twenty with a light brown complexion and dark close-cropped brown hair.

"Are you one of the detectives watching Mr. Ragen?" he asked.

I said I was.

"I think I have something I oughta tell you about."

"Well why don't you, then."

He swallowed. "Okay. After work yesterday, I was playing ball over at the recreation grounds. At Wentworth Avenue? I was playing softball. I saw these men looking at me in particular. They was watching us play ball, I thought, but they was looking at me. I had my badge on that shows I'm an employee here at the hospital." He swallowed again.

"Go on, son."

"Well, one of them come up to me and asked if I work at the hospital. I say I did. He ask me some questions about Mr. Ragen's condition. He say he was a reporter. Anyway, he ask where Mr. Ragen's room was. I . . . I told him."

"He gave you money, didn't he?"

The boy looked at the floor and nodded.

"Did you tell him?"

"Just that Mr. Ragen was on the third floor away from the fire escape."

"What did these men look like?"

"White men—real white. One had dark hair, real curly. The other had glasses and was kind of bald. They were both kinda big."

Well, what do you know.

"What happened then, kid?"

"The man had some more questions—he was the one that didn't have no glasses—and I said I didn't think I wanted to talk to him anymore. Last night I was thinking about it, and I thought, what if he wasn't a reporter? Those men didn't look like reporters. I didn't sleep so good."

"Have you told anybody else about this?"

"No, sir. I heard you was a private detective and not city. So I waited to tell you. I didn't want Mr. Ragen to get hurt, but I didn't want to get myself in trouble, neither."

I patted him on the shoulder. "You were smart to come to me."

"I don't want any money from you, mister."

"Good, 'cause I'm not going to give you any. Now go back to work."

I went down to the second floor, to the nearest phone booth, and tried to call Drury at home; his wife said he was still asleep and I told her not to wake him—I'd call back around noon. Then I walked back toward Ragen's room and plopped myself down in a straightback chair next to the cop. He was reading the morning *Tribune*. I told him he ought to be more alert than that, and took it away from him, read it myself. But all I could think about was the two guys the orderly had seen.

About eleven o'clock I glanced down the hall and noticed the fire-escape cop was gone.

"Where's your pal?" I asked the cop next to me.

"How should I know? Takin' a dump?"

"I'm going to cover the fire escape till he gets back."

I went down there and looked out the window. Down through the grating of the fire escape I could see a few psyche ward patients, in their green pajamas, enjoying the view of the I.C. tracks from their perch.

Maybe ten minutes later, a patient started up the stairs onto the third level; he was followed by another.

I stepped out onto the fire escape just as they had gotten onto the landing and said, "Nobody on this level, boys," and realized I was looking at two sallow individuals, one of whom had dark brown curly hair and a widow's peak and a wedge-shaped face, the other of whom was balding and round-faced and wore glasses, both of whom were wearing green psyche-ward p.j.s, but neither of whom were mentally sick, though I wouldn't have minded giving either one of them a lobotomy with my nine millimeter, which I was grabbing out from under my shoulder.

"Hold it right there," I said, pointing the gun at them.

They froze. The widow's-peaked guy had a big nose and bushy brown eyebrows and thick lips and bad teeth and a couple facial moles; the guy with glasses hadn't exactly stepped out of an Arrow shirt ad, either, though he had more regular features that added up to a baby face, albeit a pretty ugly baby. They both had the blankly evil expression of the business end of an automatic.

"Put your fuckin' hands in the air," I added, and they did.

I knew them. I don't just mean that they matched up with the descriptions given by Two-Gun Pete's trio of colored witnesses, and the orderly's description of the "reporters": no. I knew them from the West Side. The widow's-peaked guy was Davey Finkel. The guy with glasses was Joseph "Blinkey" Leonard. West Side boys—like me. Well, not quite like me, I hope.

"Okay, Davey," I said to Finkel, "one step forward."

With my left hand, I patted him down; under the loose green top, he had a .45 automatic tucked in his waistband—he was wearing slacks under the baggy pajama bottoms. I tossed the piece just behind me and it clanked on the fire escape floor.

"One step back," I told him, and nodded to his balding friend. "Now you, Blinkey."

I disarmed him, as well; he carried a relatively small gun, a .32 automatic, but it had a silencer attached, making it bulky. This, had I not intercepted them, would have been the murder weapon, the little darling that would've given Ragen a goodbye kiss. I tossed it just behind me, too, clanking.

"What's a couple of nice Jewish bookies like you guys doing playing torpedo, anyway?"

"Why don't you just let us lam out of here, Heller," Finkel said, in his sandpaper voice. "You won this round, okay?"

"No hard feelings," Blinkey said; his voice was higher pitched but just as unpleasant.

"I got hard feelings," I said. "You boys tried to kill me last Monday."

They shut their traps, glanced at each other, looked back at me. Finkel was scowling; Blinkey had a bland, blank expression.

"Now we're all going to step inside," I said, jerking my head toward the door to the Meyer House third floor. "You boys, first. Feel free to pull something and give me an excuse."

Just behind them, coming up the fire escape steps, came a painfully thin patient, about thirty, with a gray pallor and dazed expression and green psyche-ward p.j.s. I knew just looking at him he was a veteran; he had combat in his face.

"Can you see the lake from here?" the man said, very slowly.

"Please," I started, "get off . . ."

Finkel grabbed the skinny figure and goddamn hurled him at me, knocking me back against the fire-escape rail, hard; and quickly headed back down the iron stairway, Leonard already having a head start on him.

I brushed past the confused psyche patient and followed them down, the fire escape stairs rattling like a passing El. I had a gun and they didn't, but they stayed a landing ahead of me and on each landing were more psyche patients, and when they reached the bottom, there were more psyche patients still, a sea of green nutcases they waded into, poor goddamn innocents that were in the way of me getting a shot off at these guilty sons of bitches. They didn't head for

Lake Park Avenue, possibly because a cop was patrolling it, but to the right, around toward the Meyer House parking lot and loading area.

Their car was probably in this small lot, but it wasn't going to do them any good at the moment, because a food delivery truck was slowly maneuvering—and blocking—the narrow alley between the parking lot, the Meyer House and another hospital building. And that was the only way out.

So they were on foot, running down an aisle between parked cars, then squeezing past that delivery truck through the alley, two desperate men in green pajamas.

I followed, gun in hand, running through the parking lot, edging past the truck, following them out onto 29th; they were moving fast, but tearing at their outer covering, shedding their green tops, beneath which were white sportshirts. They crossed to Ellis Avenue, a street of two- and three-story buildings whose once proud architecture had long since decayed, cutting across a lot made vacant by an urban renewal project.

Finkel and Leonard were heavier men than me, but younger, and, so far anyway, faster. I could take a shot at them, but they were unarmed; wasn't sure I could risk it. I was breathing hard, stumbling on the rocks and rubble of the vacant lot, watching up ahead as they climbed a fence that was half-fallen down already. When I climbed it, I found myself in an alley. Soon I was trailing them through a nightmare landscape, the garbage-strewn alley running past the ass-ends of crumbling tenements whose tiers of back porch balconies sagged, their wooden slats like rotting teeth about to fall out. But it was strangely deserted—not a single colored face looked out from a window; no children jumped rope or sang songs. Yet in the distance I could hear music. A marching band was accompanying us as we ran. . . .

And, God bless John Phillip Sousa, I was gaining on them; they were glancing back, seeing that I was, some panic in their faces, and I grinned and poured it on. Then, at alley's end, they rounded the corner, on what must have been 32nd, and soon I realized why it was so deserted, understood the band music, remembered: Bud Billikens Day.

Thirty-second street itself was thronged with colored kids in Boy Scout uniforms, being lined up for marching purposes by similarly garbed dark adults; and some kind of high school marching band, in gaudy uniform, was already in rows, practicing a tune. Most of this activity was in the street itself, but there was overflow and parents and such on the sidewalks, including the two white men in white sportshirts and green pajama bottoms who went running through that crowd, knocking people aside, women and children included, and people were immediately pissed. Into that hostile arena I ran, having tucked my nine millimeter away as soon as I saw this mass of humanity, doing my best not to knock into anybody, slowing down accordingly.

And then I was at South Park Avenue, where the parade was in full swing, sidewalks packed; this boulevard, with its four lanes divided by a parkway, was thronged with colored people, in their summer finery, men in straw hats, women in bonnets, kids getting their Sunday duds stained from free ice cream and candy and pop, families filling the sidewalks, lining the parkway, as marching bands and floats streamed by.

Through this pushed my two psyche ward escapees, jostling an otherwise utterly Negro crowd that was too stunned by this Caucasian presence to do anything; I followed after, but was falling back, slowed by the sidewalk swarm. I felt hands on me, touching, slapping, but nobody outright grabbed me, or hit me, or had yet, at least. I couldn't even make out any cries of outrage, in the general confusion of band music and the crowd noise.

I'd lost sight of them, now. Hopelessness rising in me, I got to the front of the packed sidewalk and looked for white faces in a black world. It was a Klansman's worst nightmare come true.

And then there they were: they'd moved out into the street, were running alongside a float from Lake View Dairy, where a giant shredded paper milk bottle served as the backdrop for a throne for a lovely high yellow gal in a gown and crown, who was waving to her subjects.

By the time I caught up with the dairy float, Finkel and Leonard had cut across in front of it, and were up running alongside a pack of cyclists on decorated bikes. I cut in front of the float, too, fell in behind the two. They had perhaps twenty yards on me. I smiled. They seemed to be tiring; I was going to catch them after all—I was getting my second wind. People were pointing at us, shouting at us, perhaps some of them not quite sure we weren't part of the festivities.

Then I saw the two of them veer off the street and back into the crowd, on the parkway side. Getting away from the parade.

I picked up speed, and a hand reached out and grabbed me and my legs went out from under me and I rolled forward, in an awkward somersault, skinning myself on the pavement.

When I finally picked myself up, a colored cop was standing there, glowering at me. He had a nightstick in one hand; the sun was glinting off the polished copper buttons of his blue uniform.

I glanced up ahead.

My psyche-ward escapees were gone.

I felt a hand on my arm, yanking me off the street as the dairy float floated by, the high yellow queen waving, enjoying her moment.

"I don't suppose it would do any good," I said to the cop as he pulled me through the crowd on the parkway, "to mention I'm a personal friend of Two-Gun Pete."

"He's Mr. Jefferson to you," the cop said, and folded me in half with his billy club.

In the background, the colored crowd was cheering.

10

The Pershing on 64th Street, the top Negro hotel in Chicago, drew a lot of white trade at its Beige Room. On most any Saturday night, eight hundred people of both races packed themselves into this basement ballroom that was Bronzeville's swankiest nightclub. Tonight, Peggy Hogan and I, just the two of us at a cloth-covered table for four, were among them.

"I haven't been in a black-and-tan in years," she said, sipping her stinger through cherry red lips. She looked terrific, wearing a stylish beige suit, in honor of the room, a white flower in her pinned back hair; Joan Crawford would've killed for those padded shoulders. "And this is the slickest black-and-tan I've ever seen."

"Yeah," I said, trying to muster some enthusiasm, "slick as a whistle." I did not look or feel terrific. I was bruised and skinned-up and sore, from marching in the Bud Billikens Day parade (and having it march on me); if Two-Gun Pete Jefferson hadn't spoken up for me at the Fifth District Station, I'd probably still be in a cell.

Yet here I was in Bronzeville, again—at Two-Gun Pete's request, otherwise I wouldn't have come within a mile of the black belt tonight. But Pete had asked me to meet him here around ten, because the Ragen shooting investigation was "really popping." It was now ten-thirty-something.

I was already set to go out with Peggy this evening, and so I did, even though we got a late start. I had no qualms about bringing her into this part of town: she was a South Side girl herself, though obviously not from this particular part of the South Side. And besides, any effort I made on behalf of her uncle was jake with her. And I don't mean Guzik.

The Beige Room was the latest, and most elaborate ever, of these so-called black-and-tan clubs to come into white vogue. Such clubs came and went, and only the Club DeLisa, which had been around for almost twenty years, seemed an exception to that rule. I preferred the DeLisa to this place; the prices weren't jacked up there, even if the surroundings were less ritzy.

A girl with a milk chocolate complexion and a body that reminded me of a certain bubble dancer was leading a Caribbean conga line of colored babes out on the Beige Room's stage. They had an elaborate floor show here, and if the names of the performers weren't immediately recognizable, the M.C.—a smooth singer named Larry Steel—would remind you that this chanteuse was with Cab Calloway for four years, and that that comic appeared in a movie with Abbott and Costello.

The floor show had just gotten over and we were deciding whether or not to eat here or elsewhere when Two-Gun Pete strode up, wearing a flashy doubled-breasted tan suit buttoned over the bulge of at least one of his two guns, with a beautiful young light-skinned Negro woman on his arm. She was wearing a bright yellow dress that followed her curves; when she entered the dark room it was like the sun came out. She looked familiar to me, but I couldn't place her.

Pete introduced her as Reba Johnson and I shook her small, smooth hand and made introductions where Peg and me were concerned.

"You look pretty good for a man who spent the afternoon in the slam," Pete said, sitting, a smirk on that sullenly handsome mug of his.

"It was less than half an hour," I said. "But it did seem like all afternoon. They were understaffed, with the parade and all going on. It's lucky you stopped by. So. Did you run your witnesses down?"

"Well, yeah, but since it was Bud Billikens Day, it wasn't no picnic," he said, and grinned, and his date smiled and giggled. The Billikens festivities ended up with a big picnic in Washington Park, you see.

I wasn't particularly amused by anything to do with Billikens, thank you. I said, "You showed them some suspect photos?"

He nodded. "About a dozen that Drury brung 'round, with pictures of Finkel and Leonard mixed in. They both of 'em picked 'em out."

"Both? You had *four* witnesses."

"I never did track the newsboy down, and I'm meetin' with the other eyeball, Tad Jones, over at the DeLisa in about a hour. But there ain't no doubt in my mind. Finkel and Leonard was the boys with the big guns in the big green truck, all right."

"I wonder if Drury has tracked them down yet."

"I don't think so," Jefferson said.

"The dairy float queen!" I said, snapping my fingers.

"What?" Peggy said.

I pointed to Reba, who was smiling with pleasure that pretended to be chagrin. "You were on that float today!"

She smiled and nodded.

"What does that have to do with anything?" Peggy asked.

"Nothing," I said. "Just proves it's a small world."

"Yeah," Jefferson said, "but it's a big city. And Finkel and Leonard are somewheres lyin' low in it."

"I hope your witnesses hold up, Pete. Because I don't have a thing on 'em, where the attempted hospital hit is concerned."

Peggy reached for my arm, gripped it. "How can you say that? You told me you caught them dead to rights!"

"I did. But by the time I got back to the hospital, their car was gone, and so were the guns I took off them."

"Weren't there any witnesses?"

"Oh, sure. Half a dozen nutcases. Maybe a few more, if you count the ones with split personalities twice." I shook my head, chipped at my rum cocktail. "Nobody a prosecutor would dare put on the stand. And the cop who left his post, leaving that fire-escape unguarded, claims he developed stomach flu and had to head for the shitter. Excuse my French, ladies."

"You gonna have a little . . . talk with this sick cop?" Jefferson asked, with a very white, very nasty smile.

"I don't think I'll bother. I asked Drury to take him off hospital duty, and maybe Bill will do something about him. But I can't go feeding the goldfish to a cop."

"Feeding the goldfish?" Reba asked.

"He means working somebody over with a rubber hose," Peggy explained.

"How do you know what that means?" I said, a little amazed.

"I wasn't born yesterday," she smiled, demurely.

"Sometimes I think you weren't born this century," I said.

"Besides, you're not the rubber hose type," Peggy said.

Jefferson smiled at that, tried with no luck to wave a waitress down to order some drinks. I suggested we go over to the Club DeLisa, where the drinks were cheaper and Tad Jones would be showing up before long.

The Club DeLisa was, among the black-and-tan niteries of the South Side, a true survivor; when the place burned down, proprietor Mike DeLisa just moved across State Street and started again. I'm always suspicious when restaurants or nightclubs burn down and re-open, but no insurance company ever hired me to investigate the DeLisa, so what the hell. I could enjoy the sixty-five-cent highballs, no minimum or cover, with the rest of the clientele, which was just slightly more colored than it was white. The room was as big as a barn and about as fancy; it had a low, ceiling-tiled ceiling, and used the time-honored nightclub effect of dim lighting to hide its flaws.

DeLisa, our short, white, deadpan host, who pumped the hand of every male patron as he entered, regardless of race, was said to have been a pal of Capone's. That impressed out-of-towners.

"Haven't seen you here for a while, Mr. Heller," DeLisa said. He wore a dark suit and a red bow tie.

"I didn't think you'd remember me, Mike."

"Anybody who sits at Mr. Nitti's table is worth remembering."

"Anybody who sits at Mr. Nitti's table these days is dead. Got a table for four live ones? I know it's Saturday, and you're packed—"

"I got a ringside saved for Serritella, but he ain't showed yet. He's an hour late."

"Serritella?" That was sweet. "Well, give us his table, and send him over if he shows. We're old pals."

I pressed a fin into DeLisa's hand and a smile cracked the deadpan, barely, and he handed it back.

"No tip's necessary, Mr. Heller. Not for a man who's friend to both Frank Nitti and Two-Gun Pete Jefferson."

"Keep it anyway."

He shrugged and slipped it in his jacket pocket. He was from Chicago, where you rarely turn down money, and you never turn it down twice.

"Mike," Jefferson said, slipping an arm around the little white man's shoulder as he walked us over to our table, "if somebody asks for me, fella name of Tad Jones, send him over."

"Sure thing, Mr. Jefferson."

From our ringside table we watched a wild floor show—while the Red Saunders Band played, a twentyish, scantily clad colored cutie named Viola Kemp sang and danced and then stood on her head, then tied herself up like a human pretzel, legs tucked behind her head as she beamed, her face perched above her sweet bottom. Then

a guy named Harold King tap-danced on roller skates on top of a
rickety card table, blindfolded; it was the damnedest thing. Finally
some sepia babes in tutus spoofed ballet steps to the band's hot music. It was not as sophisticated a show as the Chez Paree—it wasn't as
sophisticated as the Beige Room, either—but it was sure as hell fun.

The waitresses were almost as pretty as the chorus girls, though
instead of skimpy frilly outfits they wore simple white blouses and
navy blue skirts, and one of them brought us our meals, and we all
four had the specialty of the house, thick, juicy, onion-covered steaks,
under four bucks per. For a moment I wondered why I didn't come
down to Bronzeville more often; then I moved a muscle, and the
aches and pains from this afternoon reminded me.

DeLisa was escorting our way a slightly chubby white gentleman,
perhaps fifty years of age, on whose arm was a beautiful young girl,
also white; she was as blonde as Betty Grable, but a whole lot younger, possibly a Joliet Josie, which is to say jailbait, though her make-
up sought to add some years and maturity. The part of her spilling
out the top of her low-cut blue gown did a better job of it.

The slightly chubby gentleman—who was no gentleman—wore a
nicely tailored dark suit with a red, white and blue striped tie; he also
wore wire-frame glasses with coke-bottle lenses, behind which owlish
eyes blinked. He had a weak chin and a prominent nose and a reced-
ing hairline; owl eyes or not, he looked a little like a fish, and about
as harmless.

DeLisa was gesturing toward us—pointing out the "friends" who
were awaiting the "senator" at his table—but as Serritella approached, his fish face fell. In the background, the jazz band was
playing a frantic piece, which provided an appropriately unnerving
backdrop for the first ward committeeman.

Serritella had been a political fixer for the Capone people since the
late '20s; he'd been appointed City Sealer under the incredibly cor-
rupt and incompetent administration of Big Bill Thompson, and as
Sealer had conspired with merchants to short-weight consumers.
Later, quite by accident, he made Thompson's mayoral defeat by An-
ton Cermak inevitable by causing a scandal that was outrageous even
for a Chicago administration: Serritella and his chief deputy, a Nitti
associate, were charged with conspiracy to "appropriate" funds collected for Christmas distribution to the poor. That kind of thing went
over real big in the depression.

Nonetheless, Dan had, with Capone support, gone on to serve in the Illinois legislature for twelve years. Head of the newsboys union as well, which explained his ties with oldtime circulation slugger Ragen, he was a Chicago institution; they should've bronzed him and mounted him on one of the lions outside the Art Institute.

Before our distinguished visitor could waddle away, I stood and gestured to two empty seats at our table and said, "Dan—good to see you. Join us."

Peggy looked up at me like I was crazy. It's an expression I'd seen before on any number of faces.

Serritella swallowed and whispered something to the pretty young thing and came near the table with her, but didn't sit.

"Heller," he said, his voice rather high pitched and hoarse, "I know you don't believe it, but I'm Jim Ragen's friend. I had nothing to do with what happened to him."

"Sure. Sit down. Sit down, Dan."

He thought about that, and then came the rest of the way over, held a chair out for the girl, and she sat and he sat next to her, me on the other side of him.

"We'll just stay a moment. Uh, this is my protégée, Miss Reynolds; she's in show business and I thought she might enjoy one of these black-and-tans." He directed his gaze toward Peggy. "Miss Hogan, you're looking lovely tonight."

Peggy said nothing; she was burning up, furious with me apparently, arms folded, staring straight ahead, toward where the floor show had been but where frantic jitterbugging by the patrons was now taking its place. Pete sat with his arms folded, watching me and Serritella, quietly amused; Reba, to whom our conversation must've seemed a foreign language, watched the jitterbuggers, too, but without Peggy's angry glazed expression.

"We haven't seen you at the hospital, Dan," I said.

"I, uh, didn't want to impose. I sent flowers."

"Oh, and they were lovely. They meant a lot to Jim."

"I'm glad to hear that."

"He had me flush each flower down the toliet, one at a time."

Peggy looked at me from the corners of her eyes, her attitude toward me changing.

Serritella drew back. "No."

"I'm just kiddin', Dan. He gave 'em to a nurse and asked her to give them to some worthy patient in Mandel Clinic."

"I'm sorry to hear that Jim's bitter. I passed my lie detector test, you know. Completely exonerated."

"Yeah, and I heard about the questions. 'Did you shoot Jim Ragen?' Like anybody could seriously picture you a triggerman. 'When did you last see Al Capone?' Brother."

"Well, it's true. I haven't seen Al in years."

"So what? He hasn't run the Outfit since liquor was illegal."

He straightened his tie and tried to look indignant; it didn't wash. "Well, *Jim* seems to think Al's still in charge; that's what he told the state's attorney's office."

"He told the state's attorney's office that the Capone Outfit was out to get him. There's a difference between Al Capone and the Outfit he left behind, as you damn well know."

"That's true, I suppose. But Jim did mention Capone . . ."

"Jim was just telling the state's attorney enough to send a warning signal to Guzik, but not enough to cause any real fireworks. You know that. You also know what's in those affidavits Jim's got socked away. He read 'em to you."

Serritella nodded, his owl eyes blinking, double chin jiggling. "They're dynamite. Jim should burn those. He really should."

"I think Jim may be ready to negotiate."

"Why are you telling me this?"

"I don't particularly like dealing with Jake Guzik personally. These meetings with mob chieftans look bad in my FBI file; I've been logged in surveillance records God knows how many times. They've tried to pull me in before Grand Juries because of it. Anyway, you're a go-between, Dan. Everybody knows that. Do what you do so well. Take the message."

"Which is?"

"Like I said. Jim might be ready to talk. But he needs something."

"What's that?"

"Assurance that Guzik wasn't responsible for Monday."

"Well, it was Siegel. Everybody knows that."

"Even you, Dan? Who goes to so much trouble not to know too much? Just in case you have to take a lie detector test or something? You deal with these people daily, but you're like a wife whose husband cheats but she doesn't care, she doesn't want to hear about it, what she don't know won't hurt her. Just as long as he's bringing in a fat pay check, he can screw around all he wants."

Serritella pursed his lips and reassuringly patted the arm of his blonde, who was taking this all in with wide eyes, like Shirley Temple watching Bill Robinson dance.

"You're a very unpleasant man, Heller," he said.

"I know what you mean—I can hardly stand my own company. What do you know about David Finkel and Joseph Leonard?"

He shrugged, shifting in his seat. "They're bookies, aren't they? West Side?"

"Yeah. Are they tied in with Guzik, do you suppose?"

"Geez, how should I know?"

"They're the ones who shotgunned your friend Jim Ragen. Doesn't that make you mad, Dan?"

He nodded, squinted his owlish eyes, tried to summon outrage, came nowhere near, saying, "Furious. The police should arrest them."

"That's a terrific idea, Dan. I'll pass that along to Bill Drury; he'll wish he'd thought of it. Now, from what I hear, Finkel and Leonard have dropped out of sight. It would be nice if they could turn up. Alive."

Serritella nodded more slowly. "You mean, if they showed up alive, and held up under questioning . . . without mentioning Guzik . . . maybe mentioning somebody else . . . that might convince Jim of the sincerity of a certain business offer."

"For a guy who don't know what's goin' on," I said, patting him on the back, "you got a lot of savvy, Dan."

Serritella stood, pulled out the chair for his protégée, put her on his arm, and said to me, "I'll see what I can do." Then he smiled and nodded at the others at the table, including Peggy, who smiled at him pleasantly, though her violet eyes were icy. They were no longer icy when turned my way, however.

"Nice piece of work, Daddy-o," Pete said, smiling one-sidedly, leaning back in his chair, arms folded over his massive chest. "You played that little fixer like a penny harmonica."

"I may have come on a little strong," I said. "He's a weasel, but he's a powerful weasel. On the other hand, he's used to being looked down upon by his patron saints—a guy like Serritella is tolerated by Outfit guys, never liked, let alone respected. I thought I better treat him like I figure his bosses treat him."

"Well you sure done a good job of it."

"Thanks." I looked about the room. "I don't think your witness is going to show."

"He'll show," Pete said. "Tad Jones is not gonna pass up a couple free rounds of drinks at the Club DeLisa. It ain't even midnight yet. He'll show."

"Well," I said, standing, easing Peggy's chair out, giving her my arm, "I think I'll leave him to you. Let me know if he i.d.'s Finkel and Leonard. Which he probably will. This is looking pretty cut and dried to me, now."

"You think Guzik will sell out those two torpedos?"

"Yeah—although they may just turn up dead in a ditch, especially if Guzik was who hired 'em. Will twelve cover my end?"

Pete said sure and I handed him a ten and two ones. For the food and drinks Peggy and me put away, it was a steal. And the babe who made a pretty pretzel out of herself hadn't cost us a dime.

"Nate," Peg said, later, in bed, "I want to thank you."

"Well, I think I oughta thank *you*."

Her smile was crinkly and wry. "Not about that, you goof. About what you're trying to do for Uncle Jim."

"What am I trying to do for your uncle?"

"Despite what all you've said, you really are trying to find out who tried to have him killed."

I shrugged, as best I could, leaning on my elbow in bed. "I'm curious—it's my nature. And your uncle is right, to a degree—doing business with Guzik would feel better if we knew that it was somebody else . . . Siegel, specifically . . . who paid for that hit."

"So what's your next move?"

"Nothing. There is no next move."

"I find that hard to believe . . ."

"Well, strain yourself a little, kiddo, 'cause it's true. Drury's going to nab those would-be killers and, with a little luck, and more evidence than even the state's attorney's office can ignore, he'll get an indictment and a conviction."

"Will whoever hired them be convicted, too?"

"Sure, if it's a cold day in hell. Doesn't matter whether it's Guzik or Siegel responsible, you're just not going to see that happen."

"Why not?"

"That's not the way the game works. The big boys are too well-insulated; the big boys can do too much damage to the families and friends of the small fry taking the rap. No, even if they get the chair, those two won't implicate anybody, not anybody big."

She almost looked like she was going to cry. "What happened to justice, anyway?"

"When was it, exactly, that justice was around? I must've missed it."

She sat up in bed, looking very pale, very small, just a child, holding the sheet to her breasts, looking straight ahead. "If I knew who it was, I'd kill him myself."

"That's silly."

She gave me a withering look. "It's not silly. They tried to kill Uncle Jim!"

"Hey, they tried to kill me, too. You always seem to forget that little detail."

She said nothing for a while; me, either.

Then, without looking at me, she said, very quietly, "I talked to Ginny again. Just before she left town, this week."

"Ginny?" I said. Not quietly. "Virginia Hill? What are you talking to *her* for?"

"We're friends. I'm allowed to have friends of my own choosing."

"Yeah, yeah. But she's just a hooker who got out of hand. You stay away from her."

She paused, considering, then dropped her bombshell: "She does know Bugsy Siegel. She told me."

"She does?"

"She's . . . she's sort of his girl."

"Sort of his *girl*? Oh, great. Then she *was* trying to pump you about your uncle, that time . . ."

"Maybe. But she doesn't know how I feel about Uncle Jim. About what happened to him. How close we are."

"So? So what?"

"She offered me a job."

"A job! What, riding trains with bags of mob money? Sleeping with senators?"

She ignored the nastiness of that. Said simply, "She needs a secretary."

"What for?"

"She has business interests."

"Well, where would this be? Hollywood?"

She nodded.

"You're not seriously considering . . ."

She touched my arm; cool touch. "Nate, think a minute. If I were working for Ginny, I'd be close to this Bugsy Siegel person. I might be able to find something out."

"Find something out? Are you kidding, or just crazy? You're no goddamn detective . . ."

"If I get close to him, I can find out what's he's doing where Uncle Jim's concerned."

"That's stupid. Siegel's not going to say anything around the niece of the man he wants dead—assuming he does want Jim dead. This is lunacy. Don't even think about this."

"Ginny doesn't know how I feel about my uncle. I could pretend we had a falling out; pretend to hate him."

"What is this, a school play you're trying out for? Forget this. This is stupid. You can't accomplish anything, except maybe get yourself hurt, or worse."

"I was hoping you'd think it was a good idea."

"Yeah, well it's a good idea for the radio. For real life, it stinks. I won't hear of this. I won't stand for it."

"You really feel that strongly."

"Of course I do."

"Then . . . then I won't go."

I didn't say anything. I came within an inch of saying, *you're goddamn right you won't go*. But instead, I just touched her face; smiled at her, gently. She smiled back the same way, though there was disappointment in it.

"Good girl," I said. I gave her a kiss; just a peck. I turned out the lights and pulled the covers around us, as the Morrison's air conditioning was downright chilly tonight, and we cuddled like spoons, me behind her, slipping a hand around to cup one sweet breast.

"I love you, baby."

"I love you, Nate. I really do."

We were just drifting off to sleep when the phone rang; it was after two—nobody calls me that late. I damn near ran to the phone, out in the other room, and it was Drury on the line.

"Nate," Drury said. His voice sounded hollow. "It's started."

"What's started?"

"Tad Jones is dead."

"What? Christ . . ."

"He was killed by another Negro. Drunken scuffle over a watch is the story."

"Pete was going to meet with him tonight . . ."

"Tad never showed up at the Club DeLisa. Pete's going to look into the slaying, of course. It'll be hard to prove anything. Even with Pete on the case."

"This could spook the other witnesses. Pardon the expression."

He sighed. "I know. I thought we had these bastards wrapped up in a bow. Shit."

"What now?"

"I'm not giving up," he said, as if a little insulted that I might think that a possibility, even though I hadn't suggested it, except maybe by my tone. "I'll put the other witnesses under protective custody, till we pick up Finkel and Leonard, and then we'll have a show-up. If the witnesses can pick 'em out of the line, and we can get their statements, then we might still have something."

"Damn. Is this Guzik?"

"Or Siegel? You tell me."

"Finkel and Leonard are Jews," I said, thinking out loud, "but then so are Guzik and Siegel."

"And Davey and Blinkey don't have any great ties to either of them."

"But they're bookies," I pointed out, "meaning they got *some* ties to both of 'em."

"Right."

"I'm sorry about this, Bill."

"Yeah," he said, wearily. "Well, thanks for all your help, Nate. You're a good man despite yourself."

"I'm a goddamn prince," I said, and hung up.

"What was that about?" she asked.

I turned and looked at her; she was in her little blue see-through nightie, looking about sixteen years old, a pale vision, those huge violet eyes melting me.

I told her what Drury had told me.

Her jaw tightened; her hands turned into fists. "They're going to get away with it, aren't they?"

I went to her; put my arm around her, daddy soothing baby. "I don't think so. I don't think Bill's going to let them."

She stepped away from me, just a bit. Her expression intense. "Can't *you* identify them? You recognized them, didn't you?"

"Yeah, at the hospital today—but not when they were shooting at me. I've already given a statement to that effect. Gone on record."

"Can't you say it just came to you?"

"A week later, I suddenly remember? After I have a run-in with these guys outside Ragen's hospital room? The prosecutors wouldn't want anything to do with me—once I was in court, even an inexperienced mouthpiece would chew me up, and with my checkered background, I'd be easily discredited, anyway."

Her pretty mouth was pinched to near ugly. "I wish you'd just . . . go *after* them."

"This isn't Dodge City 1880, honey. It's Chicago 1946. Which is a hell of a lot worse, in a way, but times still have changed. I'd do most anything for you, I think you know that—but I'm not going to go shooting it out with Outfit guys."

"There's no justice, is there?"

"Sure there is. It just doesn't have anything to do with the legal system."

"That's why we should do something ourselves."

"No," I told her. "We got an honest cop, who has three live witnesses. He's going to get the shooters. We're going to bed. That's all we're doing."

We did.

In the dark, she said, "Even if he does put them in jail, what about whoever hired them? What about *him*?"

Not that again.

"Baby," I said, "go to sleep."

I don't know whether she did or not. I did—slept soundly and hard and my dreams were pleasant; I was riding the dairy float and Reba was sitting in my lap. Well, part of the time she was Reba, and part of the time she was Peggy, and part of the time she was that gal who made a pretzel of herself, and also that chocolate conga-line cutie was in there, somewhere. I loved Peggy, but I reserved the right to have dirty dreams about any women I chose.

I didn't wake up till ten o'clock the next morning. Peggy was gone. I didn't think much about it. She'd done that before. Later that day, I tried to call her, at her aunt's, where she was still helping out, but she couldn't come to the phone.

Then on Monday, at the office, my secretary Gladys had a message for me from Peg, who had called.

To say she was sorry, but she'd taken a morning flight.

To Hollywood.

The beautiful nude woman was swimming under the blue water of the Olympic-size pool. Well, she wasn't entirely nude—she was wearing a white bathing cap. Her flesh took on the blue cast of the water and she looked quite unreal, much too perfect, as her arms and legs pumped ever so gently through the depths of the pool, sunlight shimmering on its surface, providing enough of a glare that you had to work to see the girl. But it was worth the effort.

It was early afternoon, on a Wednesday, and I was sitting on the patio around the pool at a sprawling white-brick ranch style home on Coldwater Canyon Drive in Beverly Hills. The home belonged to the small dark man sitting nearby in a dark blue silk robe monogrammed GR. His dark, slightly thinning hair was slicked straight back, like Valentino, a trademark that dated back to his taxi dancer days. He was still hooded-eyed and handsome, though age had exaggerated his profile, his ski nose damn near rivaling Bob Hope's. And he'd put on some weight: an extra chin, some gut pushing at the middle of the silk robe, which was sashed loosely. He sat on a deck chair near the little table, shielded from the sun by an umbrella canopy, an ankle crossing a leg, occasionally sipping a glass of iced tea, slowly shuffling cards but not playing anything, studying with a faint, seemingly dispassionate smile the girl who was now gliding on the surface of the blue water, tan arms flashing. The sound of the water as she cut gently through it mingled with big band music coming from a radio within the house.

"Glad you could stop by," George Raft said to me, flatly, in his remote way.

I felt overdressed in my brown suit. I felt like I should loosen my tie or take my hat off or something, but I didn't, and anyway my hand was filled with the glass of iced tea that Raft's big lumbering bodyguard, "Killer," who'd met me at the front door, had brought me. Killer, who was sort of a cross between a butler and Leo Gorcey, wore a blue polo shirt and white slacks and still managed to look like a guy called Killer, at least in California.

Me, I didn't want to give in to California. It was a foreign place to me. There was just no excuse for this many palm trees and this much stucco being gathered anywhere, and certainly not within the borders of these United States. The weather out here was an incentive to doing nothing. It made me want to go door to door telling people about humidity.

"That's white of you, George," I said. "It's been a long time. I hoped my name would ring a bell."

His thin line of a smile increased its curvature. "How could I forget *that* piece of business—though it woulda been healthy to."

What he and I were referring to was a job he had hired me to do, years ago, in 1933, to be exact. Only it wasn't a job I did for him, really: it was a job I did for Al Capone, who was in the Atlanta pen at the time. Raft had only acted as the go-between, a role he was as used to as his tough-guy screen persona.

It was no secret Raft had been a bootlegger, that his gangster friend Owney Madden had sent him west, pulling strings to get him going in the movies. Not that former pickpocket Raft was bereft of show business experience: he worked a Charleston act in vaudeville, and a specialty tap act at Texas Guinan's El Fay. Of course, he'd still been doing a little bootlegging for Madden on the side, as well.

"You say you'd like to meet Ben," Raft said. "I think I could arrange that. But it'd be nice to know what it's about, first."

"Actually," I said, sipping my minty ice tea, "it's personal. I'm out here on business, but that business has nothing to do with Ben Siegel. The personal matter does, though."

"Yeah?"

"I got a girl name of Peggy Hogan who came out here a little over a week ago. She and Siegel have some mutual friends. Have you heard of her, George? Met her? Has she been around?"

Raft took his eyes off the nude vision in the pool and looked at me, perhaps to let me know he wasn't lying.

"Never heard of her," he said with flat believability.

"I have reason to think she's gotten herself tied up with Virginia Hill."

Raft smiled a little. "Ginny attracts all sorts of people to her."

"And she's Ben Siegel's girl?"

"She thinks she is."

"Meaning?"

"Ben always has more than one woman in his life."

"Well, that stands to reason, doesn't it? He's married, isn't he?"

"Divorced," Raft shrugged. "From Whitey Krakower's sister. God rest his soul."

Whitey Krakower, in addition to being Siegel's brother-in-law, had been a sometime Siegel accomplice, according to the indictment in the Harry "Big Greenie" Greenburg murder, anyway. Whitey got bumped off in July 1940 in New York, after word got out he was talking. It was a hit Siegel had supposedly approved. Even arranged. Which would, I suppose, have put a certain strain on his marriage.

I was damn near a Siegel expert now. I'd been filled in by Fred Rubinski, an ex-cop from Chicago who had a small agency out here; he also owned a major piece of a restaurant on the Sunset Strip. One of my reasons for coming west was to talk to Fred about linking our two agencies; it was something I'd been thinking about for a while. Fred had an office in the Bradbury Building at Third and Broadway in downtown L.A. We were old acquaintances, if not quite friends, and he'd picked me up last night at Union Air Terminal in Burbank shortly after nine o'clock, the end of an all-day long, puddle-jumping flight that had begun at eight that morning at Midway back home.

We'd spent this morning in his office at the Bradbury, a truly weird turn-of-the-century building with wrought-iron stairwells, ornamental balconies, caged elevators and a skylight that bounced an eerie white light off the glazed brick floor of its huge central court. Fred, who was in his late forties and a hard round bald ball of a man, shared an outer office with an answering service overseen by a ditsy blonde, and the inner office was his alone. He had four ops in an adjoining office, and his business was going good. We'd discussed merging our operations once before, last year, when he came home to Chicago to visit family and friends for the High Holidays; and this morning we'd bounced it around more seriously.

But mostly I'd pumped Fred about Siegel, for whom he'd done some collecting.

"Bad checks," Fred explained. "He's got a piece of the Clover Club, you know."

"What's that, a nightclub?"

"Yeah, with gambling upstairs. It's the stars' favorite place to lose

their money. He owns part of a Tijuana race track, too, and has interests in half a dozen joints in Las Vegas."

"What else is Siegel into, besides gambling?"

Fred shrugged. "Narcotics, prostitution, diamond fencing, perfume smuggling, you name it. They say Luciano sent him out here,
in the mid-thirties, to make sure the Chicago interests didn't take
over."

I nodded. "That must've been shortly after Nitti sent Bioff and
Browne out here, selling strike prevention insurance to the movie
moguls."

"Right," Fred said, nodding back. "And word is Benny stepped in
and took over where Bioff and Browne left off, after the feds busted
their racket up."

"How so?"

"Bioff and Browne had hold of the stagehands union, right? Well,
Benny has control of the movie extras."

"I didn't know Siegel was so powerful. All I knew was he was running the West Coast end of Trans-American, the mob's race wire."

"Well, he's doing that, too. *And* building some goddamn gambling
casino in the desert. Near Vegas. Pipedream, if you ask me."

I shook my head wonderingly. "I guess I just don't know much
about Siegel—mostly just what I've read in the papers. If he's thick
with Raft, like they say, I may have an in. I did a job for George,
once."

"Raft's *real* thick with Ben. They're close pals."

Last year, it seemed, Raft had gone to bat for Siegel in court, when
Siegel and his crony Allen Smiley were arrested for bookmaking. Raft
had been present, but wasn't arrested, and later insisted on the witness stand that the three men, together in a hotel room, had merely
been placing bets on the phone for themselves. Raft had behaved like
a movie tough guy on the stand, barely skirting contempt ("Don't I
even have the right of free speech?" he demanded of the judge) and
attracting headlines, which came back to me as Fred filled me in.

"Why would Raft put his nuts on the line for a guy like Siegel?" I
wondered aloud.

"Hey, I like Benny, too," Fred said, with a shrug. "He's never
shown his temper around me—and he pays his bills. He's fun guy to
be around, too. Charm the pants offa you."

"You don't mind if I keep my belt buckled for the time being, do you, Fred? If Bugsy's killed half the people he's said to have killed, not everybody would agree he's fun to be around."

"Make up your own mind, Nate. But you're gonna be surprised."

Fred had a black book with the unlisted numbers of various stars and other celebrities and Raft was in there. I called the actor's house from Fred's office and caught him at home. Raft immediately remembered me, immediately invited me out.

Fred loaned me one of the three cars the agency owned—a two-tone gray '41 Ford sedan—and I discovered I'd been out here enough times now to find my way around okay. I pulled into Raft's driveway as a sightseeing bus went by, gawking tourists looking out the windows, squinting in the sunshine to see if I was anybody. They seemed disappointed when I wasn't, but then neither were they, so it evened out.

Raft, sitting in his poolside deck chair, was somebody. I wasn't sure for how long, though. His association with Siegel was getting him the wrong kind of press; and he was constantly studio-hopping, balking at roles, taking suspensions, battling his bosses. When he was a hot property, fresh off of flipping his coin in *Scarface,* he could get away with it.

But at fifty years of age, Raft was not the combination tough-guy and Latin lover he had once been.

The nude young woman climbed from the pool, her bare backside to us; that goddamn ass could have been made of marble, so perfect was it. Only it looked considerably softer than marble, and was tan. All of her was tan. The blue water had hidden that. She turned and faced us and stretched her arms, embracing the rays of the sun. Her pubic patch was blond. She tugged the bathing cap off and shook her long blond hair to her damp shoulders and she smiled, looking a little like Betty Grable, one of Raft's lost loves, or so the gossip columnists said.

She walked over regally and stood before the small dark man in the blue silk robe; she was taller than he was, and half his age. Hands on her hips, she said, "Thanks for the swim."

"Thank *you.*"

"Thanks for everything."

"My pleasure."

"Would you like me to stick around this afternoon?"

"No, baby. That's okay." He dug into his robe pocket and withdrew a C-note, folded in half. He handed it to her and she smiled toothily and trotted off, cheeks of her ass wiggling and finally revealing themselves to have some fat content, after all, and she disappeared inside to wherever her clothes were and where the big band music was coming from.

The girl had never acknowledged my presence. I might as well have not been there.

Raft was conscious of me, though, and as he lit up a cigarette he said, "It's easier with hookers. I had too many romances fall through. Take my advice, Nate. If you got the dough, stick with call girls."

I couldn't understand why a guy like Raft, who even at his age could obviously get just about any woman he wanted, would pay. I didn't say this. Just thought it.

But he said, "I'll give you an example. Just this week I find out I got to go to court. This night-club singer I was taking out last year is getting divorced and I'm named in the suit." He shook his head. "Stick with call girls."

"That's probably good advice, George, but I'm serious about this Peggy Hogan. I want to find her, before Virginia Hill gets her hooks into her."

"Who is this Peggy Hogan, anyway? How'd she get from Chicago to Hollywood?"

"She's Jim Ragen's niece."

"Jim Ragen . . . the wire service guy?"

"Yes."

"Ben's in competition with that guy. Didn't he get hit, what was it, couple weeks ago?"

Raft seemed to be sincere in his ingenuousness. He wasn't a good enough actor, I didn't think, to fake it so well.

"Yeah. You remember the story from the papers? Remember the part about the bodyguard whose shotgun jammed?"

He looked out at the pool, where no nude girl swam. "Naw. I don't read so good. I just heard Ragen got hit."

"Well, I was his bodyguard."

"Are you working for him, Nate?"

"Yeah. He paid my way out here. He thinks a lot of his niece. He wants me to bring her back home."

I didn't see any reason going into why she'd come out here; no need to detail to Raft the desire Peggy (and for that matter her uncle) had to determine whether or not Ben "Bugsy" Siegel had hired that hit.

"Why don't you go talk to Ginny," he suggested, smoke curling out his nostrils as he looked out at the pool, not at me. "She's probably home, or will be soon. She's renting a place in Beverly Hills."

"Peggy might be with her," I said.

"Isn't that what you want?"

I didn't know what I wanted, really; I didn't know how to go about this. On the endless plane trip I'd tried to figure what I'd say to her, how I'd get her home. I was furious with her, of course, but I was also worried. And I felt a little battered, too. She was supposed to love me. She wasn't supposed to run out on me like this.

I'd waited a little over a week before the worry and no sleep got me on a plane. She didn't call or even write, I couldn't get in touch with her, it was maddening and I was scared shitless for her, besides. Jim was concerned for her absence, too, got really worked up, especially after I leveled with him about Peg talking about checking up on Siegel, by becoming part of Virginia Hill's retinue. I didn't like seeing the patient I was guarding get upset; it couldn't be good for his recovery—even though Dr. Snaden said he thought Jim was doing much better than expected and would be going home in a matter of weeks. So I worked with Drury to tighten up security at Meyer House, putting Lou Sapperstein in charge of A-1's end, and then proceeded to go west, middle-aged man.

"I'd be glad to call over there and see if Ginny's home," he said.

"Better not," I said. "I don't know if Virginia Hill would consider me a friend. I better just go over there. Can you give directions?"

"Sure," he said. "Or just buy a movie star map. It's Valentino's old mansion."

"La Hill doesn't go second class, does she?"

"She probably uses mink tampax," Raft said. "Sometimes I don't know what Ben sees in her—she's a coarse broad. She swears like a fucking stevedore."

"I know her," I said. "Foul mouth or not, she's a babe, or used to be."

Raft smirked. "Take a look around you, Nate. Every street corner has the four most beautiful women you ever saw standing on it, and next to 'em are the four second most beautiful. Guy like Ben can pick and choose."

"What's the reason he keeps her around, then?"

"Could be business. She's tied in with a lot of his friends back east. It's a partnership. A sort of marriage. And, yeah, she is still a babe. I remember what Benny said, after that first night with her, up at the Chateau Marmont . . ."

Raft looked skyward, as if summoning a romantic memory floating on some cloud.

". . . 'Georgie,' Ben said to me, 'she's the best piece of ass I ever had.'"

Touched as I was by that, I managed to ask a question. "How long have you known Siegel?"

"Forever. Since he was a tough little kid on the Lower East Side—and I don't mean of Beverly Hills. He was always gutty and ambitious. He came out here to Hollywood because he wanted to be somebody. And he made it. He was hardly out here a few months but that I was seeing him at the track or around town with big names, George Jessel, Cary Grant, Mark Hellinger, guys like that."

"And you."

"Hey, I figured if he was good enough for them he was good enough for me. I never knew anybody who doesn't like him. He's a great guy." His expression turned sober. "Of course a lot of his friends deserted him, after he started getting bad press. Particularly after that son of a bitch Pegler took off after him, in his column. Ben had to drop out of the Hillcrest Country Club." Shook his head sadly. "Giving up golf really killed Benny."

"I've seen pictures of him in the papers. He looks like he could be a movie star himself."

Raft grinned, showing his teeth, looking at me. "He's a frustrated actor; he'd love to have a movie career." He leaned forward, sharing a confidence. "He's always coming around the set, standing on the sidelines, asking the technicians questions. He owns more cameras, projectors and other movie shit than half the studios on Poverty Row."

"What for?"

"Homemade screen tests. He had me photograph him one day. I took some footage of him with his camera in my dressing room." Raft smiled some more, and shook his head. "He re-did one of my scenes. Wanted to show me where I got it wrong."

"He isn't serious about acting . . ."

"Not anymore. This was years ago. But he showed some footage around. He let it be known he was available for parts. Nobody ever hired him. Not with his background. I'm no saint, but I don't have no rape arrests on my rap sheet."

"Is he as crazy as they say?"

"He's got a streak. But that name he hates—Bugsy—he didn't get that 'cause he's bugs, you know. It comes from when a judge at a trial, years and years ago, real disgusted, called him and Meyer Lansky a couple of bugs."

"But the name 'Bugsy' stuck, even though nobody uses it in front of him."

"Nobody uses it in front of him for long," Raft said, nodding slowly. "He's got a bad temper, all right. Particularly if you insult him. He's real vain. He dresses great. He works out every day at the Hollywood YMCA. Goes weekly to Drucker's barber shop in Beverly Hills. He showers for hours, goes to bed early, hardly drinks at all. He's real sensitive about his hair."

"Why's that?"

"Well, when he was a kid it was nice and thick and curly. But he's losing it, now. I tell you, I damn near bought it when I pulled a gag on him on his birthday last year. I sent over a gift-wrapped toup. Thinking he'd laugh. He drove over here pissed off as hell and it took me an hour to settle him down. Lucky I know what button to push with him."

"What button is that, George?"

"Well, I just call him 'baby blue eyes.' It compliments him and calms him right down. I don't think it'd work for anybody else, though."

"He sounds like a real interesting fella. I'd like to meet him—no matter how things go for me with Virginia Hill."

"How long will you be out here?"

"How long do I need to be out here?"

"Well, Ben's not in town much these days. He's in Vegas, most of the time."

"Oh, because of that casino he's building—"

"Yeah, only it's more than just a casino—it's a full-fledged resort. Hotel, restaurants, swimming pool. Gonna be a real class joint. He's putting it up out on the strip of land between the airport and Vegas. Sinking a lot of dough into it."

"His own?"

"His own and everybody else he knows. Me included. Mostly guys back east, I think; and guys from your neck of the woods. Ben says it's gonna be so fabulous it'll make DeMille look like a piker."

"I didn't know DeMille was in the gambling business."

"You don't think the movie business is a gamble? Nate, you don't get where I am unless the dice has been good to you."

Killer came out and refilled our iced tea glasses from a sweating glass pitcher. Raft asked him if he'd got a cab for the girl and the Killer said yes, then went back into the house.

I sipped my tea. "Why isn't Virginia Hill out in Vegas with him?"

"She is part of the time. But she comes back here a lot."

"Why?"

"She hates the desert."

"I hope she's not a typical customer. So, I have to go to Vegas if I want to meet Ben Siegel?"

"No, he's going to be back in town this weekend. Friday night. It's the grand opening of the S.S. Lux."

"What's that?"

"Tony Cornero's new gambling ship. Ben was one of Tony's partners on the old S.S. Rex. You want to go? You can go with me, if you want."

"That'd be swell."

"Now if you'll excuse me," Raft said, standing, tightening the sash of his robe over an expansive gut, "I want to catch a nap. I got a date tonight."

VIRGINIA HILL

12

Beverly Hills wasn't always a big deal. The Hollywood hills were where movie actors, denied access to the country clubs and social circles of Los Angeles, fled, building fabulous mansions, riding their money past stuffy respectability into cheerful decadence. One of the first of those mansions was the sixteen-room Falcon's Lair, Rudolph Valentino's home for the year or so before his death.

Perched on a Benedict Canyon hillside, on Bella Drive, the place was impressive in size but otherwise looked like just another of these overinflated mud huts to me, bleached white with scalloped burnt-red clay tile roof; it was two stories with occasional dips to a single floor, and lavishly landscaped, lots of trees doing their best to shield the mansion, but not obscuring the hilltop view of Beverly Hills, Los Angeles and even Catalina Island on this clear, pleasantly warm July afternoon. The panoramic view stretched before me like a not quite convincing miniature in a movie. That was California for you—almost like real life.

I left Rubinski's '41 Ford in the open cement area before the mission-like front of the place. No other cars were around, but a stable converted to a garage was nearby. You walked through an archway to get to the front entry, a big dark double door, a pair of Mediterranean slabs you could break your knuckles on, knocking. Which is why they invented doorbells, I guess, and Falcon Lair had one and I rang it.

And I rang it.

Raft had called ahead for me, and Virginia Hill was supposed to be home, and she supposedly knew I was coming. It had been less than fifteen minutes since Raft's call, and yet nobody was answering the door.

I rang again, the church bell-like chimes of it mellow and muffled behind the massive doors.

Which finally swung open, and there she was, poised within their V, fingers with red-painted nails caressing either door, a wry one-sided smile cracking her cool deadpan, framed by flowing shoulder-

length hair that was redder than it used to be, and green-gray eyes
that laughed. Well, they didn't say ha ha ha or anything, but you get
the idea.

And did I mention she was naked?

Well, she was. I was starting to feel like a private eye in a quarter
pocketbook. This made two naked babes today and it wasn't even
dark yet. Or maybe that was just what they were wearing in California this year. Nothing.

"Hiya, Heller. Long time no see. Come on in."

Her Alabama accent was still there, but it seemed less lilting than I
remembered it. A harshness had crept into the voice, giving it a
smokiness that was not altogether unappealing, though she was slur-
ring her words a little. If calling her drunk was less than fair, calling
her sober was less than accurate.

I followed her through a high-ceilinged entryway that you could've
put my Morrison suite in and still had room to hold a cotillion. The
place was lavish, tapestries and armor, wrought-iron wall hangings;
but it was pretty much a blur to me. I was following a naked woman
whose flesh was as creamy white as a carved ivory statuette, a few of
which graced an occasional table here in Rudy's shack.

Jiggling a bit, not being actual ivory, she led me into a big living
room where she walked to a Hoover plugged in the wall on a long
cord and began sweeping. The sound of it was fairly loud, but she
managed to bray above it: "Sorry I didn't hear you ring the doorbell,
Heller!"

"That's okay!" I yelled back.

She kept at it, sweeping an oriental carpet that extended out before
a white marble fire place and its Tara-like pillars like a multi-colored
lawn. Over the fireplace hung a dark murky painting with an Old
Dutch Masters look to it. By which I mean it was like a Rembrandt
seen through a lot of cigar smoke.

She shut the vacuum cleaner off, kicking the button savagely with
her bare foot, her long auburn hair swinging in arcs, her teeth bared
in a snarl. "I hate this fucking place," she said.

"Yeah," I said, glancing around at the smooth pastel walls and
heavy dark Mediterranean furniture, sitting on a red brocade couch
that was as comfortable as a guaranteed income. "It's a real dump, all
right."

She made a face as if she were about to spit on the carpet. The
floor on the outer edges of the carpet was polished to a gloss you

could ice skate on. The room was immaculately clean and everything seemed to be in its place. The only jarring item, in fact, was the nude woman with the vacuum cleaner.

"I told that bitch I'd shoot her," she said, pushing the Hoover to one side, going over to a heavy low-slung coffee table that ran damn near the length of the couch before me. She stood right across from where I sat and she lit up a cigarette, taken from a silver jade-inlaid box, firing it up with a silver-and-jade lighter. I could have stared right at her reddish pubic patch, which was trimmed into the shape of a heart, if I were that sort of guy, which of course I was.

She bent over, considerable breasts swaying, and poured, over somewhat melted ice, what was not her first tall glass from a soon-to-be-empty bottle of crème de menthe on the coffee table. Then she put the bottle back on the table next to a floral arrangement and a .38 Smith and Wesson revolver.

She threw back her head, and the glass too, and most of the green stuff was gone when her head and the glass returned; she filled the glass back up and killed the bottle. She looked at me curiously.

"Want something to drink?" she said.

"Sure."

"What?"

"Rum."

"Over ice?"

"Why not."

She walked to a liquor cabinet against a far wall; she moved like sex on springs. I didn't like this girl much as a human being, but I began to see how she'd gotten where she was today—even if, at age thirty or so, she was starting to show some wear and tear. Her body was holding up great, but then most women's bodies are at least five years younger than their faces.

And Virginia Hill's face, pretty as it was, was much older than the last time I'd seen it, back around '38. Her eyes were a little baggy, the laugh lines turning into plain old fashioned wrinkles, and the hard lines around her mouth marked her as a dame who had her sour moments.

But that milky body, those gravity-defying breasts and that well-tended, trimmed, hennaed valentine between her legs, could make for some sweet moments.

On the other hand, there *was* that Smith and Wesson on the table before me, like a party favor courtesy of a demented host.

Hostess.

She handed me a short fat glass with rum and ice across the coffee table.

"Bottoms up and live, pal," she said, hoisting her replenished tall glass of crème de menthe. "Tomorrow never comes and, anyway, if it does, you may be dead."

I made a "salute" gesture with my glass, saying nothing, knowing I couldn't top her cheerful toast, and sipped the rum and it was smooth, expensive stuff.

"I hope you don't mind," she said, gesturing to her nude self. Her nipples were dark, not erect, and about as big around as half dollars, but worth considerably more. "It's a little warm today and we're not air conditioned."

"I don't mind at all," I said, thinking it was fairly cool in here, a whisper of a breeze blowing in from somewhere. "I just a feel a little overdressed."

She smiled over the rim of her tall green glass. "Maybe we can do something about that."

"I thought you were Ben Siegel's girl."

"I am. He'd kill you if he found out." She said this with a smile that made it clear she found that concept very amusing and a little exciting.

"Well, I'll just keep my clothes on for right now. What's the gun for?"

"The gun?" Her eyes followed my finger as it pointed to the .38. "Oh, that. I was going to kill that bitch."

"Which bitch is that, Ginny?"

She squinted. "My housekeeper. Mexican girl. She doesn't clean worth a shit. I have to do it over, after she does, just to make sure it's right. Besides, I think she's stealing from me." She came around the table and sat next to me. Put her feet up on the coffee table. Her toenails were painted red.

"I may not look it," she said, with some defensive pride, "but I can run a household. I raised my brothers and sisters, didn't I?"

"Big family?"

"Ten of us kids and no money. You ever wake up in the middle of the night 'cause of a bad dream, Heller?"

"Sure. I have malaria flare-ups now and then, from the war. I have some doozies where nightmares are concerned."

"Yeah, well I only have one nightmare. And it's always the same.

I'm locked in a cell for a life term. The outside of the place is a prison. But inside the bars it's my shabby little house in Lipscomb, Alabama. *That* was a prison. My folks fought, mom ran off 'cause pa beat on her." She made a face and drank some crème de menthe.

This sure was a different story than she'd given the columnists. Actually, she'd given the columnists a variety of stories of her early life, over the years, but they always added up to her being some Southern heiress of the sort café society ate up in the '30s.

"My grandmother was chopping cotton for a living in Kennesaw Mountain, Georgia, when she eighty. I swore that would never happen to me."

"At this point," I said, looking at her long legs, pleasantly plump in a Petty Girl way, stretched out before me resting on the coffee table, feet near the gun, "I would think your cotton picking days are behind you."

"They better be."

"You weren't really going to shoot your housekeeper," I said. Making it sound like a statement not a question.

"Probably not," she admitted. She seemed to be sobering up just a trifle, despite the crème de menthe she was putting away. Talking about her past had done it. "Look, why don't I put something on. I'm just in an ornery mood. Looking for somebody to fuck, or fuck with."

"Why don't you put on some clothes," I agreed. "You're a great-looking woman, but I came around to get my girl back, not to bang her boss."

She looked at me sideways; her smile was wide and white and appealing—a little like Peggy's smile, actually.

"You're pretty cute, Heller," she said. "I think Peggy should've stayed in Chicago and married you or something."

"Or something," I conceded.

"But you can't hold back an ambitious kid like her."

"Ambitious kid?"

"Yeah, Peggy's got a head on her shoulders. And I'm not just talking blowjobs."

"Miss Hill, you have such a classy way of putting things."

She stood and said, huffily, "Well, excuse my fucking French," and flounced out. I couldn't tell if she was kidding or not. Either way, she had a great ass.

But I must've really been in love with Peggy Hogan, because I'd just told Virginia Hill to put on her clothes despite my having the erection of a lifetime.

Which had fortunately wilted by the time she came in, in a white two-piece outfit, halter top and shorts, like Lana Turner in *The Postman Always Rings Twice*. Remembering how that movie came out was an incentive toward keeping my pants on and my dick limp.

"You want some more rum?" she asked.

"I'm not quite through with this, thanks," I said, gesturing with glass in hand, rum swirling, ice clinking.

She still had some crème de menthe left. "I was thinking about killing my Chinese butler, too."

"Oh? Where is he?"

"He left with the housekeeper and cook when I got the gun out." She laughed; it was almost a snort. "Chickenshits. I didn't even fire a shot." She looked around the room. "I hate this fucking place."

"Why?"

"It looks like a pimp's idea of a palace."

"Why don't you redecorate? You got dough, I hear. That big handbag you lug around is usually packed with money, if the stories are true."

"They're true, all right. But I'm no fucking whore, Heller. I never asked a man for money in my life. Never had to. They just hand the green stuff over without me ever even asking."

"That beats whoring all hollow."

"I think so," she said, with no sense of irony whatever. "But I can't redecorate. Juan would kill me."

"Who is Juan?"

She shrugged; her hair shimmered, tickling her shoulders. She smelled good—a combination of crème de menthe and, my detective's nose deduced, Ivory soap. "He's my agent. He used to be a dancer and made all the premieres, first nights, parties, all the big shit events. So he ended up turning theatrical agent, and publicity man, too. This is his place."

"Does he live here?"

"Sometimes. Not right now. Anyway, he fancies himself the Latin lover type." She laughed again. "Latin lovers, you can have 'em. Who was that girl that wrote that book? *Latins Are Lousy Lovers*?"

"I don't know. I haven't even read *Forever Amber* yet."

"Well, she was right. Those fucking Italians. Peacocks, all of 'em. Needle dicks, to a man. I never knew a guy in the rackets who was well hung till I ran into Benny, and he's a Jew! Aren't you a Jew, Heller?"

"Half of me. But I got a hunch it's the top half."

"We could check that out. You don't have to be a fucking detective to tell a Jewish dick when you see one."

"Miss Hill, please. Take your hand off my zipper. I've been cir- cumcized, if that answers your question."

"It doesn't, really," she said, absently, looking away from me, glancing about the high-ceilinged room again. "This place looks like a fucking whorehouse, don't you think? Juan, Latin lover, hah—he sleeps with the gardener, if that tells you what kind of Latin lover he is—anyway, Juan has this thing about Valentino. This was the great Shiek's flop, you know. 'Cause he died after he built the joint, this castle's supposed to be jinxed. Sat empty for year. Anyway, Juan de- cided to restore it—did he best to furnish and decorate it like it was when Rudy lived here. Yecch."

"I kind of like it."

"Then *you* live here. I swear. I gotta find a decent place to live."

"Well, isn't Ben Siegel building you a place?"

"Oh, there's another dopey dream castle for you. The Flamingo. That's what he's calling it, you know. Named after those goddamn birds down at Hialeah. Except lately he's been calling *me* his pretty little Flamingo. I ask you. Does this frame remind you of one of them spindly-ass birds?"

"No," I said.

"I suppose I will move out there," she said, with a weary sigh. "He's building a suite for us in one of the buildings. Should be pretty posh, but shit. I hate the fucking desert. It's hard on my skin. I got hay fever. I got an allergy to cactus, the docs say. Hell, my idea of outdoor living is sitting on a bar stool in the cabana of a Bel Air swimming pool."

"Well, you'll just have to stay inside. It'll be air-conditioned, won't it? If it's as lavish a resort as I'm hearing, you should have a nice home for yourself."

"Everytime I'm there, I get sick. I have to take those Benadryls, and they make you feel terrible."

Particularly when you're taking 'em with liquor.

"I just thought my girl might be staying here with you," I said. "But I guess she isn't."

"Is she still your girl?"

"You tell me."

"Well, either way, she's not here. She only bunked here one night. We were in Vegas together, drove down there the day after she showed up. I came back on the weekend. She stayed."

I sat up. "Stayed where?"

"In the fucking hell hole. Las Vegas."

"What's she doing there?"

"Staying at the Last Frontier."

"Doing what in hell?"

"Heller, cool your nuts, will ya? She's my secretary."

"You seem to be here."

"She's my secretary, and she's helping Ben, because I'm associated with Ben. We're business partners, Ben and me."

"You're his partner in the Flamingo?"

"I've got some stock. I don't like the place, but it might be a good investment. People like a nice hotel. People like to gamble. I play the horses some myself—don't you?"

"Why's Peg still in Vegas?"

"She's doing secretarial work for Ben."

"For Ben. For Bugsy."

Her nostrils flared. "Don't ever call him that. That's a horrible name. He'd kill you for that. I might kill you myself."

"Well, what's stopping you? There's a gun on the coffee table."

She smiled. "Maybe I figure you'd bust me in the chops before I could fire."

"But I wouldn't do that, Virginia."

"Why?"

"Because I got a hunch you'd like it."

She didn't deny that; she just laughed a little, and leaned back in the comfortable couch. "Peg's a good secretary. I need her for things—errands and such; correspondence—I only went to eighth grade, and I need help with things like that. And she did my hair last week." She fluffed the auburn stuff. "She did a nice job, don't you think?"

"What's she doing in Vegas, Ben's hair?"

"This Flamingo hotel is a big project. It's a huge endeavor."

"That's a big word for a girl who only went to the eighth grade—'endeavor.'"

"Up your ass with a hot poker, pal. There's a lot of paperwork involved in an enterprise like that. Yeah, 'enterprise.' Just don't ask me to spell it. Ben can use a secretary."

"I don't like it. I don't like it all."

"Are you worried she's gonna get seduced by the big bad Bug? Don't be silly. Ben would never cheat on me." She shrugged. "He knows I'd kill him."

"You kids warm my heart with this great love of yours, but just the same I don't like Peg being down there all alone with him."

"There's plenty of other people around. Ben isn't looking for a new lay. He's got the best lay in the world, right here. And he's busy with his fucking Flamingo. *That's* his mistress."

"How do he and Peg get along?"

"Fine. I think she admires him. There's a lot to admire."

I didn't argue the point. I couldn't risk telling Virginia Hill that my real worry was *not* seduction by the Jewish Casanova, but Peg's own misguided search for "justice." She was obviously kissing Siegel's ass (figuratively speaking, one would hope) to get near him and try to determine if he was her uncle's would-be killer. It was a dangerous game she was playing. Only it was no game at all.

"I could drive down there," I said.

"Why bother? They'll be back Friday. For the opening of Cornero's new gambling ship. You can see her then. I can get you an invite."

"Maybe I should drive out there anyway."

"She's fine, Heller. I know she misses you, if that's any consolation."

"How do you know?"

"She told me so. She told me you were the best thing that ever happened to her. Made me curious. Why else do you think I tried to get in your pants? I'm not just another horny broad, you know. Or did you just think I was trying to give you an early Christmas present?"

I stood. "Maybe, but if you see Santa Claus, tell him something for me."

"Oh yeah?"

"Tell him there is a Virginia."

And I got out of that place. Fucking place, as she would have said. Left it to the falcons, the ghost of Valentino, the frightened servants and a beautiful woman with a lovely face, a beautiful body and a mind more twisted than the road down into Hollywood.

TONY CORNERO

MICKEY COHEN

13

The lights of Santa Monica had disappeared behind us, as our speed-boat slipped into the night, and ahead was the searchlight of the S.S. Lux, sweeping slowly over the black water like the beacon at Alcatraz looking for prisoners out for a swim. It had taken thirty-some minutes to get this far, seated on an open-air water taxi that carried Raft, his brunette "starlet" date (Judy something), half a dozen couples and myself—and the tough-looking, fiftyish customer who steered the boat, looking uncomfortable in captain's cap and a spiffy white mess jacket with S.S. Lux crest.

The couples ranged in age from early twenties into their sixties, and all were impressed by Raft's suave famous presence, his cigarette making an amber glow and rarely leaving his lips, his profile as immo-bile as a ship's prow. With the exception of Raft, however, who wore a white dinner jacket and black tie and red carnation, the other pas-sengers weren't dressed to the nines; like me, the men wore suits and ties, sure, but not tuxes, and the women—other than Judy the star-let—were smartly dressed but not in gowns. These were middle-class folks, maybe upper middle-class at best, wearing their Sunday Go To Meeting duds.

The ride had been fairly smooth—whitecaps at a minimum tonight—but the shock of the spray and the wet cold and the occa-sional lurch of the launch was enough to remind a fella he was a landlubber. So was the salty fresh smell of the ocean—for all the times I'd been on the lake, this felt different; there was a vastness, a sense of the edge of the world. A continent left behind.

After such lofty thoughts, the Lux itself was a letdown. Other than the searchlight and some blue neon trimming, the Lux didn't stand out against the night like you'd expect it to. The only sound of merri-ment was some big band music coming out of tinny speakers on deck, "I Love You For Sentimental Reasons," which echoed across the water like bad radio reception, barely heard over the motor of the launch. Any patron expecting a seafaring casino that glittered as well as floated was in for a disappointment, at least as far as the Lux's exterior was concerned. She was a decommissioned Navy mine-layer, whose superstructure had been sheared away and replaced with a wooden shed that covered the deck but for outer walkways. The Lux looked more like Noah's ark than Hollywood's (or anybody's) idea of a gambling ship.

Nonetheless, we were three miles out in a world where there was only dark water and the Lux. The ship, which wore its name on its side in huge white painted letters, was moored with iron cables and looked steadier than the Santa Monica pier. Our launch glided up alongside thick ropes that served as fenders near the well-lit landing stage. Several men in white Lux mess jackets, big enough to be bouncers but well-groomed and polite enough not to intimidate, bent down from the docking float to help the passengers up off the launch. Raft was, of course, recognized and the red carpet rolled out, figuratively that is. It would've been hard to roll anything up the steep stairs to the deck.

"You know in the old days," Raft said, as he and Judy and I walked along the narrow deckway, "there were all sorts of gambling ships out here—the Johanna Smith, the Monte Carlo, the City of Panama, and plenty more. They were real popular."

"What happened?"

"When Mayor Shaw got tossed out of office, things got moral all of a sudden. We had a crusading D.A. who wanted headlines. Him and that Attorney General character, what's his name? Earl Warren. They decided to sink Tony's fleet."

"What about the three-mile limit? How could the authorities get around that?"

"With some cockamamie law that lets 'em go outside their 'mediate jurisdiction to, whaddya call it? Bait a nuisance."

I think George meant "abate," but I got his drift.

"How did Cornero manage to get the Lux afloat, then?"

"The Rex and all that was before the war," Raft said, shrugging, tossing his cigarette overboard. "Times change. New palms make themselves available for greasing."

We went on into the main casino room, where the joint was packed and jumping. If the exterior was a letdown, the interior was quite the pick-me-up. Owner Tony Cornero, the onetime cab driver who'd become "King of the Western Rumrunners" in the twenties, had sunk nearly two hundred grand in the place, Raft said, and it showed, and it obviously attracted a crowd. Sixteen water launches were being kept busy tonight, and my guess for the number of beans in this seagoing jar would've been well over a thousand.

The upper deck's casino room was paneled in rich dark wood and was easily two hundred and fifty feet long and forty feet wide. A mirrored bar ran the length of one wall, making the room seem even bigger, and on the other wall were the slots, scores of them, like a row of metal and glass tombstones before which customers paid their respects. In between were half a dozen roulette tables, half a dozen chuck-a-luck cages, eight crap tables, a Chinese lottery, a faro bank where Cornero himself reportedly dealt.

And people. People and noise and smoke. The clink of drinks and chips, the laughter and wailing of winning and losing. I couldn't spot any celebrities other than Raft, just middle-class types like those on our launch, with a scattering of socialites in evening dress. Also, some unattached beautiful girls in their early twenties, with their chests half showing, were circulating throughout the casino; when one would see a table doing slow business, she'd go there and play. A nice, subtle way to use a shill, if you ask me. Cornero obviously knew his way around running a casino.

Despite the crowd, a few stools were available at the impossibly long bar. We took three, the little starlet crossing her legs through a slit in her gown; nice gams on her, though she had a vacant look in her very brown eyes.

"Do you think Ben Siegel's here?" I asked.

"Yeah, or he soon will be," Raft said. "It's after nine. He don't like to gamble, particularly, and he goes to bed early. He'll put in an early appearance."

"Does he have money in the Lux?"

"I don't think so. He had plenty in the Rex. He borrowed some of it from me, matter of fact, though he paid it back. For all the money he's got rolling in, Ben's always short of dough."

"Why's that?"

"He plays the stock market, and not too damn well."

"I thought you said he doesn't gamble."

"He doesn't think of the stock market as gambling. He sees it as business."

"Tell that to the guys who took swan dives out their windows back in '29."

Raft twitched a smile. "You're telling me. Me, I stick to the ponies and craps. It's more fun and you can now and then beat the odds."

A broad-shouldered, slightly stocky, roughly handsome guy in a tux eased through the crowd with a rolling gait, as if the ship were riding high waves. He came up and placed a hand on Raft's shoulder. The man was in his mid-fifties and his neatly cut and combed gray hair had traces of its original black haunting it; his eyes were slate colored and just as hard.

"Georgie," he said, with a thin wide smile; there was some gravel in the voice. "It's swell of you to come. Couldn't launch this lady without ya."

"Tony Cornero," George said, after being a gentleman and introducing Judy the Starlet to the man, "this is Nate Heller, from Chicago. Him and Frank Nitti were pals."

That was hardly the case, but I let it slide. Use whatever card you have to when you're crashing a private club, I always say.

"Welcome to the Lux, Mr. Heller," he said, lighting up at the Nitti mention, offering his hand. He had a firm grip but his hands were tapered and soft, like an artist's. "What line you in?"

"I run the A-1 Detective Agency in the Loop," I said.

"You know Fred Rubinski? He's from Chicago."

"Yeah. I'm out here to see him, as a matter of fact. We're thinking of affiliating."

"Fred's a good man," Cornero said. "He's gonna do my bad check work. How do you like this place, Mr. Heller?"

"It's a honey. Wish we had its like back in Chicago."

"Well, I treat the customer right. Out of every dollar bet on the Lux, 98.6 cents'll get returned in winnings. Try to find odds like that in Reno or Vegas."

"Why do I think, in spite of that, you've got a floating mint, here?"

Cornero smiled his broad thin smile; he was clearly in his element, enjoying this grand evening. "Because I *do*, Mr. Heller." He leaned in to whisper conspiratorially; he smelled like Old Spice—what else? "Back in the old days, on the Rex, a half million in profit in a given year, we considered slow business."

Raft said, "Whatever happened to the old Rex? I heard you lost her in a twenty-four-hour crap game."

Cornero nodded. "Yeah, after that bastard Earl Warren shut me down. That grand old girl went to war, eventually. The Nazis sunk her off the coast of Africa." He shook his head, a sad expression taking momentary hold, as he considered this most heinous of war atrocities.

"You're doing land-office business opening night," I said. "Think you can keep it up?"

"Oh Christ, yes," Cornero said, with an extravagant wave of the hand, happy again. "We'll be open twenty-four hours a day. There'll always be a full crop of squirrels to keep my ship afloat."

"Squirrels? Is that anything like suckers?"

"Naw, my customers aren't suckers. They're squirrels—you know, lookin' only for fun, entertainment. And that's what I give 'em." He offered his hand again and we shook again. "Mr. Heller, it's nice to have you aboard the Lux."

I smiled. "Always room for another squirrel, you mean?"

"Always room," Cornero smiled. Then he leaned across the bar and told the bartender not to charge us for our drinks; Raft, incidentally, was drinking soda water with a twist of lemon.

Then the stubby broad-shouldered little guy disappeared back into his sea of squirrels, happy as a clam.

"Let's see if Ben's downstairs," Raft said, edging off his stool. "Besides, we can grab a bite to eat."

"Good idea," I said, and I followed him and the starlet to a central stairway in the casino, leading down into a posh dining room trimmed in sky blue where the tables wore cloths and fancy place settings with dark blue napkins. The waiters were in tuxes and the bus boys were in white mess jackets, and it was like being in a fancy restaurant except that the air was a little dank. This dining room took up only half as much space as the casino above; an adjacent room, a five-hundred seat bingo parlor, took up the rest. According to Raft, the bingo parlor was used for off-track betting during the days, racing forms and scratch sheets provided free, cutting into Santa Anita's action by paying track odds.

The maître d' treated Raft like a god and didn't blink when he said he needed a table for eight for his party of three, in anticipation of the Siegel party joining us. We were led there, and sat, and ordered cocktails—well, Raft ordered soda water again—and then selected from the menu offering "cuisine by Battista, formerly of the Trocadero." I ordered a fish platter, since it wasn't every day I ate out on the ocean; but Raft nibbled at a small filet mignon while starlet Judy wolfed down a porterhouse that would've fed a South Side of Chicago family of six for a week.

We'd all decided against dessert when a pudgy, pasty-faced little man in a well-tailored dark gray pinstripe and blue and white striped tie, with an obvious underarm bulge, approached our table. The paleness of his flesh made his five o'clock shadow stand out, and he was just burly enough to make him seem bigger than he was. His nose had been broken any number of times, and a white scar stood out under his left eye; his mouth hung open, just a little, as if to say, I'm just a *little* thick, not terminally so. Nonetheless he looked like an exhibit for the defense in Clarence Darrow's monkey trial.

"Mickey Cohen," Raft whispered to me.

I nodded. I knew Mick from his Chicago stint; the little roughneck independent had run the biggest floating crap game in the Loop, before the war.

Cohen planted himself, smiled a little. "Hiya, Georgie."

"Hiya, Mick. Ben here?"

"Yeah. He's up top. He's et already. He wants you should join him up in the casino."

"We'll be right up. How'd you get in with a piece on you? Cornero's always had strict rules against hardware."

"Rules was made to be broken," Cohen grinned, good-naturedly. He had an edgy energy and a don't-give-a-shit cheerfulness that would make him dangerous indeed.

"This is Nate Heller, by the way," Raft said, gesturing to me. "Pal of mine from Chicago. Nate, Mickey Cohen."

"Yeah," Cohen said, squinting at me, as it dawned on him. "Heller! How the hell are ya? How's your pal Drury?"

"Still kicking," I said, smiling, shaking his hand.

"That Drury, some cop," Cohen grinned. "Hates them Capone boys damn near much as me." He gave us a little forefinger salute. "See yas upstairs."

And he turned and went off with a bantam walk.

"That suit must've set him back two hundred and fifty big ones," I said, wonderingly. "He didn't used to dress like that."

"He's a regular clotheshorse now," Raft said, matter of factly. "Ever since he got hooked up with Ben, anyway. If Ben takes one shower, Mickey takes two. If Ben gets his hair cut daily, Mickey goes twice."

"When do these guys have time for the rackets?"

"The days out here are long," Raft said, signing the check, getting up, putting Judy on his arm.

Back up in the casino, we spotted Virginia Hill, decked out in a clinging white suit with a big white picture hat and white gloves and lots of jewelry, emeralds and diamonds. Her lipstick was bright red, her wide mouth like an attractive wound. She was at one of the dice tables, shaking the bones in her cupped-together gloved hands, her smile white and a little crazed, cheering herself on, "Come seven, come on baby!" She hit her seven and hopped up and down like a kid dressed up in mom's clothes.

Standing nearby, lending support but more restrained, was Peggy Hogan. She looked great, all that hair and those big eyes and cherry-red mouth; it felt good seeing her and it hurt to look at her. She was in one of those Eisenhower jackets, they called them, a square-shouldered, cream-colored crepe blouse drawn in and tied at the waist, with a black collar and skirt; it had a fake military insignia over her right breast, and big pearl buttons. I'd never seen her in that outfit before.

She was holding onto a big black purse—La Hill's trademark bag, stuffed with cash no doubt—like the dutiful secretary she was. Neither she nor her boss lady spotted us as we moved along the edge of the crowd, heading toward the bar.

Which was where Bugsy Siegel was waiting for us.

He was perched on a bar stool, facing the casino, watching the action there with bland seeming indifference, a lean handsome man with languid light blue eyes, as sky blue as Jim Ragen's, and dark, slightly thinning hair. He looked a little like Raft, actually, giving off that same sleepy sensuality that could get a guy inside a nun's pants, a resemblance made startling by their wardrobe: Siegel, too, wore a white dinner jacket and black tie and carnation. Only in Siegel's case the carnation was pink. I didn't remember seeing a man wearing a pink carnation before, but I supposed if you were Ben Siegel you could wear a tulip in your ass if you wanted.

He had a drink in one hand and a pool cue of a cigar in the other, and didn't notice us approaching. Cohen did, tapping him on the shoulder. Siegel hopped off the stool, setting the drink on the bar, and grinned at Raft and put an arm around his shoulder and hugged.

"How ya doin', pal?" Siegel said, in a mellow medium-range voice. "Been a while."

"Nice to see you, Ben. You been a stranger lately."

"Lots of work to do on my baby, turning that desert into a paradise.

You oughta come down and see the miracles we're workin'. You'd be amazed."

They broke ground on the Flamingo last December, Rubinski had told me.

"This is Nate Heller," George said, nodding toward me.

Siegel turned his smile on me; it was a dazzler—white as winter and warm as summer. He pumped my hand and said, "It's a pleasure, Mr. Heller. Really is."

"Pleasure, Mr. Siegel," I said, smiling tightly.

He patted my shoulder, puffed his cigar, smiled around it, apparently sensing my unease. "Tell you what. You call me Ben and I'll call you Nate. How's that sound?"

"Fine, Ben."

He narrowed his eyes and made a mock menacing face. "Just don't call me 'Bugsy' or you'll find out what a crazy asshole I really am." Then he laughed quietly and motioned toward an exit. "Let's go out on the deck, Nate. I been wanting to talk to you."

"Fine. I should say hello to a friend of mine, though."

"Miss Hogan, you mean? She'll keep. She's keeping Tabby company, and Tab'll be working this room till I drag her outta here by the hair."

By "Tabby," I gathered he meant Virginia Hill, who seemed to have as many nicknames as she did personality quirks.

"Mick," Siegel said to his baboon-like bodyguard, "take a break. Have a beer or something."

"Sure, Ben."

Raft didn't have to be told that Siegel wanted to talk to me alone; he just faded back to the bar and another soda water. I hoped talking *was* what Siegel had in mind. My Ragen affiliation might brand me an enemy, after all. I hoped his affability wasn't a mask that would drop as he tossed me casually overboard. Three miles is a hell of a swim, particularly with a broken neck.

It was cool out on the dimly-lit deck, as we leaned against the rail. Big band music was still coming out the speakers, in a fuzzy, tinny way: "Am I Blue?" A few necking couples shared the rail with us, but none were close by. Siegel smiled out into the darkness, the tip of his cigar glowing red, as the blue of the ship's neon trim bathed us.

"I hear good things about you," Siegel said.

"I'm surprised you heard of me at all," I said.

"Fred Rubinski says you're one of the best in the business."

"I'm good. If I were great, I'd be rich."

"Not necessarily. To be rich you got to be born that way, or be willing to kill for what you want. You don't look like you were born with a silver spoon, and the word is you don't like shooting much."

"Who does?"

"Cowboys like Mickey Cohen. It helps to have boys like that around, sometimes, especially if they can be trusted. Anyway, story is you don't like rough stuff but you can dish it out if you have to, and can take it too. And the story also is you don't look down on people like me. You aren't too proud to do a job for a guy like me."

"It depends on the job and it depends on the money."

Siegel smiled wide again, a smile that could charm an A-plus out of the meanest old maid school teacher. "I like you, Nate. I known you, what? Under five minutes, and I already know I like you. That's a good sign. You know why?"

"Sure. It means I'll wake up tomorrow morning."

He waved that off, flicked cigar ash over the side. "Don't be silly. Guys like me and Guzik, we only kill each other. A guy like you, if he plays it straight, even if he's out on the fringes, he's not going to buy it."

"That's encouraging news, Ben. And it'll come as a surprise to that dentist who got drilled at the St. Valentine's Day Massacre. Frankly, I got a reputation for being tight with Outfit guys that ain't entirely deserved."

Long lashes fluttered over baby-blue eyes. "How'd you get that rep, then?"

I shrugged. "Mainly, when Frank Nitti asked me to come 'round, I came 'round. I didn't see any other option."

He smiled gently; the son of a bitch was almost pretty. "I suppose that's right," he said. "But word is you were privy to inside dope and you never took advantage of it, and you never leaked it. Not to the press and not to the cops."

"Listen," I said, putting as much edge in my voice as I dared. "I got friends who are cops. I even got friends who are honest cops. Don't make me out to be a wise guy. Don't trust me with any secrets. I don't want to wander off the fringes to where I qualify for the 'only kill each other' club."

He waved that off, too. "Don't worry. See, I'm going straight. I'm turning this West Coast operation, most of it anyway, over to Dragna and Cohen. I'll get my split, but the day to day shit, I'm not interested. I'm a legitimate businessman, now."

"In the resort business."

"That's exactly right," he said, gesturing with the cigar, waving it like a wand before the black horizon, as if he could make a rainbow at will. "Since the war thousands of people moved to L.A., and it's just a half day's drive to Vegas—and I'm going to make the Flamingo the greatest vacation spot in the world." He flicked a forefinger off a thumb, riffling his carnation. "Pink. Flamingo. It's on my brain—but it's only the beginning. There's Reno, there's Lake Tahoe, all fucking gold mines if you can create vacation spots where people with a little money can have good rooms, good food, good shows, swimming pools, tennis, golf, and all the gambling they want, and all the broads they want. And all that shit's legal in Nevada. And the politicians are for sale and so are the gaming licenses."

"Sounds like the ideal place to go legit, all right."

He went enthusiastically on: "I tell ya, Nate, I owe a lot of what I see ahead to my pal Tony, here. These gambling ships of his are the blueprint—he's known all along the big dough's not to be made from the highhats, or the high rollers, either—but the middle-class, the average joes, who can be sucked in to play the slots or a roulette wheel. Regular folks who ask only that a joint be clean, attractive, safe, professionally run. Tony's known from day one that a casino is a volume operation—the big money comes from a lot of little square johns on vacation with a few hundred bucks to blow."

"You and Cornero go way back."

"I had money in the Rex. I don't have any in this bucket, and that's partly 'cause I got so much tied up in the Flamingo, and also that I'm not convinced Tony's gonna get away with this."

"You think he'll get shut down?"

"I'm afraid so. Tony's a sharp guy with great ideas, but sooner or later, every time, he hits a streak of bad luck. I only tore myself away from my baby 'cause I wanted to be on board to show him some loyalty. He's an old pal, and that's what it's all about. You want to get ahead, you got to have friends, people you can depend on—you got to have their loyalty."

I wondered where that left his dead brother-in-law, Whitey Krakower.

"Well, I got to admit your Flamingo sounds like a money magnet,"

I said, not as convinced as I seemed to be. "You'll have customers lining up in the sand."

He nodded, smiled slyly. "That's where you and Rubinski come in. It's like I said, I'm strictly legitimate now. See, it's like me turning my bad check action over to Fred. Think about it. Where would you expect a guy like me to turn for action like that?"

"Well, to be honest, I'd figure you wouldn't go to a private detective, at least not a straight one like Fred. You'd use some juice collector, some arm breaker."

"Right. But a legit businessman, he doesn't do that, does he?"

"Not that I know of."

"So there are things I need guys like you and Fred for, from time to time, that if I turned over to some enforcer, or even somebody with a few brains like Mick, would be handled with no fuckin' finesse. Which is bad for business."

"Yeah, I can see that."

The sound of a motor launch approaching interrupted us.

Then Siegel said: "Fred says you used to be on the pickpocket detail, back in Chicago."

I shrugged. "That was my first plainclothes job. Most of my ops are former pickpocket detail guys. Fred isn't, though."

"Right. At the Flamingo I got a little staff of ex-L.A. and Hollywood cops who are my private police force, only those assholes couldn't catch colds. I could use somebody to teach 'em the ropes, for general security and especially at nabbing dips."

"With a resort like the one you're building," I said, "you will have a pickpocket problem. No question about it."

"Would you take that assignment from me?"

"I might be able to send a man out, or find somebody qualified through Fred . . ."

He poked the cigar at me. "I want *you*. I like what I hear about you."

"I'm flattered, Ben, really. But I'm a businessman, too, and I have an agency to run."

"I know all about being an executive. I sympathize. On the other hand, there'd be five grand in it for you for a week's work."

"When did you want me to come out?"

He grinned, making dimples that made Shirley Temple look like a piker. "You are a businessman, aren't you, Nate? I like your style.

Anyway, I'll be in touch. I plan to open before the end of the year—I won't bring you in till we're closer to being up and running."

"I think it's only fair to warn you about something."

"Oh?"

"Jim Ragen's a friend of mine. And a client. Even for five grand . . . even for more . . . I won't be party to anything that would put me in a conflict of interest with Jim."

"Of course not," Siegel said, talking around his cigar, "that would be bad business. But teaching my staff to spot and stop pickpockets has nothing to do with Ragen, does it?"

"Well, I just thought it needed to be said."

"I know about you and Ragen. I know all about it. It doesn't bother me."

"It doesn't?"

"Why should it? Ragen's no worry to me."

"Flat on his back in the hospital, you mean, all shot up?"

"I wish he was up and around."

That knocked me back a bit. I said, "Why in hell?" Thinking: *so your people can get another crack at him?*

"Ragen's business is good for my business," he said, flatly.

"That doesn't make any sense . . ."

Siegel smiled, almost to himself. He pitched the cigar over the side and turned and looked at me and put a hand on my shoulder. "I'm not a schmuck. Do I look like a schmuck?"

"No."

"You were Ragen's bodyguard when the hit went down. You swapped slugs with the shooters, who if they were my people woulda got the job done, by the way. And you been keeping guard on his hospital room. Am I right?"

"To a tee," I said, feeling very uncomfortable with that friendly hand on my shoulder.

"It stands to reason that Ragen would hire you to find out who took the contract out. I mean, you're his friend, and you're already in his employ, and you got certain Outfit connections but you're not in their pocket. Who else would he hire?"

"Pinkerton?" I asked.

"No. Nate Heller of the A-1 Detective Agency at Van Buren and Plymouth. The guy who helped nail Bioff and Browne without even pissing Nitti off, which is a fucking miracle. And which opened some doors out here for me, thanks very much. You figure—Ragen fig-

ures—this hit coulda been bought by only one of two people: me or
Jake Guzik. Guzik's probably trying to make you and Ragen believe it
was me behind it. Meanwhile he's probably trying to negotiate a buy-
out, at the same time he's trying to sneak somebody into Ragen's
hospital room to ice him. Am I cooking with gas here, or what?"

"Both burners," I admitted.

He took his hand off my shoulder; looked out into the darkness.
"From what I hear about Ragen, he must be a great old guy. I love it
the way he's standing up to those bastards. Those Outfit guys, they
always want something for nothing. Out East we learned you work for
what you get. Anyway, I'd be lying if I said I like Ragen, 'cause I only
met him a couple of times, so I can't even say I know him, really. But
I wish him the best of luck."

"You wish him the best of luck?" I asked. My mouth hanging open
lower than Mickey Cohen's.

"Sure. If he goes under, well, hell—sooner or later, I'm out of
business."

"I don't get you. He's your competition."

Siegel laughed. "He's no competition to me. Early on we had some
rough stuff, sure; Mickey roughed up Ragen's son-in-law, Brophy,
back when we were trying to break in the L.A. market. But things
have settled down since. Now, if I go in a wire room, or one of my
boys does, they buy what I'm sellin'. No questions asked. If they like
Ragen's service better than mine, well they buy his too. How does
that hurt me?"

"Not at all," I admitted.

"I'm pulling in twenty-five grand a week on Trans-American, Nate.
That's my end alone. Sweet numbers, I'd say."

"So would I."

"If Ragen sells out, or if he dies and his family sells out, the Outfit
will take over Continental and my pals back east, having business
arrangements with Guzik and the boys, will cave in and shut Trans-
American down. And I'll be out of business."

"I never of thought it like that," I said.

"I hope Ragen lives forever," Siegel said, his smile big and benign,
"and I hope he hangs on forever with his business, too, fighting those
bastards tooth and nail."

I was shaking my head, wondering why I hadn't figured it. "You
really didn't hire the Ragen hit, did you?"

"Of course not. It wouldn't make any fucking sense at all." He laughed. "You know, you got a great little girl there, Nate. I'm gonna hate to lose her."

"What?"

"Peggy Hogan. She's your girl. I know that, and not just 'cause Georgie and Tab both told me. I got my sources. I'm going to hate to lose her, 'cause she's got a great head for figures. I'd put her in charge of my whole office staff if she'd give up working for her uncle and move west permanent. But I bet she wouldn't do that, or leave you behind, either."

"Have . . . have you talked to her about this?"

"Ha! Of course not! She doesn't know I know anything about any of it. She doesn't know I know how tight she is with her uncle. She's been trying to pump me all week, sizing me up, watching me. You ought to hire her on at A-1."

"You don't seem to be pissed off or anything . . ."

"With who?"

"With Peggy. For, you know . . . checking up on you."

"Hey, I think it's cute. She's dedicated to her family. That's a good thing. It's like friendship. You can't put a price on it. Take her back to Chicago, Nate, and marry the girl, before she goes all career girl on you and you're shit out of luck. Take my advice. I know my women."

I bet he did.

"Come on," he said, taking me by the arm, "let's go back and get you two kids back together. I'm a sucker for a good love story."

14

Siegel ushered me into the casino, me on his arm like the starlet on Raft's, and with his big winning smile stopped at the crap table where Virginia Hill, having finally crapped out, was waiting for another turn, sipping one of a succession of stingers, holding her own purse while Peggy looked dutifully on.

Only now that she saw me, Peggy's mouth was, as they say, agape, which amused La Hill no end.

"What's wrong, honey?" she asked Peggy. "Aren't you glad to see your little boy friend?"

"Nate," Peggy said, her always pale face downright ashen now, violet eyes round and wet and tragic, "what are you *doing* here?"

Miss Hill pressed hand to generous bosom and laughed like a braying mule, managing to say, "I don't think she's glad to see you, Heller!"

Siegel let go of my arm and went to Peggy, who suddenly looked very frightened. He touched her arm, gently, and she flinched. He didn't let go, however.

"It's okay, it's okay," he told her. "Nate's a friend of mine. Don't worry. Everything's going to be fine. He'll tell you all about it."

He let go of her arm and nodded to me. The eyes of the nearby crowd were on us. I felt like I was wearing a fig leaf and it slipped. Nonetheless, I moved to her and she looked at me angry and hurt and confused, but I put my arm around her and walked her away from the table, from the crowd, toward the bar, where Raft looked at us, lifted his eyebrows, put them back down, and looked away.

"Come with me," I said. "Don't be afraid."

"Nate, I . . . I don't know what to say . . . does he *know* about me?"

"Yeah."

"You mean, that I was trying to find out . . ."

BEN SIEGEL

"Yeah, but don't worry. Look, there's a launch every half hour. We'll catch the next one."

In fact, the next launch took off in less than five minutes, and we made it, leaving the Lux behind, a fading blue neon-trimmed shape whose searchlight still fanned the dark sea. We sat with a few other couples, who were nuzzling, but we didn't nuzzle; we sat close, but didn't nuzzle.

The ride back was rougher; we felt the spray almost constantly, squinting into it, wiping it from our faces occasionally. We had to speak up to be heard over the motor.

"I figured you'd be mad," she said, mad. "I don't blame you for being mad. But how could you come out here and endanger me like this . . ."

I laughed harshly. "It's a little late for you to be worried about the danger factor, baby. Now why don't you shut up and I'll fill you in."

She gave me an exasperated look, but sighed and shut up and I filled her in. I told her I'd indeed come out here to retrieve her, but that I'd been careful not to tip her hand where her uncle's interests were concerned—none of which mattered a whit, I said, considering what Siegel had just told me on the deck of the Lux, and filled her in on that, as well.

She, like me, was stunned.

"Do you believe him?" she asked.

I sighed. Shook my head no, not believing I could be saying, "Yes."

She swallowed. "I do too."

"Why?" I had reasons for my opinion; what did she have?

"Ben's a good man, Nate. He's gone straight. He just couldn't have done it."

Oh. She had opinions for her reason.

And she had more: "He's an honest man."

"Well, that's rich."

"Well, he is! He reminds me . . ."

"Don't tell me. Of your Uncle Jim."

"Well, he does! I've spent a lot of time with him this week, in Vegas, at the Flamingo. He works hard. He's really . . . a very nice guy. People around him love him. He's so . . . dedicated to what he wants. He's like a . . . visionary."

"He's like a gangster, Peg."

The boat lurched and I held her, one hand on the padded shoulder of her Eisenhower jacket. She let me. She didn't seem to like it, but she let me.

"I find him charming, too," I admitted. "I think I might even like the guy, given half a chance. But he came up the hard way. Don't ever forget that. He kills people."

"I don't believe it. It's just stories."

"Well, the stories I've heard, and they're not stories, are that he likes getting into the rough stuff, personally. A boss is supposed to limit himself to ordering hits—he's supposed to plan 'em out, then get the hell to someplace where his alibi is ironclad. But don't-call-him-Bugsy went out on a contract personally a few years back; just couldn't resist, I guess, and went along with the boys to make sure it was done right, and pulled the trigger himself, and he almost went to the gas chamber over it."

"Don't be ridiculous."

"The only reason he didn't is because one witness got shot to death, a guy who happened to be Ben's brother-in-law, in case you're wondering why a charming guy like that is divorced. And also there was this hitman turned witness who got pushed out a hotel window at Coney Island a while back. Guy named Abe Reles. Murder Incorporated? Remember that from the papers?"

She folded her arms across her chest; she was squinting, not just from the sea spray that was hitting her, but from inward stubbornness. "He just doesn't seem like that kind of man to me. And, anyway, I think he's trying to make a new start of it. You should see this resort he's building. It's going to be fabulous. It's exciting just to be around it, to be any small part of it."

"Christ, you come out here to see if this guy tried to kill your uncle, and wind up president of his fan club! Did he do anything?"

"What do you mean?"

"Did you sleep with him?"

She pulled away from me, glared at me. "How can you ask that?"

"I was gonna ask if he screwed you, but I thought that might be a little on the crude side."

Working our voices up over the motor like we had to meant some of our nuzzling co-passengers heard an occasional word of ours; several of them were looking at us now and I gave them a big sarcastic insincere smile and they looked away.

She huddled to herself. "You're terrible. He was a perfect gentleman."

"You walked out on me."

"I left word."

"I ought to throw you off this goddamn boat."

She made a face at me. "Why don't you just try?"

"I oughta belt you."

"You really know how to win a girl back, Heller."

"I didn't know I'd lost you."

"I don't think you quite have, yet. But keep trying."

We sat in silence for a while—silence but for the launch's motor and the boat riding through the whitecaps. And some of our fellow passengers whispering about us. I hadn't had so much fun on a boat since the landing on Red Beach at Guadalcanal.

Then I said: "The point here is that we both believe Siegel is not who paid those guys in the truck to hit your uncle."

She nodded.

"For me it's woman's intitution," she said, putting her anger away, if not her poutiness. "What's your *detective*'s instinct say?"

I ignored her smart-ass tone, saying, "It's more than instinct. Siegel laid it out perfect—he's better off with Jim alive. So, logically, Siegel's not the guy who hired the hit."

She was nodding. "And Jake Guzik is."

"Jake Guzik is. The fat little man has been playing it real cute all along. Pulling me in, Jim's own security man, and 'confiding' in me that the Outfit wasn't behind it. Guzik even bought off one of my own men, but knew me well enough to know I'd beat the truth out of the guy, so they were careful to make all contacts by phone and money drops. And he didn't use Outfit guys for the shooters, but hired a couple of West Side bookies, to further confuse the issue. Then he sends me to Jim with a new, more generous offer, but also sends his two gunmen up the Meyer House fire escape, playing it from both ends. Those greasy thumb prints have been all over this from the beginning. I should've figured it. Took Siegel himself to wake me up."

"What does it mean?"

"It means I'm going to tell your uncle that Guzik is responsible. I'm going to tell him to keep that in mind when entering any new negotiations with him."

She looked at me with utter disbelief. "You don't think my uncle would sell out at *this* point, after hearing . . ."

The launch lurched.

"I don't know. I still think it's his best option, but with this new knowledge he can go for more money and warn Guzik that he'll cooperate with Drury and turn those affidavits over to the feds *now*, if the Outfit doesn't pay now and stay away later."

"Would that work?"

I shrugged, sighed, shook my head. "Hell, I don't know. Anyway, the stubborn old bastard will probably want to keep fighting."

She moved closer to me. "Do you blame him?"

I slipped my arm around her. "Not really. But I don't envy him, either."

Before too long we were in a warm bed in my room at the Roosevelt Hotel. The days apart, the recriminations, all of it, receded in the distance, like the Lux. Faded away, like a barely remembered bad dream. Now there was only the two of us, naked, in each other's arms, loving each other, ready to put it all behind us and go home and start over.

It was a little after midnight when the phone rang and the bad dream kicked back in.

"It's after two o'clock out there," I said to Bill Drury's staticky, disembodied voice. "What's so important it can't wait? Did you lose another witness?"

I was sitting up in bed; the phone was on the nightstand beside me. Peggy, asleep till the phone rang, was only half-awake, half-listening.

"Worse," Bill's voice said tinnily. "I've been trying to get you all evening. Didn't you check for messages when you got in?"

"I was preoccupied, okay?"

There was silence for a few moments; the phone company charges for that, too, but it was Bill's nickel so I just waited for him to speak up. Which he finally did:

"You got her back? Is she there with you? Peg, I mean?"

I smiled over at Peg and she smiled lazily at me. Did I ever mention she had violet eyes?

"Yes, Bill. She's with me. She's going to stay with me, too. I'm not giving her any choices."

"You better give her some support, Nate."

I winced. "What the hell's happened?"

"Her uncle's suffered mercury poisoning. Nobody knows how it happened yet."

"Mercury poisoning . . ."

Peg sat up in bed, eyes wide now; she held the covers to her breasts, as if seeking protection.

The voice from the phone said: "He's dying, Nate."

JAMES RAGEN SR. AND JR.

15

It was well after visiting hours, in fact approaching midnight Saturday, when Peg and I walked down the hall at Meyer House toward her uncle's room, footsteps echoing. Lou Sapperstein was standing guard, a uniformed cop sitting next to him, snoozing; Lou was in shirt-sleeves and suspenders and I hadn't seen him look so haggard since those weeks after his brother died in the war. At least this time Lou wasn't wearing a black arm band. Jim Ragen was still alive.

"I think he's sleeping," Sapperstein said. "His son Jim, Jr., is in there, keeping up the vigil. Family members been taking turns."

Peg said, "I'm going in there."

Sapperstein held open the door for her. I stayed out in the hall. This was family. I was just the hired help.

"You look like shit," Sapperstein said.

"I feel worse. If God had meant for man to fly, He'd have given airliners comfortable seats."

"All day ordeal, huh?"

"Yeah. Peg slept a lot, thank God. She was up most of last night, crying, wanting to talk it through. That made her tired enough today to sleep through most of the trip home."

Lou shook his head. "I'm sorry as hell about this, Nate. I don't know how our security could've been any tighter."

"What happened, anyway?"

"Nobody's sure. They're saying mercury poisoning, but it's a guess. Uremic poisoning I'm also hearing. He had a kidney operation Thursday. It's been downhill ever since."

"I want to talk to one of the medics. Who's around?"

"One of the two family doctors. Graaf."

"Where?"

"He's been in and out. Try that lounge area down the hall—he's probably grabbing a smoke."

I walked down there and Dr. Graff, a short, well-fed, mustached man of about fifty, in a brown rumpled suit, was sitting, smoking, looking dejected and tired.

He looked up and smiled wearily. "Mr. Heller. Back from the land of make believe."

I sat next to him. "That's right, Doc. I only wish I could make believe this isn't happening."

"You want a smoke?"

"Yeah. Why not."

He fired me up and I sucked the smoke into my lungs, held it there, let it out slow.

"So," I said, "is he going to make it?"

"If you'd asked me that Monday, I'd have said hell, yes. In a week I'd be calling him fully recovered from the wounds and the shock. Oh, impaired, certainly. But he was damn near out of this place, way ahead of schedule."

"Then what?"

He sighed, raised his eyebrows. "Then he had a sharp decrease in elimination. Blood pressure rose sharply. Decreased urine output. Bloody stools, vomiting . . ."

"This is all very colorful, Doc. But what does it mean, besides I just lost my appetite for this year?"

"Those are symptoms of mercury poisoning."

"So we're talking foul play, definitely."

"Very likely."

"How?"

"How does the poem go? 'Let me count the ways . . .'"

"I don't buy that—I set up the security here myself. We put a lid on this joint."

Graaf sighed. "Mr. Heller—mercury could enter the body through an alcohol rub, the likes of which Mr. Ragen has gotten daily; by enema; by intravenous or intramuscular injection, or absorption through the skin from an ointment."

"But not orally?"

"That's the easiest way of all. A tablet the size of an aspirin would contain approximately twice the dosage it would take to kill a man."

"That's the only other way—in a pill?"

"Hardly. The mercury could have been administered in coffee, milk, or tomato juice, or sprinkled on food. It would've been as taste-less as it was deadly."

"You're saying they've killed him."

Graaf looked at the floor. "We don't make judgments like that, not when a patient is still breathing. Tell me, Mr. Heller. In your line of work, do you ever take on a job that's more or less hopeless?"

"Never," I said, and shook his hand, and ground the cigarette out with my heel, and went back up the hall.

Sapperstein was leaning against the wall, standing next to the seated uniformed cop, who was awake now. Frankly, I trust Chicago cops more when they're sleeping.

"It's a poisoning, all right," I said to Lou. "Somebody on the hospital staff, most likely."

Sapperstein nodded. "I know. I already started poking around—they got twelve hundred people on staff, and in the menial areas, a lot of turnover."

"Yeah, but we got a restricted guest list."

Sapperstein gestured down to the clipboard leaned against the wall. "Sure we do, and that may help us find out who slipped your friend this killer Mickey Finn—but the damage is done, isn't it?"

"Yeah. It is. Damn."

"He's a tough old bird, Nate. I like him. I hate to see it end like this."

"He's an idiot. Banging his head up against the wall and expecting not to get it bloody. Goddamnit, I should never have played along on this one!"

Sapperstein, not much given to such demonstrations, put his arm around my shoulder and said, "We did what we could, Nate. I don't think anybody could've done any better. He's your friend, and your girl's uncle, and this is a tough one to lose. But you been right all along—there was no winning this game. It was rigged from the start."

I nodded. Smiled at him and rubbed my fingers over my eyes and got rid of the moisture.

Then I went into the room. Jim was asleep, all right; he already looked dead, only you could see his chest moving some. He looked skinny. Pale as milk but nowhere near as healthy. You could smell death in the room. Death and flowers.

Peg was sitting next to him, leaning in toward him, holding his hand as he slept. She was crying; not making any sound, just tears flowing. She hadn't cried at all today, before now—when she hadn't been sleeping, in the window seat next to me, she'd been angry. Not really saying anything about anything, just balling fists and shaking

them at the air, face balled up, too. That expression "You're so beautiful when you're mad" didn't apply to her; she was a lovely girl, but
anger looked ugly on her.

She wasn't mad now. She was merely devastated. It hadn't been
that long ago that she'd lost her father to a stroke. Now the man she'd
put in her father's place was slipping away from her, water through
her fingers.

Jim, Jr., sat in the flowery chintz lounge chair, but he didn't look
very comfortable. He was in his shirt sleeves, tie loosened, complexion gray, expression blank.

I went over to the boy—boy, hell, he was probably my age—and
squeezed his shoulder. "How are you holding up?"

"Okay," he said, with a small, brave, entirely unconvincing smile.
"My dad sets a good example. He never gives up, does he?"

"No. It's not in him."

Jim, Jr., swallowed. "Sometimes I wish it was."

"Yeah. Me, too. Let's step out in the hall and talk. I don't want to
wake your father."

He nodded and rose; lost his balance momentarily, and I helped
him. He'd obviously been sitting in that chair for hours.

We walked down to the lounge area; Dr. Graaf was no longer
around. We sat.

"How's your mom doing?"

"Terrible," he said. "Just terrible. She's so devoted to him. She's
not at all well herself, even without this."

"Have they got her under sedation?"

"No—she refuses that. She wants to be able to go to Dad's side, if
he takes a turn for the worse."

"I think he's taken that turn."

"I know. He's going to die, isn't he?"

"I think so. He's tough, but . . ."

"He's been poisoned. The doctors admit they 'suspect a metallic
poison has been introduced.' They think if they make it sound formal,
it makes them sound like they're on top of things. That's a laugh."

"I'm sorry, Jim. The sons of bitches got to your father, and I wasn't
even here to try to stop them."

"Heller, you've done everything anybody could. You put your life
on the line more than once. And as for not being here—my father
wanted you to go after Peggy. He's nuts about that kid. And I don't

blame him, really. She's been aces, all the way—like another sister to us."

"I'm nuts about her myself. But this is going to be hard on her. Like it's going to be on all of you."

He shook his head. "Even Danny—I didn't think he cared that much—he sat here this afternoon just telling dad how much he loved him. Crying like a baby. Dad just patted him on the head, saying, 'There, there, my lad,' comforting *him*. Can you imagine?"

"Yeah. I can. You're going to be under a lot of pressure to sell out, you know."

He bristled. "Do you think I'd do that? Do you think after all my father's been through, I'd . . ." He buried his face in his hands, bent over. He wasn't crying. He was past that. "I'm so frightened, Mr. Heller . . . I'm so very frightened . . ."

I patted his back. I couldn't think of anything to say. *There, there, my lad* was taken.

"We're going to lose him, aren't we? And I'm going to be left to try to stand up to those people."

I put my hand on his shoulder again. "When your father is dead, and the responsibility falls to you, and your brothers, then you're going to have to make up your mind what the right thing is to do."

He lifted his head and narrowed his eyes. "You're not . . . telling me to *sell*, are you?"

"I'm telling you when your father's gone, the responsibility is yours, and so is the decision. Nobody could tell Jim Ragen how to live his life. I don't think it's fair for him, even in death, to tell somebody else how to live theirs."

The flesh around his eyes tensed, momentarily, and I could see his father in his face, so clearly. Then he reached into a pocket and handed me a card. "What do you make of this, Mr. Heller?"

It was white, about the size of an index card but without lines. On it was a crude but unmistakable image: a yellow canary. The card was unsigned.

"Where did you get this? When?"

"In the mail today. What does it mean?"

"What do you think it means?"

"I . . . I think it's the underworld's way of saying my dad shouldn't have 'sung.'"

"That's right. It's a warning. For nobody else to get vocal. But it's more than that."

"More?"

"It means the Outfit is admitting, in its oblique way, that it's killed your father. He isn't even dead yet, and they're telling you they've accomplished his killing."

I handed the card back to him. He looked as if he were about to crush it in his hand, and I stopped him.

"You might want to show that to Lt. Drury," I said.

He swallowed. "All right."

"I don't suppose it came with a return address?"

Young Ragen managed a little laugh. "No, not hardly."

"Damn," I said, with mock disappointment. "Detective work is never easy."

He smiled at that, momentarily, and I patted his shoulder and rose and said, "Let's go back to your father's room."

We did. I took over for Sapperstein, tired as I was, buoyed by coffee, and Peg stayed in there at her uncle's side all night. Dr. Graaf went in a couple of times and so did several other doctors and nurses; I checked everybody against my clipboard, like a good operative. The barn door was open, the horse was gone, but I was keeping a watch on the stall anyway.

Very early the next morning, shortly after five, Jim, Jr., came out and said, "Dad's awake. He's asking for you."

I went in. Peggy was standing, holding his hand, looking down at him with what I'm sure she thought was a supportive, encouraging smile. If anybody ever gave me a smile like that, I'd call the morgue myself and save somebody else the trouble.

I went around on the other side of the bed.

"Peggy says you found some things out," Jim said; his voice was weak, but it still had some steel in it. Or maybe that was just the mercury.

"We did," I said. "I met Siegel. I'm convinced he didn't do any of this to you."

"Guzik, then."

"Guzik."

"And I'm expected to do business with that devil."

"If you do, insist on a hell of a deal."

I filled him in, some. He listened alertly, as if oblivious to his pain;

but he was feeling some, otherwise he would have interrupted more often.

"You know it does make sense, lad," he said. "When the Outfit put Trans-American together, they had to turn to the eastern boys for help. Guzik could handle Chicago and Milwaukee and so on—but he needed Lansky's help out east, and Siegel out west. That's why they want my set-up—it's national. We're everywhere."

"We can talk about this later, Jim."

"No we can't. I'm dying. Nobody will tell me, but I can feel it. They poisoned me, didn't they?"

"Yes," I said.

"How much longer do I have?"

"Do I look like a doctor, you crazy Irish bastard?"

"Don't give me that. How much longer, Nate?"

"They didn't tell me. I tell you what—why don't you just take your own sweet time about it."

"I wish I had some time, lad." He turned to his niece. "Peggy my girl—peg o' my heart. Give your uncle a kiss."

She kissed his cheek.

She stayed near him and he said, "I know I'm dying—there's an angel at my side."

"Uncle Jim, please don't say that . . ."

"Peg, you're a good girl. I told Jim, Jr., before—you're always to have a place in the family business. A piece of it is yours, my dear."

"Please, Uncle Jim. I don't care about that . . ."

"I think you do. You're not just like a daughter to me, lass. You're like a son. You could run that business of mine, if ye were."

"You can run it yourself, Uncle Jim . . ."

"I need . . . need two things from you, lass."

"Anything—"

"I want you to marry this poor excuse for a detective, here. He's going to need your help. Besides—he's a good man, even if he is only half a mick."

"I do love him, Uncle Jim."

"Good. That makes me glad to hear."

It made me feel pretty good, too.

"The other thing is something you have to do right now. You can't wait."

"Yes?"

"Find me a priest, lass."

He died at 6:55 A.M. His son had time to call Ellen Ragen to her husband's side. Also at his side were his other two sons, and one of the three married daughters.

The coroner's initial report barely mentioned the mercury poisoning, attributing Ragen's death to "hypotensive heart disease and nephritis complicated by gunshot wounds." There were "traces of mercury found in a qualitative analysis." And that was that.

But it wasn't. Lt. Drury made the point to Coroner Brodie that an important legal question needed to be definitively answered: namely, whether Ragen died due to the gunshot wounds, making for a murder case against the gunmen in the green truck; or heart disease, making it death by natural causes, reducing the charge against the gunmen to attempted murder; or nephritis brought on by mercury poisoning, making for a *different* murder case, against person or persons yet unknown.

About this time, Coroner Brodie received several threatening phone calls that he and his family were in danger unless he "minded his own fucking business" where the Ragen matter was concerned. Brodie moved to a secret office and ordered police guards put on his home, and on the vault at Mt. Olivet, too, where Jim Ragen had been recently interred, the cops protecting the vault till Brodie could receive the permission of the court and Mrs. Ragen to perform a second autopsy.

Mrs. Ragen did object, but the courts overrode it, and it turned out Jim had enough mercury in him to kill three men.

The affidavits? Ragen's so-called insurance policy? It must have lapsed, because via the family lawyer, Ellen Ragen told the press the affidavits would not be released to the authorities or anyone else. They could not, the lawyer claimed, be found.

An investigation into the hospital staff (not led by Drury, by the way) turned up nothing. Several promising leads fizzled, particularly the revelation that a tube had been inserted in Ragen's stomach to relieve gas, the night before he died, a tube containing mercury. But the mercury was a different kind than that found in Ragen's liver and kidneys, a liquid mercury that passes right through the system and can't be absorbed.

By the end of August two things were obvious: Jim died due to mercury poisoning; and the killer would never be found.

Predictably, Peggy couldn't accept that. She came storming into my inner office, on the last Saturday in August, and said, "What are you going to do about it?"

I gestured to the client's chair across from my desk and she sat. She was wearing a simple black suit with pearls and black gloves; she'd either worn black or at least an arm band every day since Jim died.

"About what?" I ventured.

"Mickey McBride just bought out Continental!"

"Really?" Actually, I knew all about it. Jim, Jr., had asked my opinion and I had told him to do what he thought was right.

The violet eyes flashed with anger. "After everything my uncle did, after all his suffering, his family sells him out! How can they be such *weasels!*"

"Peg, your uncle was murdered because *he* wouldn't sell out. Nobody else in the family, except maybe you, is dedicated to the racing wire business. It's not like it's a noble profession or anything. It's a racket."

"It's legal!"

"For the moment, and barely. This is a rough time for your aunt and her children. I don't happen to think some of 'em have a hell of a lot of backbone, myself, but young Jim seems like a good man, and I think he's worried about his mother's health. I don't think he wants to lose another parent."

"What are you saying?"

"I'm saying cut 'em some slack."

"But they sold Continental! Lock, stock and barrel!"

"Yeah, to Mickey McBride. Not to Jake Guzik."

"What's to stop Mickey McBride from selling to Guzik?"

"Nothing."

"Goddamnit, Nate—you're *impossible!*"

I gestured with two open hands. "Look, it's not going to happen right away. Even the Outfit knows if they move in on Continental now, on the heels of your uncle's murder, the roof'll come crashing down on 'em. They may cut a backroom deal with McBride, but what the hell—McBride and your uncle were business partners for years. You should be able to accept whatever avenue he decides to take the business. And you should be able to accept him as your new boss."

She folded her arms tightly across her chest. "I wouldn't work for that company now. Not in a million years. I don't want anything to do with it."

"Well, why don't you take your uncle's advice, then?"

"What?"

"And marry me. Go the picket fence route. Make little Hellers."

"Nathan, your timing doesn't exactly rival Fred Astaire."

"Sorry. So what now?"

She sighed heavily. "What's happening where those West Side gunmen are concerned?"

"Drury's case is progressing pretty well, considering he lost a witness. The other witnesses haven't backed out, amazingly enough. He's i.d.'ed the driver, another West Side bookie—who incidentally was just caught dumping something in Douglas Park Lagoon, which turned out to be a sawed-off shotgun barrel."

She sat up. "When was this?"

"Last night. Drury called me this morning about it. Don't say I never have any good news for you. Anyway, Drury's going to have no trouble getting a grand jury indictment, now."

I expected that to improve her disposition.

It didn't.

"But those men didn't kill my uncle. They tried to, but they didn't. What about whoever *did*? What about whoever *poisoned* him?"

"The cops are looking into that. You know that."

"Why don't you look into it?"

"Why should I?"

"Why don't you just go up to Jake Guzik and shoot him in his fat head?"

"That's a swell idea. Then the prison chaplin can marry you and me while I'm walking down that long, long hall. I hope you like weird haircuts."

"I don't think you're funny."

"I don't find any of this funny. There are things in this world you can't do a fucking thing about, Peggy. There are battles that can't be won. Sometimes you just got to be happy to be able to hang onto your life, for a while."

"That's you, all right. Nate Heller. You're a real survivor."

"And what's wrong with that?"

She stood. "Well, maybe I want more out of a man. Maybe I want more out of life."

"And where are you going to find *that*? Las Vegas?"

She lifted her chin and looked down her nose at me; sooner or later every woman I know does that to me. "Maybe I will. I don't like this town. I don't think I can live here anymore."

"Peg. Why don't you just sit back down . . . we'll talk a little more and . . ."

"I'm sick of you. I'm sick of my family. I'm sick of Chicago."

And she went out the door.

I thought about going after her, but I just kept my seat. She was as stubborn as her uncle, after all. And I'd had my fill of hopeless cases for one year.

But I did stand, to look out the window and watch her catch a cab. Wondering if she'd really do it. Really go running to Vegas and Siegel and that lunatic Virginia Hill, as if that were really an alternative to the madhouse of Chicago.

No, I thought. *No way in hell*.

She took the morning flight out.

Two
A KILLING IN VEGAS
DECEMBER 15, 1946 – JUNE 20, 1947

16

I got on the train at Union Station on Alameda Boulevard at a quarter to seven that Sunday morning, and promptly fell asleep in my seat. When I woke up mid-morning and looked out the window, I found Los Angeles, and civilization (not that those terms necessarily have anything to do with each other), long gone. In their place was desolation, the literal kind, as opposed to the spiritual brand the City of Angels breeds. I spent the rest of the morning watching the desert roll by my window like a bleached tan carpet covering the world. I kept trying to picture somebody putting up a casino in the middle of all that sand and sagebrush, and couldn't manage it.

It was after two when the train rolled into the modern, many-windowed Union Pacific Station at the west end of Fremont Street, and I soon found myself standing, single bag in hand, in a restful shaded park, enjoying a very dry breeze, looking down a busy street lined with wide-open casinos: the Las Vegas Club, the Monte Carlo, the Pioneer, the Boulder, the Golden Nugget. Despite the slight shock of seeing casinos sprawled over two very American blocks, I felt vaguely disappointed. While the Sunday afternoon crowds filled the sidewalks and kept Fremont's two modest lanes hopping with traffic, it nonetheless looked a little shabby, not at all glamorous. A small boy's idea of a sinful good time, complete with Hollywood-style frontier trimmings. Maybe at night, when neon lit up Glitter Gulch, I'd revise my jaded Chicagoan's opinion.

Shortly before two-thirty, a black Lincoln Continental glided up to the curb. Out of it scrambled a balding, rodent-like man in a three-hundred-dollar black silk suit. His tie was wide and red and his face was oblong and pale.

"Nate Heller?" he said, with a sideways smile, thrusting a hand forward.

I nodded, took the hand, shook it, found it moist, let go of it and, trying not to call attention to the act, wiped the moisture from my palm on my pant leg.

"Moe Sedway," he said, jerking a thumb to his chest, smiling nervously, his tiny, close-set eyes as moist as his handshake, his nose a big lumpy thing like a wad of modeling clay stuck there by some kid.

He took my bag and walked around to the rear of the Lincoln; I followed him there. He put the bag in the car's trunk, which was bigger than some coldwater flats I've seen. "How was L.A.?" he asked.

"Swell," I said.

"So you're a pal of Fred Rubinski's, huh?"

"Yeah. Business partners, actually."

"You say that like it's two different things. Where I come from business partners can be pals, too. In fact they *should* be."

I shrugged at this piece of curbside philosophy. He shut the trunk. With nervous energy to spare, he moved around me and opened the car door on the rider's side. He gestured for me to get in, smiling nervously.

I got in. He went around and got behind the wheel. "Ever been to Vegas before?" he said, lighting up a long, thick cigar that was much too big for his face.

"No," I said.

"Want a cigar? Havanas. Two bucks a piece."

"No thanks."

He'd left the car running. He pulled out and headed up Fremont Street. Mixed in among the tourists, many of whom wore dude-ranch style Western clothes, were occasional real westerners: men with the weathered faces of the true rancher or ranch hand; an Indian woman with a baby cradled on her back; a toothless old prospector who made Gabby Hayes look like a Michigan Avenue playboy.

Beyond the casinos and clubs was a business district, Western-style souvenir shops and barbecue restaurants mingling with modern offices and the dime store chains.

"What do you think of our little town?" Sedway said, blowing smoke.

"It's not Chicago," I said.

Past the downtown was an unimpressive residential district; in fact some of it was downright shabby—trailers and cinderblock houses—distinguished only by tacky wedding chapels, often hooked up with motels, that lined the thoroughfare. Pastel stucco with neon wedding bells and hearts and such. The vows of a lifetime served up like a cheeseburger at a white-tile one-arm joint.

"Yeah," Sedway said, his moist eyes dreamy, cigar between his fingers like Churchill, "ain't Vegas the greatest place?"

I nodded, and looked back out the window, the sleazy landscape blurring when Sedway picked up speed as we passed the city limits.

"Ben didn't say why he brought you out," he said, smiling over at me. He was smiling too much; I wondered why.

"I'm going to give your security people the rundown on pickpockets," I said.

He shrugged with his eyebrows. "We open day after Christmas, you know."

"I know. Should be time enough."

"How well do you know Ben?"

"I only met him once. He seems like a nice guy."

"Oh he is," Sedway said, quickly, almost defensively. "We go way back, Ben and me. I known him since we was kids on the Lower East Side."

Fred Rubinski had told me about Little Moey Sedway. He had mentioned that Sedway and Siegel went "way back"—but he had also mentioned something Sedway neglected to.

"Little Moey only recently got back in his boss's good graces," Fred told me. "For almost three years, Moey was given jobs out of Siegel's sight and told to stay away from the Bug or risk getting hit in the head."

Seems Sedway, who'd never done too well for himself despite the constant help of his boyhood pal Ben (recent failures by Little Moey included botched bookmaking operations in both San Diego and L.A.), had become a big man in little Vegas. As Siegel's on-site rep for the Trans-American race wire, Sedway wormed his way into part ownership of several Fremont Street casinos. He bought a nice house, a big car. He became chummy with the city fathers, dropping dough into charity and church hoppers. When a group of respectable citizens asked Mr. Sedway to run for city commissioner, he accepted.

And when his boss found out, the man who didn't like to be called Bugsy went bugsy, and started slapping Little Moey around.

"We don't run for office, you little schmuck!" Siegel had roared, slapping his stooge, whose name happened to be Moe, although he was getting slapped more like he was Larry or Shemp. "We *own* the politicians, you dumbass cocksucker!"

Moey had done his best to back out of the election, but his name was already on the ballot. Sedway became a laughingstock in mob circles, the butt of a much-repeated anecdote (attested to by Rubinski relating the story to me) as the only politician who ever had to spread the graft around to make sure he *didn't* get elected.

All this was three years ago, more or less, and in recent months Ben Siegel had called upon his once trusted second-in-command to come back to his side.

"You ought to be warned," Moe was saying, "that Ben's a little on edge these days. Lots of pressure on the boss. Lots of pressure."

"Why?"

"Well, you heard about the dough he's laying out on this layout."

"I heard over a million."

"He's *spilled* more than a million. I tell you, though, it's gonna be a fabulous place, this Flamingo."

"So why's he under pressure?"

"To open on time. I don't think the hotel's gonna be finished."

"Then why open? What's the rush?"

Sedway shrugged. "Ben don't like to wait on nobody or nothing. Everything's *now* with him. Here we are."

Where we were was not the Flamingo, but the Hotel Last Frontier, or so said the horizontal sign, cartoon letters of crisscrossing logs outlined in neon, resting atop a short brick wall in the midst of a vast landscaped lawn. The Frontier, and the similar nearby El Rancho Vegas, were the only gambling resorts on the so-called Strip that was highway 91, the two-lane blacktop heading southwest to Salt Lake City and Los Angeles.

Sedway pulled in the drive of the sprawling, rustic hotel past a swimming pool near the highway, where a good number of bathers were sunning and splashing. He parked and got my bag out of the trunk and we walked up to the central thatch-roofed, whitewashed adobe building, which like the other buildings was low-slung and supported by rough wood beams, decorated by wagon wheels and steer horns and other dude-ranch touches. It was all about as authentic as a Gene Autry movie, maintaining the phony cowboy airs I'd witnessed in downtown Vegas, but admittedly establishing a friendly "come-as-you-are" atmosphere. Which only made me feel out of place in my gray suit and gray skin.

"That's a nice car you got, Moe," I said, as we moved away from it. "Is that yours, or one of Ben's?"

"It's mine," Sedway said, with tight, quiet pride. "The race wire business pays good, you know."

"Yeah, I know," I said, resisting the urge to point out that an almost identical black Lincoln Continental had been driven by Jim Ragen a certain afternoon.

"Ben'll get you some wheels while you're here," he said. "He'll fix you up royal."

I followed Sedway into the open-beamed lobby; the registration desk was at the left. The Western motif continued—wood-and-leather furniture, sandstone fireplaces, pony-express lanterns hanging from wagon wheels. The rough wood-panelled walls displayed mounted buffalo heads, Indian rugs and western prints, with the directions to the casino, dining room, showroom and coffee shop burned into the walls as if with a branding iron. The desk clerk wore a string tie and a plaid shirt. He was friendly, but stopped short of calling me "pod'ner." Thank God for small favors.

If there were bellboys, I didn't see any. Sedway was carrying my bag and I let him lead me down a hallway and up one flight of stairs to my room, 404. The numbering apparently had something to do with which wing you were in, because not only was I not on the fourth floor, there wasn't any fourth floor.

My room was nice enough—not small, not large; modern furnishings and rustic walls and a print of an Indian chief. Sedway put my bag on a stand and I sat on the edge of the bed.

"What now?" I said.

"Ben may stop by and see you tonight," he said, shrugging.

"Where is he now?"

"Up the road."

"Up the road?"

"At the Flamingo. Working."

"Doing what, exactly, Moe? This is Sunday."

"Not at the Flamingo it ain't. Workers are working damn near 'round the clock, up there. And Ben's supervising. That's his big problem, you know."

"What is?"

"He wants to keep his eye on everything, his finger in all the pies. He's hardly getting any sleep. Running himself ragged." He made a *tch-tch* sound, and shook his head, trying to convince me he cared deeply about his boss's health. Sure.

"And you think he ought to delegate authority, more," I said.

"What?"

"He ought to trust the people around him. Give them some responsibility."

"Yeah," Moey said, smiling, nodding. "He ought to do that."

"Don't you still handle the local end of Trans-American for him?"

"Sure. He gets out of my way on that. It's just the Flamingo he don't want anybody touching. You'd think he was a goddamn artist. You'd think it was a goddamn picture he was painting."

"Maybe to him it is."

Sedway shrugged. "Maybe. But it ain't his *paint*, entirely."

By that I took him to mean the money Siegel was spending was mostly that of the boys back east. Lansky and Costello and Adonis and Luciano—although Luciano wasn't back east, anymore, unless you viewed Sicily as east of New York, which I guessed it was. Whatever the case, the deported "Charlie Lucky" was said to still be running things, albeit at a distance.

"What am I supposed to do till Ben comes around?"

"Have some fun. You can run a tab on anything except gambling. Food's good here. Hit the bar. Ride a horse. Have a swim."

"I didn't bring bathing trunks. Never occurred to me." Back in Chicago, there was snow on the ground. A lot of it.

Sedway was turning to go. "You can get a suit in the gift shop. I got to hook back up with Ben. I'll leave you to it."

"Why don't I just come with you. . . ?"

He stopped and turned and looked at me. "Look, Nate. You better get this straight right now. You do things Ben's way when you're in Ben's world, which is where you are. Ben wanted you to relax after your long train ride. So that's what you're going to do. Is relax."

He pointed a finger at me and went out.

I slept for an hour, in my clothes, and then got up and undressed and showered and unpacked and put on a sportshirt and slacks and prowled the place. I had a rum cocktail in a replica of a forty-niner saloon, complete with bullet-scarred mahogany bar and saddle-shaped leather bar stools; then I rode on into the main casino, where the ceiling was covered with pony hide and the walls ornately papered and peppered with bawdy house nudes in heavy gold-gilt frames. Despite these distractions, I played blackjack for a couple hours and ended up ahead a few bucks. I bought a swimming suit in the gift shop, or rather charged it to my room, where I went back to put the thing on, feeling somehow foolish to be wandering across a landscaped lawn with a towel around my waist in the middle of December.

But the pleasantly warm desert air took that thought away, and for a moment I wondered if I was still asleep, as this seemed nicer than real life; when I dove into the blue pool, the cool water refreshed and awoke me, making me realize I was not dreaming. I was in fact in a desert oasis, getting paid for this.

I stretched out on a deck chair on the sandstone apron by the pool and let the sun have at me. It was getting late in the afternoon, but I could feel the warmth on me, like a soothing blanket. Maybe my Chicago pallor would go away. I would walk into the A-1 office a bronze god, and sweep that pretty secretary of mine off her feet. Fat chance.

I was sleeping again. It was my third nap of the day. But then for months now I'd been sleeping more than usual. My habit was to sleep six hours or so each night, especially since the war, after which I'd started having cold-sweat nightmares. Actually, immediately after I got back from St. Elizabeth's Hospital, I'd had mostly sleepless nights. It had taken a good long time to work up to six hours per.

But lately I'd been sleeping twelve hours. And catching naps, too. I was working hard, sure, but no harder than normal, and doing damn little field work. Why was I so tired?

Hell, I wasn't tired. I was escaping. I was at a point in my life where I'd rather be asleep than awake. Where I'd rather be out like a light than alert and thinking.

When I was asleep I was safe, safe from memories and pangs. I was kind to myself in dreams—with the exception, of course, of the occasional combat nightmare—and when Peggy came to me, in dreams, it was as a lover, not as a love lost.

She would speak to me in my dreams. Tell me she loved me. Call out to me.

"Nate," she'd say. "Nate. Nate!"

I opened my eyes, slowly.

Before me, in the soft focus of Hollywood and the half-awake, was a vision of Peggy. The sun was behind her, making a halo around the dark curly mane of her hair; her skin was golden, not pale, but her eyes were as violet as ever, her mouth scarlet and smiling, teeth white as purity. This wasn't Peggy. Not the Peggy who'd bolted from my office, hating me. This was the Peg of my heart. Of my dreams.

"Nate!"

I blinked. Sat up on the lounge chair.

"Peggy?" I said. My mouth was thick with sleep. It tasted as bad as she looked good.

And did she ever look good. She loomed over me, little woman that she was, her trim figure caught in a damp black swim suit, top half of her breasts peeking out whitely above the black. She was still smiling, but she'd hidden the white teeth away for the moment. She'd plucked the dark eyebrows some, making them more conventionally curved. The sun had made her freckles stand out more. She was a little thinner, the chipmunk chubbiness of her cheeks gone. She at once looked younger and older than I remembered her.

She sat on the edge of the lounge chair.

I ran a hand through my hair, waking up, wishing I could brush my teeth.

"How are you, Nate?" she asked.

"Okay," I said. "Okay. How are you?"

"Okay," she said.

She smiled tightly at me.

I smiled tightly at her.

"I didn't write," I said. "I didn't know where to write."

"I know. I didn't write, either." She shrugged. "I thought a clean break was best."

I said nothing.

She said, "You're not surprised to see me, though."

"I thought maybe you might still be out here," I admitted.

"Didn't you know?"

"How could I?"

"You're a detective, aren't you?"

"Yeah, not a psychic. You didn't even tell your family where you were. You dropped off the face of the earth."

She shrugged again. "I just dropped off the face of Chicago."

"Same difference. Anyway, you look great."

"You look good, too."

"No I don't. I'm fat."

A half-smile crinkled one cheek. "You are a little pudgy. How much do you weigh?"

"Almost two hundred pounds."

"How do you account for that?"

"I'm just your typical successful businessman. Fat and sassy."

"Really."

I sighed, smiled one-sidedly myself. "All I do these days is eat and sleep. It's my way of compensating."

"Compensating for what?"

"The loss of my girl."

Her smile disappeared, then returned briefly, just a twitch, and she said, "I hope you didn't come looking for me."

"I didn't. I'm here on a job."

"I know. Ben hired you. For pickpocket work."

I nodded. "He approached me months ago. Back on the S.S. Lux."

"Did you say yes then?"

"More or less. He approached me again, through Fred Rubinski, who I'm in business with now. The money is good. It's cold in Chicago. Good time of the year to go west. As Elmer Fudd says, west and wewaxation at wast."

She shook her head, smiled again, sadly. "I think you came looking for me, Nate."

"So do I. But I also came for the money, and the sun."

"The sun. How many times last summer did I get you to the beach?"

I thought. "Three times?"

"Once," she said. "Nate, it's a mistake."

"What is?"

"Coming here. A part of me still loves you, but it's over. I don't want either one of us to get hurt. It's just not going to happen again, do you understand?"

"I don't understand, but if you want me to keep my distance, fine. I may be pudgy these days, but I still don't have to force my intentions on women."

"You're a good-looking guy, a good catch for any girl." She pointed at her half-exposed bosom, which was droplet pearled. "Except this girl."

"You got a new guy, is that it?"

"That's not really any of your business, at this point, is it?"

"No need to get nasty. Just don't tell me you want us to be friends, Peg. I'm not good at that."

"I know. Me too."

"It runs too deep. I can't turn it into being pals. I might be able to turn it into hate. I could work on that, if you want."

She swallowed. Her eyes were as wet as her swim suit. "I don't think I'd like that."

"Okay. Then why don't I just love you at a distance, and you can feel about me however the hell you care to, at a distance, and I'll do this job, and put half a continent between us as soon as possible."

She nodded. She stood. "I think you should pass on the job, too."

"Why?"

"This is a bad time to be around Ben."

"I hear he's under a lot of pressure."

She nodded. "He's very brave, and very smart. But I'm afraid for him."

"Well, if he called me out here to be his bodyguard, I'll be on the next plane out. The last time I took a job like that, everybody got burned."

"Including . . ." She shook her head. Not finishing it.

I finished it for her: "Including your uncle. You know, if you insist on getting attached to headstrong gangster types, you're going to spend a lifetime crying over spilt blood."

"You can be cruel sometimes."

"Sure. I learned that from life. And from Chicago."

"Same difference," she said.

"Are you still Virginia Hill's secretary?"

"No. I'm working for Ben. His confidential secretary."

"That sounds very high-tone. What about La Hill?"

"She's in and out of here. She's allergic to cactus, doesn't like the climate."

"But she doesn't like leaving her boyfriend's side, either."

"No," she admitted. "She goes on buying trips. She's helping him decorate the Flamingo. The hotel part, anyway."

"Is she here now?"

"Yes. She's over there with him this afternoon."

"That must be hard on you."

"What?"

"Knowing he's with her."

"What do you mean?" She bit off the words.

"Well, you love him, don't you?"

She squinted at me. Hatefully. Upper lip curling. But she said nothing.

"I thought so," I said.

"It's none of your business," she said, and she turned and walked quickly away. Her legs were tan and bore not a trace of fat; the cheeks of her sweet ass showed under the cut of the black swimsuit. I wanted her, in every way you could want a woman.

I dove back into the cool water, but it didn't do any good. I was a goddamn detective with a detective's goddamn instincts. I climbed up on the side of the pool and water ran down my face, from my wet head, although a salty taste was mixed in.

"I thought so," I said again, to nobody.

17

The rest of that afternoon slipped away from me. I left the pool and returned to my room, dressed casually and found my way to the moderately busy casino, where I played blackjack till I lost what I'd won earlier, drinking several rum cocktails brought to me gratis by the cowgirl waitresses who kept the customers well lubricated and free spending.

At around seven I was back in my room and, thanks to the free drinks and a general glumness that had settled over me, I managed to fall asleep again, taking nap number four of the day. When I awoke, the room was dark but for a bathroom light I'd left on, and it was after eight.

Must've been hunger that woke me, because my gut was burning. The last food I'd had was a sandwich and fries on the dining car of the train. I couldn't quite bring myself to wear a sportshirt to supper, so I put on my other suit, which had hung out pretty well by now, and went down to the restaurant.

Like the casino, the Last Frontier's dining room was doing good if not spectacular business. I wasn't the only guy wearing a suit in the rough-panelled room, but apparel again was definitely dude ranch, not Monte Carlo. I helped myself to the elaborate "chuck wagon buffet," which I was relieved to find was not serving up the sort of pork-and-beans and barbecue fare one might expect. In fact, there was an ice sculpture of a swan lording it over a lot of fancy food items, particularly salads and cold cuts, fussily arranged on platters by a chef who obviously did not have "Come'n get it!" in his vocabulary.

I was sitting in a booth by myself, working on my second plate, seeing just how much rare roast beef a human could eat, when Ben Siegel and his party came in.

Siegel, looking very tan, was wearing a maroon sports jacket and navy slacks and alligator shoes; he wore no tie, the points of his off-white shirt's collar reaching down so that one touched the embroidered BS on his breast pocket, from which came a slash of lighter maroon silk handkerchief. On his arm was Virginia Hill; she was wearing a black halter-top and matching slacks, her reddish brown hair pinned up. She wasn't tan at all, her mouth a scarlet gash in her pale face; she'd put on some weight but carried it well. She didn't look hard to know, as more than one mob guy had put it. Bringing up the rear was Sedway, in his black suit and red tie, and Peggy who alone among them looked touristy in her white eyelet blouse and full blue-and-white vertical-striped skirt. Peggy was not on Sedway's arm; in fact, she stood apart from the mole-like Moe. Her make-up was subdued.

Siegel didn't notice me at first; Virginia Hill did. She tugged his sleeve and pointed me out. He smiled like he'd spotted an old friend, and motioned his party over to the table reserved for them, and headed my way.

I patted a napkin to my mouth, slid out of the booth and shook hands with him.

"Good to see you, Nate. Why don't you join us?"

Without waiting for my answer, he stopped a passing waiter and instructed him to move my food and iced tea (I'd had enough cocktails for one day) over to the larger table across the room where his party was even now ordering drinks.

He slipped an arm around my shoulder and we walked over there.

"I'm glad you decided to take me up on my offer," he said. "I don't think you'll be sorry. We're making history, and you're going to be part of it."

"I'm not all that interested in history," I said, good-naturedly. "I'm more interested in money."

"We're going to make that, too. Sit down, sit down."

Siegel took the head of the table. Virginia Hill was at his left, and the chair at his right was mine. Next to Miss Hill sat Sedway, and across from him—next to me—sat Peggy. I nodded at her and smiled politely; she smiled the same way, and looked away, as if fascinated by the activities of a waiter clearing a table nearby.

Siegel sipped his wine and smiled his dazzling smile. He was the same handsome, charming soul I'd met aboard the Lux, with one exception: beneath the almost feminine long lashes and baby-blue eyes were dark circles; he tried to cover that up with powder or make-up or something, but he couldn't fool me. I'm a detective.

"Did you hear about Tony?" he asked me, the smile settling in one corner of his mouth.

"Tony?" I asked.

"Cornero," he said, as if I should've known. "The Coast Guard shut the Lux down a couple weeks after she launched."

"You had a hunch that would happen," I said.

"Yeah, those gambling ship days are over. You're sitting in the middle of legal gambling in America. Say, uh, I'm very sorry about your friend Ragen."

I nodded my thanks. Peggy lowered her eyes.

"That's that bastard Guzik for you," he said.

I said nothing.

He clapped his hands, dismissing that subject. "Ready to get to work?" he asked. "You only have ten days to whip my little police force in shape."

"It won't take me long," I shrugged. "I assume there's not much for them to do till you open—that I can have their full attention for a while."

"Whatever you need."

"Should be no big deal. They're ex-cops, aren't they? They should pick up fast on this stuff. They probably had some pickpocket training already."

"They're good boys," Siegel said, nodding. "They've been on my payroll for years."

"Anybody mind if I eat?" Virginia Hill asked, with poor grace.

"Feel free to feed your face, Tab," Siegel said, just a little snidely.

"Just be more of me to love," she said, and rose.

Siegel and I stayed behind, as the rest of his party went to the chuck wagon buffet. Siegel ordered off the menu—a steak, medium rare, and a salad; he was drinking a single glass of white wine. "Tabby," as he referred to Miss Hill, had already run through her first two stingers.

"I may have some other work for you, Nate," Siegel said, now that we were for the moment alone.

"Oh?"

"I may have a little security problem that can best be served by somebody from the outside—somebody like you."

"I don't understand. You said the boys on your security staff are longtime, trusted employees . . ."

"I don't remember saying I trusted them. These *are* ex-cops, remember. They're tied to me by the juice I spread around when they carried badges. These boys are, remember, what washed ashore after the shake-up in L.A. when his honor Mayor Shaw got booted the hell out. The rest are vets of a similar house-cleaning in Beverly Hills."

"What sort of security problem are we talking?"

He sighed, sipped his wine, shrugged with his eyes. "Priorities," he said, disgustedly, shaking his head. "Trying to put up the Taj Mahal in a fucking desert in eight months is enough of job, let alone having to goddamn do it whilst dancing around postwar priorities. Building materials and labor . . . both in short supply." He shrugged with his shoulders this time. "But I'm getting the job done just the same."

"How?"

"How do you think? Pulling strings. Paying top dollar. You know who Billy Wilkerson is?"

I nodded. He was the publisher of the Hollywood *Reporter* and the restauranteur behind Ciro's and the Trocadero. I'd seen the little man in the latter nitery, a few years back, kissing the collective ass of Willie Bioff and George Browne, Frank Nitti's Hollywood union bosses.

"Wilkerson's one of my investors," Siegel said. "He's got influence on the movie execs. He got me lumber, cement, pipe, and you wouldn't believe what all, right off the studio lots. And I got enough political clout in this state to get me steel girders, copper tubing, fixtures, tile and so on."

"Sounds like you got it dicked."

He sighed. "It takes dough, but yes, I do. And Moe's been on my case because the community's unhappy—VFW here held protest meetings, 'cause they couldn't get materials for their new homes when I could for the Flamingo. I tell Moe, let 'em thank me for the money I'm gonna be pumping into the town. But some people can't see something that's right in front of them, let alone the future. Anyway, thanks to those protests I ended up having to do some dealing with fucking lowlifes to get materials."

"Black marketeers, you mean."

He nodded, frowning. "And I'm getting suspicious."

"Of?"

"Of why I'm spending so goddamn much money on materials."

"You think maybe you're paying for the same materials twice."

He leaned forward, cocked his head. "A truck pulls up, and it's full of lumber, and I pay for it. How am I to know where they got it? They could've got it the night before from our own construction site."

"It's a common enough scam," I granted him. "Who's in charge of purchasing and receiving?"

"Me. I am."

The others were returning now, plates of food in hand. Both girls had modest platefuls; my guess was Virginia Hill's added weight came from drinking. They all took their places, the conversation going on, as if Siegel and I were still alone.

I sipped my iced tea. "Handling the purchasing and receiving yourself . . . don't you have bigger fish to fry?"

His smile was disarming but also, I thought, mildly crazed. "Nate, I fry *all* the fish at the Flamingo. I'm where the buck starts *and* stops. When we're up and running, well, sure I'll hire some people to take care of the day-to-day proceedings. Down the road, I will. But this is my dream, and it's up to me to make it come true. It's up to me to supervise the kitchen crew, hire the big name entertainers, appoint the pit bosses, choose the decor for the hotel rooms . . . not a single employee is getting hired without my personal approval."

"You've hired a hotel manager, and a casino manager, I assume . . ."

"No. That I'll get around to. Down the road. For the time being, I'm it."

"You have an accountant, for Christ's sake . . ."

He smiled over at Peggy and she smiled briefly, nervously, back. Virginia Hill smirked and sipped her latest stinger.

"Miss Hogan is helping me look after the books," he said, toasting her with his wine glass. "She's got a background in that area. Down the road, we'll hire somebody, or maybe I'll put Peg in charge and get myself another secretary. But right now I need to have my finger on the pulse, so to speak."

I sighed. Said, "Look. Mr. Siegel. No offense meant . . ."

"Keep it Ben, and speak your mind, Nate."

Sedway, concentrating on his food (or pretending to), lifted an eyebrow and put it down.

"You can't handle a job this size by yourself," I said, "and expect not to get taken advantage of. How much have you spent so far?"

A waiter put Siegel's salad in front of him. "Well over five at this point," he said, picking at the lettuce with his fork.

"Five? Million?"

"Million," he said with some condescension. "You don't build palaces for peanuts, you know."

"Where has it gone?"

"Where hasn't it gone? Hell, I spent a million bucks on plumbing alone."

"Plumbing?"

He grinned, flushed with pride. "Sure. Every one of my two hundred-and-eighty hotel rooms has its own private sewer system, its own private septic tank."

"Ben," I said, trying to keep my jaw from scraping the floor. "The best hotels in *Chicago* don't have that."

"That's good enough for Chicago, maybe, but not the Flamingo," Siegel said, flatly confident, eating his salad. "That place is going to stand forever. No goddamn wind or earthquake is going to blow *that* place away. I built the walls out of concrete—double thick."

What particular advantage that would be in a climate this mild, where chicken wire and plaster would suffice, I couldn't guess. But I didn't say anything. I'd been in this conversation long enough to know that disagreeing with Bugsy was like arguing with, well, with a cement wall. A double-thick one.

A waiter removed Siegel's half-eaten and pushed-aside salad and put the steak before him. "You wouldn't believe what I been through here," Siegel said, ignoring the steak. "Everything went wrong . . . take the other day, the fuckin' drapes. Turns out they're highly flammable and got to be shipped back to L.A. for chemical treatment. Then they install the air-conditioning system with intakes but no outlets and that all has to be ripped out and re-done. And when the heating equipment shows up, the concrete housing in the boiler room turned out to be too goddamn small and had to be built over. Jesus, there's no end to it. I been paying fifty bucks a day to carpenters, bricklayers, tinsmiths, steelworkers. Twelve hour days, seven days a week. With this labor shortage, I have to fly most of 'em in, from all over the country. That means paying bonuses, providing living quarters . . ." He was working himself up into a lather, and sensed it apparently, because he backed off, shrugging. ". . . but the job's getting done, that's the important thing."

"Moe here said the hotel may not be ready in time."

Sedway flashed me a dark look, as if I'd betrayed a confidence.

"It'll be done," Siegel said, his eyes narrowing momentarily, looking down at Sedway, who by this time was giving all his attention to his plate of food. "Tomorrow they're doing the landscaping. It'll be done."

"If it isn't," I said, "can't you just postpone?"

"I'd lose face," Siegel said, "and that's the one thing no gambler can afford to lose. Look, I'll be straight with you, Nate . . ." He lowered his voice to a near whisper. ". . . I got construction costs I gotta cover. Del Webb's threatening to put a half-mil lien up against the place. If I can open up, take advantage of the holiday crowds, get the money flowing, then the people I owe will back off."

By that he meant Lansky and company.

I said, carefully, "I take it you can't go to your investors and ask for more . . ."

"You can only go to the well so many times." His mouth tightened. "Besides, those thick-headed, unimaginative bastards, it's them I want to show. They don't think I know what I'm doing. Hell, I know exactly what I'm doing."

"I'm sure you do," I lied.

"There's money to be made in the fucking desert. Just take a look around you." And he gestured around at the rustic surroundings. "This place is fine, for what it is. But it's the wrong fantasy. You want to take money away from people and make them smile while you're doing it, give them Hollywood, not Tombstone. Give 'em chrome and winding staircases. Swirling silk, marble statues, Greek urns . . ."

"How much *does* a Greek earn, anyway?" Virginia Hill asked, stinger poised.

He ignored her. "Picture it, Nate: revolving stages with *top-name* entertainment. Water ballets for the chorus girls. Wheels of chance spinning every night, night and day, in a dream setting, a place where time stands still, 'cause there's no goddamn clocks. It's gonna make Monte Carlo look like a penny arcade. And it won't just be the Flamingo, no. You'll see this whole three-mile strip out to the airport lined all along with luxury hotels and fabulous casinos. Legal. All of it." He smiled like a naughty child. "The beauty part is you can use it for a money laundry. The government's got no idea how much the tables take in. You can skim the hell out of it and then write off other shit. It's the perfect set-up. That's what going legit can do for you, and one day, before you know it, the boys back east are gonna wake up to it."

I chewed on that for a while. Then I said, "I want to ask you something, Ben—and I need a very straight answer."

"Ask and I'll answer," he shrugged. "Straight."

"If I find out somebody's been screwing you, where your black market supplies are concerned, what are you going to do about it?"

"Put a stop to it, what else? Oh. I get you. You don't want to be part of any rough stuff."

"I understand Miss Hill is allergic to cactus. Well, I'm allergic to being an accessory to murder."

He shook his head. "Don't worry about that. I'm on my good behavior out here. I'm a legitimate businessman, after all. I'm building a tourist trap, Nate—neither me nor my backers are about to spill *any* blood in *this* sand. The only killin' in Vegas is gonna be the one *I* make when the Flamingo opens, day after Christmas."

Virginia Hill, smirking as she sucked up her sixth stinger, said, "Me, I wish you'd just sell the crummy joint, before you fall the fuck apart."

Siegel whipped his face around till it was bearing down on hers; his baby blues had turned to ice. Sedway was eating his food, calmly, seemingly oblivious to all this; Peggy was obviously unnerved. As for La Hill, she smiled at Ben blandly, untouched by his withering gaze.

"I'm not falling apart, and don't ever call the Flamingo a crummy joint, understand?"

"Sure, Ben, sure."

"Falling apart," he said. "What the hell do you know about it?"

All the insolence melted away in her expression and she took his chin in her fingers and beamed at him in an apple-cheeked way that belied everything I knew about her. "I just think you deserve a rest, honey, that's all. I think you should think about handing the Flamingo over to the boys—*and* take a piece of the action, a nice piece, for putting your heart and soul in it. And then go to Europe and live a little. Rest a little. You've earned it, the easy life."

His expression softened and he smiled back at her, the long lashes fluttering over the no longer icy blue eyes. "Maybe down the road. Right now, I don't want to think about that—my baby ain't even born yet. But thanks, Tab. Thanks for thinking of me."

"Your best interests are all I ever have in mind, baby," she said, butter wouldn't melt.

I thought I saw something like a smirk, and a disgusted one at that, pass over Peggy's face; but it was momentary and she returned to picking at her modest plate of food.

"So, Nate," Siegel said, turning his benevolent gaze on me, "tomorrow morning we get started?"

"Sure," I said. "But I got to caution you—I have a work problem that may take me back home on short notice."

"Oh?"

"You know how it is," I said, evasively, "when you run your own business. Damn thing's falling apart without me."

He nodded that he understood, said, "But I'd be very disappointed if you didn't stick around."

At least there was no menace in the voice.

I said, "I'd have Fred Rubinski send somebody top-notch to replace me."

"You're who I want, Nate."

I waved it off. "It probably won't happen, but I just wanted to be up-front with you, Ben."

"I appreciate that," he said, and he finally began to eat his steak, which was surely cold by now.

After dinner, he painted a picture of the gala opening he was planning, including dozens of Hollywood stars that George Raft and Billy Wilkerson were lining up for him. He had Jimmy Durante and Xavier Cugat booked in as the floor show.

He was still holding court, the little group drinking cocktails, when at a few minutes after ten I stood and excused myself.

"Where you headed?" Siegel wondered.

"To my room," I said. "Train travel tires me out."

"I'll walk you there," he said, and he did.

As we ambled down the hallway to 404, he put his hand on my shoulder and said, "I wanted to ask you something in private, Nate. Something personal."

"Sure, Ben."

"Did you take this job to get near Peggy Hogan again?"

"No," I lied.

"I wouldn't stand between you two, if . . ."

"There's nothing between us anymore," I said. That, I feared, was no lie.

He took his hand off my shoulder. He seemed almost embarrassed as he said, "I figured maybe this afternoon you might run into her, and sort the thing out . . ."

Had he planned it?

I said, "I did run into her. But like I said, there's nothing between us, now."

"Maybe you still got feelings that she doesn't." He made a clicking sound in his cheek. "That kind of thing can be rough. I figured maybe that was why you said something about going back to Chicago. Maybe the situation was making you uncomfortable . . ."

"I thought Virginia Hill was your girl, Ben."

He shrugged, smiled his usual dazzling smile. "She is. And she's a lot of girl. A lot of woman. Ain't she a handful? She'd tell the Pope to go to hell."

"What about Peggy?"

He shook his head no, the smile gone. "There's nothing between her and me, either—strictly business." And the smile reappeared, but a modified, only moderately dazzling version. "I think maybe she's kind of sweet on me, but I'm not gonna take advantage of that, cute kid though she is. She's gonna go far with my organization, if she wants to. Normally, I'm not much on career girls, but she's got a good business head. Maybe it's because she's got Jim Ragen's blood in her."

"I can remember having Jim Ragen's blood *on* me."

His eyes narrowed. "What do you mean by that, Nate?"

"Nothing. I just . . . I'm just not crazy about getting involved in your business, Ben. Even though you are legit, these days. I'd like to shake this rep I have of being a mob hanger-on. Doing work for you isn't going to help that."

He was looking at me carefully, like a bug collector studying a specimen. "You did come out here to take her home, didn't you? And you found out she doesn't want to go back with you, and now you want to run out on me?"

I let out a sigh that must've betrayed how weary I was. "I don't know, Ben. It wasn't exactly like that. But it wasn't exactly not like that, either."

"Stick around, Nate. Time is short, and I need your help—a couple ways. There's ten grand in it, if you stick it out till after the opening."

That was a lot of money. Normally, I would've done jumping jacks in the nude in Marshall Field's window, for dough like that. But in my present mood I didn't much give a shit.

I said, "I'll give you my decision first thing tomorrow morning, Ben."

"I'll respect what you decide, whatever it is. I like you, Nate. I think we could work well together." He extended a hand, and smiled again, and we shook hands, and I found a smile to give him back. He walked back down the hall—swaggered, actually—and I shook my head and went into my room.

I sat on the edge of the bed; the Indian chief on the wall was staring at me balefully. Peggy wasn't what was bothering me. Siegel himself was. He'd bitten off too much, here. Like all bad executives, he wanted to run his whole operation; thought he had to do every little job himself; thought only he was up to the job, any job, every job. For a smart guy, it was a stupid way to do things. And it would kill him.

Maybe literally, considering the people backing him. Six million bucks was a lot to spend pursuing a pipe dream, particularly when you don't know what the fuck you're doing where making it a reality is concerned. I'd seen first hand that the Last Frontier, while doing okay, was not exactly attracting land-office business. Siegel looked at the stretch of desert that was highway 91 and saw some vision of the future, a neon mirage that might or might not turn real someday. Whichever, I had a very strong feeling that this fabulous arena Siegel was erecting was nowhere I wanted to perform.

Peggy was a lost cause. And Siegel was playing a losing game.

There was no reason for me to get caught up in any of it.

I nodded, stood, and began to pack my bag. There was a midnight train back to L.A., where I could touch base with Fred, get a replacement lined up for Siegel, and fly home.

I had just latched my suitcase when somebody knocked at my door.

I answered it, wondering who the hell it could be.

And who the hell else could it be, the way this day had gone, but Virginia Hill.

She was a little swacked, but what else is new? She looked sexily zoftig in her halter top and slacks, her pale, slightly plump tummy pulsing.

"Can I come in?" she asked, and did.

I shut the door.

"I hope you came out here to take that little cunt back home with you," she said, leaning against the door.

"What are you talking about?"

"I'm talking about that fucking little Irish slut. If you still care about her, take her home, get her the fuck out of here."

"That isn't up to me, Ginny."

"Well, I'll tell you this, pal: if she's banging Ben, I'm gonna bang her."

And, with a sneer as nasty as she was drunk, she raised her hand and made a gun of it and shot at me, saying, "Bang. She's fucking dead."

She went to the door, opened it, looked back over her shoulder at me, like a parody of a pin-up pose, and said, "Word to the wise."

And she shut the door. Hard.

I stood looking at it.

Then I unpacked.

18

The sign said F
       L
       A
       M
       I
       N
       G
       O,   and poised above it as if considering flight was a
neon-outlined caricature of that unlikely long-legged bird that so em-
bodies both awkwardness and grace. Its pleasure palace namesake
had neither of these, but did manage to marry two contrary qualities:
stark lines and soft pastels.

A ghostly olive-green structure in the modern geometric mode, the
Flamingo sprawled across a stretch of sandy nothing along a blacktop
road to nowhere, a.k.a. Los Angeles. It was on the left, several miles
beyond the Vegas city limits, its Frank Lloyd Wrightish lines an aber-
ration against the timelessness of the desert and the purpleness of
Black Mountain shimmering against the morning sky, a morning that
was blowing some, sending sand and stones and sagebrush skittering
across the highway, some of the gritty tumbleweeds piling up in balls
against the Flamingo's foundation, as if nature were trying, without
much luck, to topple the structure. Nature simply didn't have the
determination of Benjamin Siegel.

Off to the right was a lot where I parked the used Buick I'd been
provided. Not surprisingly, that lot was fairly empty, but for a few
pick-up trucks and other vehicles that probably belonged to those few
workers within who were local. Siegel was putting his mostly imported workers up at motels and rooming houses in town, and bringing them in to his forty-acre playground by bus and truckload each
morning.

Past an imposing stone waterfall and under a *Flamingo* canopy, the
fancy brick front entry led into a lobby lined with slot machines; a

small check-in counter for hotel guests was at left, but at right, going down five steps, was the vast casino, with its various tables (21, roulette and craps), its plush carpeting and green leather walls, looking, in this somber unoccupied state, like a museum of gambling. There was no whir of the roulette wheel, no metallic ka-chunk from the one-armed bandits, no silver-dollar clink, no business-like dealer voices calling out, "Are your bets down? The number is—," and no crowd noise, winners and losers mixing together like equals in the din. Nothing but the echo of hammering from some other part of the building, as workmen tried to pound Bugsy's dream into reality.

I found him behind the dining room beyond the casino, in the kitchen, which was a good-size, modern affair, blinding white formica here, shining stainless steel there, and not a chef in the place.

Unless you counted Ben Siegel, who was wearing a snappy gray suit and dark blue tie and pale blue shirt.

I was wearing a suit and tie, too, by the way—though hardly as natty an ensemble as Siegel; but I couldn't get into the "Come as you are, pod'ner" swing, either. I was working.

"Much better," Siegel was saying, to nobody in particular, hands on his hips, beaming, basking in the glow of the spotless kitchen.

"Ben?" I said.

He looked at me and grinned and waved me over. "Look at this," he said. He was pointing to two facing walls of ovens. "Plenty of room there, wouldn't you say?"

"Sure."

"Before I had 'em do it over, these ovens opened right onto each other. What kinda layout is that? I'm not paying the top chefs in the business so they can fry their asses off!"

"What did this little remodeling job cost?"

"Thirty grand," he shrugged. He looked tan and fit, but his eyes were bloodshot as well as bagged. "Come on, you need to meet somebody."

He led me out through the restaurant area, where the smell of paste was in the air, half a dozen wallpaperers in white coveralls and painter's caps at work, dealing with heavy brocade material that had to be tricky as hell. The plush carpet was covered by tarps; nonetheless, Siegel stopped in mid-track and bent and flicked at several spent cigarette butts, like Sherlock Holmes examining a muddy footprint.

"Hey!" he yelled.

The men, several of whom were up on ladders, stopped their work at once; turned in the direction of what by now was surely a familiar voice.

Siegel stood, having scraped the butts and ashes into his palm. "I'd like to catch the dirty pig who dropped these," he snarled. Then he wadded the butts in his fist and walked over to a waste barrel and dumped them in.

The men exchanged looks and one of them, presumably the foreman, muttered, "Yes, Mr. Siegel," and they turned back to their struggle.

Immediately pleasant again, he led me through a corridor of slot machines, saying, "The dining room is very important, you know. You can't hope to make a profit on it—it's a come-on. Food service has got to be tops for the high rollers, but at the same time the prices can't scare away the two-dollar customers, either."

"Keep an eye on your chefs," I said.

"Why's that?" he said.

"A chef can steal from you a hundred different ways. Kickbacks from suppliers. Selling prime cuts of meat as scrap. Lots of ways."

"I'll keep that in mind," he said, giving me a pleased, appraising look. "You do know your stuff."

"Security's my racket. I can tell you right now that you need more people under you—people you can trust. Or everybody and his dog is going to steal you blind."

He nodded. "And I'm gonna do that, Nate—down the road. Come on out and see the pool."

We walked out onto an immense patio that led to a luxurious Olympic-size pool, the edges of which had a scalloped design; below the blue ripples of sun-reflecting water you could make out a mosaic pink flamingo. This patio was an oasis in the midst of a vast well-trodden expanse of barren desert real estate. Over to the right of the aridness, as I stood with the casino and restaurant complex behind me, was a rambling modern building which here was two-stories, there three-stories, and in the middle four, making it the tallest structure on the grounds. A crew of trowel-wielding plasterers on scaffolding was giving the massive building a skin of stucco, which clung to wire mesh covering the building's cement surface.

A small fat man in an Hawaiian swim suit was sitting under an umbrella beside the pool; he had a bottle of beer on the table next to him and he was wearing sunglasses. He was as brown as a berry. His body was round and hairless, a beach ball with legs. And he had the face of a self-satisfied bulldog.

"This hardworking gentleman," Siegel said good-naturedly, "is Bud Quinn, formerly of the LAPD."

"Don't get up," I said.

Quinn smiled widely, making his cheeks tight, and it should have been a jolly smile, but it wasn't really a smile at all. It was an expression the hard fat little man had adopted to use at appropriate times, to affect humanity.

"You'd be Nate Heller," he said, removing the sunglasses, thrusting a pudgy hand forward.

Reluctantly I took it. Shook it. It was as moist as Sedway's, and even more repellent.

"I didn't know you were working for Ben," I said. "Let alone his top security man."

Piggy eyes narrowed in pouches of fat. "Have we met?"

"No. I've just heard about you." I turned to Siegel. "I take it you haven't mentioned to Fred Rubinski that Quinn's in your employ."

"Why, no," Siegel said. Then with a little edge in his voice he added: "I didn't know I needed to clear my staff with Fred."

I shrugged. "It's just that Fred's late partner and Lt. Quinn had their share of run-ins."

Quinn grinned yellowly. "Jake took a likin' to my rubber hose. I never knew a boy who took to the goldfish like Jake."

I pointed a finger at him. "Have some respect for the dead. You're going to be that way yourself some day."

"No disrespect meant," Quinn said, standing now, gesturing with both hands, trying to smile away my ill will. "I liked Jake. He was a good boy. He put money in my pocket, time to time."

Siegel, frowning slightly, said, "Is it going to be a problem, you fellas working together? I had no idea there was bad blood . . ."

"There's no bad blood," I said. "We don't even know each other. Forget I said anything."

Quinn smiled magnanimously. "No hard feelings, Nate. Mind if I call you Nate?"

I did, but said, "Not at all, Bud. We'll get along fine, you and me."

"Good," Siegel said, putting a hand on either of our shoulders. "Bud isn't working today, but I asked him to stop by so you two could get acquainted—set up a time to work with his people."

"I hear you're gonna teach us all about pickpockets," Quinn said, in a sing-songey way. Pretending to be friendly but reeking condescension.

"Just a few pointers. Is this afternoon too soon?"

"Not at all," Quinn said. "I got a few boys on the grounds, keeping an eye on the hired help and the delivery people. Can't be too careful—pilferage can be a problem, you know, with all this building material here, in such short supply elsewhere."

"Right," I said. "What about the rest of your staff?"

"They've all settled in," he said. "Found apartments and homes. Regular Las Vegas residents, now, looking forward to a long and happy association with the fine, fabulous Flamingo club."

"Hotel," Siegel corrected.

"Hotel," Quinn amended.

"Why don't you call 'em all in so we can meet here around one-thirty," I said. "In the casino—it's not being used for anything, and the construction there seems complete."

"Nothing left but to put the new fireproofed curtains up," Siegel said, smirking to himself.

"Casino'll be just dandy, Nate," Quinn said, putting his dark glasses back on. "Looky here, I'm sorry about your friend Fred's partner. No offense meant. Got run down by a car, didn't he?"

"Well, Fred's more than a friend, Bud. He's vice-president of my detective agency, and that makes his late partner an associate of mine, even though we never met."

"That don't make sense to me," Quinn said, thoroughly puzzled, and a little disgusted.

"It does to me," I said. "That's what counts."

Siegel was watching me warily, and then said, "You want to come along with me, Nate? I can show you around a bit."

He took me across the stretch of scalp-like ground to the building where the plasterers on scaffolding hovered like a dozen Harold Lloyds as directed by Busby Berkley. We went inside, where a carpet layer was at work in the small lobby; the ceiling rose through the floor above, creating a circular balcony, making room for a fancy chandelier. The sounds of carpentry echoed down, making the chandelier's crystal shake and shiver. The carpet layer, on his hands and knees, looked up at Siegel and smiled and nodded, saying, "Mr. Siegel."

"What the hell is this?" Siegel snapped.

"Pardon?" The man had to work to get his voice over the hammering coming from above.

"Are you responsible for this?" He was pointing to a sooty palmprint on an as-yet-to-be-painted plaster wall.

"No, Mr. Siegel."

"You tell your foreman for me that I'll kick his ass back to Salt Lake City if I see that sort of thing again. What, do you people think you're working in a cheap bar somewhere? This is the *Flamingo*—and don't fuckin' well forget it!"

He stalked up the nearby stairway. I shrugged at the kneeling carpet layer and he shrugged back and returned to his work and I followed our mutual boss up the stairs.

"What is this building, Ben?"

"The hotel. The check-in's in the main building, but all the rooms are here."

No carpet had been laid on the second floor, or the third, but when we got to the fourth, via a narrow out-of-the-way staircase, a plush money-colored carpet appeared. In fact, it began on those narrow stairs, which took us to a door, which Siegel unlocked, and he ushered me through a side entry into a penthouse suite that was entirely finished and furnished. More money-color carpet with lighter, pastel green walls.

We entered next to the well-stocked bar; to our right, picture windows looked out on the swimming pool. The room was tastefully if sparsely decorated, not at all garish; it reminded me a little of Ragen's room at Meyer House. Siegel lounged on a chintz-covered sofa and grinned.

"There's four bathrooms in this dump," he said.

I wondered if each had its own septic tank.

"I'm moving in with Tabby later this week. Some of the furniture hasn't arrived yet."

"It's quite a spread, Ben."

"There's four ways out of here."

"That's good to know."

"Only thing is," he said, looking upward, "that fucking beam."

There was a massive central concrete beam, in the white plaster ceiling, running down the middle of the spacious living room, cutting it in half; it dipped low enough that a man six feet or more would have to duck some.

"I told 'em to tear the goddamn thing out," he said, "but they said it was a support beam. It coulda been done, but it would've cost twenty-five grand or so. And there just wasn't time." He looked up at it with regret. Let out a weight-of-the-world sigh. "What the hell. You got to draw the line somewhere."

No shit.

He slapped his thighs, stood, said, "Come on, Nate—I'll finish the tour."

He showed me throughout the facility, most of which was done, except for the hotel building; and he rattled off his plans for the months ahead: a wedding chapel; private cabins; a health club with gymnasium and steam room; courts for tennis, badminton, squash and handball; a stable with "forty head of fine riding stock"; a nine-hole golf course; and shopping promenade—nine "major stores" already signed up.

"When do you expect to have all that up and running?" I asked him.

"June," he said. "Late June it'll be finished."

At a loading area behind the kitchen, a truckload of silverware and glassware, come from L.A., was being delivered. Siegel signed for the stuff, after examining several boxes. Two delivery men were doing the unloading. One of Quinn's security people was keeping an eye on them. Neither he, nor anybody else, saw me mark the sides of several boxes with a grease pencil.

Later a big truckload of linen, for the hotel, arrived, and Siegel signed for that as well. He did the same for a load of lumber, around by the hotel building.

At lunchtime, Siegel drove me down to the El Rancho Vegas, the other rambling rustic resort on the Strip, which had in fact preceded the Last Frontier; its chuck wagon buffet, however, was similarly not very frontier-like.

"What do you think of my baby?" he asked, pouring himself some tonic water. He had a meager plate of cold cuts before him.

"The Flamingo? I think it's pretty amazing. I think you're going to make some dough."

"So do I."

I was working on a heavy plate with something of everything from the considerable buffet; the ham was very good (I'm only technically a Jew). "Do you really think your hotel's going to be ready in time? It's clear you can open the casino and restaurant, but . . ."

"Once the landscaping's done," Siegel said, impatiently, "rest'll be

a piece of cake. So what do you think, have I got a pilferage problem?"

Piece of cake; that was a good idea—I'd have to get one. "I think
you're spreading yourself too thin; you shouldn't be the guy who
signs for fucking linen, for Christ's sake."

"Never mind that. Do you think they're robbing me?"

"The chief of your security force is so crooked he can kiss his own
ass without turning around."

"You think I don't know that? But those boys are used to working
for Quinn . . ."

"I don't mean to be critical. Anyway, I got it covered. Put it out of
your mind."

Siegel smiled; sipped his tonic water. "I knew my instincts about
you were right."

"Where was Sedway, today? And I didn't see Peggy Hogan around,
either."

"Peggy's doing some business over the phone for me, out of her
suite. Moe's tending my Trans-American interests."

"I see."

"It's going to be a little dusty and crazy around the Flamingo today,
anyway. I didn't figure Peggy would appreciate that. Though I don't
think it will interfere with your pickpocket school."

"What will?"

"I told you, didn't I? We're doing the landscaping today." He
checked his watch. "The trucks left L.A. early this morning—they
should start showing anytime."

We pulled into the Flamingo just as the fleet of trucks began arriv-
ing, thundering down highway 91 like the invading force they were,
grain trucks filled with topsoil, gravel trucks hauling sod, tank trucks
of water, flatbed trucks bearing imported trees (Oriental date palms,
cork trees from Spain, among fifteen other varieties of fully-grown
trees). Scores of trucks began roaring into the Flamingo parking lot
and up onto the grounds, as dungaree-clad workers in tin hats
hopped out of the vehicles and began getting to work.

And soon Siegel was leading them, Patton in a suit, his thinning
hair blowing in the dry breeze, as he mingled with the foreman,
pointing here and there, sculpting in the air, shaping his dream, an
architect seeing to it his exact bidding was done.

I shook my head and went into the casino, where I found that
Quinn—now dressed in a baggy brown business suit and an appropri-

ately ugly tie—had gathered his staff of twenty, most of whom were casually dressed. They were sitting at a cluster of 21 tables.

I introduced myself and got quickly into it. I gave them the basic lecture on the whiz mob and solicited a trio of volunteers to stick around after, so we could work up for tomorrow some examples of typical two-handed, three-handed and four-handed stall and tool routines. (The stall sets up the mark for the tool, who works the mark.) By the time my session with the whole group was over, and training the volunteers was accomplished, it was early evening.

I thanked the three men, who faded away, and went over to Quinn, who'd been watching me work with them.

"You know your stuff, boy," he said, pretending to be impressed, a stogie in the corner of his mouth.

"Yes I do," I said, "but I could use some advice."

"Glad to be of help."

"This pilferage problem you mentioned . . ."

He shrugged expansively. "Well, I suppose a little of that's natural in a undertaking this size."

"I suppose so. But Mr. Siegel has asked me to help him curtail that little problem. Now, there's several ways I could go about that. I could stick around at night and wait and see if trucks come back and pick up things they've already delivered one day, to deliver again another. I could treat some of the delivered goods with a slow-drying dye, or a dry dye, to stain the hands of thieves. Or I might use your so-called non-apparent dye, the kind that doesn't show up to the naked eye, where you need ultraviolet light? That technique works even after the hands are washed."

Quinn's eyes were narrowed to slits. His stogie hung like a limp dick.

"It's possible I've even already marked some of the goods delivered today," I said. "By one of those methods, or some other one."

His mouth twitched a humorless smile. "Your point being?"

"My point is this. Going to all that trouble—surveillance, dyes, ultraviolet light—it's such a bother. We're here in the sun. This beautiful weather. Swimming pools, pretty girls. We should enjoy life."

Quinn was smiling knowingly, cheeks fat and taut. "You mean, you figure there's enough gravy to go around."

"No. I tell you what I figure. I figure if anymore pilferage goes on, any at all, I figure to tell Siegel you're responsible."

His mouth dropped open and he lost his stogie. "What proof do you have . . ."

"None. But I know that this couldn't be going on without your benign neglect, which is a commodity you'll gladly sell for a price. It's on the same shelf as your integrity, right above your self-respect. So, anyway—I'm putting you in charge of putting a stop to the theft."

"And if I don't?"

"I'll turn you in to Siegel. I don't need any proof, though I'm sure I'll have some. But I got a hunch he'll take my word for it. And then you'll be fertilizing some rose garden out by that pool you love so dearly."

"Listen to me, you little son of a bitch . . ."

"No. You listen to me. I'm going to check up on these various shipments of materials and supplies. At random. If I come across one missing towel, one missing dish, one missing spoon, you're history, asshole. You'll take the rap for all the stealing that's been going on. And you'll answer to Siegel."

He looked hurt. "What have you got against me, anyway?"

"Fred Rubinski thinks you killed his partner."

And now he laughed. A snort of a laugh. "Maybe I did. They say it was hit-and-run, but maybe I was drivin'. Maybe you shouldn't oughta fuck with the likes of me."

I poked him in his fat chest. "Maybe you shouldn't oughta fuck with the likes of Bugsy Siegel."

He swallowed thickly and finally nodded.

"I'll take care of the situation," he said.

"I know you will."

And I walked outside, through the front doors of the Flamingo, out into a night lit up by blinding floodlights. The landscaping crew was still at it—they would work through the cool night, under the hot lights, dumping the truckloads of rich soil, terracing it, laying acres of lawn, planting entire gardens of exotic flowers and shrubs. Caterpillar tractors were pushing earth around; gravel trucks were spreading topsoil; trees, their roots bagged in burlap, were being eased down planks from the backs of flatbeds. Just before me, a small palm tree in a wheelbarrow was being guided past me by a young man in dungarees.

Ben Siegel showed him where to plant it.

I shook my head and smiled and, stepping over a tangle of electrical wiring, found my way to my Buick in the parking lot.

MEYER LANSKY

19

On the day after Christmas—a Thursday—Ben Siegel unwrapped his gift to the people and himself, flinging open the doors of the fabulous Flamingo to an apparently eager public. Even the colors of this glittering night suggested the Flamingo was Bugsy's great big Christmas present to the world: forty acres of desert transformed into vivid, terraced green, imported shrubbery and trees back-lit by red-and-blue lights. Meanwhile, klieg lights stroked the sky, Hollywood-opening style, creating a veil of light that made the Flamingo, its Grand Opening banners fluttering, visible for miles. Lines of automobiles coming from both directions converged and jammed, while a couple of off-duty Las Vegas traffic cops (who just that afternoon had been moving along a prospector on a burro holding up the downtown flow) somehow coped, though obviously stunned by the size of the throng storming this castle on the sand.

The only opportunity Siegel had missed to further light up his big night was leaving the fountain, out front, dark. The imposing structure was designed to keep water tumbling twenty-four hours, with spotlights throwing color onto its waterfall.

I had been with Siegel that afternoon when he went to watch the fountain's inaugural moments. But the groundskeeper was down within the bowl of the thing on his knees, looking inside the rock-plaster-and-lumber affair.

"What the hell's the deal?" Siegel asked him. "Are you ready to turn this baby on or not?"

"All set, except—"

"Except what?"

"Well, Mr. Siegel, we're gonna have to flush out that damn cat first."

"Cat?" Siegel stepped back. "Where in hell?"

"In the sump. Cat crawled in there last night and had kittens. We'll just have to flood 'em outa there."

"Listen," Siegel said, pointing a finger like a gun, "you drown those cats and you're out a job."

"You're the boss, Mr. Siegel," the groundskeeper shrugged, "but you won't have a fountain at the opening tonight."

"Fuck the fountain. It can wait."

As we walked away, I said, "You don't look like the animal-lover type."

"I hate cats. They make my skin crawl. But it's bad luck for a gambler to touch a cat."

I presumed this didn't apply to "Tabby"—although I had a hunch he would've been better off if it had.

Despite the dry, dark fountain, Ben Siegel's fabulous Flamingo was having a bang-up opening night—even if Jimmy Durante was heard to say, on his way to perform in the red velvet-draped showroom, "Da place looks like a cemetery wid slot machines!"

The Schnozola was referring to arrangements of fresh flowers littering the lobby and main casino, tributes from the movie industry and the underworld. Representatives of the former were due in for Saturday night's "big gala Hollywood premiere"—posters around the Flamingo promised the presence of Veronica Lake, Ava Gardner, William Holden, Lucille Ball and a dozen others.

The only representative of the underworld, that I knew of, was a small dark man in his mid-forties, registered at the Last Frontier Hotel as George Lieberman.

"You know who that is?" Moey Sedway, bedecked in a tux, asked me smugly.

"Your brother?" I asked. Both men were tiny Jews with close-set eyes and prominent noses, though this other man had an air of quiet authority that Sedway could only hope for.

"I wish he was," said Little Moey. "I could use being born next to that much dough." He paused for effect, then said: "That's Meyer Lansky."

I looked at Sedway like he was crazy. "That pipsqueak?"

"I wouldn't call him that to his face," Moey advised. "They come bigger, but they don't come no more powerful."

Lansky, in dark suit and dark tie, was smiling faintly, having a pleasant conversation, in low tones, with the wide-smiling Ben Siegel, who looked spiffy as hell in his white dinner jacket with red carnation in the lapel.

Surprisingly, Lansky didn't seem to have any bodyguards, but then neither did Siegel. With the exception of his security force of ex-cops—whose job was watching the casino, after all—Siegel lacked the armed retinue you might expect. I'd figured Sedway was his bodyguard, at first, till I found Moey never carried a gun; besides, that little weasel couldn't have cut it as bodyguard to a department store Santa.

I'd been around my share of mob guys, but Ben Siegel had me stumped. Despite occasional flare-ups of temper, he just didn't gibe with the stories I'd heard about him. Look at him and Lansky stand-ing there schmoozing. Lansky might have been a moderately suc-cessful garment-district businessman; Siegel someone from the movie industry, a director, a producer, perhaps. Were these two men really the founders of Murder, Incorporated? Was Lansky truly an under-world financial wizard the likes of which made Guzik seem an ama-teur? Was Siegel really the man who controlled narcotics on the West Coast?

Whatever the case, tonight Ben (Don't-Call-Him-You-Know-What) Siegel was a charming, gladhanding host, although as Sedway and I stood along the periphery of the lobby, looking over the packed ca-sino, Siegel did show his colors, momentarily. A heavy-set man in a plaid jacket, looking very out of place in this world of evening wear, was standing in front of a slot machine lackadaisically lighting up a cigar—and not a Havana like Sedway and Siegel smoked. Siegel ex-cused himself from Lansky and walked over to the man.

"You're blocking the machine," Siegel told him. "Play, or move it along."

The bewildered patron in plaid just moved it along.

I thought I could sense disapproval in Lansky's deadpan; but the little man was smiling again, however faintly, when Siegel ap-proached him and put a hand on his shoulder and led him down and through the big casino.

"You won't see Meyer Lansky at the Saturday night grand open-ing," Sedway said.

"Why's that?"

"That's when the reporters are going to show. And Mr. Lansky doesn't like publicity much."

"Ben doesn't seem to mind it."

"You're tellin' me. He got himself a goddamn press agent, the other day."

"Yeah, I know. I met him. That guy Greenspun. Don't you think a place like this *ought* to have a press agent, Moe?"

"Sure. But I don't think some of the, uh, investors knew Ben was going to be so . . . prominent, in the scheme of things. Newspaper articles. Greeting guests at the door. Mingling."

"Telling 'em to move it along."

Sedway laughed shortly. Then he decided he'd said enough to me, and excused himself to do some mingling of his own.

There were plenty of people to mingle with. Earlier that week Siegel had been concerned about a rumor that Las Vegans would boycott his pastel palace. Resentment over the political strings he'd pulled to get building supplies was part of it; the rest came from a whispering campaign about the Flamingo being a den of gangsters, begun by his downtown competitors. These "short-sighted fucking vultures," as Siegel referred to them, didn't understand that (as Ben saw it) he would only bring them all more business by attracting more gamblers to Vegas.

Apparently the rumor had been just that—a rumor—or else the resentment and whispering campaign had been overcome by curiosity and Siegel's pro-Las Vegas advertising: "The Flamingo has been built *for* Las Vegas . . . the Flamingo owners believe in Las Vegas, its future as the greatest playground in the universe . . . the Flamingo will bring Las Vegas the best money can buy and brains can conceive."

Siegel wrote most that himself, of course. He even told his PR guy what to do and how to do it.

Me he'd left pretty much alone, to do my job. Right now I was keeping an eye on the security people, seeing if my training over the past ten days or so had done any good. It was crowded enough tonight to make pickpocket control difficult, which would be a nice final exam for my ex-cop students. Some of them were posted here and there, others were mingling. All wore tuxes—all of Siegel's staff did. Siegel himself had interviewed and hired, after Sedway thinned the pack, the eighty-five dealers, eighteen pit bosses and box men, and three slot-machine supervisors. All of whom, if you asked me, looked uncomfortable in their monkey suits.

Former LAPD lieutenant Quinn, looking in his tux like a tan but sickly penguin, came up to me and smiled and asked how I was doing. He'd been trying to be friendly ever since we tangled. I hadn't gotten rough with him again, because I was pretty sure the pilferage had stopped. My spot checks of boxes I marked (and I'd marked some every day) indicated such, anyway.

Quinn assayed the casino. "Think my boys'll find any dips workin' the room?"

"If they can't, they couldn't find their ass with two hands."

He couldn't resist some sarcasm. "You really think there's gonna be a 'whiz team' in the woodpile?"

"That's the surest bet you could make here tonight."

And I moved away from him. I don't mind your average crooked cop; I used to be one myself. But a guy like Quinn gives corruption a bad name.

I walked out on the patio, which was lit in a soft-focus way by more red-and-blue spots spotted around. Around the pool, as if sunning in the moonlight, were various young women, all of them lovely, shapely, in bathing suits, mostly two-piece, lounging on the chaises. These women were in Siegel's employ, although in what capacity exactly I couldn't say. They'd been posing around the pool all week, for cheesecake photos for the wire-service boys. I knew some of these bathing beauties doubled as cigarette and change girls. Only a few were waitresses, from the lounge; the dining room was served exclusively by waiters, in tuxes, natch. (Siegel had drilled the waiters himself, until they worked with the precision of a Marine platoon.)

One of these women sunning in the moonlight, one who had not done any cheesecake posing earlier in the week, worked as Siegel's confidential secretary.

"You look like a movie star," I told Peggy.

She was wearing a dark blue two-piece.

"Thanks," she said. Her reply was a little chilly. But then so was the air; it wasn't cold out, but if I had a quarter for every erect nipple around this pool, I could've fed a slot machine till midnight.

I got down on my haunches next to her. "But isn't this a little beneath a businesswoman like you?"

She looked down her nose at me, smiling with no warmth. "I don't think so. Ben wanted some pretty girls to sit around the pool tonight, and I think I qualify, thank you."

I pulled up a lounge chair. "Sure you do. I just thought you might have played a slightly more conspicuous, more important role in this grand event."

She seemed to be studying the red and blue lights as they shimmered on the water in the pool.

"Certain parties wouldn't have liked that," she said.

"And yet, at the same time, by sitting here in your near altogether, you're sort of thumbing your nose at 'certain parties.' I like that. You still got some of that Chicago fuck-you spirit. The desert air hasn't dried you out entirely."

Sadness tightened her eyes. "You hate me now, don't you?"

I shook my head, smiled a little. "No. Are you still angry with me?"

She gave me a quick, burning look. "I should be. You had no right getting . . ." I think she was about to say "so personal," but reconsidered, since that was absurd on the face of it. She just let her thought trail off and looked out at the pool again.

She was referring to a short conversation we'd had, in a Last Frontier hallway the second day of my stay, in which I had said to her as follows: "I don't know if you're sleeping with Siegel or not—but if you are, take my advice: don't, at least not when 'Tabby' is in town."

"Is that right?" she'd coldly said.

"That's right. But if you can't help yourself, do it on the sly, and be goddamn careful."

"Really?" Anger bubbling.

"Really. That cunt is capable of murder, you know."

For a moment I'd thought she was going to slap me; but she just glared at me, tightly, and stalked off. We hadn't talked since, except occasional polite, meaningless dinner table conversation, when Siegel held court nightly at the Last Frontier's restaurant and, in these last pre-opening days, at the Flamingo dining room, where we had a few trial meals. Pretty good, too. Siegel's French chef knew his stuff.

"Look," I said. "I know it hasn't been easy having me around. Anyway, I know it hasn't been easy for me to be around . . ."

She looked at me and her expression softened; I could see in it the ghost of her love for me. And I wondered if it haunted her like it did me, at all.

"I'll be going home soon," I said. "Probably Monday, after this grand opening weekend's dead and gone."

"Why did you take the job, Nate?"

"Money."

"I don't believe you."

"Come on, baby. You know me better than that. Name something that matters to me more than money."

She turned away and looked out at the pool. I thought maybe her lower lip was quivering. Maybe not.

I stood.

I was just going when she said, "I think you stayed to keep an eye on me."

I couldn't think of anything to say.

"You . . . you think you're protecting me, don't you?"

"Don't be silly."

"You've been keeping an eye on me. I know you have."

I didn't say anything.

She looked at me. "You really think Ginny's dangerous, don't you?"

"Don't *you*?"

"No. She's all mouth. Big mouth. Ben can't stand her."

"Oh, really?"

"He's just putting up with her."

"Why's he doing that?"

"She has her hooks into him. Monetarily. She has money in this place, you know."

"So does George Raft, but Siegel isn't sleeping with him."

She looked away again. At the pool. "You know how tight she is with Ben's people back East."

"You mean gangsters? Is that what you think, he's putting up with her, because she's the darling of the syndicate? Maybe he keeps her around because he knows that she's spying on him for them—and that lets him control what she reports back."

"Well, doesn't that make sense?"

"It's bullshit. She was a courier for those guys; they trusted her. And they used to lay her, most of them, but now she's Ben's girl, and that's all she is. You're kidding yourself. Why don't you go back to Chicago where you got family and friends?"

"Nate. Don't . . ."

"I'm not talking about us. I'm talking about you. About putting a life together for yourself, a real life that isn't the ersatz Hollywood your dreamboat's trying to turn this desert into."

She gestured around us with one hand, smiling wryly. "I think he's done pretty well."

"Tonight it looks like it. Looking at these palms and terraces and this swimming pool, sure. But you know better than I how wrong this is going."

She swallowed. "I don't know what you mean."

I pointed over to the hotel building. "He didn't make it, did he? His personal deadline. That hotel isn't going to be open for weeks— maybe months. He had to book rooms at hotels all over town, when people called for reservations."

"So what? You saw those crowds in there. The casino's open. The restaurant. The showroom."

"He's not going to make any money on the restaurant; like he says, it's strictly a come-on. Nor the showroom—he's spending thirty-five grand a week on Cugat and Durante and the rest. Top-name talent don't come cheap. So it's all riding on the casino—and these opening-night type crowds aren't going to hold up. Not even on opening night."

"And why not?"

"Aren't you listening? Aren't you paying attention? He didn't get the hotel open in time—the Flamingo drew people in, but those people are staying at other hotels, most of them at the Last Frontier and the El Rancho Vegas, which have their own casinos. The other hotels are close to all those open-door casinos downtown. People gamble where they're staying, Peg. They may come to the Flamingo for an hour or two every day while they're in town, but they're going to do most of their gambling where they're staying. That's basic."

She was shaking her head no. "He'll make a go of it. You wait and see."

"I don't know. You notice that little guy he's been talking to?"

"Mr. Lieberman?"

"That's right, only it's Lansky. Meyer Lansky."

Her eyes narrowed. "Isn't he . . . a gangster?"

"Isn't Rita Hayworth a woman? I don't think his being here is a good sign."

"Maybe it's a show of support."

"I don't think so. I don't think Ben has much time left to make a go of this place. He's sunk six million bucks of mostly mob money into the Flamingo, and I have a hunch the boys want some results, fast. They want to see that Ben's running this place to their satisfaction."

"You think that's why this . . . what is his name?"

"Lansky."

"You think that's why this Lansky is here. Checking up on Ben."

"Possibly. Possibly warning him. They're partners. They go way back."

"You almost seem . . . worried about Ben."

"I like the guy. Don't ask me why. By all accounts, he's a murderer and a narcotics trafficker, among other niceties, including he's in my ex-fiance's pants. I oughta hate him."

She winced at my remark about her pants, but was expressionless when she said, "But you don't."

"No. I kind of admire his chutzpah. And maybe he'll pull this stunt off. Maybe. But I'm not waiting around to see. I'll be in Chicago before you know it."

"I love him, Nate."

"You fall in love a lot, don't you, kid? Me, it doesn't come quite so easy."

"I'm not going back to Chicago with you."

"Well, here's my advice, then. Stay out of Siegel's bed. Tell him you'll get back in, when Virginia Hill's out of his life. Tell him you aren't prepared to play side dish to her main course."

"You're cruel."

"Not as cruel as you, and you aren't even trying. Do what I said, and maybe you can hang onto your job here. Siegel does seem to respect you for your mind as well as your body. Be a career girl, if you want. You just might be in on the ground floor of something."

"Why do you . . . why do you still care about me?"

"I haven't the faintest fucking idea," I said, and I went back into the casino.

Where Ben was in his element. He was shaking hands with guests (those who weren't in plaid jackets, anyway), and on his arm was Virginia Hill, looking resplendent in her thirty-five-hundred dollar flaming orange-red gown; a diamond necklace caressed her bosom, and who could blame the lucky rocks? She seemed in *her* element, too, tapping back into her days as the belle of the social ball, when she was posing as an Arkansas heiress. Gone, for the moment, was her disdain for Siegel's pastel dream castle. Here was a beautiful woman, charming, funny, and so very desirable. The psychopath was hiding.

I stayed away from her. I saw Lansky two more times that evening; in both instances he was speaking, off to one side, with Moe Sedway.

My pickpocket school graduates did all right. They stopped one whiz team, and two single-handers. They followed my suggested procedure and did not confront the dips till they had left the premises; that prevented any nasty embarrassing scene within the facility itself.

As I suspected, the crowd thinned out early, for a joint that never closed. People headed back to their own hotels, where they'd probably gamble some more before retiring.

A little after three A.M., I found Siegel in the small main counting room off the casino. Boxes of money were on the table before him. He and the top pit boss were counting the take. But I could see from Siegel's fallen face that something was wrong.

"This is impossible," he said, ashen.

The pit boss shrugged.

"I'll, uh, report in later," I said.

Siegel looked at me with the expression of a man who has been struck in the back of the head with a plank.

"We're down almost thirty thousand," he said.

"What?" I said.

"We lost tonight. How the fuck does the *house* lose?"

I didn't know.

But the way Siegel's luck had been running, I wasn't surprised he'd found a way.

20

"The place ain't exactly hoppin'," George Raft said, lighting up a cigarette as he viewed the moderately attended casino floor from the slightly raised perspective of the lobby. It was early Friday afternoon, and Raft had just arrived from Hollywood; he'd driven over in his shiny cobalt-blue Cadillac, only it wasn't so shiny after the desert had been at it for seven hours. He was wearing a dark blue sportshirt and a lighter blue jacket and seemed tired; his hair was slicked immaculately back, but the rest of him looked slightly out of focus.

"Come evening it'll be jammed again," I said. "Without the hotel open, days are bound to be slow."

He nodded. "How's Benny holding up?"

"He's a little frazzled. This morning he chewed out some poor customer who had the bad judgment to go up and call him 'Bugsy.'"

"Ouch," Raft said.

"And, too, he was down thirty grand last night."

Raft gave me a disbelieving look. "Down?"

"Yeah. Partly it's the pros from downtown coming in and playing smart. That includes his supposed pal Gus Greenbaum."

The gregarious, fleshy Greenbaum ran the Arizona branch of Trans-American for Siegel.

"Even the savviest gamblers are still up against house odds," Raft said. "What's *really* going on?"

"I think I know," I said. "I'm just not ready to spring it on Siegel yet."

Raft nodded again. "Where is he? I got more bad news for him."

"Well, if that's the case, I'm going to make myself scarce . . ."

"Too late. Here he is."

Siegel was striding through the casino, wearing a tux with a red carnation; he was beaming, gladhanding, putting on a good front, but just the way he walked was a tip-off. This guy was teetering.

But he grinned widely at seeing Raft and said, "Georgie! Georgie,

FLAMINGO POOL

how are ya? Thanks for coming," pumping his old friend's hand. He didn't seem to notice how forced Raft's smile was.

"Let's talk," Raft said.

"Fine!"

"Private, someplace."

Siegel shrugged. "Sure."

"I'll see you guys later," I said.

"Naw," Siegel said, "Georgie and me got no secrets from you, Nate." And, Raft staying dutifully at his side, Siegel eased his arm around my shoulder and walked me to his small office behind the hotel check-in counter.

Siegel's desk was cluttered with notepad notes to himself; there were four phones, making it look more like a hole-in-the-wall bookie joint than some big shot's office. The pink plaster walls were decorated with framed photos of Ben and his Hollywood pals, chief among them Raft, including a portrait of the two of them smiling at each other after Raft stood up for his childhood chum in court.

Behind the desk, Siegel leaned back in his swivel chair and lit up one of his Havanas. Normally the health-conscious Bug only allowed himself one a day; the last several days I'd noticed he was going through them like he was chain smoking Camels.

Raft took a chair across from Siegel while I stood in the corner, next to a signed, framed Cary Grant 8" by 10" glossy.

Siegel pointed at me with his pool cue cigar and showed off his patented dazzling smile. "I oughta put you in my will, Georgie, for introducing me to Nate, here. He's just about the most valuable guy I got around this joint."

I swallowed. I didn't know whether to say aw shucks or go screaming into the desert.

"He's straightened out my pilferage problem overnight. He's turned those flabby ex-flatfoots on my private police force into something like a real security staff. You used to be a dip, didn't you, Georgie? Well, don't try it around here—Nate's got his boys trained to spot ya. Nate doesn't know it yet," he confided to Raft, as if I weren't there, "but I'm going to offer him a permanent position."

I said, "I'm flattered, Ben," and let it go at that.

Raft said, "Hear you had quite a turnout last night."

Siegel gave with a magnanimous wave of his cigar. "Jam-packed. Couldn't ask for better." His expression darkened momentarily. "We had a bad run of luck at the tables . . ." And then he brightened, or pretended to. ". . . but the house odds'll turn that around."

If he was counting on that, he was making a mistake, at least potentially so. Sure, assuming his tables were straight, the odds would even out in the house's favor; that was a tide that would inevitably turn. But as over-extended as he was, his bankroll might be expended before said tide came in.

"Everything's set for tomorrow night," Siegel said. "I chartered a TWA Constellation to bring your pals down, and anybody that doesn't want to fly can come by train, at my expense."

"Ben," Raft said, shifting in his chair, "we got a little problem."

"What kind of problem?"

"A few people can't make it."

"Like who?"

"Well. Like almost everybody."

Siegel's face went expressionless; and then it began to burn.

Raft seemed very uncomfortable. "It's not easy for me to tell you this, Ben."

"What's the matter with those jerks? Since when don't Hollywood wanna come to a big party?"

Raft shrugged, tried to find something to say, couldn't. It was very strange seeing George Raft nervous; it made me at least as uncomfortable as he was.

Siegel gestured to the framed photos around him. "What about your buddies at MGM? Joan Crawford, Greer Garson, Spencer Tracy, Ronald Colman?"

"Ben. Look. Old man Hearst passed the word around the studios. He's against the whole idea of stars coming out here for this—everybody's been told to stay away."

Siegel slammed a fist on his desk and his framed photos rattled. "That lousy cocksucker! What's he got against me?"

"I don't know, Ben."

"It's that fucking Louella Parsons. She's always on my ass. Calls me a gangster, in print!"

"What can I say? *I'll* be there."

"Who else?"

"Lon McAllister, Sonny Tufts, Charlie Coburn . . . a few others."

Siegel's face had slowly gone from red to white. "I advertise Ava Gardner and instead give 'em Sonny Tufts, is that it?"

"Hell, I think it's white of Tufts to show, considering the pressure."

Siegel, calming, said, "Yeah, you're right. I'm not gonna take it out on the ones with stones enough to show. What about Jessel?"

"He's coming. He's set to emcee."

"Yeah, he can deliver the fuckin' eulogy."

"Ben, there'll be enough stars to justify your advertising and everything. And Wilkerson says that all the reporters you invited are coming."

Siegel smirked humorlessly. "After the free ride I promised 'em, you can bet on it. I sent out cases of whiskey to a couple dozen of the bastards." Abruptly he stood, looked sharply my way. "Have you seen Chick around?"

Chick was Virginia Hill's twenty-one-year-old brother, a nice enough kid, who was working as a robber, that is, one of the trusted hands who emptied the slot machines and hauled the bags of coin to the counting room.

"Yeah," I said, "he's working. If he isn't on the floor, he's in the counting room."

"Get him, would you?"

I didn't much like playing gopher to Siegel, but I didn't much feel like telling him to go fuck himself, either. I found Chick in the counting room and hauled the boy back.

"What do you need, Ben?" he asked. He was wearing a white shirt and black pants—which was one of the two standard casino employee uniforms, the other and more common being a tux; even just the modified formal wear looked odd on Chick, who was a kid with dark blond hair, slicked back in the Raft manner, and pointed, callowly handsome features.

Siegel, still standing, dug in his pants pocket; he withdrew a wad of bills and peeled off ten one-hundred dollar bills; he scattered them on his desk like more notes to himself.

"There's a grand," he told the kid. "Take it and do some shopping in L.A. Get some nice presents for the reporters, the columnists. Neckties, shirts. Oh, hell, you know."

"Sure, Ben. Should I drive, or what?"

"Naw, I want you back by tomorrow afternoon. Catch the first available flight." He peeled off another hundred.

Chick collected the money, smiled goofily like a teenager whose

dad just handed him the keys to the new DeSoto. He stood there
with the money in his hands for a few moments, until Siegel rather
irritatedly waved him off, and the kid slipped out the door.

"We'll keep these reporters happy," Siegel said. Then he put his
cigar out in a tray and came out from behind the desk and Raft stood
and the men went out into the lobby; I trailed behind, not having
been dismissed yet.

"Let me show you the pool," Siegel said, his arm around Raft now.

I was about to fall away, but then decided to go along. I wanted to
see if Peggy was playing bathing beauty today.

Turned out she wasn't. Just a bevy of waitresses, cigarette girls and
hookers, soaking up the winter sun.

So was a guy in a tux, his tie loose around his neck.

Siegel's face reddened again.

He broke away from Raft and went over and kicked the chaise
lounge, whose pale, round-faced, startled occupant sat up and looked
at Siegel with wide, terror-filled eyes.

"What the hell do you think you're doing?" Siegel snarled.

"Just—just s-sitting here . . ."

"Get back to work, you bum, before I boot your ass out on the
highway."

The round-faced man looked at me and then at Raft, whom he
obviously recognized but was too bewildered by Siegel's performance
to be impressed by the presence of a mere movie star.

The man could only stutter: "B-but I'm a ga-ga-ga . . ."

"Spit it out!"

"Guest!"

"What?" Siegel said. Taken aback.

"I don't work here . . . I'm a guest."

Raft covered his mouth but I didn't bother. My hand wouldn't
have been big enough to hide the grin.

Siegel, very embarrassed, started brushing off the shoulders of the
guy's tux, as if it had gotten dirty, which it hadn't. He did his best to
make it up to the guy, handing him one of the same courtesy cards
the newspapermen got, giving him a free ride on everything except
gambling itself.

We walked back into the casino and Siegel said, "Brother, is my
face red."

Frequently.

"I guess I oughta watch my fuckin' temper . . . *shit!* Do you see who that is?"

A tall, slightly heavy-set man in a pinstripe suit, with satanically shaggy eyebrows, was standing at a slot machine, studying it like a sociologist might a pygmy hut.

Raft said nothing, but the mask of his face was grim.

"Pegler," I said.

Siegel looked at me with a vicious, self-satisfied smile. "Westbrook Pegler is right."

I shrugged. "Well, you wanted to attract newspapermen."

"That bastard's been cutting me up. Called me a hoodlum and carpetbagger. Called me Bugsy. In syndication."

I could see Siegel's shoulders tensing; his hands were fists.

Raft put a hand on Siegel's arm. "Ben—he's been cutting me up in his column, too. Ever since that gambling bust, but so what? That's his racket. Live and let live."

"I'm going to kill him," Siegel said, quietly, smiling, "I'm going to kill him. I'm going to kill him."

It was times like these I wished I'd taken my father's advice and finished college.

"You're not killing anybody," Raft said. "You're going to ruin it for yourself, if you do. Get a grip, baby-blue eyes."

Siegel visibly softened.

But he walked over to Pegler, who had inserted a quarter into the slot machine and was yanking back the arm.

Raft and I followed; we seemed to be backing Siegel up, but in reality we were poised to grab and brace him, if necessary. Pegler, who I'd had a run-in with in Chicago back in '39, looked right at me and didn't recognize me. Like him, I was older and heavier, now.

"Mr. Pegler," Siegel said.

"Yes?" Pegler said, losing his quarter, turning his gaze on Siegel, eyebrows raised, voice patrician. Pegler was one of those columnists who made a big deal about being for the common man while at the same time considering himself above just about everybody.

"My name is Ben Siegel."

Pegler began to smile; he was searching for the right pithy comment, when Siegel stopped him.

With Pegler's own weapon, words: "This is my casino. If you're not out of here in five minutes, I'm going to take you out. Personally."

Pegler's smile wilted. He looked at Siegel carefully, slowly. Siegel's back was to me, so I don't know what expression he was showing Pegler. Whatever it was, it was enough to make the powerful columnist swallow thickly, tuck tail between his legs and go.

Siegel turned to us and opened his two hands like a magician displaying something that had disappeared. "See? I can control my temper when I want to."

"Good," I said. "Because it's time you knew something."

"What's that?"

I turned to Raft. "Why don't you park yourself at a blackjack table or something, for a while? Your face attracts too much attention. We need to be a little less conspicious for a few minutes."

Raft shrugged. "I'll try the chemin-de-fer room."

"Good idea," I said.

Then he moved off, and I took Siegel by the arm. "What do you have in mind," I asked him, "where these gambling losses are concerned?"

"In mind?"

"What do you intend to do about it?"

He shrugged facially. "Well, we're switching dice more frequent. Cards, too. Tonight I'm gonna move dealers from table to table . . ."

"Some of your dealers need to be moved farther away than that."

"What do you mean?"

"If you patted them down on their way out the door, you'd find subs full of chips." A "sub" was a hidden pocket.

His eyes tensed. "You've seen this?"

"Have you got your temper in check?"

"Nate, I'm cool as a cucumber."

"Good, because the answer is yes, I've seen half a dozen dealers sweeping chips into subs."

"Christ, I interviewed them all myself!"

"Never mind that. Just take a look there."

I nudged his attention to the roulette table where I'd been leading him; we were now about five feet away from it, behind and to one side of the croupier, a thin, hawk-faced man who was pushing chips across the table to a pockmarked heavy-set gentleman in a brown suit. The problem was, the pockmarked heavy-set gentleman who was having chips pushed his way was not winning.

"That guy isn't hitting any winning numbers," Siegel whispered harshly to me, after a while, his eyes large.

"Right," I said. I nodded toward the croupier. "You get the pit boss to take him off the table. I'll handle the phony player."

Siegel, eyes narrowing, nodded. He turned away.

I walked up to the pockmarked player, thinking Siegel was off getting the pit boss.

But the Bug had changed his mind, because he was standing right behind the hawk-faced croupier.

"I oughta kill you, you son of a bitch!" he said, and punted the croupier's ass.

It lifted the man off the floor and sent him skidding across the table, chips scattering. When he came to a stop, his hawkish nose pointed to the double-00 on the numbered felt.

"You lose," Siegel said, and reached over and picked him up like baggage and hurled him into the aisle.

Without looking back, the ex-croupier picked himself up and ran. The astonished onlookers—and the very pleased Ben Siegel— watched the guy hurtle up into the lobby and out the front doors.

Siegel gestured big with his hands, like a ringmaster. "No cover charge folks!" he said, letting loose his dazzler of a smile.

And people, smiling too, if not dazzlingly, shaking their heads, chattering amongst themselves, turned back to their gambling.

Siegel came over to me and slipped his arm around my shoulder. "Let's go have a talk."

We walked across the terraced green grounds that not so long ago had been barren, and he walked me across the painted, carpetted lobby of the unfinished hotel and took me up the elevator to the penthouse suite.

We sat on the chintz-covered sofa. He was drinking tonic water; I had some rum on ice.

He was shaking his head. "I hired those guys myself, Nate."

He meant the dealers and other casino floor people.

"Most of them local?" I asked.

"Right. I screened them all personally."

"After Sedway thinned the pack, you did."

"Right." His eyes slitted. "What are you saying?"

"I think there's widespread cheating going on out there. And I don't think it's random."

"You mean, it's organized?"

"Yeah. I think so."

"Moey?"

"Who else?"

"What about Quinn?"

I shook my head no. "He's not smart enough, and besides, I put him on notice. He's too scared of you to pull anything. He's even scared of me. Moey? Moey resents you, and that breeds a kind of bravery."

"Moey resents me?"

"I think it goes back to that scuffle you had over politics."

He sat and thought about that.

I went on: "I think he's angling to take over. My guess is he's trying to make you look bad to your friends back east."

Siegel's face tensed with thought. "And if he convinces them I'm a bad manager, they'll ask him to step in?"

"Yeah. He seems to be in pretty thick with Lansky."

Siegel nodded. "He is at that. You know what Meyer said to me last night? He said, 'Ben, you're a smart dreamer, but a lousy engineer.' Can you imagine?"

"Ben, none of this is my business . . . I've told you what I know, and what I think." I was getting uncomfortable being privvy to Siegel's inside thoughts.

But he pressed on: "He just got back, Meyer did, from Havana. They just had a big meeting down there, with Charlie Lucky."

Luciano. A big secret syndicate confab in Havana, and I knew about it. Great.

I rose. "Ben, you're getting into areas . . ."

"Sit down, Nate. I trust you."

"That isn't the point . . ."

"Sit down, Nate."

I sat.

"Meyer said the boys aren't happy with me, the money I spent, here. They want me to bring in a top hotel man. They want to hire somebody from one of the downtown joints to run my casino." He grinned but there was desperation in it. "You know what else?"

I said nothing.

"You'll get a kick out of this, being Ragen's pal and all. They want me to fold Trans-American up. Guzik has control of Continental now, through that McBride character. I told Meyer, sure—just buy me out."

My mouth was dry. Nonetheless, I managed to ask, "How much did you ask?"

"Two million."

Jesus.

"I'm pulling in twenty-five grand a week," he said. "Why should I give it up, otherwise? They'll make their money back in less than two years. It's a fair offer."

I didn't say anything.

"I need the money," he said. "This place eats money."

I didn't say anything.

"Moey, huh?" he said. Then, reflective, he went on: "Meyer said they heard bad things about me. Some of the boys said they heard I was skimming off the top of the construction money. Jeez!" He shook his head, gestured toward the two picture windows, out of which the terraced lawn and the scalloped-edged pool could be seen. "Those wop bastards, don't they know I put every available penny into this place, including my own? And my heart and my fuckin' soul? This is my . . . what, monument, the thing that'll be around when I'm gone that'll make people know I was here."

"When you get the kinks ironed out," I said, carefully, "it'll be a great success, I think."

"I think so, too. But Meyer's putting the pressure on me. Something else they heard was I got half a million stashed away in Switzerland. I sent Tabby to Zurich to pick out some furniture for the hotel rooms and from that they figure I'm stuffing their dough in a numbered account. Jesus!"

"What pressure are they putting on you?"

He sipped his tonic water, shrugged. "They expect me to make a good showing, quick."

I smiled thinly. "That seals it. Sedway."

He looked at me and slowly began to nod. "Sure. He's saboToging my casino—that's where I gotta make it to make it."

"Right."

Siegel stood and walked to the window, surveyed his kingdom with a smile. "I'm gonna fool the bastards. I'm gonna pull it off."

I stood. "I hope you do. Look, I'm going to go back to the casino and keep an eye on the security staff."

He turned back to me. "Nate, I was serious about giving you a permanent position, here."

"Well, uh, I was serious when I said I was flattered . . ."

"I know, I know, but you don't want to work under Quinn. Well hell, I plan to fire the fat little crooked son of a bitch, anyway. You

think I don't know how you managed to stop the pilferage so goddamn fast? You weren't here five minutes before you spotted the
problem."

"You would've, too, if you weren't trying to do so much."

"I know, I know. And I will hire some of those people the boys
want me to hire, hotel man, casino manager, down the road. I'll start
hiring now, right this minute. How's this for openers? Stay on and be
my security chief, Nate. It'll pay you sixty grand a year and fringes.
You can live right here at the Flamingo."

"That's good money. That's attractive. But I have my own business."

He shrugged. "You could keep it going. Own it, keep an eye on it,
but put somebody you trust in charge. Like Fred's going to run your
west coast office."

"Fred's a partner. That's different."

He patted the air with one hand, setting his tonic water on the bar.
"Just think about it. For the time being, let's go back to the casino
and see if there's anymore dishonest dealers who need a kick in the
ass."

I laughed. "I imagine the cheating's been cut way back since that
little scene."

"It's what the cops call a deterrent, right?"

"Right."

Siegel laughed and we went out a side exit that led down a slanted
ramp-like passageway that opened at the side of the hotel nearest the
main building. We walked back toward the pool.

Sedway was standing near one of the youngest-looking of the
bathing beauties, a little busty blonde number, coming onto her as
subtly as a safe falling out a window; but then she could see it coming
and didn't seem to be moving out of the way, so what the hell. He
was wearing a white jacket with a red carnation, similar to Ben's apparel of the evening before; but a weasel in a dinner jacket is still a
weasel.

"Moe!" Siegel called out.

Moey looked over at Siegel and gave him a slippery sideways smile
and reluctantly left his quiff and trotted over.

"Yes, Ben?"

Siegel put a hand on the little man's shoulder. "What's the idea
badmouthing me to Meyer?"

Moey's eyes began to move back and forth. "What do you mean, Ben?"

"Don't shit me. You think Meyer would keep something like that from me? You know how far back Meyer and me go? They used to call *him* 'Bugs,' too, you know."

"Ben, I don't know what to say."

Siegel's hand began to squeeze the shoulder, like an orange you want to turn into a glass of juice. Pulp and all.

"Tell me, Moey. I already know, but I wanna hear it from you."

The rat-faced little man swallowed and said, "I just told 'em the truth. That I thought you were dangerous to their interests."

"Really. Because I ain't up to running a big place like this, is that it?"

"Well, I think you need more help, anyway. I don't mean any offense."

He didn't let up the pressure on Moe's shoulder. "You don't mean any offense. Going to Meyer and Christ knows who else behind my back. They were voting down there whether to have me hit or not, Moey. Down in Havana? Bet you didn't tell 'em you were fixing my casino room so I'd lose, did ya? Or that you were setting me up with crooked dealers?"

Moey's face fell; he tried to move back.

Siegel said, "Goodbye, Moey. If you ever set foot at the Flamingo again, I'm gonna break the rules. There's gonna be a killing in Vegas, and you're the guy that's gonna get killed, and I'm the guy that's gonna do the killing."

He let go of Moey's shoulder and Moey turned and moved quickly away, disappearing into the casino.

Siegel sighed, looked at me, shaking his head. "It ain't easy being an executive," he said.

And we walked back inside the fabulous Flamingo.

SIEGEL AND RAFT

21

Even with Sedway's absence, the Flamingo's losing streak rolled on. And I knew why: the dealers, alerted by the literal booting out of one of their own, not to mention the ousting of Sedway himself, would only do their cheating all the more carefully now; and members of the security staff, whose attention I'd called to the problem and who were supposedly keeping an eye out, might well be in on the scam. In the case of either or both, Siegel was flat out screwed. Short of firing everybody on his casino crew and closing down and starting over after rehiring—which Siegel of course could (or anyway, would) not do—there was no way around it. Friday night the house didn't lose as badly as it had Thursday, but it did lose. To the tune of fifteen thousand dollars.

On the surface, at least, the evening's "Hollywood Premiere," which of course was the grand finale of Ben's gala opening, was going well. Newspaper, magazine and freelance photographers converged en masse, snapping leg art of the girls around the pool (Peggy not among them). Columnists and other newshounds were on hand to do write-ups and interviews, giving rave reviews to an especially demented Jimmy Durante, who hurled into a stunned and delighted audience beat-up old hats, a perplexed Cugat's sheet music, and bits and pieces of a piano he was seemingly dismantling, only to be topped by the former child-star Rose Marie, looking a glamorous young woman now, nonetheless doing an uncanny showstopping imitation of the Schnoz.

A few more of Raft's Hollywood friends showed than had been anticipated; not the glittering array Siegel had been promised—and had promised his patrons. But the respectable likes of George Sanders, Vivian Blaine and Eleanor Parker, as well as the expected Sonny Tufts, Lon McAllister and Charles Coburn, and a few others.

And the place was packed, with Hollywood industry figures like Jesse Lasky and Sid Grauman scattered amongst a crowd that mingled rank and file with Los Angeles society types. Siegel had instructed the security staff to enforce a dress code of sorts; it was vague—one of the few specifics was that men had to check their hats, which annoyed the natives who were used to wearing their Stetsons just about everywhere, bed and bathtub too I suspected—but it was working to the extent that the majority of patrons tonight were in formal wear.

Even I was in a rented tux, provided by Siegel, and I was determined that this would be my last night in his service. I'd trained his people and otherwise helped him. If nothing else, spotting the cheating on the floor, and helping him zero in on Sedway as his betrayer, had earned me my paycheck.

But I wasn't confident that Siegel could keep his head—not to mention his temper—in the face of the pressures ahead, not the least of which was his conflict with the boys back east. Meyer Lansky, Lucky Luciano and the rest obviously wanted three things from Ben and the Flamingo: fast results on their investment; a slowdown on spending; and no more embarrassing publicity. They also wanted him to shitcan Trans-American, which had after all been intended as merely a stopgap measure till Ragen's Continental could be bought out or taken over.

I wasn't convinced Ben Siegel could deliver on any of those things. And I knew he was dreaming a bigger dream than the Flamingo itself in thinking the Combination would buy him out of their own race wire for two million. One determined man standing up against his old mob cronies who, past friendships or not, wanted him to hand over his race wire, well—that was where I came in. I wished him luck, but didn't want to be around when, inevitably, the bullets would start flying. Sixty grand a year and fringes was nice. But breathing had it beat all to hell.

And Peggy? I wouldn't be taking her home. That was the best bet of the night.

I spent the evening moving through the crowded casino, posting myself here and there, watching the dealers and croupiers, not spotting anything untoward; nor did any dips seem to be working the room tonight. Maybe the word had got around.

Shortly before midnight the Hollywood guests—Sonny Tufts and the rest of the luminaries—trooped out through the lobby, shaking hands, smiling, flash bulbs popping, Siegel lording over it all with a big shiteating grin. He was in the white dinner jacket again, tonight, with a pink carnation in his lapel, like that first night on the S.S. Lux. (Speaking of which, earlier that night I noticed Tony Cornero, looking gray and defeated, standing at one of the craps tables, looking for some luck. I doubt he found it.)

Raft and Siegel were bidding the stars goodbye, limos waiting outside to drive them to the nearby airport, where the chartered Constellation would wing them home. Standing near Siegel was Peggy, wearing an off-the-shoulder emerald green taffeta cocktail dress with a flamingo-shaped jeweled brooch. She looked very chic, short black gloves, hair piled high, tight curls framing her sweet face. God, it's annoying still loving a woman after it's over.

I was down in the casino, but well within viewing range. I wondered where La Hill was keeping herself. She'd been playing chemin-de-fer earlier, looking opening-night lovely in her white crepe formal gown, aglitter with gold sequins. And an hour ago or so I'd seen her in the bar, in a not untypically sloshed condition, buying the "best champagne in the house" for a honeymooning couple—using a thousand-dollar bill to do so. She'd moved on, latest stinger in hand, and left the $900 change on the bar. She was known to be a good tipper, but the bartender had nonetheless paged Siegel to pick up the dough.

I assumed Ben had tracked her down and deposited her in their penthouse suite. He would not want her at his side on this big night, not that drunk. Maybe Peggy was chosen as Ginny's stand-in, so the boss would have a lovely woman at his side as the Hollywood crowd was bid fond farewell.

They were just going out the door, Tufts and all, photographers following on their heels (a fortunate break, as it turned out), when trouble came from the other direction, through the lobby, entering from the patio. At the very moment, so luck would have it, that Siegel was slipping an arm around Peggy's waist and leaning over to give her a peck on the cheek.

Virginia Hill, legs swishing in the expensive crepe gown, saw this and was rolling inexorably toward them, bumping patrons out of the way like bowling pins. Her face was distorted by drink and anger.

I moved through the casino-floor crowd up the five steps to the lobby.

I was just in time to see Tabby attack with both clawed hands, her painted nails like ten scarlet knives. First she snatched the jeweled flamingo off Peg's breast, tearing the taffeta, and hurled the bauble at Siegel. Then one hand scratched Peg's face, viciously, leaving trails of red behind, and the other grabbed a handful of that curly hair and yanked.

Peg yelped and a stunned, silent crowd looked on, fascinated. This was better than the Christians versus the Lions.

Siegel was momentarily frozen as his two girl friends went crashing to the lobby carpet. Virginia sat on top of the dazed Peggy and smacked her with a small hard fist, twice, and then Peggy fought back, grabbing onto Virginia's dress and ripping, exposing a breast. Then they were rolling over, biting and gouging and punching, Peggy screaming, Tabby growling.

We pulled them apart, Siegel yanking Virginia back roughly, and me cradling a shaking, stunned, bleeding, bruised Peggy in my arms; Peg was a tough cookie—she wasn't crying. But she was badly shaken, and clung to me, without exactly knowing it was me, I think.

Siegel slapped Virginia Hill. It was a hard, ringing slap, and she looked at him, covering her exposed breast with one hand, with big eyes and a hurt expression that had nothing to do with the pain of the slap.

"You ain't no fuckin' lady," he told her.

"Ben . . ."

Siegel swallowed, suddenly aware of the many eyes upon him, the awful silence around him; only the casino sounds, and even they seemed hushed, continued.

Quietly, under his breath so that only those nearest by could hear, he said to her, "You made me look like a bum."

Trembling now, she covered her mouth with one hand, the other hand still protecting her breast, and with a rasping cry, she rushed out.

He looked after her with a scowl. Then he faced his public. He couldn't cover for such a disaster; there was no dazzling smile to pull out of somewhere, no crack about "no cover charge, folks." Just an angry and, somehow, hurt Ben Siegel.

Slowly, the crowd went back to entertaining themselves. The photographers came in from shooting the departing stars, not knowing they'd missed anything.

Siegel turned to Peggy, who I had up on her feet, now. Her hair had come undone; she looked generally undone, actually. He touched her shoulder.

"Are you okay?" he said, his voice soft now, seeming genuinely to care.

"I—I think so."

He put his hand on her shoulder, gently. "Maybe we oughta get you to the hospital. Have you checked up."

"It's not that serious, Ben. I'm just . . . embarrassed."

"Sure you are." He smiled a softly wry smile. "Who isn't?"

She managed to smile back at him, despite the caking blood on her cheek.

"Nate," Siegel said to me, "why don't you drive Miss Hogan back to the Last Frontier. She needs some rest."

"Sure," I said. "If that's okay with Miss Hogan."

She nodded, smiled bravely.

Siegel patted her cheek—the unbloodied one—and gave her a warm smile. His blue eyes seemed almost to twinkle. Fuck him, anyway. I had more hair than he did.

I walked her out to the Buick I was using. Guided her by the arm; just being helpful. Strictly business. Siegel's gopher. Until tomorrow, and the hell with this noise.

We drove in silence; it wasn't far.

I walked her to her room.

She paused at the doorway, her back to me. "Thanks, Nate."

"Are you okay, kid?"

"Not really."

"I'd offer you some company, but I don't think you really want any." Not mine, anyway.

"No . . . I don't. But thanks. Thanks for not rubbing it in."

"That's okay."

"You said all along she was dangerous."

"She is dangerous. It could be a gun next time."

She nodded. "I know. I'll be careful."

"Do that, would you?"

She went in, and I walked away.

Then she called out to me. "You could see I was right, though, couldn't you?"

"What?"

"He doesn't love her. He hates her. It was me he was concerned about."

Right. That's why he had his gopher drive you home.

"Sure, baby," I said, and walked on out.

When I got back to the Flamingo, Siegel was sitting in the bar. It was not his usual wont to hang out there, nor was it his wont to drink a double Scotch. He was doing both.

"Rough," I said.

"Yeah," he said. He gestured to the stool next to him.

I sat. "How's Virginia?"

He shrugged. "She's sleeping it off in the penthouse. I went up there and we went a few more rounds. I belted her in the belly and she puked. Got it out of her system, anyway."

Ain't love grand.

"Ben, uh . . ."

"You're not gonna take my offer, are you?"

I shook my head no.

"You don't like it."

"What?"

"Me and your ex-girl."

"Well, I'm not going to scratch your face over it, Ben. But I probably like it just a little less than Ginny does."

He sighed. Nodded. "Fuckin' broads, anyway. Too bad."

"You mean it could've been the beginning of a beautiful friendship?"

He smirked. "Something like that, pal." He raised his glass to me.

"Besides," I said, not having a glass to raise, "I'm like you. I like running things. I like having my own agency. It started out just me, in a little ratty office, fourteen years ago. And now I got people working for me, and I'm moving into a big modern office. I got dreams, too, Ben. And they don't include the Flamingo."

He was nodding, slowly. "Fair enough. When you leaving?"

"Monday. And I don't particularly want to work tomorrow."

"Fine with me. I haven't paid you yet, have I?"

"Just expenses as we've gone along. You promised me ten grand, you know."

He nodded again. "Yeah, and you earned it. I oughta pay you a bonus, but I been told to watch my spending."

I gave him a rueful grin. "Just my luck I'm where you decided to start."

Of course, bad as my luck had been running, it was still better than Siegel's. He told me to meet him in the counting room at 3 A.M., and he'd pay me, in cash. And I found him there with that familiar, sick, ashen look.

"Fuck," he said, sitting at the table, money boxes before him, pit boss lurking nearby, staying out of the boss's way but ready to be at his beck and call.

"How bad is it?" I asked, leaning against the table.

"Bad. Another thirty grand."

"Christ . . ."

"If this keeps up, I'll be down a hundred thou by weekend's end."

"You got to close up, Ben. You got dishonest sons of bitches on that floor, watched over by other dishonest sons of bitches, I'm afraid."

"I'll put the fear of God in 'em," he said, with nasty resolve. "Better still, I'll put the fear of *me* in 'em."

I ignored that. "I think you ought to close up, and do some new hiring, and wait till the hotel's open."

"What the fuck do you know about it?" he spat.

I shrugged. "Why don't you just pay me and I'll go. Pay me while there's still some cash in the till."

He shook his head, his expression softening. "Sorry, Nate. Sorry. I'll think about what you're saying. Your advice has been good so far. I'll think about it."

"Good enough, Ben."

He counted me out nine grand in hundreds, and another grand in fifties and twenties and a few tens.

"Let me know what you're gonna declare on your taxes," he said, "so we got our stories straight."

"Good idea," I said, folding the hundreds into one thick wad, the other grand of smaller bills into another. Put them away. A lot of money, but I earned it.

I was shaking hands with Siegel when Chick Hill came rushing in.

"Benny!" he said. "You gotta come quick! She's killed herself, I think she's killed herself!"

"Tabby?" he said, standing, eyes wide.

Chick nodded, pointed back behind him.

"Nate," Siegel said, his eyes desperate, moving away from the table, "can you lend a hand?"

I nodded, and we rushed out through the lobby around to the patio and across the terrace garden to the unfinished hotel building.

"She's swallowed a bottle of sleeping pills," the frantic Chick explained. "I don't think she's breathing . . ."

"How'd you happen onto her?" I asked him, as we crossed the lobby to the private elevator.

"I wanted to check up on her," her brother said. He looked with wounded eyes at Siegel, as we boarded the tiny elevator. "I heard you beat her up, Ben."

"Shut-up, Chick," Siegel said tightly, looking upward, as if willing the elevator to rise more quickly.

We found her on the pink sheets of the big bed, on her back; she was still wearing the torn gown, one breast exposed, her eyes closed, a faint bluish tinge to her cheeks. Siegel bent over her.

"She's breathing," he said. "Shallow but breathing—get me some cold wet towels!"

Chick wetted some down in the nearest bathroom, on the floor of which I found the empty pill bottle. The kid handed Siegel the towels and he began slapping her with them.

"Wake up!" he said. "Goddamnit, wake up!"

Chick stood off to one side, helpless, near tears.

I said, "Ben, look, let's get her to the hospital, get her stomach pumped. I can pull my Buick in the construction access out back. I'll go right now, what do you say?"

He was cradling her in his arms now; he looked up at me, with a haunted expression, and nodded.

"Can you two haul her down okay?" I asked.

Siegel nodded, said, "Go on, get the car!"

I did.

Southern Nevada Hospital was five miles away, on Charleston Boulevard. Traffic was heavy, and I had to weave in and around it, hurtling along at upwards of eighty miles an hour.

Virginia Hill, dead to the world, was between Siegel and me in the front seat; he had his arm around her, holding her close to him, soothing her like a sleeping baby. Chick was riding in back, nervous with worry.

"Step on it!" Siegel yelled at me.

"I am."

"Goddamn stupid bitch," he said, but quietly, in that previous, soothing voice. "Why did she have to do it?"

I pushed the Buick harder; the speedometer's needle quivered at ninety. A siren cut the night behind us.

"Damn," I said. "A cop . . ."

"Screw the cop," Siegel said, holding her to him. "Keep stepping on it."

The cop didn't catch us till we pulled in the emergency entrance, by which time he'd more or less figured out what the score was; just the same, Siegel quickly, pointlessly, handed the guy a C-note, which would buy you twenty traffic tickets in Chicago.

The orderlies lifted Hill's slack body onto a stretcher and wheeled her into the emergency room and before long we were in a private room and Siegel was shaking the hand of the doctor who had pumped Mrs. Siegel's stomach.

You see, Virginia Hill, it turned out, was Mrs. Benjamin Siegel. That was the name she was admitted under, anyway.

"Doc," Siegel said, turning on the charm, dazzling smile and all, pumping the man's hand harder than Ginny's stomach had been, "thanks a million. I just might donate a new wing to this joint."

Virginia Hill, groggy, looked up and said her first words since rejoining the living: "Give 'em the fucking Flamingo for a wing. To hell with that dump. Get out, Ben, before you're dead! Before you're dead . . ."

And she was crying.

He began comforting her, and the doctor and Chick and I slipped away.

I said to Chick, "They're *married?*"

Chick shrugged affirmatively. "It isn't common knowledge. They did it in Mexico a while back."

"Why's it a secret?"

"It's not exactly a secret, but I don't think some of Ben's friends back east approve of my sister."

"Hell, I thought she was in tight with them."

"That was before she and Ben got so close. She hasn't done any business with them since."

A few minutes later, Siegel came out. He smiled a little; it was almost a nervous smile, and I wondered why.

Then I found out.

"Nate," he said, "I want you to take that little girl of yours home."

"That little girl of mine."

"Peggy Hogan. It's just not going to work, having her around. It's just gonna be a burr under Tabby's saddle."

Our voices echoed a little in the hospital corridor.

"Well, we can't have that, now," I said. "But what if Miss Hogan doesn't care to go?"

"I took care of that already. You just go back to the Frontier. Knock on her door."

"Christ, it's almost four o'clock in the morning, Ben!"

"Do it, Nate. She's up. I called her." He swallowed. Then, as if mildly ashamed of himself, he grinned like a chagrined kid. "Tabby made me call her."

But I didn't knock on her door. I went back to my own room at the Last Frontier. I'd had quite enough emotional bullshit for one night.

And I was between the cool sheets of the warm bed, just tired enough to go right to sleep in spite of it all, when somebody knocked on my door. I let some air out. I stared up into the darkness where the ceiling was. And somebody knocked again, kept knocking. Then I hauled myself out of bed. I was in my skivvies but I didn't give a damn.

I opened the door.

She was standing there in a dressing gown, her hair a mess, her face scratched, not a trace of make-up, her expression blank with despair. I couldn't help myself. I touched her cheek, gently, where it was scratched.

"I'm sorry, Peg."

Her voice was the voice of a small child. "Will you take me home, Nate?"

"Sure, baby."

Her violet eyes stared into nothing. "Thank you. I really appreciate it."

She turned to walk away. Her steps were halting. I went to her; I was in the hall in my underwear, but at this time of night—of morning—who the hell cared? I put an arm around her.

"Are you okay?"

"No," she said, in the same small voice.

Then she tumbled into my arms. Grabbed me, like she was grabbing for dear life, and she wept. She wept.

I drunk-walked her back to my room, sat her on the edge of the bed, sat next to her, and let her cry into my chest as long as she wanted, which was a good long while.

"He . . . he called me . . . and said we were through."

"I know," I said.

In the midst of the emotional pain, she still managed to hear that; she squinted at me and said, "You . . . you *know*?"

I told her briefly about the suicide attempt.

"He . . . he was calling me from her hospital room, then?"

"That's right."

"She was there."

"Sure."

"You know what he said to me?"

"No."

"He said she told him that he had to choose. That it was her or me." She swallowed. "And he chose her."

I said nothing; she had stopped crying.

"Can you beat that?" she said, wonderingly.

"I think I can," I said. "They're married."

Her eyes went wide and, finally, angry. "Married?"

I nodded. "Married. Mexico. A while back."

"I've been . . . having an affair with a married man. And I didn't even know it."

"That's it."

She sat there and brooded for a while.

Then she stood. She stripped off the dressing robe; the garment made a pool at her feet. She had her short sheer blue nightie on underneath; I remembered it well.

"Take your things off," she said, through her teeth.

"Okay," I said, and did.

She stepped out of the nightie. She was tan, now, except the patches of creamy pink where her two-piece bathing suit had been; the bushy triangle between her legs was startling against the pale flesh.

"Do it to me," she said, laying back on the bed, parting her lips, her legs, herself.

She just wanted revenge on Siegel. I knew that.

But I'd take it anyway I could get it.

I plunged into her like a knife and took my own sweet revenge, and she was crying when she came. I didn't give her my tears; I gave her my fucking seed. That was enough.

Then I held her in my arms, cradled her, soothed her, like Ben had the unconscious Virginia Hill, and she fell asleep there.

On Sunday, the day of rest, we made love half a dozen times, in

between some silly bursts of sightseeing—Boulder Dam, anyone?—
and yanking the arms off slot machines downtown and buying stupid
touristy souvenirs for the folks back home. And then on Monday,
before we caught our train, we found our way to one of those stucco
and neon wedding chapels and did the deed. It was her idea, but I
was game; what was Vegas for, if not to take a gamble?

22

The following June, on a warm but not scorching Friday afternoon, I was once again in Los Angeles, comparing notes with my partner Fred Rubinski in his fifth-floor Bradbury Building office. We were both pleased with the way our little merger had worked out. Technically, I was the boss, because I had bought fifty-one percent of his business; but I'd made him vice-president of A-1 Detective Agency, leaving him full rein over the L.A. end of the firm. The reality was our two agencies ran as independently as ever, only with me getting a piece of his action; and the appearance of being a nationwide agency now (I was working on lining up an office in New York, as well, which would make it more than just an appearance) was increasing business on both our ends, as well as making easier any investigations spanning both our parts of the country. I was up to ten operatives and Fred was up to half a dozen.

Business out of the way, talk turned social—although in our case such talk still ran to cops and crooks.

"I understand Bill Drury's got himself in a jam," Fred said, frowning, emphasizing the deep lines of his weathered face which so contrasted with his smooth shiny bald head.

"Sad but true," I said. "And no surprise. State's Attorney's office has him up on charges."

"What sort of charges?"

"Conspiring to obtain an indictment on false testimony. Two of Bill's colored witnesses on the Ragen shooting went public about Bill offering 'em part of the twenty-five grand reward."

"Shit. Great. Can he beat the rap?"

"I don't know. And both colored witnesses recanted, to boot, so those three West Side bookies who pulled the shooting are home free."

"What a world," Fred said, shaking his head. "Drury may go to jail, and the shooters walk. How do you figure it?"

VIRGINIA HILL'S PLACE

"I figure I'm better off in the private sector. If Bill shakes loose of this thing, I'm going to try to get him to come aboard A-1."

"I'm for it," Fred said, with a tight smile, nodding. Fred's intercom buzzed and he answered. "Yes, Marcia?"

"A gentleman's here to see you, Mr. Rubinski."

"Does he have an appointment?"

"No . . ."

"Well, I'm in conference. Make an appointment."

"It's Mr. Siegel, Mr. Rubinski."

"Ben Siegel?"

"Yes, sir."

"Send him in."

Ben entered, looking dapper as ever in a gray plaid suit and a dark blue tie; but he'd lost weight, had a pallor odd for a guy who operated out of sunny Vegas. And he wasn't even bothering to use make-up on the darkness circling his baby blues.

His smile was as dazzling as ever, though. "Nate Heller! Jesus, this is a pleasant surprise . . ."

I stood and grinned at him and we shook hands.

"What's this I hear about you gonna be a father?" he said, still pumping my hand.

"It's a fact," I said. "Late September, if the docs know what they're talking about."

He pulled up a chair, and I sat back down. He said, "The little woman must not be so little, these days."

"She's out to here," I admitted.

"You gonna name it after me?"

"Only if it's a girl."

Siegel frowned. "Just so you don't call her Bugsy."

And then he laughed and so did I.

Fred, smiling, said, "What's the occasion, Ben?"

He pointed a thumb behind him. "I stopped in to see my lawyer, Joe Ross."

Ross also had an office in the Bradbury Building.

"Went over the account books," Siegel went on, "and some legal problems concerning the hotel. Joe's doing Virginia's tax returns, for one thing."

"How's Ginny doing?" I asked.

He shrugged, smirked. "She's in Paris. We had a fight and she took off. She'll get over it."

"Hope it's not serious."

"Naw, it's nothing. I'm even staying in her place. So, how are you guys getting along, now that you're in bed together?"

"Fine," I said.

"No complaints," Fred said. "I'm glad you dropped by, Ben. You probably want to find out how I been doing with your checks."

"That's right," Siegel said, smiling, but a little anxious.

"It's not good news," Fred said, with a fatalistic shrug. "All I've got is five hundred dollars for you."

Siegel's mouth twitched disappointment in what was otherwise a business-like expression. "Hell, Fred, you've got better than one hundred thousand bucks worth of checks you're working on . . ."

"There's not much we can do. It's not a violation of the law in this state to refuse paying gambling debts. Of course, these welshers can't go back to Nevada, but if they were still in Nevada, you wouldn't need me. We can call them, write them letters, go 'round and see them; but we don't go in for bullying tactics. You knew that when you hired us."

"That rough stuff's no good for business, anyway," Siegel said, distantly.

"More than that, I was informed just yesterday by the Bureau of Standards that our detective license doesn't permit us to collect bad checks."

"So," Siegel said, a hint of irritation entering his voice, "you're just going to kick 'em back to me?"

"No, not exactly," Fred said, soothingly. "We're just going to farm them out to a collection agency. Mutual. Any objections?"

Siegel shook his head no, his expression a little glazed. The baby blues looked quite bloodshot.

"How *is* business at the Flamingo, Ben?" I asked.

"Bad," he said, distractedly. Then he turned his gaze and his smile on me: "Actually, real good. That advice you gave me to close up and clean house and start over was just the ticket."

Siegel had closed up less than two weeks after his gala opening; he had re-opened in March, the hotel completed, a largely new staff in place.

"We cleared three hundred thousand in May," he said, proudly. "Problem is, we still got a lot of creditors hounding us. And then that fucking Wilkerson . . ." Bitterness twisted his mouth. ". . . he gets a phone call from J. Edgar Hoover and pees his pants."

"What?" I said. "Hoover called Wilkerson?"

"Yeah," Ben said, waving it off. "Hoover calls Billy and asks him if he knows he's 'in league' with a gangster. And the little fucker pretends he never knew a thing about my background. So he decides he has to get out of the Flamingo 'immediately if not sooner,' 'cause of how it 'might look,' publisher of the Hollywood *Reporter* 'hobnobbing with unsavory characters.'"

"Christ, he was one of your first investors."

"Well, all I know is, before I die, there's two guys I'm gonna kill. Sedway and Wilkerson, the two biggest bastards that ever lived."

I was used to hearing him say things like that, but it was still a little chilling.

Fred said to me, "Wilkerson insisted Ben buy him out, overnight, and said if he didn't, he'd blackball him with the press."

"Over a hundred grand, it cost me," Siegel said.

"How's the situation with the boys back east?" I asked.

"They know I've turned the corner," he said, trying to sound confident and not quite making it. His smile was not dazzling at the moment, more like a wrinkle in his thin face.

"I understand Trans-American is still running," I said.

He nodded. "I compromised. I withdrew my demand of two million dollars to shut the wire down. Instead, I just asked 'em to let me keep it running for one more lousy year. That should catch me up, financially . . . of course there's some grumbling over my price hike . . ."

"What price hike?"

He shrugged matter-of-factly. "I doubled the cost of the wire to the bookies. That brings me over fifty grand a week, from Trans-American. A year of that, and a year of the Flamingo on a roll, and I'm in like Flynn."

"How, uh, are your customers taking the price hike?"

"Who the fuck cares? Those bookies are rolling in dough. And so will I be, with their help—and now that the summer tourist season's in swing."

I couldn't imagine the bookies would sit still for this gouge, nor
that Lansky, Luciano and the Combination would approve. But it was
none of my business, so I said nothing.

"Well," Siegel said, slapping his thighs, standing, "I guess that's it.
You gonna keep me posted about the bad-check situation, Fred, or
somebody at Mutual?"

"Mutual," Fred said. "They'll be contacting you." He stood behind
his desk and shook hands with Siegel.

Who crooked his finger at me, smiling a little, and said, "Walk me
out, Nate."

He went out and I followed, looking back at Fred and shrugging
some.

Outside the office, dappled with sunlight filtering in the Bradbury
Building skylight, Siegel put a hand on my shoulder. "What are you
doing tonight?"

"Nothing," I said, shrugging again. "Maybe I'll go to Grauman's
Chinese and see if my feet fit Gable's."

"I got a better idea. Let me buy you some supper. We'll talk old
times."

"Sure," I said. "Shall I meet you somewhere?"

"Good idea. We're trying a new place called Jack's-at-the-Beach."

"Where's that?"

"At the beach, schmuck. It's in Ocean Park."

"Where's Ocean Park?"

"Santa Monica. You can find the place. I got faith in you. You're a
detective."

He flashed his smile and walked over to the open cage of the elevator. He was alone; no bodyguards. Despite his pallor, his loss of
weight, his obvious lack of sleep, he didn't seem worried for his life. I
guessed it was safe to eat with him.

So I ate with him. Him and Chick Hill and Chick's girlfriend, a
cute little redhead who had taken over for Peggy as Virginia Hill's
secretary, and a smooth, silver-haired guy named Al Smiley, who
was a business associate of Ben's and wore a snappy checked jacket
and snazzy blue patterned tie. Jack's-at-the-Beach was an ex-
clusive little joint, with rough-hewn wood and seafaring touches.
We sat near a window where we could watch the waves roll slowly,
foaming up onto the sand. It was peaceful, soothing, steady. The
sea, the beach, were bathed in silvers and blues, thanks to a clear

night and the moon and stars. I had the feeling of being on the edge of the world; and the feeling that that world was a tiny insignificant place in a vast universe. Of course, I'd had several glasses of wine, when all this occurred to me, so I wouldn't put a whole hell of a lot of stock in it.

"Ben," I said, after the remains of our seafood dinners had been cleared away and we sat chatting, "if you don't mind my saying so, you look a little tired. Getting the Flamingo up on its feet's been an ordeal for you. Why don't you take a rest or a vacation or something?"

Siegel, who was sipping his single glass of wine for the evening, smiled almost shyly. "I am tired, Nate. And I am going to get away for a few days. My two daughters are coming out from New York by train. To meet me here."

"Well, that's great."

He smiled more broadly, nodded. "They're great kids. I promised to take them to Lake Louise up in Canada."

"Now you're talking," I said, smiling back at him.

He glanced at his watch. "It's early yet. Not even ten. How about coming back to the house with us? I got something I wouldn't mind running past you."

"I don't know, Ben . . ."

He stood, picking up the check. "Aw, come on. Georgie's gonna drop by around eleven or so, and we can play some cards or something."

I hadn't seen Raft this trip; I wouldn't mind seeing him.

"Sure," I said. "What house is this where we're going?"

"Virginia's bungalow," he said. "Follow us up Wilshire. We'll show you the way."

Thirty-five minutes or so later, give or take, we drew up in front of the Beverly Hills haunts of La Hill, hardly a bungalow, rather a Moorish castle of pale pink adobe with a red tile roof on North Linden Drive. The near mansion had obviously cost big bucks, but it was surprisingly close on either side to its next-door neighbors, and the sloping lawn was relatively modest. I left my A-1 Agency Ford at the curb across the way, while the powder-blue Cadillac driven by Smiley (whose car it was) went up into the car port alongside the house.

Ben and his little party of three came down to greet me at the sidewalk and go up the short flight of cement steps to the walk, where at the front door Siegel produced a solid gold key (a gift from Tabby). Chick and Jerri, who seemed to be an item, had their arms around each other's waists; Smiley had a newspaper, the early edition of tomorrow's *Times,* courtesy of Jack's-at-the-Beach. The night air was full of night-blooming jasmine.

Siegel unlocked the door, stepped inside, flicking on the hall light, and we all followed him into the spacious living room.

Which wasn't a particularly attractive room, despite Virginia Hill's redecorating efforts. I couldn't help but think how classy Falcon's Lair had been (a "dump" to Ginny) and how tacky this room was, with its bronze cupid statue, marble Bacchus statue, oil painting of an English dowager on the wall over the fireplace fighting a nearby art deco study of a nude with wine glass, French Provincial coffee table, the flowery chintz divan clashing with the flowery drapes of the windows behind it.

Siegel settled on that divan, at the right end of it, taking the newspaper from Smiley, who sat down at the divan's left end. I took a comfortable easy chair to one side of Siegel, who said to Chick and his girl, "Why don't you kids go upstairs? I want to talk some business with Al and Nate."

Chick was agreeable to the notion of going upstairs with his little redhead—who wouldn't have been?—and the redhead was equally agreeable and, so, they disappeared. Ben was glancing at the paper as he spoke: "I'd like you to come to work for me, Nate."

"Ben, we've been down that road before . . ."

"No we haven't. I'm not talking about security work." He looked at me; bloodshot they may have been, but those baby blues were magnets when he trained them on you just right. "I think you got a lot on the ball. You gave me good advice at the Flamingo, when everybody else around me was either kissing my ass or stealing from me—or both, like Moey."

"It was just common sense."

"Yeah, well I seen how you're doing with your own business. Which is to say, very well. I have a lot of legitimate business interests, now—that's why I wanted you to meet Al, here. We got some feelers out on an oil deal; and we got a legitimate business in salvage materials called California Metals."

Smiley was smiling, nodding. I didn't know much about the guy,

although Fred had mentioned this "business associate" of Ben's had a
rap sheet as long as a player-piano roll.

"Anyway, I want you to consider getting involved with me on a
management level. An executive level."

"That's flattering, Ben—but I don't really want to be doing business with the likes of Jack Dragna or even Mickey Cohen . . ."

"You won't be. Those guys are involved in areas wholly outside
what you would be. Nate, consider this . . ."

Glass crashed as gunfire rocked the room, shook Ben like a ragdoll,
his right eye flying, nose crushed, and I hit the deck; so did Smiley,
who yelped, a bullet nicking his arm. Rapidly, the gunfire, from a
carbine, a .30-30 from the sound of it, chewed up Ben and the room,
another slug entering from behind his head and turning his face into a
mask of blood. Smiley was scrambling across the floor, like a crab,
moving past the couch and the dead Siegel and from where I was
plastered to the floor; he crawled inside the fireplace. I wish I'd
thought of it.

Marble statues shattered; bullets ate patterns in the walls; the
dowager in the picture took a slug; so did the nude with the wine-
glass. Meanwhile, Ben's head rolled back against the divan as if he
finally had found time to rest, but his body danced as more slugs
came tearing through the couch behind him, cracking ribs, shearing
muscle and organs.

Then silence.

There had been nine shots—a full carbine clip—and I waited, flat
on my face on the floor, to see if another clip would follow.

Then Chick, in T-shirt and boxer shorts, was running into the
room, a .38 in hand.

"Get down!" I yelled, and he had sense to.

A minute later, though, I moved toward the kid, staying low, and
put my hand out. "Give me that—I'm going after them."

"Who?"

"Whoever killed Ben. Give it to me!"

He did, and I crawled across the room and got up against the wall
and edged along till I was next to the windows, that is the yawning
place where the window glass had been. I thrust myself into that
firing line, .38 held out in two hands, faced the jagged-edged former
window, but there was nobody there: just the rose trellis beyond,
where the carbine had no doubt been steadied.

I jumped out, feet landing on cement and glass, the latter crunching under my shoes.

I could see a figure moving across the enclosed back patio, by the pool; then he was hopping over the cement fence and into the alley, where a car no doubt waited.

Chick was looking out the window.

"Call Cohen," I said. "Find out what he wants done, and then call the cops."

"Why do it that way?"

"Because it's what Ben would want. Do it!"

I didn't wait for a response. I ran down to my Ford and got in and started it up. I did not turn on the lights. I sat and waited and watched the intersection of Linden and Whittier to my back. Seconds later a battered green Pontiac—very wrong for Beverly Hills—went lumbering by. In no hurry.

I was in no hurry, either. I did a slow, easy U-turn and turned past the small dividing island onto Whittier, a wooded, winding street, expensively residential. I kept my lights off. The Pontiac was up ahead.

Perhaps two minutes later, they turned right on Wilshire. I kept well back. At times I turned my lights on. Other times I pulled over and parked and waited while they (I could make out at least two shapes in the car) were stopped at a light. Westwood Boulevard was one such stop; Bundy, another. I kept at my quiet pursuit as Wilshire dropped ever so gradually to the ocean, through toney residential districts and blocks of apartment houses and a business district now and then. I kept thinking of that newspaper Ben had been reading, which had wound up bloody in his lap. The paper, given him courtesy of the restaurant's management, had been stamped: *Good night. Sleep well with our compliments.*

I wanted a smoke, but I didn't have any. We passed a military cemetery at Veteran and Wilshire, an infinity of white crosses; soon we crossed through a sprawling complex of modern wooden buildings, a V.A. hospital. I'd been following the enemy—and I hoped that was who they were, I hoped my instincts about the battered Pontiac were correct—for fifteen minutes, now.

Maybe there were some cigarettes in the glove compartment, yes! Camels, and I didn't even have to walk a mile for them. I lit one up, sucked the harsh smoke into my lungs. Sweat beaded my forehead.

The night was pleasantly warm, rushing in my rolled-down windows, but my eyes were burning.

I got up fairly close behind them, in Santa Monica. Three of them. Three shapes. I checked the .38. Six bullets.

Resting the gun on the seat beside me, I dropped back, kept my distance as they led me from Wilshire to Palisades Beach Road and up Pacific Coast Highway. The world had become strangely desolate, suddenly; the lights of Santa Monica winked in my rear view mirror, civilization bidding me a wry farewell, but to my right was a cliffside, and to my left, not more than five hundred yards, was the water line, waves beating against the shore every twenty seconds or so, sounding distant and yet a roar. That, and the hum of the motor, was all that kept me company on this eerily quiet drive along the coast; oh, and the sight of the red rear lights of the car glowing up ahead. I was driving with my lights on, now, but I was back well enough, and there was some traffic out here to cover me. Not much, though. Not much.

Just past where Sunset Boulevard emptied out, a busy street dissipating down to the middle of nowhere, the Pontiac pulled over, off the road, onto the sandy shoulder. They had another car waiting there. A dark blue Plymouth parked there, newer than what they were driving, which was either stolen or black-market untraceable.

I glided past them, and saw them, bathed in moonlight, one man in a Hawaiian shirt, two others wearing sportjackets, getting out of one car, heading to the other.

Old friends. Small world.

The man who'd been driving was Bud Quinn, formerly a lieutenant with the LAPD, formerly an employee of the late Benjamin Siegel; it was Quinn wearing the Hawaiian shirt, of course. His two riders were boys from out of town who needed a savvy chauffeur like Quinn.

They were from Chicago. West Side boys. Like me.

Well, not quite like me. They were bookies. Name of Davey Finkel and Joseph "Blinkey" Leonard.

And this time they'd pulled off a hit without a hitch.

Almost.

I slowed, threw it in reverse and hit the pedal.

The car had screeched to a stop just next to them, as they froze in their procession toward their nearby second car, and their eyes were wide and white in the night as I leaned out the window and said, "Any of you boys know the way to the V.A. hospital?"

Widow's-peaked Finkel was just opposite me, and I opened the car door into him, hard, throwing him back, hard, onto the sandy ground. I jumped out, .38 in hand and before I could tell them not to, both Quinn and Blinkey went for guns, Quinn to a .38 stuck in his waistband, Blinkey clawing under his unbuttoned jacket.

Quinn I shot in the head, right above the bridge of his nose and he went back hard in a mist of red and thudded in the sand, his gun in hand, at the ready. Blinkey, having trouble maneuvering his gun from his shoulder holster, thought twice and ran, heading toward the beach and the lapping waves. Finkel was still on his back, but was making a move for his gun; I kicked him in the head and he stopped.

I ran after Blinkey; he had his gun out, now, and was looking back at me, moonlight glinting off the glass of his glasses, and he was shooting back at me, the gunshots sounding strangely hollow in this big empty landscape. We ran in slow motion, the sand under our feet making a mockery of the chase, but when he reached the shoreline, he seemed to pick up speed, feet leaving impressions in the wet sand, foam flicking his ankles, and he was smiling crazily as he looked back at me and aimed and I put a bullet in one of his eyes, glass cracking. His howl could barely be heard over the crash of the surf, and he went splashing back into the sea, his feet on the sand, toes up, his body covered, and then unconvered, and then covered by the tide.

I was walking back toward my car when another shot rang out, and I felt a bullet hit me just above the left temple; it threw me back, on my ass, and blood streamed down into my face, into my left eye. I wasn't dead or even dying; it had to be just a bad graze, and I was pushing up with one hand when I saw Finkel looming above me, his impressively ugly face a symphony of bushy eyebrows, thick lips, and facial moles, his rotten teeth pulled into a ghastly smile. His head was bleeding some, too, from where I kicked him; he wasn't dead, either, or dying, and he seemed to take glee in pointing his automatic down at me.

I shot him in the smile and his teeth went away and so did he; he went back, hard, though the sand cushioned the blow, not that it mattered, as now he was dead, or dying, and I struggled to my feet, wiping the blood off my temple and forehead, getting sand in the wound, blinking, the sand under my feet slowing me down as I moved toward my Ford.

I got behind the wheel. Put the gun on the seat beside me. Lit up a cigarette. Sat and smoked and glanced out at the landscape, littered with bodies, turned silver and blue in the moon and starlight.

Then I drove away.

23

I drove north. By all rights I should have headed back to the city, but I drove north. I was bleeding. Blood was flowing gently, not gushing or anything, just trickling down over my eyebrow into my eye. I held a handkerchief to my head and drove with one hand. The ocean at my left remained a constant, reassuring presence; to my right the cliffs moved gradually back and became hills.

Finally there was a T intersection with a diner and a gas station and a phone booth. I stumbled into the latter, feeling woozy.

I had enough change to put a call through to Fred Rubinski, at home.

"What the hell is it, Nate?" he said thickly. "It's after midnight . . ."

"Do you have Cohen's number?"

"What are you talking about?"

"Mickey Cohen's number. Can you reach Mickey Cohen?"

"Sure, yeah, I suppose. I got his unlisted number in my black book. Why?"

"Call him and give him this." I read off the pay phone's number. "Tell him that's where he can reach me. Tell him to call right away."

"Okay, but what's up?"

"They hit Ben Siegel tonight."

"Jesus!"

"He was sitting on the couch in Virginia Hill's place and somebody outside the window with a carbine shot him, good and dead."

"Jesus. Jesus. Where do you fit in?"

"What you don't know can't hurt you. But why don't you get dressed and go over and sniff out the situation. Protect my interests."

"Well, Christ, Nate, just how do your interests need protecting exactly?"

"Just do it, Fred. Play it by ear."

"Were you there when it went down?"

"I don't know yet. That's one of the things I gotta find out."

"Oh, brother." He paused. "You know, you don't sound so good. Are you all right?"

"I'm on top of the world. Call Cohen."

I hung up.

I sat down in the booth, my butt inside it, my feet hanging out onto the cinder parking area of the diner. Nobody tried to use the phone, or if they did, saw me sitting there and said the hell with it.

My teeth were chattering, and my head was burning. What was this, a fucking malaria flare-up? Hell of a time. Why wouldn't my forehead stop bleeding? I didn't feel so good.

The phone rang.

"This is Heller."

"This is Mick. What the fuck happened?"

I told him.

"Fuck a duck! You nailed all *three* of 'em?"

"That's right. So what's the score? Do I go to the cops, Mick, or do you just clean up after me?"

"Nobody saw it happen? Not a soul?"

"Not a living one."

"I got to talk to somebody."

"Who? Dragna?"

"What you don't know won't hurt you, pal."

Where had I heard that before?

The phone clicked dead.

I hung up, sat down and waited some more. I still felt punk; feverish. Was I in shock? Did I have a concussion? Did I still have a screw loose that triggered some kind of ersatz malaria flare-up after a "combat" situation? Totally sane people don't get mustered out on a Section Eight, after all.

The phone rang.

"You was never there."

"Never where, Mick?"

"Anywheres. Not at Siegel's house or the beach, neither. In fact, nothing happened at the beach."

"If you say so."

"What was you usin'?"

"A .38 I got from Chick, at Siegel's house."

"You're calling from where, exactly?"

"I don't know. I'm not exactly a native. Somewhere near Malibu, I suppose."

I read off the name of the diner and the gas station.

"Toss the piece in the drink," Cohen advised, meaning the .38.

"Just that easy, huh? Then head back to L.A.?"

"No. Keep driving. Before long you'll see a motor court. El Camino Motel. Don't even check in. You'll find unit seven unlocked."

"I could use some rest," I admitted. "But I want to get out of here soon as I can. I got a flight out Sunday morning."

"Good, 'cause with that wound of yours, you got to duck the cops."

"But, Mick, I was seen with Ben at that restaurant."

"Right. So they're gonna want to talk to you. Fine. Just get out of town before they have a chance."

"Maybe I ought to just drive back to the city and check in with the cops . . ."

"You just killed three guys. You left the scene of a shooting. Two shootings. You was with Bugsy Siegel when he was hit. Any of this sound like anything you wanna be tied up with in court? In the papers? Any of this sound good for business?"

"No," I said.

"No is right. Meantime, we'll get a doctor for you."

"I don't need a doctor," I said, blinking blood out of my left eye.

"Jack says you got to have a doctor. We got our own guy who don't report gunshot wounds, you know?"

"It's just a graze," I said, but my legs were wobbly.

"Better safe than sorry. Now do it."

"Okay," I said, and hung up.

I walked back to the car, feeling shaky, wondering if my judgment was worth a fuck. Was this a set-up? Was I a loose end they were going to tie off?

No. That wasn't like Cohen at all. He was a straight shooter, and he hated the Capone crowd like poison—and this hit had obviously gone down from the Chicago end, either at the request, or with the complicity of, the east coast Combination.

As I mulled this over, behind the wheel of the Ford, I realized I was feeling better. The gash at the edge of my forehead had clotted over; no more blood in my eye.

I drove easily, but my thoughts were racing. Cohen and Dragna

were Ben's partners. I'd play it their way. If I got tied up with another mob killing this major, I'd never shake the "mob guy" reputation. That was not what A-1 needed right now. That was not what
Nate Heller needed, either. I was going to have another mouth to
feed, soon.

The motor court was on the right of the highway, with a view of the
beach, a dozen stucco cottages lorded over by a neon sign incorporat-
ing a clock with the cursive neon letters, EL CAMINO MOTEL. I parked
in front of unit seven, found it unlocked and went on into the small,
clean room with its plaster walls and ranch style furniture. It had a
phone, a radio, a shower. This much civilization under one little red-
tile roof was comforting to me, about now.

I stripped to my T-shirt and went in the john and threw cold water
on my face, looked at my head, where it was grazed, which was scab-
bing over. I sat on the edge of the bed, still feeling shaken, but
better. Better. What had happened on that beach, perhaps forty minutes ago, seemed distant. Unreal.

The lamp by my bedside had a three-way switch; I turned it to its
lowest setting and sacked out on the bed, on top of the nubby spread.
I felt bone tired but couldn't seem to doze. I wished I could call
Peggy, the nearby phone tempting me; but I didn't dare. It was two
hours later back there, anyway.

I hadn't even faced yet whether this was something I would tell her
about; of course, she'd be glad to hear the men who shot her uncle—
two of the three involved, anyway—were gone. I'd probably be a
hero to her. Nice to get *something* out of killing three people.

Finally I did doze, but the knock at my door ended that.

I sat up, tasting the film in my mouth, and took the gun off the
nightstand and answered the knock.

"I'm the doctor," the man standing there said. "I presume you're
the patient."

He was a thin, dryly tan man in his forties, wearing thick-lensed
glasses, a yellow short-sleeve sportshirt and tan slacks, and carrying a
black medical bag in one hand. He might have stepped off a golf
course, but for that bag, and a drowsy air of having been rudely
awakened for a house call.

"I'm the patient," I said, narrowing my eyes, studying him, making
way for him as he came in.

I knew him. I knew this guy.

"Why, you're Nate Heller," he said, pointing at me, smiling. "Well, small world."

He extended his free hand and I shook it, moving the .38 over into my left hand.

"Dr. Snaden," I said, gun back in my right hand again. "I'd forgotten you were heading out to California."

"Gave up my Miami practice, yes. Isn't this the most amazing coincidence," he said, shaking his head, heading for the bed, where he opened the medical bag.

"An amazing coincidence," I said. "I haven't seen you since Meyer House. Since Jim Ragen died."

He was sticking a hypodermic into a small bottle, filling it up with clear fluid. "Jim was a fine man. That was a rough one to lose."

"You know, frankly, Doc, I think you're wasting your time. I feel fine. It's just a graze. I'm not bleeding. Why don't you just go on home and back to bed. Sorry to bother."

I was standing by the door.

"Nonsense," he said. "You need something for pain, and for tetanus. I have my instructions."

I trained the .38 on him. "I bet you do. Now, just get the fuck out of here. You wouldn't be the first son of a bitch I shot tonight."

His eyes were big behind the thick lenses. "Mr. Heller—what in the world is wrong?"

"You were Jim Ragen's doctor in Miami. Christ, I should have known. How stupid could I be? You were a mob doctor down there. You moved there from Chicago, didn't you? Capone, Nitti, Fischetti, it's been an Outfit convention in Miami for twenty years. With Jim's Outfit ties, who else would his Miami physician be but connected?"

"This is foolish."

"Put the needle in the bag."

"Mr. Heller . . ."

"Put. The. Needle. In. The. Fucking. Bag."

He put the needle in the fucking bag.

"All my precautions," I said, smiling bitterly, "monitoring who goes in and out of that room. All the investigating trying to figure who could've poisoned Jim. Was it in the food? A salve some nurse rubbed on him? Hell, no. It was his own goddamn family doctor."

He seemed calm, but there was nervousness underneath. "Maybe

I *should* leave. Even though it's clear you're in shock from your trauma . . ."

"I heard you were moving your practice out to California. I didn't think much about it, at the time . . . but I'm thinking, now. I'm thinking your big-money Miami patients are thinning out—first Nitti up and dies, and then Ricca and the rest go to stir. And I hear a lot of the east coast boys are spending time on the west coast these days . . . business interests, homes in Palm Springs, and so on. Moving your practice out here starts to make sense."

"You're obviously very . . . disoriented right now, Mr. Heller . . ."

"This isn't Cohen's work, is it? Dragna, then? I don't know much about him, though I've heard he has some east coast ties. So maybe that makes sense, too. But he slipped up sending *you*. You didn't know it was me who was wounded out here, did you? And whoever sent you didn't know that the two of us had run into each other before. Christ, did you do Cermak, too? You were one of his doctors. This is a consultation that's been overdue for about thirteen years, Doc . . ."

He swallowed. Smiled, in a twitchy way, cracking his parchment tan. Said, "Perhaps I will just go. You're a very confused man. I do recommend you see a physician tomorrow, as soon as possible."

"Hey, heal your fuckin' self, Doc." I gestured toward the door with the gun. "Now get out of here before I give you the cure to everything . . ."

He snapped the bag shut, swallowed again, nodded to me, and moved quickly toward the door; as he opened it with one hand, he swung the black bag with savage speed and force and clipped me right on the head, where the wound was.

Gun flying from my fingers, I hit the wood floor on my back with a teeth-rattling thump, blood running down my face, into my eyes, consciousness slipping away . . .

Something was squeezing my arm.

I opened my eyes; I was still on my back, on the floor. A rubber strap was around my left forearm, tight, my veins standing out like a bas-relief map.

Thin, tan Snaden was leaning over me, looking like a mad scientist, eyes wide and intense behind his thick lenses, sweating, hypo in hand; with his thumb he tested it, and a little squirt of the stuff he intended for me ejaculated prematurely.

I watched this through slitted eyes; his big eyes behind the glasses were looking at my arm, one hand cradling it, as his other hand with the needle descended.

My other arm was free. And I lashed out and latched onto his wrist, gripping as hard as I could; he was surprised, and in the moment his surprise gave me, I brought up my knee and kneed him in the stomach. It sent him back, rattling into some furniture, knocking a chair over, and he hit his head; it stunned him. He wasn't unconscious, but he was good and goddamned dazed. He was that way when I sank that needle into his own arm, pushing the plunger in all the way, covering his mouth with my hand to stifle his scream.

I don't know what was in the hypo.

I only know it took him less than three minutes to pass out. He spent those three minutes weeping—"What have you done, oh God, oh God what have you done"—a pitiful pile of humanity on the wooden floor of the motel unit, a sack of flesh full of angular bones tossed up against an upended chair. Only I didn't pity him. He had killed Jim Ragen and God knows how many others. And he had tried to add me to his list of patients who hadn't pulled through.

He had some cigarettes in his breast pocket. I took the pack, Camels again, and shook one out and sat on the edge of the bed and smoked it, feeling calm; blood was caked on my face, but it wasn't running down from the wound any longer. My heartbeat was slowing to normal. I didn't feel feverish. I didn't feel woozy.

I felt just fine.

After the smoke, I tested for a pulse in his neck and there was none. I went in and splashed some water on my face, washed the blood off. Then I wiped the room of prints, leaving the .38 in his medical bag; perhaps he'd get tagged for what I'd done on the beach; perhaps this would be written off as suicide. That was up to the cops, and the mob boys who threw the party.

I drove to another motor court, five miles up the highway, and checked in and slept till three the next afternoon. At a nearby diner, where I convinced them to serve me breakfast, I read the papers and Ben's death was all over them. I wasn't mentioned in any of the accounts.

Nor was Dr. Snaden's death reported. Nor was there any mention of two West Side of Chicago bookies and one former LAPD police lieutenant being littered along the beach like so much bloody drift-wood.

So I drove back to Los Angeles, and on the way stopped at the place where it had happened, the crime scene if you will, and the beach stretched to the ocean like a pristine blanket of sand. There wasn't a single crumpled candy bar wrapper, let alone a corpse, and certainly no cops marking off the area for investigatory purposes. Nothing. Just the sound of gulls and the reflection of the sun off the sea and the gentle crash of the surf.

I touched my head where the grazed area was, scabbed over now. I did feel a little shaky, still. A warm breeze calmed me. Had all that happened last night? On this lonely stretch of sand? Or perhaps it was all a dream.

Like Ben Siegel's Flamingo.

Something interesting had happened, the night before, that only days later, via Fred Rubinski, became known to me.

Twenty minutes after Ben Siegel's handsome face was shattered by carbine fire through the window of Virginia Hill's home, Moe Sedway and Gus Greenbaum walked into the Flamingo and, in the name of its eastern investors, took over operations.

Less than twenty-four hours later, a stockholder's meeting was called. Greenbaum was put in charge of the resort; Sedway remained affiliated. The resort, after yet another million dollars was sunk into it, began to flourish. Hotels sprang up like cactuses on the strip, albeit gaudy ones: the Thunderbird, the Desert Inn, the Sands, the Sahara.

And the Stardust, which was Tony Cornero's last great dream. Tony dreamed even bigger than Siegel, envisioning the biggest resort hotel in the world. Working from a base of only ten grand, Tony got the 1,032-room hotel off the ground by luring in small investors via billboards and newspaper ads; unfortunately, the U.S. Securities and Exchange Commission didn't like the way he was going about it, including his not having registered with the SEC. "I'll win this battle or they'll carry me out feet first," Tony said, shortly before stepping up to a Desert Inn table where, while shooting craps, he fell across the green-felt table, dead of a heart attack.

Trans-American, of course, died just as suddenly; it was buried with Ben. Continental, run by Mickey McBride with certain silent partners, continued its land-office business until heat from the Kefauver Senate Crime Investigating Committee got it shut down.

Siegel's funeral was attended by his ex-wife, his brother (a respectable, respected doctor), and his two teenaged daughters. Virginia Hill was not there; nor was Raft or Cohen or Smiley or Chick or me; nor was anyone who worked at the Flamingo.

I was never drawn into the Siegel shooting, other than having a deposition taken at Central Headquarters in Chicago, where the cops didn't even ask about the bandage on my forehead; the deposition covered the dinner at Jack's-at-the-Beach and nothing else. According to the papers, neighbors reported seeing a man fleeing the house out the front, taking off in a Ford, but this stopped short of a viable physical description and a license number.

Dr. Snaden's death was ruled a suicide; the three dead men at the beach simply fell off the edge of the earth.

And I did tell Peggy about the beach shooting, and the "consultation" with Snaden, and she was delighted by the outcome of both, though reassuringly horrified by my having been through such scrapes.

My forehead remains scarred.

The indictment against Bill Drury was dropped due to a general unreliability of the two witnesses, but Bill was then called before a Grand Jury which demanded he reveal his dealings with those witnesses. Bill said he would gladly do so if he were promised immunity, should he reveal things indicating he might have been "shading" the law. Immunity wasn't granted, Bill refused to testify, and was dismissed from the force by the Civil Service Board for refusing to give testimony before a grand jury.

Bill did come to work for A-1 for a time; and he worked for the Chicago *American*, as well, doing crime exposés. He was about to give testimony to the Kefauver Committee when he was murdered in his car by hitmen with shotguns—a familiar enough scenario.

Bill had brought Mickey Cohen into the Kefauver fold, but after Bill's murder, Mickey turned out not to have anything much to say to the Committee. Incidentally, the Mick assured me, every time I encountered him in years to come, that he'd had no part of the attempt on my life at the El Camino. I believed him. When the clotheshorse roughneck died in 1976, I was sorry.

Mickey died of "natural causes"—not everybody in the rackets went out bloodily like Ben Siegel. Many a mob guy went quietly into that good night, including Meyer Lansky himself; Luciano, too; Sedway stepped off a plane in 1951 and had a heart attack and died (his partner Greenbaum, however, had his throat slit).

One evening in 1956, Jake Guzik died with greasy thumbs intact, having a heart attack while in the midst of pork chops and pay-offs at St. Hubert's; he was buried in a five-grand bronze coffin, and one of the boys mourning him was heard to say, "Christ, we coulda buried him in a fuckin' Cadillac for that!"

As for Virginia Hill, she became, of course, a star witness at the televised Kefauver hearings, managing to say very little while achieving a big celebrity. When next heard from, she'd taken a new husband and, fleeing the IRS, was living in Salzburg (Virginia had written the tax boys to tell them she'd not be setting foot in "your so-called Free World again," concluding by saying, "So fuck you and the whole United States government"). Forty-nine years old, less beautiful, less ornery, she swallowed sleeping pills that March morning in 1966, and lay down in the bed of snow by a stream in the woods and watched the clouds until they turned forever dark.

A year or so ago I visited Las Vegas, my second wife and me. The place seemed full of old people, myself and the missus included. Vegas all seemed so innocent now, and the neon, the glitter, seemed faded, shopworn. Jimmy Durante was dead. In his place you got Wayne Newton and faggots making tigers disappear. I wondered what Ben Siegel would've thought.

Hell, he probably would've loved it. He would take one look at Caesar's Palace or Circus Circus and be in heaven (as opposed to where he likely was now). He would ride up and down the wide neon-flung Strip and feel proud of what he'd accomplished with his life.

Funny, isn't it? The mob had worried about the bad publicity Ben was generating, afraid it would scare customers away; but it was the urge of Puritan Americans to take a safely sinful time-out that drew them to Lost Wages. It was a killing in Vegas, by way of Beverly Hills, that sparked their morbid curiosity, sent them flocking to the Flamingo in the wake of Siegel's bloody demise. To see where it all happened.

They still talk about him at the Flamingo Hilton, staff and guests alike; a flower bed near the pool is whispered about as being the grave for some hapless Siegel foe. Most of all, folks still want to see, even stay in, the penthouse (the Presidential Suite, now) where Ben and Tabby loved and fought.

You can see it, as clear as neon at night, can't you?

It wasn't Ben's life that gave birth to Vegas.

It was Bugsy's death.

I OWE THEM ONE:

Despite its extensive basis in history, this is a work of fiction; some liberties have been taken with the facts, though as few as possible—and any blame for historical inaccuracies is my own, reflecting, I hope, the limitations of my conflicting source material, and the need to telescope certain events to make for a more smoothly flowing narrative. In life, the intertwining stories of James Ragen and Benjamin Siegel had large casts of characters and complexities of event that defy the more necessarily tidy shape of a novel, requiring, upon occasion, the use of composite characters and compression of time.

It should be noted, however, that even the wholly fictional characters in this novel have historical counterparts, including Heller himself. James Ragen did indeed hire private detectives to serve as his bodyguards, and the portrayals of the shoot-out and Ragen's hospital stay in the first section of this novel are based tightly on fact. Readers who have, from time to time, accused Nate Heller of being a convenient witness to history—which he of course is, in a literary tradition that goes back at least as far as Alexandre Dumas—might consider that in every one of his "memoirs" to date, Heller has filled a role that a detective did, more or less, fill in the real-life events from which the novels are drawn.

Similarly, while Peggy Hogan is a fictional character, Jim Ragen's real-life niece was a secretary for Ragen's lawyer, and the situation described herein about the threats toward the lawyer and the secretary are based upon fact. The characterizations of Ellen Ragen and James Ragen, Jr., must be viewed as fictionalized ones, my imagined portraits drawn from sketchy newspaper accounts; Danny Ragen is a fictional character, although the number of Ragen children, their sexes and ages and so on also have been drawn from newspaper accounts of the day. Dr. Snaden is a fictional character, but Ragen was, during his hospital stay, attended in part by his doctor from Miami, who just happened to be in town, and who had indeed been one of

Mayor Cermak's attending physicians. From such factual acorns do fictional trees spring.

Again, I must single out my Chicago research associate George Hagenauer, whose role in shaping these novels is considerable. George goes beyond digging out research—which he does better than anyone—by discussing that research with me, exploring the potential for fiction in fact. I am grateful for his continuing efforts to make Heller's world real and interesting.

More than the usual thanks for support and help must go to my wife, Barb Collins, whose suggestions inevitably improve my work. I am especially grateful for her patience in allowing our trips to Las Vegas and Hollywood to be consumed with research—exploring bookstores and antique shops, conducting interviews, locating and "casing" sites of events, digging out and evaluating information; the one-armed bandits of Vegas that swallowed our silver were photocopy machines at the public library.

My thanks to Mary Bryant of the Flamingo Hilton, for her graciousness and generosity in providing background information and photos, as well as arranging a visit to the Presidential Suite (a.k.a., the Bugsy Siegel Suite).

I am especially grateful to Nate Schlaifer, who was at one time a dealer at the Flamingo and a personal friend of Ben Siegel's. Sitting on the terraced garden of the Flamingo, looking out on the pool, Mr. Schlaifer reminisced, confirming some legends and dispelling others, and generally bringing Bugsy to life. And if Siegel has come to life here, in these pages, it is at least partly due to Mr. Schlaifer's gracious help. And a tip of the fedora must go to Charlie Stump, formerly of the Four Queens, for bringing Nate Schlaifer and Nate Heller together.

Screenwriter Steve Kochneff gave generously of his time and expertise in the California portions of this novel; thanks, Starko. Thank you also to Steve's writing partner, Frank Esposito. Others who answered research questions include Lynn Myers, my guide through the Bradbury Building (via Carlisle, Pennsylvania); David Burns, archivist, Michael Reese Hospital; Jane Crawford of AAA Travel, Muscatine, Iowa; and my musical collaborators Ric Steed and Chuck Bunn.

Special tips of the fedora to Dominick Abel, my agent, and Tom Dunne, my editor, for their continued belief in Nate Heller and his ghost writer. And a thank you, too, to Michael Seidman and Tom Doherty of TOR Books for giving Heller a paperback lease on life.

The photos of James Ragen and of James Ragen and his son are copyrighted by the Chicago Tribune Company, Sept. 5, 1940, and June 24, 1946, respectively, all rights reserved, used with permission. Other photos selected by the author for use in this edition have been selected from private collections. Efforts to track down the sources of certain photos have been unsuccessful; upon notification, the author will list these sources in subsequent editions.

Five book-length nonfiction works about Ben Siegel and Virginia Hill proved of considerable help, most notably Dean Jennings' *We Only Kill Each Other* (1967). *Bugsy Siegel: The Man Who Invented Murder, Inc.* (1974) and *Virginia Hill: Queen of the Underworld* (1975), both by David Hanna, were also helpful. So were *Bugsy* (1973) by George Carpozi, Jr., and *The Mistress and the Mafia: The Virginia Hill Story* (1972) by Ed Reid.

Hundreds of books, and magazine and newspaper articles (from the *Tribune, Daily-News, Herald-American* and other Chicago papers, as well as the Las Vegas *Review-Journal*) have been consulted in researching *Neon Mirage*. Among the magazines are issues of *Ebony* (particularly the January 1950 issue, which features an autobiographical article by Sylvester Washington, the real-life police officer whose exploits inspired the fictional Two-Gun Pete Jefferson) and *Our World*, another Black-audience magazine which provided background for the Bronzeville section.

Despite the extensive list of books below, the bulk of research on this (and the previous novels from the "memoirs" of Nathan Heller) has been derived from newspaper files. Often the history books are at variance with eyewitness accounts as reported in papers of the day. For example, the commonly reported "fact" that the gala opening of the Flamingo was a poorly attended, dismal flop is dispelled by contemporary newspaper accounts (and the reminiscences of Mr. Schlaifer). No books, to my knowledge, have been written about James Ragen, and the first section of this novel draws heavily upon newspaper accounts, accordingly.

I am indebted to the anonymous authors of the Federal Writers Project volumes on the states of California and Nevada, which appeared in 1939 and 1940 respectively. Other books that deserve singling out include: *Chicago On Foot* (1977), Ira Bach; *Easy Street*

(1981), Susan Berman; *Las Vegas Playtown U.S.A.* (1955), Katharine Best and Katharine Hillyer; *Mickey Cohen In My Own Words* (1975), Mickey Cohen as told to Peer Nugent; *The California Crime Book* (1971), Robert Colby; *A Two-Dollar Bet Means Murder* (1961), Fred J. Cook; *Mafia* (1973), Fred J. Cook; *Captive City* (1969), Ovid Demaris; *The Last Mafioso* (1981), Ovid Demaris; *Meyer Lansky: Mogul of the Mob* (1979), Dennis Eisenberg, Uri Dan and Eli Landau; *The Luciano Story* (1954), Sid Feder and Joachim Joesten; *Hollywood Confidential* (1976), Jeffrey Feinman; *The Art of Detection* (1948), Jacob Fisher; *Hollywood Lawyer: The Jerry Giesler Story* (1960), Jerry Geisler as told to Pete Martin; *All of Our Lives: A Centennial History of Michael Reese Hospital and Medical Center, 1881-1981* (1981), edited by Sarah Gordon; *Where I Stand* (1966), Hank Greenspun with Alex Pelle; *Sunshine and Wealth: Los Angeles in the Twenties and Thirties* (1985), Bruce Henstell; *Uncle Frank: The Biography of Frank Costello* (1974), Leonard Katz; *Crime in America* (1951), Estes Kefauver; *Chicago Confidential* (1950), Jack Lait and Lee Mortimer; *USA Confidential* (1952), Jack Lait and Lee Mortimer; *Lamparski's Hidden Hollywood* (1981), Richard Lamparski; *Sagebrush Casinos: The Story of Legal Gambling in Nevada* (1953), Oscar Lewis; *The Grim Reapers* (1969), Ed Reid; *Chicago: Growth of a Metropolis* (1969), Harold M. Mayer and Richard C. Wade; *Lansky* (1971), Hank Messick; *The Mob in Show Business* (1973), Hank Messick; *Meet the Mob* (1961), Frank Mullady and William H. Kofoed; *Headline Happy* (1950), Florabel Muir; *The Legacy of Al Capone* (1975), George Murray; *The Madhouse on Madison Street* (1965), George Murray; *Investigation Hollywood* (1976), Fred Otash; *The George Raft File* (1973), James Robert Parish; *Las Vegas Is My Beat* (1973), Ralph Pearl; *Barbarians in Our Midst* (1952), Virgil W. Peterson; *This Is Costello* (1951), Robert H. Prall and Norton Mockridge; *Inside Las Vegas* (1977), Mario Puzo; *Viva Vegas* (1953), Paul Ralli; *The Green Felt Jungle* (1964), Ed Reid and Ovid Demaris; *Las Vegas: City Without Clocks* (1961), Ed Reid; *Mickey Cohen: Mobster* (1973), Ed Reid; *Get Me Giesler* (1962), John Roeburt; *Chicago Blues: The City and the Music* (1975), Mike Rowe; *This Is Hollywood* (1978), Ken Schessler; *Crime, Inc.* (1984), Martin Short; *The Encyclopedia of American Crime* (1982), Carl Sifakis; *Syndicate City* (1954), Alson J. Smith; *No Innocence Abroad* (1953), Michael

Stern; *Murder, Inc.* (1951), Burton B. Turkus and Sid Feder; *Gamblers' Money* (1965), Wallace Turner; *Organized Crime in America* (1962), Gus Tyler; *Frank Costello: Prime Minister of the Underworld* (1974), George Wolf with Joseph DiMona; *Fallen Angels* (1986), Marvin J. Wolf and Katherine Mader; *George Raft* (1974), Lewis Yablonsky.